EMPRESS OF FAE
BRIAR BOLEYN

For more information, email: author@briarboleyn.com

Cover Design by Artscandare Book Cover Design

Proofreading & Editing by

Flourish Art by Polina K, Emmie Norfolk, Gordon Johnson (GDJ)

ACKNOWLEDGEMENTS

To Rachel (Rychel) who has been there since the Regency!

And to my very own Rose Court, the most incredible Street Team an author could ask for. Thank you for joining me on this journey through Eskira, Myntra, and beyond. May you each continue to cast your brilliance across the universe.

CONTENT & TRIGGER WARNINGS

Blood of a Fae is a dark fantasy romance series that deals with topics which some readers may understandably find triggering.

A trigger and content warnings list may be found at the end of the book.

Please keep in mind that the content warnings list will spoil certain plot elements. Avoid reading the trigger warnings list if you do not have any triggers and do not wish to know specific details about the plot in advance.

JOIN MY NEWSLETTER

Grab the FREE bonus scene and hear about the latest new releases, giveaways, and other bookish treats:

http://briarboleyn.com

Find me on Instagram or contact me via email to join my Street Team:

https://www.instagram.com/briarboleynauthor/

author@briarboleyn.com

CONTENTS

THE CHARACTERS

At the Court of Umbral Flames
KAIROS DRAVEN VENATOR, Crown Consort
LYRASTRA VENATOR
ODESSA DI RHONDAN
CRESCENT DI RHONDAN
GAWAIN
TAINA
HAWL, an Ursidaur
ULPHEAS, a Royal stitcher

At the Rose Court of Camelot
MORGAN LE FAY, Empress of Myntra
ARTHUR PENDRAGON, King of Pendrath
BELISENT, Queen of Pendrath
ORCADES, Morgan's sister
KAYE PENDRAGON
FENYX, Lord General
MERLIN, former High Priestess of the Temple of the Three
TYRE, High Priest of the Temple of the Three
CAVAN, High Priest of the Temple of Perun
SIR ECTOR PRENNELL, a loyal knight
GALAHAD PRENNELL, his son
DAME HALYNA
LANCELET DE TROYES

GUINEVERE OF LYONESSE

JAVER, Royal Mage of Myntra and magical hitchhiker

The Creatures

NIGHTCLAW, an exmoor

SUNSTRIKE, his mate

TUVA, eyes of the High Priestess

The Deities

ZORYA, goddess of the dawn

MARZANNA, goddess of death

DEVINA, goddess of the hunt

PERUN, their brother

NEDOLA, goddess of fate

VELA, high goddess of the fae

KHOR, her mate

At the High Fae Court

GORLOIS LE FAY

RYCHEL, a lost girl

PRONUNCIATION GUIDE

Aercanum: AIR-kay-num

Agravaine Emrys: Ag-ra-VAYN EM-ris

Ambrilith: AM-bri-lith

Atropa: uh-TROH-puh

Avriel: AV-ree-el

Bearkin: BEAR-kin

Belisent: buh-LI-sent

Brasad: BRAH-sad

Breena: BREE-nuh

Cavan: KAV-uhn

Cerunnos: Ser-UHN-os

Devina: DEH-vee-nuh

Ector Prennell: EK-tor Pren-ELL

Eleusia: EL-oo-see-uh

Enid: EE-nid

Erion: EH-ree-on

Eskira: es-KEER-ah

Ettarde: eh-TAHRD

Exmoor: EX-moor

Fenrir: FEN-reer

Fenyx: FEH-niks

Florian Emrys: FLOH-ree-an EM-ris

Galahad Prennell: GAL-uh-had Pren-ELL

Gawain: GA-wayn

Gelert: GEL-ert

Glatisants: GLAH-tis-ants

Gorlois: GOR-lwah

Halyna: Ha-LEE-nuh

Hawl: HALL

Haya: HI-uh

Idrisane: ID-ri-zayn

Javer: JAH-ver

Kairos Draven Venator: KAI-ros DRA-ven Veh-NAH-tohr

Kastra: KAS-truh

Kaye: KAY

Khor'a'val: KOR-a-VAL

Khor: KOR

Khorva: KOR-vuh

Lancelet de Troyes: LAN-suh-let deh TROYZ

Laverna: la-VER-na

Leodegrance: lee-oh-de-GRANS

Lucius Venator: LOO-shus Veh-NAH-tohr

Lyonesse: LEE-oh-ness

Lyrastra: LIE-rah-struh

Malkah: MAL-kah

Marjolijn: mar-jo-LYN

Marzanna: mar-ZAH-nuh

Medra: MEH-dra

Meridium: MEH-ri-dee-um

Myntra: MIN-truh

Nedola: NED-o-la

Nerov: NEH-rov

Noctasia: nok-TAY-zhuh

Nodori: no-DOH-ree

Numenos: NOO-meh-nos

Odelna: o-DEL-nuh

Orcades: OR-kay-deez

Orin's Horn: OR-inz HORN

Pelleas: Pel-LEE-us

Pendrath: PEN-drath

Perun: PER-uhn

Rhea: RAY-uh

Rheged: RAY-ghed

Rychel: RYE-chel

Selwyn: SEL-win

Sephone Venator: se-FOHN-ee

Siabra: SHAY-bruh

Sorega: soh-RAY-guh

Tabar: TAY-bar

Taina: TIE-nuh

Taryn: TAIR-in

Tuva: TOO-vah

Tyre: TY-ruh

Ulpheas: UHL-fee-us

Ursidaur: UR-si-dor

Uther: OO-thur

Valtain: val-TAYN

Varis: VAR-is

Vela: VAY-luh

Verdantail: ver-DAN-tail

Vesper: VES-per

Vespera: ves-PAIR-uh

Ygraine: Ee-GRAYN

Zephrae: ZEF-ray

Zorya: ZOHR-ee-uh

BOOK 1

BOOK I PROLOGUE

T he trees were whispering. The moon was rising.

Deep in the heart of an ancient oak grove, a stone altar sat waiting.

Behind the altar stood three trees holding three bound women. White robes covered their youthful forms.

A man stepped forward. The grove itself seemed to hold its breath.

The eyes of the three women were wide and watchful.

There was a great darkness in the grove, despite the starlight in the space above the trees. And amidst it all, a feeling ominous and terrible.

The moon reached its zenith, climbing over the tops of the oaks, full and painted red as if it had been marked with blood.

The man drew a silver blade. Its hilt was made of bone.

One of the women spoke.

"Father, please. You don't have to do this."

For a moment, the man paused. His eyes flickered briefly to the woman on the tree. Her hair was black as night and silver as the moon. She was very beautiful and very young and one of her names meant death, though she had known little of it.

Something not so dissimilar to grief shaped itself in the man's eyes as he looked upon her. Then it was gone.

The world was very young.

The world was just beginning.

Evil was being born tonight, born into a world that might have been spared from ever seeing its face.

CHAPTER I - DRAVEN

My wife was gone.

I smashed my fist into the black marble pillar.

My wife was *gone*.

I hit the pillar again, knuckles smashing resoundingly into the hard surface. Then stood, watching as a spindly crack began to form. White spiderweb against the gleaming black.

Morgan didn't want to be your wife in the first place, a gnawing, cruel voice in my head reminded me. Isn't that why she had fled? Preferring to throw herself into a portal that hadn't been used in decades rather than remain another minute by your side?

What was it she had said?

"This isn't a marriage."

She had accused me of destroying her trust. Of ruining all that had been growing between us.

And just what had that been exactly?

I vividly remembered the last words she had murmured as she kissed me.

"You're all I think about. You're all I see. I'm so tied to you, I barely know who I am anymore."

But the words were faint comfort. Moments later, she had run from my arms.

Followed only by that fool of a court mage, Javer, who had probably died throwing himself in after her. Even now, the portal frame she had passed through was singed with smoke. She had destroyed it rather than allow me to follow her.

I knew some of my friends believed Morgan's departure to be the greatest act of betrayal. After all, she was my wife. She was their empress. She should have stayed.

But that wasn't how I saw it.

I had trapped her. Not once but twice. Caught her in a complex web of snares.

The greatest webs of all.

Marriage.

And an empire.

Yet somehow she had broken free. I had known she would, even as I had struggled to wrap the invisible bindings around her.

Had a small part of me hoped it might be otherwise? Of course.

And if it had simply been marriage and not the empire... Well, who knew.

But she had chosen neither for herself.

Both choices had been mine.

And make no mistake, I would make them again.

I hadn't been able to save Nodori. But I had saved Morgan.

If her hating me was the price I had to pay, so be it.

And in saving her, I had seen the chance to save a rotting, corrupt empire.

I had fastened onto that hope like a drowning man to a rope. I had tied Morgan to that rope, forcing her to try to pull us aloft.

Instead, she had cut the rope and run.

Clever, wicked, beautiful woman. Brilliant, brave wife.

Perhaps I was doomed to always be left by the women I loved.

Nodori, my sweet childhood friend and first bride. A gentle flame burned out too soon.

Nimue, my precious daughter, her life smothered mere moments after her birth.

I felt my heart constrict at the thought. Rarely did I allow myself to dwell on them at all. But it seemed fitting to consider the three women I considered my truest family together.

Now Morgan.

My throat felt constricted as the image of my wife appeared in my mind.

Her long, silver hair cascading like a silken waterfall. Her skin, a shimmering canvas of gold that defied the boundaries of beauty, mortal and immortal alike. Tall and statuesque, she moved with the regal poise of a queen, her figure a perfect blend of strength and grace.

I had watched her wield a sword with the precision of a master. I had watched her spin naked flames from the palms of her hands.

But it hadn't been her beauty alone that had ensnared my heart in the first place.

Her wit cut through the thickest of shadows. Her strength was indomitable. Her determination made her a force to be reckoned with.

And the fire that burned within her... She was a brilliant enigma born of starlight and fire. Within her, I saw the potential for greatness beyond measure.

She was fated to cast her brilliance across the universe.

Without her, I was a void once more. Missing her with an ache that gnawed at the very core of my being.

She haunted my soul. She was my constant reverie. The vision of all I longed for.

She was the constellation that guided my destiny.

I had stood so close to her fire, I had thought I might ignite as well.

I wouldn't have minded if I had.

I raised my fist a third time, hoping this would be the instance that drew blood.

Instead, a slow clapping sound made me pivot towards the door.

Odessa stood there, her arms crossed. I recognized the look on her face. It was one of patient restraint. Not something the warrior ordinarily excelled at.

Not that I could claim to be much better.

"I knew you wanted to bring down the establishment, but I didn't think you meant it so literally."

She looked past me to the cracked pillar. "You could come to Steelhaven if this is what you're looking for."

"For?"

"To bleed," she clarified.

I averted my head. "Don't be ridiculous. Besides, Steelhaven is for women."

"We'd make an exception. For you. We wouldn't go easy on you either. No one would feel sorry for you."

"I wouldn't expect them to," I snapped.

Odessa didn't rise to the bait. Her dark eyes were sharp as a raven's as she watched me. "Or perhaps you could spar with Gawain. I know he's missed—"

"No," I cut her off.

She deserved better from me. They all did.

Odessa cleared her throat. "You miss her. We all know that."

I grimaced in the direction of the pillar I'd been torturing. They'd have had to have been blind not to. "Now's the point where you say 'Do you think this is what Morgan would have wanted?'"

Odessa was quiet for a moment. "I'm not particularly interested in that."

"No? She's your empress."

"Only because you arranged it so that she had no other choice."

The accusation hung in the air.

"No one who desires power should ever have it," I repeated the refrain I had told myself was ample justification for my actions.

She shook her head. "But that's just it. You never did. Desire it, I mean. Can you really look me in the eyes and say you did?"

I touched the pillar with my knuckles, resisting the urge to give it another good tap.

"And giving power to one who has no desire for it?" Odessa continued. "Who has no investment in its outcome? Are there any wise proverbs about *that* sort of folly?"

"She's invested. She cared about all of this. All of you," I retorted.

Odessa shrugged. "Perhaps. Perhaps in time she might have. Even so, thrusting the rulership of a continent into the hands of a woman who was just beginning to come into her own power... Well..."

"Well?"

"It seems unwise. I'm surprised you didn't foresee this outcome. You're usually...more astute."

It was a bitter compliment. A jab. I could take it. She was right, after all.

"I didn't say I thought she'd embrace the position with open arms," I muttered.

Odessa cocked an eyebrow.

"Didn't think she'd flee across the world either," I clarified.

"Part of that was due to Beks," the dark-haired woman said with surprising softness. "You couldn't have anticipated his death."

"Ah, but I should have," I said bitterly. "That's just it. She thought I should have. She blamed me for Beks. Not just Javer. And she was right. He was a child. A child I sent to the front lines. A child I allowed to die. She was right to blame me."

"You trusted Javer's judgment. You believed him when he said Beks was ready." Odessa sighed. "No one could have held that boy back. He was..."

"A force to be reckoned with. Sounds familiar." I punched the pillar again. I couldn't resist. The column trembled.

Dust trickled down from the gold inlay ceiling.

"I'd prefer it if you didn't bring the roof down on our heads while I was here," Odessa said. "Common courtesy."

"Sorry." I steadied the pillar with both hands, then glanced upwards.

It wasn't the only pillar in the room. The structural integrity of the chamber should be all right.

Although, with the recent attack, I supposed I couldn't be too certain. The palace had lost some structural soundness in spots. In more ways than one.

"Is this what you want?" Odessa's eyes were still fixed on the pillar. "To bring us down? To watch us crumble?"

"Of course not."

"And yet you would topple the Siabra court without a care. Even now, we stand on the brink of chaos. Unguided, unled. Our former regent locked in the palace dungeons. Our new empress gone. Meanwhile, our prince spends his days alone." She gestured to a table laden with untouched trays. "You don't eat. You ignore friends who try to visit."

"I didn't ignore you. We're talking now, aren't we?" I scratched my head. "But then, you didn't bother to knock."

"The time for knocking is past, Draven. You have an empire to oversee."

My jaw clenched. "Morgan's empire."

"Not Morgan's. Yours." Her voice was gentle. Gentler than I deserved. "You made this mess. You'll clean it up now."

It was very close to what Morgan had said. The words hit home. Not to mention how much Odessa was reminding me of my old governess.

"You sound almost maternal, Odessa."

"Save the insults," she snapped, finally losing a little of her carefully maintained control. "If I have a maternal bone in my body, then it serves this empire. Our people. Just as you should."

"Admirable," I acknowledged. "You're right."

"You made choices. Only you can say if they were the right ones, the only ones you could have made." She drew a deep breath. "Nevertheless, Morgan is your wife and my empress. So, tell me this. The bond—you can sense her through it? Is she... alive?"

"The bond is weak," I hedged. "But yes. She lives." I could sense that much, even from this distance.

She nodded, a small hint of satisfaction on her smooth, mahogany face. "It will grow stronger with time. We both know this, even if she does not. And the sooner she accepts it, well..."

There were ways a bond between mates that had been forged in the way ours had been could be strengthened or enhanced.

Not that Morgan seemed keen on finding out what those ways were.

"I doubt she'll accept it anytime soon," I said, not a little sourly.

I had told her that I loved her.

She hadn't exactly returned the sentiment.

It shouldn't have changed how I felt—and it hadn't. But still, the words she'd used had hit me like a blow to the gut.

She'd confessed she felt the same emotion. But it was false, she'd said.

False.

Odessa waved a hand dismissively. "Who knows what that woman will do? She's nothing if not unpredictable. Regardless, she's not coming back anytime soon. I think we can agree on that."

My lips thinned. "Agreed."

"Then perhaps it's time you took up the mantle and began to rule."

"Rule? I'm not the emperor, Odessa."

Odessa's mask of patience dropped. "If *she* is the empress, then *you* are her consort. In her absence, the throne is yours. That is, unless she specifically decreed otherwise before she left. Did she?"

"Not precisely..." In fact, Morgan had said much the same thing Odessa was saying.

"Or assigned someone else as regent?"

"No, but..."

"I didn't think so. Because she assumed you would do what needed to be done." A distinct look of impatience crossed her face. "I wonder what she would say if she could see you now."

"Smashing pillars and feeling sorry for myself, you mean?"

Odessa sniffed and looked around the suite. "One might think you were a true Siabra nobleman at the rate you're going. All you need are decanters of wine to slosh all over the room."

I felt my cheeks redden. I might have been reduced to punching pillars, but I hadn't become a drunken wastrel yet. The worst Odessa saw were the trays of untouched food and clothing tossed onto chairs instead of neatly folded. And the pillar.

Thank the gods that my pacing back and forth across the room for hours on end had left no discernible trace.

A small smile appeared on Odessa's face as her eyes landed on the uneaten trays of food, and I glowered. "What?"

"Does Hawl know you aren't eating?"

"Breena takes the trays away…" I began defensively.

"Before Hawl can see them? Oh, ho, you've been spared so far. But I don't think that will last." Odessa's smile became gloating.

"What do you mean?"

"I mean I asked Hawl to join us."

"You did what—" I started to say, just as the door from the connecting room that led to the kitchen exploded in a fulmination of brown fur.

"We'll discuss the trays later, princeling," the Bearkin bellowed. "Now duck."

It was fortunate Hawl had directed their command towards Odessa and not to me, because while the Steelhaven warrior immediately bolted to the side, I continued to stand there, embarrassingly transfixed as the Ursidaur barreled into the room, a silver tray outstretched in one clawed paw.

Before I could say another word, the tray was released. It flew across the room towards the spot where Odessa's head had been a mere second before.

The flat piece of metalware collided with its target with a sickening thud.

There was a muffled cry, and a figure came into view along the impeccable gold and emerald encrusted rear wall—a few feet behind Odessa's last place. The form of a slender man clad all in black fell to the floor, blood dripping from an unhealthy-looking dent in his forehead.

"Intruders," Hawl roared, as if we weren't already aware, and continued to charge forward.

With signature grace, Odessa slid out of the way as the Bearkin pulled a kitchen cleaver from the pocket of their loose, white apron. A large cast-iron pan had also appeared as if by magic in their other paw, and now they swung this up and over their head, then downwards.

There was another sickening smack, and a second figure in black fell to the floor along the wall.

"Like swatting flies," Hawl roared gleefully.

Another smack.

I glanced at Odessa. "Shouldn't you be…?"

She raised her eyebrows. "Helping? Hawl seems to have everything under control. Indeed, I believe they're even enjoying themself."

"I certainly do," Hawl roared as they struck down a fourth shadowed intruder along the opposite wall. "And I most certainly am."

Odessa gestured at me. "Or are you suggesting you'd like to join in the fun? You're not too tired from all that pillar pummeling?"

"Pathetic, these creatures," Hawl declared. "Not tiring in the least. Too easy by far. Stay where you are, my prince. This will be over in a moment. Now, where's their queen bee?"

"Queen bee?"

A shadow flickered on the opposite wall. A faint mist began to form.

I grimaced. Ah, I was beginning to see the full extent of the plot now. Perhaps Odessa was right and all of the time I'd spent sequestered away was taking its toll.

Ordinarily, I would have easily anticipated this and met it head-on. Much like Hawl was so eagerly doing.

Odessa sighed as she saw the new visitor. "I'll take care of it."

A slender stiletto blade had appeared in her palm.

She moved across the room like a hawk smoothly diving—and just as swiftly, her prey was trapped mercilessly in her grip.

"Hello, Stepmother," I said.

Odessa held her blade carefully against Sephone's porcelain skin, just at the temple.

"It seems your security could stand some improvements, Odessa," Hawl boomed. "Not that I mind the diversion."

"It certainly could. I believe 'ensconced comfortably in the dungeons' were the words used?" I said, raising my eyebrows at Odessa.

"Can anyone really be comfortable in the dungeons?" Odessa shot back. "Especially the ones your father built. They're always full of rats and spiders. Or so I'm told. Care to weigh in, Sephone?"

I half expected Sephone to hiss and spit like a cat. Her eyes were wide and furious. Her plan to murder me while I was alone in my rooms had been foiled, and she was evidently still reeling with disappointment. Her dark red hair had been pinned back from her face. She was dressed more plainly than I had ever seen her before. But then, even though I had instructed the guards to make her comfortable, this had not extended towards her ordinarily jewel-laden silk gowns.

The former Queen Regent bared her teeth with a hiss of venomous steam. There it was. The poisonous breath she was so renowned for.

But with the knife at her temple and Odessa's arm tight around her throat, a small puff was all she dared release.

"She has supporters, it would seem," Odessa noted.

"Not particularly clever or well-organized ones," Hawl growled.

"Well, they did get her out of the dungeons." My eyes narrowed. "You don't look particularly surprised by that, Odessa."

The warrior woman looked slightly chagrined. "There's only one good way to test your own security."

"By springing a trap for yourself," I finished.

"I wasn't certain she'd manage to get this far," Odessa said. "I'm almost impressed, Sephone. Your supporters are well-funded. It will be a pleasure to hunt them down and lay these corpses at their feet."

"Before you turn them into corpses themselves. This does create a problem, however." I ran a hand over my jaw.

"Since you'd have preferred to leave her to rot and not deal with her treachery in an overt way, you mean?" Odessa said sweetly. She met Hawl's eyes. "Look, I know she's your stepmother, but she's also a treacherous bitch who has now spat your pity right back in your face. Quite literally." She gave Sephone's neck a slight squeeze.

Sephone's eyes narrowed in rage. "The only treachery here is on your part," she hissed. "You would annihilate the Siabra, destroy us all. Have us become feeble and weak-hearted. You would have placed that outsider bitch upon my throne. My throne!"

"Decidedly not your throne," I interrupted, mildly.

Her eyes flared. "Avriel would have made a strong emperor. And with me by his side…"

"Yes, but he's dead now. So that won't be happening. That 'outsider bitch,' as you called her, saw to that, remember? Anything else you'd like to say in your defense?" Odessa nudged her slightly forward.

"Defense!" Sephone managed to eek out a bitter laugh. "I need no defense. And when the court realizes the extent of our prince's weakness, why, they'll *beg* for me to resume my duties as regent of this court and to lead them into battle as we retaliate against the Valtain and bring your deviant little sister back for her well-deserved execution for treason."

"As I recall, she wasn't the only one who committed what you might call 'treason,'" I reminded. "Trying to kill the new empress…"

A puff of steam. "Stop calling her that."

"I believe a very powerful being confirmed you should leave Morgan well alone, Sephone," I said.

"What sort of a being?" Odessa's eyes flickered with interest.

I shifted uncomfortably. "I'm still not entirely sure. Certainly not a mortal one." Though it had displayed no qualms in possessing mortal forms. Each time, taking up residence in a dead body temporarily. First the child, Odelna. Then the corpse of a soldier in our royal guard.

"You have more important things to do than deal with Sephone and her plotting. Or overseeing her trial," Odessa pointed out.

"The former regent has made one good point, my prince," Hawl growled. "We were indeed attacked."

I met the Bearkin's eyes. "Indeed, we were."

"In our home. Our royal court. Above and below. Siabra and mortals," Odessa said carefully. "We lost... people."

"Indeed, we did," I said softly. I met her eyes. "And you would have me do something about it."

"I would have you not waste any more precious time," she said simply.

I saw her point. Now I would have to spend my time dealing with our former Queen Regent. First, she would have to be escorted back to the not-particularly-secure dungeons. Then, a trial would need to be arranged. Her treachery would be put on display for the court. A court of her peers, half of whom would be plotting her return.

And then, of course, there would eventually be the formal execution. All the while dealing with pleas from her supporters to stay her trial and allow her back into the court.

I would have to oversee the proceedings and deal with the machinations of the court... all while remembering that Sephone had tried to murder Morgan and myself and was unlikely to ever stop trying.

Odessa was watching me. "There's a simple way around all of that, of course."

"Oh? And what's that?"

"I let her go."

And then she did. Releasing her grip, Odessa stepped back, the stiletto disappearing once more into a side pocket of her leathers. She even folded her arms casually over her chest.

Without her captor to hold her, Sephone surged forward eagerly towards me.

I saw the glint of lethality in her eyes. The familiar mist hovered in the air around her mouth.

I felt her hatred and pure desperation. She wanted me dead, very badly.

I knew what I had to do. With a sigh, I braced myself.

The mist swirled.

A cleaver flew through the air.

The meat-smacking sound came again.

"You're welcome," Hawl announced as Sephone pitched lifelessly to the floor.

The Bearkin stalked towards the table in the corner. "All of these platters. Do you mean to say you've eaten nothing I've made for you? Where do the trays go?"

I swallowed hard, unable to consider eating at that precise moment. "Breena takes them away."

"That wretched housekeeper. Trickery and deceit!" Hawl glared at the table of covered trays.

"Blame me, not Breena." I glanced down at the cleaver lodged in Sephone's head and gagged slightly. "Really, Odessa? Was this what you had in mind when you planned your visit?"

The warrior tilted her head, eyeing Sephone's corpse not without a little displeasure. "Not entirely, no, but I won't deny it's convenient. I am still in charge of security for this palace, am I not?"

"The palace. The city. The continent. The job is yours if you want it," I said, waving a hand. "I doubt anyone else does."

"The continent is your problem. But Sephone was easy to turn into mine. Hawl was only too willing to help. We'll save time now that she's... disposed."

She studied me carefully. "Don't tell me you have regrets."

"About Sephone?"

"She was your stepmother. Your aunt."

I met her gaze. "And she wanted me dead. Always has. Is that what you want me to say?"

"It's only the truth. There was a time..." She paused. "When you might have already dealt with the problem yourself."

"I've gone soft. Is that what you're saying? You wish me to be a more brutal sovereign? Like my father, perhaps?"

"Not like him, no. Like the man you used to be. I want you to remember who you are. No more, no less."

I scowled. "I wasn't aware I had forgotten."

"You've gone through more than most mortal men do in a lifetime, Kairos. You've lost a wife. A child. You've slain a brother. You've lived in exile." She paused. "Now you've returned."

"Returned. Lost another wife. Killed a stepmother."

"Don't take credit for my work," Hawl complained. The Bearkin was nibbling at some of the untouched food. I watched as they grunted in satisfaction.

I shook my head. "I need to be more swift in my judgment. Harsher. More brutal. More violent. More... Siabra-like. Is that what you're saying, Odessa?" The criticism stung. I couldn't deny it.

Odessa took her time replying. When she did, her words shocked me.

"We stand on the brink of something. The world is about to change. I can feel it. Can you?" She looked back and forth between Hawl and me. The Bearkin was silent, listening carefully. "When you returned to us, you brought back a lost object of untold power."

"The grail," I said softly.

"And now, it's gone. Taken by your sister. Given back to a people who are, arguably, our greatest enemies."

I opened my mouth, but she held up her hand. "And don't say that it may be all they wanted. You know better. They have Rychel. They have the grail. We've had our peace for one hundred and fifty years. That peace is about to end. I can feel it. Tell me I'm not the only one." She looked at Hawl, almost pleadingly.

The Bearkin nodded slowly. "War comes."

"War comes," Odessa repeated. She looked at me. "But it may not come to Myntra first."

I stared. "Eskira? Pendrath is already at war with its neighbors."

"An ordinarily peaceful kingdom engaged in a reckless battle with its neighbors," Odessa said slowly, as if teaching a small child. "A continent in chaos for the first time in a century."

"But the war is between mortal lands. The fae had nothing to do with that..." I trailed off as I saw her face. "You think they did."

"Remember your history, prince," Odessa said softly, her eyes sharp and penetrating. "The land of Valtain may have been abandoned. A slight of hand, nothing more. The Valtain fae will rise. Of that I have no doubt."

"They cursed us. They left their land. We have no idea where they are now." I heard the words for what they were. Weak protests.

"They've made a new stronghold. I have no doubt they're as powerful or more than they were when they fought your father."

"One hundred and fifty years ago." I shook my head. "You and I grew up on these tales."

"We lived in the aftermath. We should know better than anyone how real the threat still is. But the Siabra, for the most part, have chosen to forget. We are steeped in our bitterness, sullen in our tragedy. Resting on the laurels of our blighted conquest, assuming it is enough. We do not age, but we do not create. The curse of childlessness has left us weak and rotting in indolence and indecision. We believe the worst that can happen is to go on as we are."

"But it's not the worst, is it?"

She shook her head. "Recall your history. The fae were once one. And when the fae were united..." She paused significantly.

"Mortals were below us," I acknowledged. "In all ways."

"All creatures," Hawl growled. "All creatures served the fae. Whether they wished to or not."

Utter subservience. That was the relic of our brutal past. One I vaguely remembered learning about as a child. Even now, I knew that some of the most long-lived of the Siabra secretly recalled those ancient days with fondness. The days when all creatures had served us, worshiped us, lived solely for our pleasure.

A time of stark divisions. When to be fae was everything, and to be mortal nothing.

A time when slavery was so commonplace, the concept did not even exist. One was simply fae, or born to serve and die.

I remembered what I had promised Morgan. To help her end the war in Pendrath. All of Myntra's resources would be at her disposal, I had sworn. We would set things right in Eskira.

A hefty promise. I had meant what I said. But now, looking at Odessa, I realized I had no idea where we stood.

"You believe the war in Eskira is not of mortal design. That there is more at play here."

Slowly, she nodded. "Some things are too great to be coincidence. You sought a weapon of great power."

"Excalibur." I had not forgotten. I had met my mate along the way to that cursed sword. Some day, I looked forward to telling Morgan's brother face-to-face just how overvalued the blade was compared to his precious sister. Some day.

"But all along, it was being sought by another. A mortal king who had been schooled in its usefulness."

"Fae and mortals have both used that sword," I pointed out.

"When was the last time all three items were together?" Odessa asked. "Excalibur slipped from your grasp."

"I saved Morgan Pendragon instead," I reminded her.

"The blade's worth pales in comparison to her life. I am well aware. Yet you returned here with the grail. Now the grail and sword are gone."

My sister had taken one. Morgan's sister had taken the other. Ironic? Perhaps. Depending on who they had taken them to.

I gave a short laugh. "And here I thought you'd balk at getting the Siabra involved in an intercontinental conflict. You *want* us there."

"I *want* us ready," Odessa replied. "I want us prepared. We are nowhere near that point."

I stared at her. "What do you mean?"

"The Siabra barely retain a hold on the city above us. Let alone this continent. We are polarized, disorganized, and yes, shockingly weak."

"Do you really think Sephone cared for anything outside of this court?" Hawl growled.

"She did not have your father's... grasp... of politics. Or logistics," Odessa clarified. "She let many things fall by the wayside during her term as regent."

"Including our defenses," I said as understanding dawned.

Odessa nodded. "Our defenses are practically nonexistent. As you know, various Siabra nobles rule over their own smaller courts across Myntra. All of them owe allegiance to the Umbral Throne. But it has been a very long time since that allegiance has been tested. Since any of them have had to pay anything but the minimal fealty."

"And our army? Our resources here, in Noctasia, and in the ports of Sorega?"

"All sorely diminished due to a lack of support and funds. There is much work to be done if we are to face the Valtain on firm footing, whether here or on the battleground of Eskira."

I glanced at my stepmother's body lying on the floor. There was no point in blaming her now.

I felt no remorse as I looked at her form. No grief. Her end had been a long time coming. Hawl had acted ruthlessly. But at least the death had been swift.

There was a time I had similarly excelled at delivering swift and merciless deaths to my foes.

But since returning home to the Court of Umbral Flames, something had hindered me. I had stayed my hand more times than I could count. And my friends had shielded me despite this. Morgan had shielded me.

I looked at Odessa. "I swore I would be at her side. I swore our power would be her power."

I had also told Morgan I wished for peace.

I still did. But based on what Odessa was suggesting, peace was no longer a likely prospect. At least, not yet.

Only from the crucible of battle could the elixir of peace be distilled, my old tutor had claimed.

"And it will. Now you can get down to the brass tacks. You won't have to waste time giving Sephone a trial she didn't deserve in the first place, or lose time listening to her sycophants and dealing with more assassination attempts from her delusional supporters."

"Instead, you want me to move ahead and do what?" I already knew where I longed to go. Now I wondered how I'd managed to hesitate this long.

Odessa gave me a cool, frank look. "Well, besides staving off future attacks from our enemies or going on the offense and developing a strategic military plan, you could start by eating your dinner and making Hawl happy."

"And then?"

"And then I'd say a trip to see your sister-in-law is in order."

"Excellent idea," Hawl huffed from where they were rapidly piling trays one upon the other. The Bearkin began to stride back to the door they had emerged from carrying the large pile. "I'll bring something simple but warm. Soup perhaps."

But my eyes were still on Odessa. "Go and see Lyrastra?"

Annoyance flashed in Odessa's eyes. "Lyrastra, yes. Perhaps you've heard of her."

"She was... injured," I said slowly, forcing myself to remember.

"Her arm was shattered," Odessa snapped.

I winced. "Of course. In the competition. I had thought that she would have…"

Odessa's eyes blazed. "What? Recovered? Like you have? Moved on? Like you have?"

"Fair point," I admitted.

Odessa's face softened slightly. "I know you miss Morgan, Draven. But there are many worse off than you."

"Also a fair point."

"And they need you. They need you to lead. You may not be emperor, but you're the next best thing." She folded her arms over her chest, her lips set stubbornly. "So step the fuck up and stop the bullshit. Morgan is gone. You are not. Deal with your people. Put your house in order. Make arrangements. And then…" She paused.

"Yes?"

"Well, you *are* going after her, aren't you?"

All I could do was stare.

I had been trapped in this room, trapped in my own indecision for far too long. Along the way, I had apparently also become blind. Unable to recognize that leaving Myntra was inescapable.

I had never imagined that my friends already knew this, too. That they would see my departure not as abandonment or betrayal but as a simple inevitability.

"I've waited my entire lifetime for Morgan," I said simply. "I'll go after her even if she doesn't want me. Even if she runs in the opposite direction. I'll follow her to the ends of Aercanum, and I'll never stop."

Odessa's dark eyes gleamed. "Now there's the prince I remember. I never expected you to say anything less."

CHAPTER 2 - MORGAN

"*M*organ!"

I knew the voice. Boyish and high-pitched. So familiar.

"Morgan, I see you. Can you see me? What is this place?"

I struggled to open my eyes. A trickle of light filtered in, blinding me. A pile of burning rubble.

I had set something on fire, I remembered. The arch.

"You have to stop him, Morgan. He's going to kill us all."

The smell of singed feathers filled the air.

I shook my head in confusion, looking around.

A stone floor. The scent of burned flesh and fabric. The acrid scent of crumbling stones turned to powdered ash.

A man lay near me. His clothes had been on fire. Now the fire was out. He was groaning.

I kneeled beside him.

Javer lifted his head. His black, pointed beard was singed. Skin blackened with soot, he looked up at me, dazed.

"Oh, you stupid, stupid man."

My voice echoed loudly off the stone walls of the windowless room.

There was a creaking sound from far above us.

I whirled around. A door at the top of a set of narrow, stone stairs was opening.

A figure stood silhouetted in the frame.

They stepped forward. Light from behind illuminated their figure and lit up their face.

A ripple of disbelief went through me. Any words I might have said dried up as my breath caught in my throat.

"Morgan?" Lancelet stepped into the chamber. "Is it really you?"

I was back in Camelot. And Lancelet was alive.

CHAPTER 3 - LANCELET

To whom did one pray after being dead and returning to life?

Marzanna was queen of eternal rest. Death was her dominion. She embraced rotting flesh and chiseled bones. She swung a sickle.

Was she to whom I should now pray? Or had she discarded me like ashes, like carrion, like a worthless corpse?

Or perhaps it was Zorya to whom I owed my devotion, my gratitude? Was it she who had reclaimed me, queen of light and life? Had she pulled me into her warm embrace, refusing to let the shadows carry me away?

If so, damn her to hell. Damn them both.

Life was unexpected. Death was supposed to be a certainty.

You made a choice—or someone made one for you—and your last breath was gone before you knew it.

I had known it. I had felt mine going.

By rights, I should have died back in that place. Back in that tomb. Back in Meridium.

Yet here I was. Made new. Reeking flesh and full of holes.

A brand new Lancelet.

No one could tell me why I was here, how, or for what purpose.

I couldn't remember crawling through that arch. I couldn't remember being alive enough to do so.

Yet, somehow, I had passed from death to life.

I could swear I had died. Or had been close enough to it to have made no difference.

Yet here I was, forced back into the land of the living.

So, to whom did I pray?

Did I pray for gratitude, guidance, or forgiveness? Did it matter? Was there anyone listening at all?

I had seen the face of the gods in the mouths of those hungry children. The power and the horror. The helplessness and the futility.

The *divine* was a gaping, hungry mouth.

The divine was nothingness.

I had wanted to sink down into that nothing. To let it consume me.

But then I had seen *her*.

Fragile like a bird. Wings broken but healing. Trying to fly.

Was that what I looked like?

She was far more beautiful than I had ever been. Her face was full and curving, like a golden crescent moon. She walked, and the light followed her.

Only shadows followed me. My heart was iron, cold and heavy.

But her heart—I could practically see it beating. Glowing with an insurmountable light.

Something in me had stirred itself and sparked.

If I could not live for myself, could I live for her?

For her, I embraced the shadows.

For her, I welcomed the dark.

I followed her like a silent wraith. I became her sworn protectress. Whether she knew it or not.

So when I looked down the staircase and saw the other woman I had sworn my entire life to protect, my heart skipped a beat and red flared up before my eyes.

Morgan Pendragon.

The bitch who had left me for dead.

CHAPTER 4 - GUINEVERE

C ould one forget how to be free?

Could the belief be lost, never to be regained? Could the feeling of freedom be unlearned in just a few short months?

I was reared in extravagance. I came of age in luxury. My existence was one of privilege and ease. I was the beloved eldest daughter of a summer court. A princess of the highest rank.

Little did I know that the high honor of my birth would become the very reason for my debasement and downfall.

Lyonesse, so sure of its own security and prosperity, was only too easily caught in the trap the young king of Pendrath set for it.

A king utterly lacking in honor who had broken the most fundamental of all laws when he betrayed the guests he had welcomed into his land, his court, his home.

For when the delegation from Lyonesse had joyfully arrived to celebrate the spring rites of Marzanna with the Rose Court, they had met treachery instead.

My father, Leodegrance, could not conceive the truth of what was occurring. Instead, he misinterpreted it as the false steps of a young and overly eager king.

So when Arthur demanded that Lyonesse send additional nobles as "surety" for the safekeeping of the ones who had already been taken, my father stupidly complied. Worse, he went so far as to enter into a marriage alliance with the king of Camelot, offering his only daughter as a token of Lyonesse's continued friendship.

The bargain was struck.

I was the dice tossed onto the table to be shuffled back and forth. My fate was thrown from my father's once-loving hands into those of a cruel stranger.

Marriage to Arthur might not have been so bad. He was not who I would have chosen, but I had always known my marriage would be arranged for me and was likely to be to a man.

But what happened was far worse than my wildest imaginings.

The marriage never occurred.

The wedding night did.

My father did not deliver me unto evil himself. He sent his most trusted ambassador for that.

Lord Cumbrage's head now hangs outside the king's wall alongside a number of other familiar faces from Lyonesse.

But before that dark conclusion, there was mirth and merriment—all forced and false, of course.

Gifts were exchanged. The betrothal documents were signed. A dowry contract was drawn up.

How much was Lady Guinevere of Lyonesse truly worth? Five hundred plots of rich fertile farmland? Or six? Three gold caskets filled with sea pearls? Or four filled with rubies harvested from the coastal mines?

Of course, King Arthur and his court covered me in finery while I waited for all the negotiations to be sorted. Noblewomen were assigned to clothe and tend me, draping me in lush robes and decking me in precious jewels. All fit for a queen.

Arthur greeted me in a formal welcome ceremony.

I looked into his cold, handsome face and saw my future torment foretold in his eyes. My freedom dried up like dew on blades of grass.

The members of our court who had been held hostage by Pendrath stood around us, their faces expressionless. They knew I was there to redeem them with my freedom. With my very life.

A princess of royal blood could do no less for her people. Could she? My father certainly did not think so. Or else why would he send his daughter to the man who, by rights, should have already been his enemy?

I lifted my chin. I carried on. I prayed in the temple by Arthur's side, begging the goddesses' blessing upon our marriage. I joined Arthur in supplications to his new god, Perun, in rituals led by the new High Priest, Cavan, in the newly constructed temple as well.

I touched my head to the cold stone, and I prayed.

I stood in banquets and I supped at feasts. I danced in courtly dances, my hips swaying in memory if not in happiness.

Finally, the day of the ceremony arrived. The day in which rings would be exchanged, vows made, and a new queen crowned.

Except all broke into chaos.

Arthur's displeasure rang out through the castle, and the marriage festivities sank under the weight of his fury.

A covert attack force led by my father and eldest brother had attempted to infiltrate the Pendrathian border on the day of my wedding.

They were struck down, of course. My father? Killed. I was told it was instant.

His torment was over much quicker than mine.

The alliance was off. The marriage? Worth less than nothing.

But my value as a hostage, a symbol of Lyonessian resistance? Satisfying and crushable.

Arthur took great pleasure in beginning my vanquishment that very night.

It was supposed to be our wedding night. The most sacred night of my married life. The night I gave myself to my husband, my king.

Though, had I not already been given to him by another? Bequeathed like a casket of rich jewels?

Now my maidenhead was stripped from me like the stolen treasures of a kingdom's vault.

All while a group of male advisors from the king's court sat in the adjoining room, official witnesses to my desecration.

My tattered wedding dress was sent back to my family in Lyonesse. I assume they placed it on the funeral pyre alongside my father's body. That they burned both together, my freedom and his life.

Instead of an honored pawn, a noble queen, I had become—in the span of a night and a day—a cruel king's plaything. The subject of his abuse. The target of his rage.

For surely, Arthur accused, I must have known what my father and brother had planned all along. Surely, I must have arrived in Camelot carrying the knowledge of my own betrayal like a poisonous seed.

When I could offer no new knowledge, no information in my defense, Arthur gave up and instead directed his ire towards the other Lyonessian nobles. The ones who had been eagerly counting the days until our wedding, waiting for the time when they would finally be released and permitted to return home.

Half of their heads hang on the castle walls alongside Lord Cumbrage's.

The women... Well, most of them fared worse.

Above ground, the Rose Court is a beautiful place. Below ground, not even the strongest whitewash can cleanse the charnel house of horrors that Arthur has created for his amusement.

My cage was bright and gilded. Rays of sunshine filtered in, illuminating my pain as I waited day after day for the man who was not my husband to return at night to use me as he saw fit.

Until, one day, a voice spoke to me. A voice I had heard before but only in my dreams, always wise and gentle—but this time, above all else, brave.

It urged me to flee. It showed me the way.

I took it.

I left my people behind.

In my gilded cage, I had dreamed of death. I had not dared to dream of freedom.

And now that freedom is mine again, I am not sure I wish to keep it. This punishment of existence. This belonging of myself to only me. It is not a self I want. It is not a self I chose.

All the while, *she* looks at me. Her eyes deep and guarded. Guarding me.

She guards me, even against myself.

CHAPTER 5 - MORGAN

We were divided by oceans, and there was no going back.

I had made sure of that, hadn't I?

Kairos Draven Venator—my *husband*—was back in the Court of Umbral Flames below the city of Noctasia on the continent of Myntra.

While I... I was back in Camelot. In the Temple of the Three.

The year I'd left Camelot by Draven's side, spring had just arrived. We had traveled through spring and all of summer before arriving in Valtain and finally reaching Meridium.

After my failed attempt to claim Excalibur, Draven had taken me home. To his home in the Siabra court. The court of claws and fangs and talons. Of hissing poison and glistening scales.

Nevertheless, it was a court I had almost begun to think of as "home."

Until I had found out I was married to its crown prince. In a wedding no one, fae or mortal, had witnessed—not even myself. We were bonded. Fused through some rite I still didn't fully understand.

Then, Draven had made me an empress. Tricked me into doing what he had known I would be unable to help myself from doing: protecting him at all costs.

In the process, I had inadvertently sold my soul and become empress of the Siabra fae. A position I had no intention of fulfilling.

And when Beks had died... had *withered* like fresh fruit on a toxic vine, as he fought with everything he had to protect the city he loved and the court that didn't deserve his love. Well, after that, it hadn't felt much like home.

The Siabra were bloodthirsty. They had stripped Beks of everything he had. A mortal child, drained of his magic as he protected them.

I had felt the same happening to me.

I choked. I fled. I ran.

There was just one small problem.

I wasn't sure there was a *me* without *him*.

And even though I had traveled thousands of miles to extricate myself from his grasp, I couldn't help but feel a lingering certainty that there was nowhere I could go that he would not somehow find me.

Even now, I could feel the tendrils of his awareness reaching out to me, coiling like a mist around my being and reminding me that, like it or not... we were *bound*.

"Morgan?"

Merlin's voice was as gentle as I remembered, perhaps more so. But she was looking older. And much wearier.

I met her concerned gaze and forced a smile.

The wheel had turned full circle. I had finally come home.

But it was not the homecoming I had expected.

"We're going in now," she murmured. "Are you ready?"

I could do nothing but nod.

Behind me, I sensed Javer. Wary and watchful. I ignored him.

He had chosen to follow me. I hadn't asked why. Truly, I didn't care. If he had died coming after me... Well, perhaps it would have been better for us both. I believe he'd had the same thought. But he had lived. To trail after me in this strange land where he knew no one else. I wasn't about to turn to him as a confidant, however. He was alive, and he was permitted to remain in the temple by Merlin's grace. That was more than enough, as far as I was concerned.

Merlin raised her hand to the massive oak doors and pushed them open.

As the doors yielded to her touch, I followed her into a room of the temple I had never been in before.

A grand chamber unfolded before us. Hewn from the heart of ancient stone, the room exuded an air of timeless mystery. Carvings of ivy had been cut into the stone walls. Tall, graceful columns stood sentinel-like around the edges of the room, their marble surfaces gleaming white.

But it was the object in the center of the chamber that caught my eyes and held dominion.

A colossal, round, stone table, its surface worn smooth by the caress of countless centuries. Etchings of thorns and roses were carved into the table's stone perimeter, flourishing for all eternity.

Looking at the table, one could almost hear the echoes of hushed deliberations and whispered discourse as the destinies of kingdoms and fates of rulers were shaped and history inscribed, all around the border of this circular stone.

Gradually, I realized the table was not empty. Those seated around it had risen to their feet and now stood, staring at me with a mix of expectancy and shock.

Unspoken questions hung in their eyes as I slowly looked from one face to the next, a lump growing larger and larger in my throat.

Sir Ector's was the first face I saw. His weathered, warm, brown complexion seemed unchanged, as timeless as the walls of the temple itself. His features were as familiar as they had always been, etched with the wisdom of years past. His polished onyx eyes, full of experience and compassion, looked into mine, and I swallowed hard. He was the compass I had not known I'd needed until I'd lost it. He was the steadfast rock on turbulent seas upon whom we could always rely. He was my protector, my mentor, my friend.

His tightly-curled, salt-and-pepper beard was, if anything, a little longer than I remembered. And perhaps there were deeper furrows around his brow than there had been when I'd left.

But the same could be said of Merlin.

The strain of war had left its mark. A few deeper creases here. A few more white hairs there. What of the marks that were not so easy to discern?

Sir Ector smiled slowly at me, his eyes crinkling in the corners. A warmth started to spread in the center of my chest.

I looked past him to the young man standing by his shoulder, and that warm feeling vanished.

Galahad.

Gone was the laughing friend I had left behind all those many months before. A mantle of sorrow and solemnity had draped itself over Galahad's shoulders since our parting. His face, the same rich, warm brown hue as his father's, was now etched with tributaries that hinted at untold tales of loss and sacrifice. His lips, once always curved in a ready smile, were now straight and contemplative.

Only his eyes still held a hint of their former sparkle. And as he looked at me, I watched his lips turn up ever so slightly.

Then he glanced away, his fingers grasping the familiar talisman I remembered. The little sun symbol that hung around his neck on a leather string, the symbol of his faith. Some things had not changed. Galahad may be burdened beneath new sorrows, but if he had retained the talisman, then he had retained his faith—and a source of comfort I had always envied.

My eyes lighted upon the woman beside Galahad.

Dame Halyna. I had to suppress a grin. The woman had all but terrified Lancelet and me when we were younger.

Lancelet... I resisted looking across the table where I sensed her standing.

Instead, I met Dame Halyna's gaze and nodded respectfully. The weathered knight slowly nodded back, her eyes watchful. She looked much the same as she always had. Short, cropped, light brown hair tinged with a touch of gray. Her expression stern as stone and just as unwavering. Her fair skin had always been touched with red and was weathered with crisscrossing lines and scars, like a battle-worn flag that bore the colors of a life fiercely lived. Sturdy and athletic, every sinew in her frame spoke of the lifetime she had spent honing her skill. She was a master of the blade. She had trained countless knights before Lancelet and I had even been born.

Unlike Sir Ector, Dame Halyna still wore her royal armor. The silver suit had been polished to a fine gleam. A cloak of deep crimson flowed from her shoulders.

I thought I understood. Even as she stood on the precipice of rebellion, her armor was a testament to the honor she had sworn to uphold. The honor my brother was lacking.

My breath caught in my throat as I saw the man who had risen from his seat to stand beside Halyna.

Caspar Starweaver. Master of Potions. My uncle.

The hooded, purple, velvet robe he wore hung loosely on his frame. I watched as he smoothed his long, white, braided beard and then clung to the edge of the stone table for support. His hawk-like nose and weathered, creased skin had always suggested knowledge and wisdom to me.

But now his once-proud stature had given way to frailty. His hands trembled where they touched the table.

He looked at me with a wry expression, then, with an effort, lifted his hands palms up.

"We will talk later, niece," he said. "I know I have been... remiss. There is much to discuss."

Remiss? Was that what we were going to call it? Call him helping Arthur to kill me painfully with poison? Call putting iron shavings into the "medicine" I had trusted to protect me?

There was guilt in his eyes. He made no attempt to disguise it. This, more than anything, led me to nod briefly and then move on.

My eyes passed to the girl standing beside him, watching me steadily from out of large, doe-brown eyes. She was small in stature with a round figure that curved softly in a pale blue gown trimmed in dove gray. Dark, lavish lashes brushed against the honey-toned canvas of her rosy cheeks. I might have described her as sweet or even beguilingly pretty, were it not for the chopped, curly, brown locks that touched the tip of her chin. The hasty cut revealed jagged edges and loose long strands, as if she had taken a knife to her own tresses in an impulsive, violent attack.

There was something on the girl's shoulder. No, not something. A bird. An owl.

The owl clung to the blue linen gown the young woman wore, delicately gripping the cloth with its curved talons.

The bird's plumage was a study in earthy elegance, a composition of intricately patterned gray, gold, and brown mottled feathers. Luminous, burnished gold eyes stared back at me, framed with stark-white feathers in the shapes of perfect circles, like lanterns bright with ancient wisdom. Delicate, peaked, horn-like tufts crowned its head.

As I watched, the owl let out a low, haunting hoot and then spread its wings. Lifting off into the air, it glided across the room and came to rest on Merlin's shoulder.

Reaching a hand upwards, the High Priestess gently caressed the owl's feathers.

"Her name is Tuva," Merlin said to me briefly, meaning the bird, before turning back to the companions standing around the table.

I glanced one last time at the girl in blue.

There was a story there. Perhaps even more than one. But as I noted the figure standing to the girl's right, I knew I was only piecing together a small part of it.

"You wouldn't have met Guinevere yet," Merlin said quietly from beside me, indicating the girl in blue. "Guinevere..." To my surprise, the high priestess looked discomfited. "As you already know, Guinevere comes to us from Lyonesse."

"Lady Guinevere, it is an honor to greet you in person," I said, meeting the eyes of the petite young woman. "I am well aware of your noble family. I wish we were meeting under happier circumstances."

From the corner of my eye, I caught Merlin pursing her lips. "Indeed," she murmured. "Perhaps we'll leave it at that for now."

I nodded and saw Guinevere nod briefly, too. "Very well."

Fleetingly, I let my eyes rest on the tall and slender woman standing to the right of Guinevere of Lyonesse.

Lancelet de Troyes had been my closest friend and companion. Now she would not even meet my eyes.

Like many in the room, she had changed.

Before her harrowing ordeal, she had been strikingly beautiful and glowing with good health.

She was still lovely to my eyes and always would be.

But the horror that had befallen her had left indelible marks. Her face bore the worst of the scars. Most notably, a jagged, puckering wound along one of her cheeks that was edged with the unmistakable marks of small human teeth. Fresh, pink flesh around the scar's edge hinted at the hope of healing, but for now, the remnant of the nightmare lingered. Her short, sun-streaked hair had been pushed back off her forehead and tied with a simple braided piece of leather, but even this could not hide the cruel gaps of pink flesh where her beautiful hair had been violently torn away.

I had no wish to gape, but neither did I wish to permit myself the luxury of turning away.

So I held my gaze, waiting for Lancelet to return it. Observing how closely she stood to the petite girl from Lyonesse.

As close as a king's guard might stand to the king while they passed through a chaotic crowd. Was that how Lancelet saw herself? As Guinevere's protector?

Finally, Lancelet's eyes flickered over to me. Her mouth hardened into a grim line.

Still not pleased to see me then. I could understand and accept that. For now. Not forever.

Merlin stepped forward. "Shall we come to order?"

As Merlin raised her hands for silence, I watched as her fingers moved through the air, noting their delicacy, their frailty. The blue veins showing through the pale brown skin. Merlin, I realized with chagrin, was getting old. She could not live forever. And serving as High Priestess in times like these could not be easy for her.

But then, she was not High Priestess any longer, was she? Arthur had stripped her of that noble position. One she should have rightly held all her life. He had appointed another in her place.

A man.

One man to replace Merlin in the Temple of the Three. And another high priest to lead worship in the newly constructed Temple of Perun the king had built on the banks of the Greenbriar River.

A hush spread like ripples on a pond. I watched as, one-by-one, the guests standing at the round table took their seats.

Merlin approached her chair, her gray and white linen robes sweeping around her sandaled feet, and gestured to a curved wooden chair next to her own. I sat down gratefully beside her, barely registering as Javer scrambled into the seat to my right without a word.

But before we could begin, the doors behind us creaked open.

"Have I missed anything? Oh, you're just getting started. Excellent, excellent."

I turned my head as a jovial, smiling priest bumbled into the room, his arms full of scrolls. Irreverently, he kicked the heavy, oak doors shut behind him and jostled his bundle of parchments higher in his arms before they could topple onto the floor.

His cheeks were flushed, and his thin strands of hair a mess, as if he had just come in from the wind and rain outside. Dumping the pile of scrolls onto the table, he began to tug off the cloak he had been wearing, revealing a stocky, portly figure.

With a sigh, he eased himself into a chair on the left side of the table near Sir Ector and began to fan himself with one of the scrolls. The older knight eyed the priest with a hint of amusement.

Merlin smiled slightly. "Morgan, this is Tyre, my successor. High Priest of the Temple of the Three."

Tyre leaned forward to look at me with interest, then winked. "I think we all know who the Three take their marching orders from, and it's certainly not me."

If he could have said anything that would have instantly endeared him to me, it was this. I grinned at Tyre. "I couldn't agree more, Your Eminence."

Tyre burst out laughing. "Your Eminence. Oh, ho, she's a feisty one, isn't she, Merlin. I can see why you're happy she's returned."

"Morgan would have made a wonderful addition to the temple," Merlin said a little primly. She looked at me with affection and regret in her eyes. "Though I see that is not to be your path, as it turns out."

I felt myself blushing. If only she knew. A chaste priestess's life was decidedly not my path.

Since I had arrived back only yesterday, we had not had a great deal of opportunity to talk. Javer's injuries had needed to be seen to, first and foremost.

Before he and I had even made our way to the top of the stairs from the stone chamber below, it had been clear from Lancelet's odd behavior that the temple was not the same place it had been when I left.

Hardly speaking, she had carefully chosen an empty corridor and escorted Javer and me to a secluded wing of the temple and then summoned Merlin.

Next, a close-lipped priestess had arrived to dress Javer's wounds. His injuries were apparently worse than I'd initially thought, for at one point, he'd lost consciousness from the pain, something I observed with cool detachment.

At least Javer was still alive to feel pain. Beks was not.

Merlin had embraced me, held me close for a moment. The sentiment had been unexpected but not unwelcome.

And yet, somehow, I knew she had not been surprised to see me. Relieved perhaps, but not surprised.

I had sped quickly through a brief explanation of where I had been, leaving out any detail I thought would upset her.

Including the small detail of my being married against my will to a Siabra fae prince.

Or becoming the Empress of Myntra.

Or learning my mother and father may have both been Valtain fae royalty.

I would bring up everything when the time was right, I decided.

And the time had not been right. Before we could say much more to one another, Merlin had been called away to deal with something urgent elsewhere in the temple. I had fallen asleep in the little room she had left me in, my dreams a chaotic jumble of a world on fire and Beks' small face lifted up to the flames.

Fortunately, Draven had not been a part of them.

Now, as I sat at the round table, I swiveled towards Javer, conveying a silent, intense reminder with my eyes that he was not to mention a thing of his own initiative. He got the message. One I had already hammered in, tersely and bluntly, that morning. He nodded almost indiscernibly. If I had to guess, I'd have said that for once in his bitter, miserable life, he was leaning towards a self-imposed period of extended silence. Thank the Three for that small blessing, since I trusted the loathsome toad about as far as I could throw him.

And yet... he had been a trusted member of Draven's inner circle, I reminded myself. But that didn't mean he had to be a part of mine.

I looked slowly around the table. Was that what this was?

Merlin had declared she would convene a small meeting. She had not said of whom or for what.

Now, as I looked from face to face, I wondered if these were the only allies I could hope to find in Camelot—or perhaps even in all of Pendrath.

There were ten of us in all. And one of the ten was still looking at me with unmistakable animosity.

"I've just come from the castle," Tyre said, rifling through his scrolls. "I had an opportunity to visit the library briefly as well. The king is fortunately not overly concerned with its contents." He glanced at me reassuringly. "Nor does he have any inkling that you have returned, Lady Morgan."

"Only those present in this room have that knowledge," Merlin said quietly. "As well as a few of our most trusted priests and priestesses. And we have precautions in place to ensure it stays that way."

"Of course, Merlin," Tyre said quickly. "You may wish to begin with another topic than my research. I defer to you completely on this, as always."

While it was reassuring to hear this—to see that Merlin was being treated with the respect and deference that I believed would always be her due—I had my own ideas as to where this meeting should begin.

"Wait," I said, holding up my hand. "Where is my brother Kaye? He should be here." I glanced at Merlin. "If at all possible. I know he is young, but—"

"Morgan," Merlin said, her face slightly stricken. "I thought Lancelet had already informed you. Kaye is not in Camelot."

I stared at her. "But... I heard him. He told me..." I shook my head. Now was not the time to spill the contents of my dream in hopes I'd be believed. "I need to see him. As soon as possible. No matter the risk. He is the reason I returned. The first and foremost reason."

"I can understand that." Merlin's voice was gentle. "But—"

"He's on the front lines," Dame Halyna cut in.

My head shot towards her.

"Safe," she clarified quickly. "At least, last we heard. But near the front lines on the border of Pendrath and Tintagel."

The border I had seen in one of my dreams. I remembered the village on fire. The people's screams.

"No," I whispered.

"He is not fighting, as far as we understand." Dame Halyna glanced at Sir Ector as if for confirmation, and he nodded.

"We've been told by our sources that Arthur is using him as a figurehead more than anything else," Sir Ector chimed in. "Kaye is not required to fight. He is paraded in front of the troops as a reminder of what they are fighting for. But he is kept in relative safety, behind the lines in the camp."

Kaye must have be hating every moment of it. Being forced to represent the king and royal family in a war he knew in his heart was completely wrong and unjust.

"From what we understand," Dame Halyna said softly. "He is...cooperative. Arthur is pleased with his younger brother's service."

I snorted. "Pleased, is he?" I clenched my fists. I would show Arthur 'pleased.' "Arthur dares to send our younger brother—his heir—to the front lines, does he? It's too dangerous."

Was this why Kaye had called to me in my dream? Was he in more danger than Dame Halyna and Sir Ector were letting on?

"Not his heir for much longer."

The words were said so softly, I might have been forgiven for not hearing them.

"What was that?" I demanded, looking across the stone table to where Guinevere sat with her eyes downcast. "What do you mean?"

Slowly, she lifted her eyelids to look at me from under long, dark lashes. "Merlin, I..."

"It's all right." Merlin rose hastily to her feet beside me. She put a hand on my shoulder lightly. "There was too much to tell you last night, I'm afraid, Morgan."

"I suppose I could say the same."

She nodded. "There is much to discuss. Much to inform you of. Just as I am sure you will have much to tell us of your travels." She looked around the table. "Morgan has been a guest of the fae, you see. Not the fae of Valtain, but of another land entirely. She has returned to us from across the Kastra Ocean. From Myntra."

The table erupted.

"The fae!" That was Sir Ector. He did not sound particularly pleased. "Damn that guard. I knew him for a liar."

"Myntra! How fascinating." That was Tyre. He was looking at me with an academic tilt of his head that reminded me painfully of Rychel.

Where was she now? That clever, curious girl. How I hoped that wherever she was, she was safe.

"The fae of Myntra," my uncle murmured. I looked at him long and hard then. But his face was inscrutable.

Was this it? Was this when I told them?

But what good would doing so serve?

So I kept my own counsel and said nothing.

"You look very different, Lady Morgan."

The table subsided back into silence. The words had been spoken by Dame Halyna. She was looking at me curiously now.

"Yes, I suppose I do," I acknowledged.

I stood up, stretching out my arms from beneath the sleeveless tunic I wore. "You mean this, I suppose."

I let them take a good look at the golden tinge of my skin and the tapestry of symbols that gleamed like silver paint along my arms. I touched my hair.

"Or I suppose you might mean this." My hair, which had been what one could only describe as an elderly shade of gray when I'd left Camelot, had metamorphosed into a pearly silver. Perhaps not a shade everyone would find pretty, but it had grown on me.

I hesitated. Did I tell them that I no longer believed I was Uther Pendragon's trueborn daughter? Did I tell this room full of mortals that I was not half-fae but fully fae?

I bit my lip, and as I did, my uncle caught my eye. He rose to his feet, clearing his throat and swaying slightly.

"I believe I can explain Morgan's transformation." He met my eyes. "And a lovely one it is, may I say."

"A killing compliment," I said with deceptive gentleness. "One I would have been only too happy to receive before I left Camelot."

His face fell, haggard and old. "I understand, my dear. Believe me, I do."

To my surprise, Guinevere, seated beside him, touched his arm. "Perhaps sitting down would be easier," she suggested. Her voice was soft and melodic, like the ringing of chimes.

My uncle nodded almost absent-mindedly and sat back down.

"What do you mean, Caspar?" Merlin's voice was crisp and cool. "What do you have to do with any of this?"

My uncle sighed. "Perhaps some of you were already aware of the medicinal tonic that Morgan was prescribed as a young girl. From an early age, her father had me craft and concoct a potion that would discourage latent tendencies Uther had no wish to have displayed."

"Her fae attributes. Yes, I recall the potion," Sir Ector noted. Beside him, I saw Galahad nod. His eyes were thoughtful as he looked at me.

"For more than a decade, my niece drank this concoction. It subdued her fae features. When my nephew had Morgan leave on his questionable assignment, he instructed me to strengthen the tonic to a lethal level of toxicity that would render his sister weak, leading to illness, and eventually death."

The room became very still.

"This I did," my uncle said softly, "to my great shame, but also with hope in my heart."

"Hope that I would die along the way, you mean. I'm sorry to have disappointed you." To my mortification, I felt the prickings of tears. I lifted my chin so Javer wouldn't see. As a girl, I had believed my uncle to be a fount of wisdom. I had trusted him. Now, looking at him across the table, I felt betrayed all over again. I had not made my peace with his great deception.

"Not at all, my dear. I had hoped you would live."

"And yet you admit you poisoned me at Arthur's request. Gave me a tonic so toxic you knew it could kill me."

"Indeed, I did. There is no denying it. But, my dear, I also knew who was accompanying you."

My heart sped up. "Whitehorn. Agravaine's man."

My uncle grimaced. "Not that dimwitted brute. The other."

"The Captain of the Royal Guard?" Sir Ector was frowning. "A liar he might have been, but Lancelet has already told us that Halyna and I were wrong about his intentions. He behaved with surprising honor and protected the group. Even aided a small refugee girl."

Draven. They were speaking about Draven. My Draven. My... husband.

My mind raced with conflicting thoughts and emotions.

"Aye, Kairos Draven. Arthur had appointed him captain just before assigning him to join Morgan on her quest," my uncle said, his eyes intelligent and beady. "A very convenient appointment. Swift, too. Rarely have I seen a man advance through the ranks so quickly."

I shot to my feet. "Are you suggesting you had something to do with it?"

"I had everything to do with it," my uncle said. "Regardless of whether or not you will believe me, it was I who orchestrated his hiring in the first place."

My jaw may have dropped. "I don't believe you."

He rubbed his temples. "I don't expect you to believe me. At least, not yet. Nevertheless, it is the truth."

"Your optimism is misplaced. Why would you do something like that?" I demanded.

Caspar Starweaver was quiet for a moment. "We all serve in our own way, Morgan Pendragon."

"I don't see how bringing Draven to Camelot served your king whatsoever. If you really *knew* this man as you claim to, you would know this already," I snapped.

"Ah, but I did not say it was Arthur I serve," my uncle said mildly.

I stared. "Then... who?"

His face hardened. "I serve the throne of Pendrath. I serve this kingdom. I serve the best interests of our people. Do not tell me you have ever believed your brother had those interests at heart, Morgan."

"Well said," Sir Ector said. "As do we all, Caspar. Pendrath. Pendrath is my mistress. And Morgan Pendragon is the one who should be seated on that throne, not her treacherous, traitorous whelp of a brother."

The room exploded with sound.

I held up my hands. "Stop! Please. I mean it." I met Sir Ector's eyes. "I have no wish to sit on that throne, Sir Ector, though I am grateful you think so highly of me. But I will say this once. The throne should be Kaye's. Years ago, my father set me aside. You all know this. What's done is done. I will never be queen. But Kaye... Kaye deserves to sit on that throne. Kaye would be a good king."

The room fell into a surprising quiet.

"What? What is it?" I asked, looking from face to face. "What are you not telling me?"

It was Lancelet who broke the silence.

"While you were gone, Arthur wed," she announced bluntly. "His new queen is with child. "

My eyes widened. "Arthur is married? To whom?"

Ironic that my brother and I had both been wed while I was away. I did not voice the irony.

"His bride is something of a mystery," Merlin admitted. "Originally, a marriage alliance had been arranged with... Well, he had a traditional marriage planned."

"Traditional?" I raised my eyebrows. "And this marriage was not traditional?"

"It was... hasty," Merlin hedged.

Lancelet snorted from across the table. "You can say that again. The bans were not read. There was no announcement. No one was told. Not until after the wedding had already happened."

"We have absolutely no idea who the new queen really is," Merlin admitted. "Simply that her name is Belisent. She appeared by the king's side on the steps of the castle, and that was when most of the kingdom first learned they were married."

I felt dizzy. Camelot had a queen again. Kaye... Kaye was displaced. Or would be as soon as Arthur's child was born.

"How?" I said sharply. "The High Priestess performs royal weddings. That's how it has always been done." I looked in Tyre's direction.

He raised his hands quickly. "Don't look at me, milady. I was not asked to perform the nuptials, and believe me, I thank the Three for that every day. I believe I would have vomited all over the bride's gown."

I couldn't help a small snicker at that mental image.

"There is another temple now, Morgan. Cavan, the High Priest of Perun, performed the ceremony from what we understand," Merlin explained, looking immensely uncomfortable.

I began to understand. "Is that why the temple is so empty?"

The day before, Lancelet had searched for an empty corridor, seemingly to try to avoid the eyes of visiting worshippers, but she hadn't had to look far to find one.

Merlin nodded reluctantly.

"Simply replacing Merlin with a High Priest was not enough for your brother," Tyre said, his normally pleasant voice tinged with a hint of bitterness. "I was not enough. For do we not still primarily serve the Three here? Three women?"

"Three divine goddesses," Merlin said, her voice sharper than usual.

"Of course," Tyre assured her. "Three most deserving goddesses."

"But Arthur has become obsessed with Perun. And he's forcing the people to worship him, too. Yes, I understand." I rubbed my temples.

"He credits Perun for the blade," Merlin said softly.

"Excalibur?" My eyes widened. "You mean he has Excalibur? She brought it to him?"

"She?" Merlin looked confused. She shook her head. "We do not know how he got the sword. Lancelet could not explain it either. But it is in the king's possession."

"You're sure of that?" I insisted. "You've actually seen the blade? You know it is Excalibur, for a certainty?"

I thought of Orcades. None of this made any sense. She was fae. Arthur hated the fae. He did not seem to have stopped hating the fae while I was gone or just because he had gotten married.

Of course, there was only one way to be certain.

"This woman Arthur has married," I said carefully. "What is her name? What does she look like?"

Merlin frowned thoughtfully, then opened her mouth to speak. But it was Guinevere who answered.

"Hair as black as night. Lips as red as rubies. Eyes bright as a bluebird's feathers. Skin as pale as porcelain," Guinevere recited dully. "Queen Belisent is perhaps a few years older than you or I."

"I see," I said slowly. "Thank you, Guinevere." That didn't exactly match the description of Orcades, who, last I saw, had preferred the color amethyst to match her vivid, purple hair and violet eyes.

"So, Kaye is on the front lines. Arthur is married. His wife is pregnant." I ticked the items off on my fingers. "Arthur also has Excalibur, or most likely has it. And I assume Arthur hates the fae as much as he always has?"

Some of the faces around the room flickered with confusion, but Galahad answered, "We assume that he does. But he has not targeted the fae specifically while you have been gone."

"No, he's saved his hatred for people like us above all," Lancelet spat, looking down the table at Galahad who immediately seemed uncomfortable.

"Men who love men and women who love women, you mean," I said softly. "I am... sorry. Galahad, I still remember the night Lancelet came to us in the forest and told us you were no longer permitted to serve in the temple."

Galahad nodded. "It was a blow."

I looked around the room, my mind racing. What were my options here?

I wasn't exactly powerless.

I could leave the temple and storm into the castle, destroy Arthur with my fire magic—provided I could rely on it to work, though my confidence had grown in recent days. Then I could stop the war, go and extricate Kaye from the military, and... Put him on the throne? What of the new queen and her child? What of the many soldiers I would have to face down?

Or, I could sneak to the front lines. Rescue Kaye. Avoid Arthur altogether. And then what? Take Kaye where? Do what? Pendrath was at war with two kingdoms. Was I really going to leave my country in conflict without trying to stop it?

I clenched my jaw uneasily. There was another option. Would killing my brother Arthur put an immediate end to that war?

But what if Arthur did have Excalibur? And what if he already knew how to wield it?

Would I be any match for him if that was the case? Or would I be destroyed in an instant, leaving Kaye completely defenseless and Camelot exposed to Arthur's continuing evils?

Meanwhile, back in the Umbral Court, would Draven feel my death?

What was he doing, anyhow, while I sat here at this stone table conferring with Pendrath's most loyal?

I shifted uncomfortably in my seat. Did I even want to know? Did he miss me? Or was he simply furious that I had left him, refused to become his empress?

Or was he devastated? Sorrowful? Full of regret?

No, that didn't sound like the Draven I knew.

Or... A strange feeling prickled in my stomach. Or was he plotting even now how to reach me? I had destroyed the arch in the Siabra temple. But surely there were other ways. Even if he had to take a ship from the coast of Myntra to Eskira.

Would he do that? For me?

He had sworn to lay his armies at my feet. To help me destroy Arthur and save Kaye.

But instead of taking him up on that generous offer, I had simply left. Alone.

No, that wasn't true either. I glanced sourly at Javer who was studying his steepled fingers. I had one Siabra by my side. An unwanted one.

Across the table I heard Sir Ector clear his throat. "Your noble companion..."

"Who? Him?" I scoffed. "I wouldn't call him noble." I narrowed my eyes. "Are you noble, Javer? Is that how you would describe yourself?"

There was an awkward silence. I knew I was being rude and that no one else knew why. No one but Javer himself.

"Would you like to introduce us to your companion, Morgan?" Merlin said, full of tact as always.

"Not particularly," I said flatly. "But I suppose I must. Unless he would like to do it himself..."

To my surprise, Javer rose to his feet. "Javer is my name, good people of Pendrath." His voice was low and quiet. He kept his head down, his hands hanging by his side. The picture of contrition.

I shook my head. I wasn't falling for it.

"Back in Myntra, I had the good fortune to be called Wielder and Mage of the Court of Umbral Flame of the Siabra Fae under the benevolent auspices of His Majesty, the Crown Prince Kairos Draven Venator..."

I made a shushing noise, but it was too late. Javer's eyes flickered to me with panic.

A roar of voices arose around the table.

"Did you say Kairos Draven? *The* Kairos Draven who served in our guard?" Dame Halyna demanded.

I slouched in my chair. "One and the same, I'm afraid," I admitted. I snuck a glance at my uncle. There was a small smile on his face. I swore silently in my head.

It was almost as if the bastard had knownDraven was fucking fae when he had Arthur hire him.

And had my uncle anticipated that I'd wind up married to the morally gray asshole? I suspected *that* part of things would still come as a surprise to him.

"If I may finish," Javer protested weakly, raising his hands.

"Quiet down, everyone," Merlin beseeched. "Let us finish hearing what this gentleman has to say, if you please." I caught a twinge of pity in her eyes as she looked at the court wielder.

"Thank you, my lady." He waited until there was silence. "I have told you who I was. Now hear who I am."

He looked down at me, and I winced. I had a bad feeling about what was coming. Was it too late to gag Javer? Perhaps I should have done that from the start. Why, oh why hadn't I waited a few more seconds to destroy the arch? Then I could have shoved Javer right back where he'd come from.

But then Draven might have snuck through, a small voice in my head reminded me.

I clenched my jaw and waited.

"I stand before you, humbled and penitent, renouncing the titles and privileges that were once bestowed upon me. For in my pursuit of power, I lost sight of the sacred responsibility entrusted to me by my prince."

Beks. He was talking about Beks.

"The most sacred duty of all..." By the Three, the bastard's voice actually broke. Was he an excellent actor, or was I supposed to believe he truly cared?

Javer paused to collect himself.

I said nothing, simply crossed my arms over my chest, feeling murderous. I could feel everyone in the room staring at us.

Javer drew in a deep breath. "In the wake of my failure, I make new vows, here, today, in the presence of you, witnesses. No longer shall I bear the weight of titles and rank. Instead, let me be known simply as 'Javer the Penitent.'"

I bit my lip hard. Across the table, Lancelet's face caught my attention. She was looking back and forth between Javer and me. She seemed confused.

"My days of wielding magic for glory or prestige are over. Henceforth, I serve one person. Our young..." He hesitated.

I looked up at him, practically screaming with my eyes. Don't you dare say "empress," I silently prayed. Don't you fucking dare do that to me, Javer.

"Your young Morgan Pendragon," he corrected. He looked around the table. "With my last breath, I will serve and protect her. All I do shall be for her sake. I am her humble servant. May my actions henceforth speak louder than any words of contrition."

Javer dropped back down into his seat, his relief palpable. I watched as he wiped the back of his hand over his brow. The man was truly sweating. At least that was authentic if nothing else was.

Another awkward silence filled the room. I could almost feel the questions hanging in the air. What terrible thing had this man done to make him so contrite? What had happened before we'd arrived here? And why in Aercanum had he now made it his life's mission to tag along after *me*?

That last one was my most pressing question.

"Thank you, Javer. We are honored to have you here, amongst us." Merlin arched a brow at me, as if asking if there was anything I wished to add.

I knew I wasn't being very gracious, but I just shook my head, feeling like a small child, sullen and petulant.

I blamed Javer for Beks' death, yes. But I blamed Draven more.

Suddenly, I remembered what I had said to him. What I had let him say. He had all but called himself Beks' true murderer. And I had *let* him. Then I had left.

When the truth was... What was the truth?

We were all to blame.

Beks should never have been out there.

My heart clenched. Just like Kaye should not be out there right now, anywhere near a battlefield.

What the fuck was Arthur thinking?

He was thinking he would have another heir soon.

"We need to get Kaye away from the front lines," I spoke up, not caring if I was interrupting someone else. "We need to stop Arthur. We need to take back Excalibur. And we need to stop this fucking war."

"I don't think anyone in this room would disagree with you, Morgan," Merlin said with just a hint of tartness.

I flushed.

"And how would you propose that we accomplish all of that, O wise one?" Lancelet demanded, leaning across the table, her blue eyes blazing. "I mean, you've only just seen fit to come home to us at long last. But I assume you have a plan for how to solve all of our problems. After all, you wouldn't have come back otherwise, would you? So, please"—she stretched out her arms—"enlighten us. What's the plan, Morgan?"

I stared at her. At the woman who had been like my sister. There was cold bitterness in her voice. Such fury in her eyes.

And could I really blame her?

No, I could not. She was entitled to all of this. The accusations. The anger.

And I... I had to take it. Just like Draven had taken everything I had thrown at him, had let me attack him, had let me blame him. It didn't matter that I had been wrong. He said he loved me—*loved* me—and so he had stood there and let me do it.

I felt a pang of incredible shame. For Draven. For Lancelet.

So, I would not defend myself. I didn't deserve to.

"Enough," Merlin said to Lancelet.

The blonde girl sat down, her face still flinty.

Merlin looked at me calmly. "We are open to your ideas, Morgan."

I cleared my throat, then stood up slowly. "You're right, Lancelet. I should have been here. I *wanted* to be here. More than you know. I doubt I'll ever be able to convince you of that. I wish I'd never left your side."

It was the truth. Emotion caught in my throat. I forced it down.

"I'm back now," I went on. "And I swear I'll do my best to be what you need. What all of you need. But Kaye... Kaye is my priority. He's so young."

He was so young. And I loved him. And he had called out to me in my dreams.

Merlin touched my arm gently. "We understand."

"No, you don't," I said hollowly. "Because I know Kaye *can't* be my only priority. I want to run to him, but I can't."

I looked around the room. "He's not the only one who is suffering. Many people are. All of you have, in your own ways." My eyes rested on Guinevere briefly. She had lowered her head again. "So while all I want to do is go to my little brother, I know we have to deal with Arthur first. He's the cause. He's the reason for all of this. And we have to stop him."

I started pacing behind my chair because I couldn't stay still any longer.

"I can't explain it all now, but I don't come to you... completely empty-handed. But the tools I have at my disposal..." I thought of my powers. "I don't know if they would be best used right now. I want to hear from all of you. I need you to tell me how you want to use *me*."

CHAPTER 6 - DRAVEN

A contingent of Royal Guards burst into the room first, leaving the chamber doors swinging open behind them with a dramatic flourish.

Two small Royal Pages marched in next, playing their golden trumpets a little too loudly and a little too gleefully as nine-year-old boys were wont to do.

Close enough behind to supervise, followed the Royal Herald, looking arrogant and imperious and distinctly bored.

Next came the Court Mistress of Ceremonies in a long robe of emerald and gold, twirling a gilded staff and smiling broadly. It had been a long time since she'd had an opportunity to participate in a formal occasion that was not scheduled to include bloodshed, and the change seemed to be a welcome relief.

Behind them followed some highly underutilized members of my late father's court—the jesters. A troupe of acrobats, no less. They entered with wild abandon, whooping, capering, and somersaulting through the doors. The suits of gleaming gold and silver metallic fabric they wore were adorned with bells and ribbons that jingled and fluttered with every gravity-defying flip.

They tumbled to the ground at the foot of the bed in a perfectly executed pile of lithe bodies, then bounced to their feet with a grin and a flourish, leaving the two young pages laughing their approval while the coterie of guards looked on with undisguised smiles.

Amidst all of this, I walked in last.

Catching the Royal Herald's eye, I nodded my approval, ignoring the commotion that was occurring in the large bed that occupied the center of the room where a single occupant had been lying down and was now endeavoring to push themselves upright.

The Royal Herald cleared their throat and turned to face the occupant of the bed. Unfolding a long parchment covered with elegant calligraphy, they began to read.

"Let it be known unto all present in this august assembly and in accordance with the solemn rites of our most revered traditions as well as the immutable decree of the Crown Prince and Royal Consort, Kairos Draven Venator, Noble Warden of Myntra, Protector of the Siabra and First of His Name, that it is my esteemed privilege to declare that..."

A furious hissing had been emanating from the bed and now reached a crescendo.

"Stop, stop, stop! What the fuck is this?"

The Royal Herald trailed off, looking down his long, aquiline nose at the figure in the bed with distinct disapproval.

"If you would remain silent, Madam, you would be certain to find out," he replied, his voice clipped.

"Not you, you nitwit," the woman in the bed snapped. "I'm speaking to your master."

My sister-in-law, Lyrastra Venator, was glaring at me with an expression of extraordinary fury.

"Lyrastra," I said, taking a step towards the bed. "It's good to see you, too."

She made a sharp sibilant sound as if a tempest of fire and venom had been ignited within her. Though I did not think we were the first to light that spark.

Long, glossy, black hair framed her pale, delicate features. She had always been a beautiful woman. Now she was a vision of haunting vulnerability as she pushed back against the plush pillows supporting her. Her vividly hued, serpentine eyes of purple, green, and gold were clouded with pain and frustration.

With determined resolve, she finished pushing herself up in the bed, her one remaining arm trembling from the effort. The empty sleeve of the mulberry silk robe she wore hung forlornly where her missing limb should have been, a stark reminder of the horror she had been through.

And the sacrifice she had made.

For me.

"You are here to mock me. Is that it, Kairos?" I watched her draw a long, shuddering breath as if to gain her composure.

"Not at all. That is the furthest thing from my mind," I replied. Her eyes dilated angrily, and I quickly added, "I simply wished to get your attention."

Her nostrils flared. "You have it. Now get them out."

I turned to the Mistress of Ceremonies apologetically, trying to ignore the crestfallen look on the poor woman's face. "I assure you," I murmured. "There will be... other opportunities."

She smiled stoically and then ushered the two pages, the offended herald, and the acrobats from the room.

The group of guards were the last to go. All female, they hailed from Steelhaven, and I knew they took their job of protecting me with the utmost seriousness. After consenting to have them take up a station just outside in the corridor, I closed the heavy, oak doors to the bedchamber and turned back to Lyrastra.

"You didn't let the herald finish," I said.

"Fuck the herald."

"Tsk, tsk. That's not very nice. Though I suspect he'd likely be willing. Shall I call him back, and we'll find out?"

"Don't you dare," Lyrastra snarled.

I didn't bother to hide my grin. "Are you sure? It might improve your spirits."

"My spirits are fine."

"The decree stands whether you heard the full thing or not, you know." I leaned casually against one of the wooden pillars holding up the canopy bed. "You're looking well."

"I look like shit, and you know it." She scanned me up and down. "You look like shit, too."

I winced. "Fair. I'm working on it. We can't be our best selves when we've taken up brooding in bedrooms, now can we?"

For a second, she looked curious. "Is that what you've been doing?"

"Brooding, yes. Not literally lying in bed while brooding, no."

"Fair," she muttered. "You have me beat then, I suppose."

Cautiously, I took a seat on the edge of the bed. When she made no sudden, violent move, I let my body relax slightly.

"It's time you were up and about. Don't you wish to know what the herald was about to say?"

Lyrastra turned away, studying the closed curtains over the window across the room. "I don't care."

I followed her train of vision. Rising to my feet, I crossed the room and yanked the curtains open. Light flooded into the chamber. I turned back to see Lyrastra squinting.

"It'll do you good. Be careful, or I'll send Breena to you next," I warned her. "Now, are you going to let me finish, or do I have to bring back the entourage?"

Lyrastra's eyes flashed. "Don't you dare let anyone carrying a trumpet set foot in this room again, Draven, or I swear to Vela, I'll send them wailing to their mothers, one and all."

I snorted. "Never took you for the devout sort. I doubt Vela honors that sort of a threat."

Lyrastra's eyes narrowed. "Where's Morgan? Oh, that's right. I hear she left you."

I swallowed, trying not to react. "That's right."

"You made her your wife. Without asking, might I add. You made her our empress. Also without asking, might I add. And now she's gone." She shook her head slowly. "No wife. No empress."

"Yes. I am... bereft." It was true, but I said the words lightly.

Lyrastra shrugged. "So, you rule in her stead. It's the way it ought to have been all along. It was idiocy to try to change it. You should have been satisfied with winning and taking the throne on your own, not tampering with fate."

"She *is* your empress," I said softly. "And she *will* return."

"Perhaps in a few hundred years. If she lives that long," Lyrastra said sarcastically.

"I'll be bringing her back long before that," I said, meeting her eyes steadily.

She froze. "You're... leaving?"

"I am."

Her eyes narrowed. "And I..."

"You're remaining. You'll continue to convalesce as you rule the empire just as the decree said, if you'd waited to hear it read. I've appointed you the new Regent. You may thank me at your leisure."

"You've... what. I don't fucking think so."

"You don't need to think about it at all. It's not a request, Lyrastra. It's a command. I'm not asking."

I'd known she would be reluctant. That she'd do her best to refuse. I was prepared for that.

Her face flushed. "You knew I'd throw you out, so you came in with that... that mummer's farce!"

"I knew you'd try. I figured I'd give you a few people you could throw out. And one you couldn't."

Slowly, she moved her hand to the empty sleeve of her robe and shook the place where her arm should be. "I'm hardly fit. Ask someone else."

"Last I checked, one didn't need two arms to do the job of regent. One didn't even require half a brain. Just ask Sephone."

"How can I ask her? I understand you've had her summarily executed."

"I won't apologize for that. She tried to assassinate me. I'm sure you'll hardly be surprised. Hawl and Odessa were with me. Swift action was required, and we took it."

Well, Hawl took it, and I suspected they'd also have enjoyed taking all of the credit. But I didn't particularly want it to get out that the only Bearkin in the court had killed the former regent. Siabra could be very vindictive, and Hawl was already not especially popular. Not that they cared.

"Smart," Lyrastra said, lifting her chin. "Brutal but fair. Very Siabra. Wasn't sure you still had it in you. She didn't deserve better. And here I was, worried you'd coddle her and cater to her until she'd have you wrapped around her finger and regained her freedom again."

I coughed. "You're probably right. It was better this way."

When Morgan did finally return, she wouldn't have to worry about Sephone ever again.

One less person trying to harm my mate.

"But the answer is no, of course. I won't be your regent," Lyrastra said, sighing and turning her head away again. "Ask someone else. Ask Odessa. Ask Rychel. Oh, wait, you can't. She left you, too."

I grimaced. Lyrastra was being more brutal than usual, but I supposed I had it coming. "She certainly did. Another reason I must go. But you've misunderstood if you continue to perceive this as a request. Perhaps you should consider Sephone's demise more carefully. You *are* the regent. The herald's announcement is going out to the rest of the court at this very moment while you and I speak in this room."

That got her attention. Her sleek, black head whipped around to face me, wrathful once more.

"Don't make me threaten to have you executed, Sister," I said. "The court would enjoy that too much. Simply take the position and recognize it for what it is."

"Oh?" The green in her eyes blazed. "And what's that?"

"An honor," I said simply. "There are few I would trust on the Killing Throne."

"What if the power goes to my head? What if you come back to a sea of blood?"

"I'm sure you won't do any real damage. If there are a few executions here and there..." I shrugged. "Well, I'm sure they'll have had it coming."

Her lips twitched.

"I understand Laverna came to visit you."

Lyrastra's lips became a hard line.

"And you turned her away," I continued. "Why?"

The serpentine eyes flickered closed. She was shutting me out.

"The healers say you frequently bar the doors to them. They might have done... more for you."

Her eyes opened. "More?" She struggled against the pillows, pushing herself higher against the headboard. "More? They could have done more?"

I stood up as the bed quavered with her movements.

"What more could they have done? Could they give me my arm back? Could they restore it to me?"

"Did they say that was an impossibility?" I asked, my voice low. Such matters were not outside the realm of the possible. It depended upon the healer, yes, but just as much upon the patient. Not all fae had the potential to self-restore as I had when it came to parts of themselves. Now, I caught Lyrastra looking up at my horns, her face savage.

"Such a trivial part of you. A part you might have lived without. But me. My arm." She met my eyes. I held her gaze, unswerving. Her voice broke, "My arm, Draven."

"I know, Sister. It is a hard loss. I cannot imagine how great the pain must be," I said gently.

"That's a lie."

I frowned. "What do you mean?"

"You're missing half of yourself."

My face softened. "Morgan."

"You'll leave us? Go to her?"

"I'll go to her. Then I'll go to Rychel. I must find them both, Lyrastra. Tell me you understand."

She looked at me for a long while before she replied, "I understand."

"There is no one better than you to leave as regent. I truly believe this, Lyrastra."

"Things must be a dreadful mess if you have to tell me such lies."

I made a face. "They are. Sephone was not an ideal caretaker of the empire. She avoided everything of a practical nature, caring only to sustain the court and keep its favor. The army and navy are in shambles. Our vassals across Myntra, each in their own courts, are untried and untested."

"Should it come to war, you mean?"

I nodded. "Should it come to war."

"So, you believe... what? That the Valtain will invade here?" Lyrastra looked incredulous. "I thought that attack was random. Fleeting. They came to retrieve something, and they left."

"Perhaps. Perhaps not. They've left us alone for this long." I hesitated. "Odessa believes they have their sights set on something else right now. Some*where* else."

Lyrastra looked thoughtful. "Eskira?"

I nodded. "And if that's the case, then it's even more reason why I must go. If Morgan has returned to Pendrath, she's beset on all sides."

Not to mention from within her very own family.

"What do you need me to do?"

"I need you to keep order," I said. "To keep the court from imploding while we're gone. To keep treachery in check. No, more than that—to root it out and stop it from gaining a foothold in our absence. By whatever means you deem necessary. You know there are those amongst us who would have no issue with infighting and backstabbing. It's a way of life to them. But others want peace. And they deserve it. Those outside of the court, in Noctasia—the fae and the mortals alike—deserve it the most. In the past, Siabra court machinations have spilled up to the surface and infected the city like a disease. Sephone allowed this. Even encouraged it. I want you to prevent it."

"Such a small task," Lyrasta murmured sardonically.

"I would also have you rebuild our forces. Begin an immediate restoration program. Begin a sweeping wave of recruitment. We need the best from across Myntra. Fae or mortal. Or Bearkin for that matter. No discrimination, simply the best we can get. Request recruits from the vassal courts. Politely once, then with force if necessary. It's the least they can do, and they should be well aware of this. Remind them that the empire's defenses protect us all."

"You want me to be your general?" Lyrastra said.

"Not you. You'll have help. Odessa."

"Ah. She's not going with you."

"She wants to. But... no. Not this time."

"Just who are you taking along? Or are you going on this romantic redemption quest solo like an utter fool?"

I had been tempted. But in the end, common sense had won out.

"I won't take risks with my person if I don't need to. Not yet. Not if it means I risk not getting to Morgan," I said quietly.

Lyrastra was watching my face like a hawk. "And when you reach her? What then?"

"I stay by her side," I said automatically. "Whether she wants me there or not. She's not getting away from me again."

"If she's even alive," Lyrastra said brutally.

My nostrils flared. "She lives. I know that much."

Lyrasta's expression turned curious. "You feel her then? The bond... She rejected it but it still tells you that much?"

"She didn't reject it. I don't think she even knows how to do that." If Morgan truly wished to in the first place. And I hoped she did not. "But yes, I can sense it."

"And if she's in danger..."

My senses roared as I imagined it. "If she's in danger, I slaughter everyone who stands between us without hesitancy. The trials were a mere preview of what awaits those who dare to make an enemy of me by laying hands on my mate."

Lyrastra smiled. "You'll do all that single-handedly, will you?"

"I'll do what needs to be done," I said, my patience snapping as I imagined the worst-case scenarios, the ones I wouldn't let myself play out in my head but which ran in my dreams every night. "Shattered or whole. Kneeling or standing. I'll get to her, and I won't ever leave. This time, I'll make her understand what we are, together. And if anyone dares to hurt her, I'll burn them to the ground without a second thought."

"Burn them, will you?" Lyrastra's eyes were shrewd.

"You know the potential of the bond," I said, my voice lethally soft.

"Oh, I've seen the bond's potential firsthand. But does *she* have any real idea?"

"She's seen a preview. You know what we did in Noctasia. We did it together."

"I've heard the stories. Even if I had no wish to, the chattering of the servants was unstoppable. The Flame Empress, they're calling her." Lyrastra gave a short laugh. "She ran from them, but most of the commoners in the palace love her already. She ran from the big, bad, dark prince."

I was taken aback. "Is that how they see it? Is that what they're saying?"

"The prince who murdered his brother, his stepmother, and countless others as an assassin in exile? Yes, some of them. Others see it as romantic. After all, you chopped off pieces of yourself for her." Lyrastra rolled her eyes.

My horns. My heart. There was nothing I would not have done.

Lyrastra was nothing if not direct. She smiled wickedly at me. "Well, you *are* big and bad, aren't you? Isn't that what you were just saying?"

I leaned towards her. "And you're cool and cruel and sharp as a razor, and you're going to be the most efficient damned regent that Myntra has ever had."

She smiled, finally. "It's true. I will."

"That said... Be cruel to those who deserve it and only those. I don't want to return to a repeat of my father."

Lyrastra looked sick at the thought. I found this heartening. "Fae forbid."

"Fae *don't* forbid," I said sourly. "That's the problem. We don't forbid ourselves anything."

"Hmm," she said. "You still haven't told me who will be going with you."

I must have looked hesitant because her eyes narrowed. "What is it, Draven?"

"Gawain wishes to come. He's a formidable warrior. A good friend."

"Yes? So, what's the problem?"

"Crescent is insisting on coming along as well. He won't let another stitcher take his place."

"So? Oh. I see."

"Yes. Taina."

"She can't possibly go with you."

"No, she can't. She'll be... remaining here. With you."

"Me?" The word was practically a shriek. "I'm no nanny."

"Odessa will assist you," I said soothingly. "She's the girl's aunt, after all. But officially, I'll be leaving you as the girl's protector. After all that's occurred, Crescent and Gawain may have enemies they don't even know about. If any should seek to harm them through their daughter..."

Lyrastra's face hardened. "Just let them fucking try."

"That's the spirit I was looking for," I said.

"Fine," she said, her expression still sour. "I'll watch over her. Her and the entire continent. For you."

"And I'll love you for it." I grinned in a way I hoped was cheeky.

Her face softened. "We only have each other now. Out of this entire miserable fucking royal family. All the rest are dead."

I nodded. "They weren't all miserable."

She cast her eyes downwards. "No, I suppose they weren't. Two of them, at least."

I wavered, then asked, "Is it strange... My being... Well, married again. After Nodori..."

Her eyes flashed. "No. Why should it be? Nodori... Well, she was always the better half. You know this. She was better than you. Certainly better than I. She would have wanted... She would have wanted you to be happy again. You know this." She raised her eyes to my face. "And I know you never would have been happy with her. Not really. Between the two of us, let's be truthful about that at least."

There was a tight feeling in the center of my chest. I thought of Nodori. I thought of Nimue.

"I... might have been," I said carefully. "I'll never know."

I knew less about being happy than most people, I suspected. But I wasn't about to say such a self-pitying thing to Lyrastra in her current state.

Oh, I'd felt true happiness a few times in my life. Always with the same person.

Lyrastra's face filled with pity. I knew she was thinking about Nimue, too.

"Well, one thing is certain," she said. She flipped back the silken coverlet that lay over her lap, and to my surprise, began sliding to the edge of the bed.

I stepped back, knowing she would not want my help. "Oh? And what's that?"

"We're better off the way we are now," she said firmly. "Whether it's Morgan or you or me on that cursed throne, it's better than Sephone or Avriel or your father or Tabor." She gave me a crooked smile and started walking over towards her wardrobe. "And I'll have Odessa to keep me in check. Don't think I don't know that."

"You'll keep each other in check."

She stopped abruptly. "I want Breena."

"Breena?" I was confused. "My housekeeper?"

Lyrastra nodded. "I want her. She's a no-nonsense type, and I need that."

"I'll speak with her," I promised. "I'm sure if I asked her, she'd be honored to serve the new Regent."

"And just Regent," Lyrastra clarified. "Not Queen Regent or any of that nonsense. I'm keeping the spot warm, I'm not keeping it."

"You have your own life to lead, and I understand that," I said, holding up my palms. "That said... If there's anyone you would like beside you for companionship."

I meant Laverna, of course.

Lyrastra tilted her head. "I'll consider it. Thank you."

CHAPTER 7 - MORGAN

Merlin was speaking, and I was trying to listen. But my entire body was humming, buzzing, bursting with distraction. I had been prepared for some... discomfort... at being separated from Draven. But I had expected it to have taken some time before the feeling became anything more than a slight nuisance.

This... This was something else entirely. Just now, when I had stepped away from the table to stretch my legs, I could have sworn I felt his fingers caressing the back of my neck. The phantom touch left me shivering with disquiet—and with stark need.

Then there were the whispers in my mind. Like a distant echo of someone else's thoughts. Not clear enough to put into words or ideas, but faint and unsettling. The barest sensation of his voice in my head, a distant echo.

And this was only the second day apart.

How much worse would it get?

I forced myself to focus on what Merlin was talking about. Not to think about Draven. His scent. His voice. His touch. The way he would turn over in bed at night and wrap his long legs around mine, then throw a heavy arm over my chest and pull me tightly against him until I could hardly breathe. Oddly, I'd enjoyed the sensation. Two bodies, intertwined. The beating of his heart as his chest pressed against my back. And then the inevitable. The swelling hardness against my ass as our close contact raised him to arousal even in his sleep. The sweet feel of his teeth as he nibbled on my skin, as the palm of his hand cupped my breast through my thin night dress...

"What you're saying would be suicide." Sir Ector's voice broke through my reverie. "I won't allow it. Absolutely not."

"Shouldn't it be Morgan's decision?" This was Galahad, gentle but stubborn.

"Indeed." Merlin, calm, patient as ever. "The choice is hers in the end."

"The girl has been through enough..." Sir Ector sounded as if he were on the brink of losing his temper.

"The girl will decide for herself," I said. "Thank you, Sir Ector. You have no idea how much I have missed you. I can always count on your protection, and for that, I am eternally grateful." He looked gratified.

I looked around the table. "All of you." I let my eyes linger purposely on Lancelet. "I am grateful for all of you."

"All of us?" Tyre piped up.

I smiled. "Well, most of you."

"He grows on you," Dame Halyna said, smiling faintly.

"Like a wart," Tyre agreed, chuckling heartily.

Merlin smiled, but I sensed she was growing impatient with the delay.

"You wished to send me back to the castle? Directly to Arthur?" I said, repeating what she had just been suggesting.

"A spy in the king's court, yes," she said, meeting my eyes. "A dangerous plan. I admit it."

"Dangerous, yes, but bold, too. And where else would I go? I can't just hide in the temple..." Too late, I remembered Lancelet and Guinevere. Wasn't that what they were both doing? Or seemed to be doing? I pressed on. "If that's where I can best serve you all, then—"

"It's a foolish plan." Lancelet's voice cut in. "And not for the reasons you think."

"Oh? No?" I tried to keep my voice polite.

"No. Look at you." Then she turned to the rest of the table. "Look at her. She's practically glowing. If Arthur hated her when she was hiding her faeness before, what would he think now? And where will she say she's been? Obviously he'll suspect the worst based on how she looks. That she's been conspiring with his enemies."

"Fae enemies?" I tilted my head. "Does Arthur believe he has any? I thought his foes were all mortal—and all his dear neighbors."

Lancelet shrugged. "He's a mad man. Who knows what he thinks. He's *your* brother."

I tried not to lose my temper. "Right."

"She has a point," Merlin said, touching a finger to her chin. "But there is a way around it..."

"I don't think Morgan will agree to that again," my uncle spoke up, his voice firm. "And for once, I would agree with her."

"The medicine," I said, understanding. "You think I should hide what I am?"

I tried to imagine taking the potion daily as I had done all throughout my childhood. The concoction that had almost killed me.

I imagined my golden skin fading, the silver markings disappearing. My hair reverting back to a sickly, colorless gray.

But worse, I imagined my powers dwindling. Being helpless and vulnerable to anything that lay before me.

I could still carry a weapon. I could fight. But in many ways, I knew I'd feel impotent after having access to the kind of power most could only dream of.

Arthur had no idea what I was capable of now. And truth be told, neither did I. Not fully. But that didn't mean I wanted to hide my capabilities completely. Or lose all access to them.

And what of this connection to Draven? If I began to take the potion again, would it suppress that, too? This bond, irritating though it may be already, was also a lifeline back to Myntra. Back to him."

"I'd have to think about it," I said slowly. "I'm not sure I could... do that again."

"Completely understandable. Of course. You must consider it," Merlin said, nodding. My uncle's face was grim as he looked across the table at me.

"Still," Merlin sighed, "think of what you could learn if you went back. If you could make Arthur trust you again. Not to mention if the king really does have the sword..."

"Chances are that I would be nothing more than a well-treated captive, Merlin," I said carefully. "I think it's safe to say that Arthur never truly trusted me. And as I didn't bring him back the sword and I've been missing for months, he has no real reason to start even if I suddenly reappear and try to play the devoted sister."

"Still, if we could think of a reasonable excuse to explain your disappearance. Something convincing."

"It's not a terrible plan," Dame Halyna agreed, her voice gruff. "At the very least, Morgan could get close to the new queen. Perhaps she'd learn something that way. And she'd be closer than any of us to Excalibur. Or," she amended, "to at least finding out where the king keeps the damn thing."

"You want me to try to steal it, don't you?" I realized.

A spy and a thief. Was this what I had returned for? I reminded myself I had returned to be whatever they needed me to be.

And in the end, there were worse things they might have asked me to do.

Like kill Arthur outright. In a way, I was surprised no one had suggested this yet.

Looking at Lancelet's face, I was fairly certain she wanted to but knew Merlin would erupt if she dared.

"It's the first way to weaken him," Merlin said. "None of us can imagine the consequences of him possessing such a weapon. Every day I thank the Three that he has not found some terrible way to use it yet—against our people or against his perceived enemies. Can you think of a better way?"

"No," I admitted. "It's... not a bad plan."

"Well, well, we've given Lady Morgan a great deal to think about," Tyre said cheerfully, rubbing his hands together. His words seemed to be a subtle hint.

Merlin nodded and rose to her feet. Tuva the owl was still perched on her shoulder. The bird seemed in no hurry to fly off.

The High Priestess hesitated, then placed her hands on the stone table.

"We'll adjourn for today. I know for some of you, our plans move too fast. For others, not fast enough." I caught her quick glance at Lancelet. Was she worried my friend would protest, disrupt the meeting's conclusion somehow?

If so, she was right.

"Once again we've accomplished precisely nothing." The words were spat bitterly.

I caught others glancing away, not wishing to meet Lancelet's merciless stare.

"Arthur has *killed*. And he has *maimed*. And he has *taken* from us. From all of us. From some more than others. And yet still we do not act. We stew in indecision. We hesitate. We—"

There was a small commotion near where Lancelet stood as Guinevere rose to her feet and pushed past her without speaking or raising her eyes.

She came around the table and reached the door, fumbled for the latch, then pushed open one heavy, oak panel and slipped out into the corridor beyond.

But before she'd disappeared, I had glimpsed her face. Caught the sheen of unspent tears in her eyes.

Silently, the bird on Merlin's shoulder lifted into the air and flew from the room in the direction Guinevere had taken.

Lancelet looked briefly shaken, then enraged again. "We are all cowards," she hissed furiously. "Sitting here, pretending we have any choice in what we must do next."

She glared at each of us in turn, her eyes filled with condemnation.

I resisted the impulse to squirm under that glare. Was I not the most deserving of her censure? I, who had only just returned and who had done the least of anyone to stop Arthur's mad course?

"Rushing in with a hot head is a good way to return headless." I turned to see Tyre looking at Lancelet with a reproving expression.

Next to me, Merlin touched the table's surface again as if to steady herself.

"Tyre speaks truly," she said slowly. "Oh, bold-hearted Lancelet. Make no mistake, your courage serves you well. But spend it wisely. Conserve it until the time is right, then strike true and strike hard. We would not see you make a futile attempt only to be felled for it, never to rise again."

The words hung in the air like a solemn warning.

Slowly, Lancelet sank back into her seat. Her face remained sullen, but the fire had gone out of her.

"This table," Merlin continued, her hands still upon the stone, "has sat within the walls of this temple for hundreds of years. There was a time when no monarch of Pendrath would have failed to consult here with the High Priestess and other wise advisors before taking any significant course of action for the kingdom. Before beginning a negotiation, forging a new alliance, or entering into a war."

It went without saying that Arthur had broken with tradition. I wondered if our father, Uther, had ever sat in the room.

"Within the courts and palaces of the world, few such tables as this will be found," Merlin went on. "Why? Because the table is round. There is no head, and there is no foot. Where an individual sits at the table says nothing about their rank or their value. All places at the table are equal. All voices are equally important. That is the significance of this round table, this piece of circular stone that has witnessed so much of our history."

Her fingers lingered on the stone surface with affection—and with fatigue. I was touched by the weariness I saw in her face.

Reaching out a hand, I laid it upon her arm. "Was there a name for the collective when they would meet here, Merlin? What was it called in my father's day?"

It was inaccurate to continue thinking of Uther Pendragon as my father—and yet, he was the only one I had ever known in that role. The only one I could clearly remember, I corrected myself.

Merlin smiled wanly. "I cannot say I recall, Morgan. In your father's day, this room was seldom called into use. Uther preferred to hold meetings in his own chambers. He was not really one for temple visits."

No, that was true. Uther Pendragon tolerated the goddesses. He had not bowed to them except when he'd had no other choice.

"What would you call us, Morgan? Would you have us come up with some trite name?" Lancelet's voice was tinged with sarcasm. The words stung, as she had meant them to. "Knights of the Round Table, perhaps? Or some other silly nonsense?"

I opened my mouth, but it was Galahad who spoke first.

"We are not all knights. Some of us are priests." He looked at Tyre. "And priestesses." He nodded at Merlin. "We have an apothecary among us as well. And a king's brother." This was to my uncle, Caspar Starweaver, bastard brother of Uther Pendragon. "As for myself... Well, I am not sure where I fit in. I am neither knight nor priest."

"Nor am I," I said quietly, meeting Galahad's eyes.

He nodded and smiled slightly.

"Nor is Guinevere," Lancelet said, begrudgingly.

"Yet knights have long been the symbol of nobility in Pendrath," Galahad continued. "We look up to them, for they are meant to personify our most beloved ideals."

Was I imagining it, or did Lancelet look slightly chagrined as she said this?

"Knights are to be courageous, virtuous, and chivalrous," he went on. "They are to protect the weak and the defenseless."

"Don't forget loyalty to their monarch," Lancelet said, almost despondently. She was looking down at the table with her arms crossed over her chest.

"Loyalty to the crown. Of course," Galahad replied. "But when the monarch is a scourge of the people? When the monarch terrorizes those he is sworn to protect? Well, then I would argue a knight no longer owes loyalty to such a lord and should feel no shame in breaking their oath. As Morgan has said, Kaye is the rightful heir. The one whose throne we must protect, whose people we must serve. And with this in mind, I humbly suggest the name you facetiously posed was truly fitting, Lancelet."

She looked up, surprise on her face.

"The Knights of the Round Table," Galahad continued. "It is a good name. For we are all acting as knights of Pendrath. Are we not swearing to serve and to protect with our very lives if need be?"

Galahad sank back into his seat as if embarrassed for having spoken for so long. I watched as Sir Ector gave him an approving clap on the shoulder.

"I like it," Tyre said loudly. "Let's keep it."

"If there is no objection, I don't see why not," Merlin said, looking around the table.

"Guinevere is not here..." I started to say.

"It's naive and stupid... just like all of us," Lancelet muttered. "Perfect." I wasn't sure anyone but me had heard her. I hoped they hadn't.

The group rose and began to disband. Merlin stayed close by my side, not allowing anyone to steal me away.

With relief, I watched my uncle nod at me, then slip outside.

I caught sight of Guinevere standing a little way down the corridor with Tuva on her shoulder. She leaned against a pillar, looking down at the acolyte garden below, absentmindedly trailing her fingers over the owl's feathered head.

Lancelet brushed past me. In an instant, she had taken up a position on the opposite side of the arch, her expression terse and watchful.

"What is with them?" I murmured to myself.

"What was that, my dear?" Merlin touched my elbow.

I nodded towards the two women. "What's going on with... you know."

"Oh." Merlin nodded. "Yes. Lancelet and her Guinevere." She smiled fondly, then gestured for me to follow her down the hall.

"You will not have heard Guinevere's sad story yet." She kept her voice low.

Javer had been trailing me—I turned to him with a silent frown, and he scuttled in the opposite direction down the corridor. I had no idea where he planned to go, and I honestly didn't care.

We passed a young acolyte with a gray hood pulled up over her head. She bobbed a curtsy, then hurried past, hardly sparing me a glance. I looked questioningly at Merlin.

"The novice? She will be discreet. Any who you meet in these halls are aware of who the four of you are and may be trusted." She hesitated. "It's been a long time since you and I walked through this temple alone together, Morgan."

"It has," I murmured.

"Perhaps you'll recall that the last time you were here with me, I asked you about your own magic."

For a moment, I was uncomfortable, wondering if she was about to ask me the same question. What a different answer I would have for her now, if I were to answer honestly.

But Merlin apparently had something else in mind.

"I was not... entirely forthcoming with you then," she said. "About my own abilities."

My heart sped up. "What do you mean?"

She hesitated. "For your own good, I allowed you to believe my abilities were as dormant as your own."

Dormant. An excellent word choice. Did she know how apt it was?

She raised her eyes to mine. "But the truth is that there are those in the temple conclave who foresaw your brother's actions a long time ago. Those who were prescient enough to realize that any son of Uther's... Well..." She paused.

"Don't stop on my account," I said wryly. "I know only too well what he was like..." I stopped. Choked more like it, as memories came flooding back in a torrent.

"I saw your torment, Morgan."

The words came as a shock.

"When you were a child. You and Arthur. We all saw the sort of father Uther was to you both." Merlin's face was full of regret. "No one dared step in. Oh, how I longed to. But I dared not. My place was so precarious. Uther... Well, he was not a friend to the temple. Not like kings and queens before him had been."

My throat was dry. "I understand." I forced myself to shrug. "My father died when I was quite young. I hardly think of him now."

"Yes," Merlin said quietly. "He did die. Very fortunately."

Her eyes held mine. Intense and prodding. I looked away.

Did she know? Did she understand what had occurred that day? The day I'd believed Arthur was dead, killed in a violent fit of rage by our father, Uther?

Even now, the memory of Arthur's small body lying on the ground as my father kicked him with a booted foot was enough to make the bile rise in my throat.

"My father killed my mother," I said directly before I could stop myself. "He nearly killed Arthur."

Merlin's face remained unchanged. No shock. No surprise. "I believe you. And no one stepped in."

"I was too young to step in when he hurt my mother." The words were a rough rasp. "I hid under the bed. I couldn't help her. I was too little. He didn't know I was there."

What was I doing? Why this sudden urge to confess?

"You were right. You did the right thing."

The words kept coming. "Then, with Arthur. He nearly killed him. My brother. I tried to stop him then. I couldn't let him kill Arthur, too."

The sorrow and empathy in Merlin's eyes became almost unbearable. "Of course you couldn't, Morgan. Whatever you did, I know you did the right thing."

"How?" I choked out. "How can you know that? Look at what Arthur has become. Maybe it would have been better if..."

I couldn't finish that sentence.

"No," Merlin said firmly. "You were both children when your father died." She was careful not to say "when you killed him."

She placed her hands on my arms. "No one could have known what Arthur would become, Morgan."

"But you just said..." I protested. "You said it was foreseen."

"'Foreseen' is not the same as 'came to pass,'" she said, releasing me. "Predictions were made about futures that were more or less likely. It is a tragedy, really, that this is the one that has played out." She raised a hand and touched my cheek gently. "Two children. Both raised in violence and blood with a cruel father. Who could have said which one would nurture the violence they had borne and which one would repel it?"

I was shocked. "Do you mean there were prophecies and predictions about me as well as about Arthur? That I might have been the one to go down a dark path?"

"There are those in the temple who peered down every path," she said carefully. "It was their task to do so."

"Who? Who looked? Was it you?"

"Tyre was one such." She smiled faintly at my expression which must have been one of stark surprise. "He is older than he may look. As am I. As for the foretellings, well, there were many prophecies made when you were born—and when your brother was born. Some have come true. Some have come close to true. And others will never come to pass."

She looked at me carefully. "I tell you this here, in this space where to speak of such things is safe."

"What do you mean?"

"I mean, Tyre and I have warded the temple and placed any who will come across you and the others under seals of silence. They cannot speak of what they know, even should they wish to." She smiled faintly. "Your uncle is not the only one who possesses such talents."

"I see," I said. "I had no idea you could do such things." I looked at her pointedly.

"No, I never wished for you to know. There was no need. We had hoped there never would be."

"And if Arthur had known that those who served in the temple were capable of more than he thought, he would have been certain to use you however he could," I concluded. "He would have conscripted you, demanded you do his bidding. I understand."

"I thought you would. I make no apologies for keeping these things from the king. Such matters are deeper and more significant than one man alone."

She was leading me into a different part of the temple. We passed along a covered walkway and through a garden where clusters of fruit trees and an herb garden lay surrounded by low stone walls and arched pillars.

Then we were back under the dome of the temple. I followed her through the purification room and into the room where I had once watched her pour a libation offering, my senses prickling with anticipation.

She pushed open a door on the far side of the sacred room, and I gasped. Just as I had the first time I had seen it.

I stood within the arched corridor lined with fantastical mosaics once more. On either side of me, the fae were depicted. To my left, the fae were beautiful and regal. To my right were fearsome fae of tooth and claw.

And in the center of the passage, beneath the ceiling lined with precious jewels and costly stones that glowed with a life of their own, stood my uncle, Caspar Starweaver.

CHAPTER 8 - MORGAN

H e pushed back the velvet hood of his cloak.

"An ambush?" I glanced back at Merlin.

"Forgive the subterfuge," she said. "He wished to speak with you... and I believe there are things you need to hear."

"As it happens, I wished to speak with him, too," I said. "So I'll forgive your methods, Merlin... this time. Next time, simply ask."

Merlin nodded. "I understand. You are no longer a child."

Then, to my surprise, she turned back to the door and left the passage.

My uncle and I were alone.

I turned to face Caspar Starweaver.

"You nearly killed me."

"I am glad I was not successful," he said calmly.

I crossed my arms. "I'm to believe you planned not to be?"

"It's the truth."

"So you somehow... what?" I shook my head. "Manipulated Arthur into hiring a royal guard who you already knew was not what he seemed? *Sir Ector* didn't even know the truth."

He and Dame Halyna had thought they'd peeled back the truth, and Sir Ector had told me Draven was an assassin-for-hire, a ruthless one. "So you somehow knew that Draven was posing as a royal guard who was posing as a brutal assassin but that he was... neither of those things."

"How well do you know him?"

I flinched. It was an excellent question. But not one I wanted to face.

My uncle's eyes swept over me thoughtfully as if he were seeing much more than I was saying. "Even now, you are not sure, are you? Yes, I knew. That said, he really is quite a talented assassin. Perhaps not as cruel a killer as Arthur was led to believe, however. Or Sir Ector for that matter. I'm sorry about that. Tricking Sir Ector was not my primary intent, of course. But it can help to be thought of as worse than you are." He smiled slightly.

"You would know, I suppose? Just how much about Draven do you know, really?"

I thought about all of the things Draven was. The list was lengthy.

Fae.

Crown prince.

Royal guard? For a time.

Assassin? Apparently before he'd come to Pendrath. In that shadowy period where he'd been banished by the Siabra court for his brother's murder.

My protector? Always. Whether I wished it or not.

My husband. But in the royal courts, women often had husbands they hardly knew and did not love. Marriage did not make them true partners. It did not make them mates. Was Draven? Was he my mate?

I looked at my uncle, wondering just how much he'd seen, suddenly feeling strangely exposed.

"He did what I hoped he would do. He kept you safe."

My eyes widened. "Are you saying you had no idea what he would really do? That you hadn't actually spoken to him about it?"

"How could I have possibly spoken to him? It would have put him in a very dangerous position. As well as myself."

"So you sent me off with a man you *hoped* was not as brutal as the rumors claimed. And with a potion you *knew* could kill me."

"I had heard enough of Kairos Draven to know he was much more than he seemed—and that a man of strength and some decency lay beneath."

"'Some' decency," I muttered.

A smile flickered over my uncle's face. "Too much is not always a good thing."

"He's just as brutal as the rumors," I snapped. "Perhaps you got a lot wrong."

"Not, however, a slayer of infants." My uncle's smile became annoyingly cherubic.

"Not that I've been able to confirm," I said, narrowing my eyes.

"Nor have I," my uncle said. "A rumor I highly doubt has any basis in reality. But your brother enjoyed hearing it." His eyes fastened on mine. "Convincing him Draven was a cruel man made it easier when I suggested that the guard captain be the one assigned to assassinate you if the need arose."

"Well, did you want me dead or not?" I exploded. "Was I supposed to have died from the potion or from Whitehorn or from Draven? Or perhaps the sword was to have done me in at the end?"

My uncle tilted his head to one side. "To tell you truly, I don't think even Arthur could tell you that."

I looked at him. "What do you mean?"

"I mean your brother has very confused feelings about you, Morgan. I don't think he knows himself if he wants you dead or alive. Which is why his instructions to Whitehorn were one thing and his instructions to Kairos Draven quite another."

I wondered if my brother was smart enough to have known that Whitehorn had been too much of an idiot to succeed. Perhaps he simply sent him to weaken Florian's father, Agravaine, his most trusted advisor—and one who held a great deal of sway at court.

Though if it weren't for Draven, Whitehorn might have succeeded. I hadn't exactly been in any condition to protect myself when Whitehorn had tried to strap me to his horse.

"Forgive me if I don't find that particularly heartening," I said.

"No, I don't suppose you would," he murmured. "Family is such a complicated thing, isn't it? Still, I hope you will believe that this old man would have been very regretful to hear of your passing, and that it was never my intention to do you long-lasting harm, niece."

Long-lasting harm. I supposed in the Pendragon family, that was as good as it was going to get.

I snorted without meeting his eyes.

"You traveled to Valtain. You saw the ruins of Meridium," my uncle said, his gaze becoming a little more astute, a little more prodding. "You must have learned a great deal. Seen much."

"Meridium was only the beginning of what I've seen."

He smiled. "Ah, so you have met the Siabra then."

If I'd been drinking a beverage, I would have spewed it across the passage then.

"You know of the Siabra?"

He gestured to the mosaics that surrounded us. "Why do you think I chose this place for our meeting?"

"Merlin said the mosaics showed the two sides of the fae. The dark and the light."

"Well, in a sense they do. Don't they?"

This dancing around was becoming exhausting. I decided to be blunt. Very blunt. "How much do you know, Uncle? Do you know who I am? Truly?"

The smile again. But it was a sad one. "Who do you think needed that foul potion badly enough to create the recipe in the first place, Morgan?"

I stared. "My mother. You said she..."

"Yes, she needed it. Wanted it most desperately. For reasons I have never been able to fathom. She loved your father. And she loved you. She wanted..." He took a deep breath, as if it pained him. "She wanted to be able to fit in, I suppose. And she knew it was not likely to last long."

"What do you mean?"

"She knew the refuge she had found here was only temporary. Sooner or later, something was bound to snap. Either Uther's temper as he realized the truth or..."

"The truth? What was the truth?"

"She had placed him under a glamor, you see. How else would a man such as Uther have been able to bring back a fae bride when he found her while out hunting one day? He was lovestricken. Quite infatuated."

"And? Was it real?" Did I care? If a man like Uther had been tricked into falling in love? "He must have known I wasn't his child. All along."

My uncle nodded slowly. "When they brought you back to the palace, you were very young," he said softly. "Hardly more than a toddling baby."

A baby who had spent over one hundred years in some liminal place between worlds. What had my mother been doing for all of that time? Had she simply slumbered alongside me? Or had she been watchful, active?

"Uther announced you were his. There was no fanfare and absolutely no challenges. Few would question the king on such a matter. You were named his heir then. Your mother was... gratified."

"To think I might someday sit on a throne? Or to think the spell she had cast over him was working so well?"

I knew she had done all of it to protect me. She hadn't wanted to marry Gorlois. And she probably hadn't wanted to marry Uther either. She had simply chosen another powerful man. One she had gambled would be able to protect her. But she hadn't bargained for the fact that he would wind up being the man who broke her heart and took her life.

So why did I feel so angry with her now?

"She might have done more, Morgan," he said quietly. "But that was the limit of her powers. You see, she had given all she had left to you."

"I don't understand..."

He gestured. "The markings. On your arms. Surely you must have wondered what they were."

I touched myself. "She did this?"

He nodded. "A very old, very powerful form of magic. She covered you with protective wards and imbued her magic into the runes. She poured everything she had into you. Then she began taking the potion."

"The potion you already had on hand." I stared at him. "Why? Why did you already have it?"

He sighed. "Haven't you already figured it out, my dear?"

Slowly, he pulled back the folds of his cape, pushed aside strands of white hair.

The pointed tips of his ears.

"Oh, I haven't bothered taking it for some time," he said lightly. "I never had what you might call prominent features. Besides, Arthur rarely deigns to visit. Nor does he look at me particularly closely. I might shave my head or dance through the castle naked." He paused, thoughtfully. "Well, that second one might get his attention. But I prefer nude cavorting under the moonlight, between you and I."

I couldn't even muster a chuckle. I simply gaped at him. "You're... fae."

"Part-fae. Just part. On my mother's side, of course." He shook his head. "This penchant for fae women. It's not a particularly good look coming from men who always claim to hate the fae, is it? Not a set-up for a particularly healthy relationship."

"No," I said. Then I thought of Florian. "But... You wouldn't even put wards on my door when I asked you."

A shadow passed over his face. "A miscalculation. Perhaps a cruel one. I thought you could deal with that particular problem on your own."

"I did," I said coolly. "But first he gave me this." I pulled down the neckline of my tunic to reveal the scars on my chest.

My uncle studied the marks in silence. "I have made many errors in my lifetime, Morgan. Let us call this another one. Truly, I am sorry. I was not ready to tell you then, you see. You were leaving. I thought there was no need, not yet. And I admit, there may have been fear behind my reluctance. Your brother..." He sighed, shaking his white head.

I tried to understand. What would it have been like to grow up in Uther Pendragon's shadow? To have had such a man for a brother? My uncle could not have had a happy family life either.

"But now..." he continued. "Well, I did not wish to speak of it openly at the meeting, but I have done what I can to protect you. If anyone tries to divulge your whereabouts to Arthur, they will find themselves quite inexplicably unable to utter or inscribe the words. Instead, they will find themselves filled with a strange but undeniable compulsion to throw themselves into the Greenbriar River." He smiled softly. "My small contribution, niece. Too little, too late though it may be."

I nodded. He wasn't actively trying to harm me, and he had apologized for the past. It was a start.

"Your mother and mine would have had a great deal in common, I believe," he said with a wistful expression. "If they could have spoken."

"What do you mean?"

"Both fled the Valtain court. I have never figured out just who or what my mother was in relation to those in power, but she must have surely been close to the throne, or why run away as she did?"

"So the Valtain were—are—as brutal as the Siabra?"

My uncle looked slightly surprised. "Oh, much more, my dear."

"The last Siabra emperor..."

My uncle waved a hand. "Brutal, yes. But a pawn. He hardly weakened the Valtain as much as the Siabra may like to think."

"Does it matter?" I said thoughtlessly. "What matters is here, now. What matters is what Arthur is doing."

Impatience flashed in my uncle's eyes. "But it's all connected, child. Surely you can see that now. There is more at play than mortal and fae, Siabra and Valtain. More at stake than any mortal war. When the very instruments of the gods themselves begin to play a part in the workings of mortal man..."

"You mean the sword?" I said. "But Arthur has that."

"And what of the grail?" My uncle's gaze fell sharp as a whip upon me. "You have seen it, have you not?"

I nodded slowly. "But it's gone now."

"Gone? Gone where? *He* was supposed to take it, safeguard it."

"Draven brought it back." I stared at my uncle, aware that there was more at play here than I could guess at. "He brought it back to the Siabra court. But his sister stole it. She took it to the Valtain." I paused. "Or they took her. It wasn't... clear."

That was probably more charitable than Rychel deserved.

"Back to the Valtain?" For a moment, my uncle looked almost frightened.

"Does it matter?" I said. "What do any of these things matter when people are dying? When Kaye is not safe?"

My uncle's expression turned thoughtful. "Beware the dread curse of Three," he recited.

"The sword, the spear, the grail's mystery.
Blood calls to blood, the dark shall rise,
Forged by the gods under sacred skies."

"I've heard that before," I said. "It was written on the stone. The stone that held Excalibur."

"I'm not surprised. It's an old prophecy."

"What does it mean?" I demanded. "Rhyming words. But what does it tell us exactly?"

"At the very least, it tells us that objects better left lost are in motion once more. Playing into powerful hands. Converging upon one figure."

"Upon whom? Arthur? He doesn't have the grail. Only the sword."

"Not Arthur, girl," my uncle said. "Arthur is a fool and always has been. Toying with matters he hardly understands."

"Rychel took the grail to the Valtain," I said slowly. "She was trying to undo what had been done to the Valtain children by the Siabra."

My uncle looked stupefied. "By the Three, and I thought there couldn't be anyone denser than your brother."

I scowled. "Rychel isn't stupid. She's extremely clever. And she...cares."

"Cares? Bah! So she gave the Valtain exactly what they wanted? She betrayed her people? Doesn't sound like the cleverest girl to me." But his voice was a little milder.

"Well, perhaps she was right," I said, grasping at straws. "Perhaps they'll help her use it to... somehow cure the children."

My uncle tilted his head skeptically. "You've seen the children, have you not?"

"I have. Why? Have you?"

"I'm aware of what they are reported to have become. Of what exists in Meridium, yes." He gave a dark laugh. "But if your Rychel thinks the Valtain will help her fix those children, she is bound to be terribly disappointed."

My heart sank. "Why?"

"Because it was the Valtain who were responsible for their creation in the first place."

My eyes widened. "That's not possible. What kind of people would do that to their own children?"

"Oh, not the Valtain as a whole. But their ruler? The fae monster who has ruled for millennia?"

My head was spinning. "Are you talking about the man my mother ran from?"

He looked at me steadily. "I am talking about your true father, yes. Gorlois le Fay. King of the fae. All of them. Since before there were Valtain or Siabra."

I swallowed. "That's not possible. Is it...? He'd have to be so old... And besides, none of this makes sense. Draven's father used the grail against the Valtain. He did that to the children. It was a terrible, terrible mistake."

"The children's souls were removed."

"What?"

"Their souls. Their essences. What makes us... us."

"Yes, I know what a soul is," I snapped. "I've been to the temple."

My uncle's eyes twinkled briefly. "Of course you do. And did you learn in the temple the considerable power that a soul has?"

"A power that can be taken?" I asked.

"Ah, now you're catching up. The Emperor of the Siabra, Lucius Venator." So strange to hear someone else say Draven's father's name. "He was tricked into using the grail for something it should never have been used for."

"And who stood to benefit?" I said coldly.

"Now *that* is the key question. I suppose the one who has the grail now. The one who has been seeking it all these years."

The one who must have lured Rychel away with false promises and false hope.

"My father," I said quietly.

Caspar Starweaver nodded. "The grail was used to take power that should never have been taken."

"The power of the souls of innocent children," I said, hardly registering the horror of the words. "But Gorlois lost the grail. It was missing. Draven found it, somehow. He brought it back to the Siabra. It should have stayed there."

"It should have indeed."

"You didn't factor in Rychel and her tenacity, did you?"

He looked chagrined. "I did not. I knew the grail would be used by the Siabra at times..." I thought of Sephone raising the grail as she opened the Blood Rise competition. "But I never dreamed it would be snatched from Myntra."

I thought that was saying quite a lot—considering just how far-reaching my uncle's dreams must be to have recruited Draven and somehow gotten the grail into his hands in the first place.

"You hoped I would find Excalibur with Draven and go back with him to Myntra, didn't you?" I said carefully. "Then two of the three objects would be far from Arthur."

"It was a hope," Caspar acknowledged. "And as it turned out, not as far-fetched as I might have feared. For you did go back with him, didn't you?"

I didn't bother to deny that I'd been in Myntra. But neither did I offer more information.

"Why would anyone want this much power? And what kind of power is it exactly? The power of souls?"

"Innocent souls," he corrected. "Pure souls."

I shuddered. "Yes, innocent children's souls. I don't need reminding."

"As for what the power does..." He shrugged. "I don't particularly want to find out. But I suspect that's an indulgence I won't be permitted. Clearly he has some purpose in mind, or why strive to accumulate such power?"

I swallowed. "I suppose this tells me the sort of man my... father is."

Caspar's eyes turned cold. "He's not a man, Morgan. He's hardly even fae. He's a *being*. He lives. That's the most that can be said about him."

"What do you mean?"

"I mean when one has been alive as long as Gorlois Le Fay, one wants and one takes. Whatever one pleases. Have you never wondered about the world before this one, Morgan? The world before the Siabra and Valtain split and the Siabra retreated to their far-off continent?"

I shook my head. "Most of our books don't go back that far. Or if they do, it's very vague." I hesitated. "And in Myntra... Well, there wasn't time for many history lessons." Though I had visited the library on one memorable occasion.

"It's incredible, really, how much can be forgotten in a few generations." My uncle shook his head. "The world was not one you would wish to see, Morgan."

"My father... he's that bad then?"

"He makes Uther Pendragon look like a soft kitten and your brother Arthur, a puppy," he said bluntly. He began to move towards the door. "Now, we will speak again. But in the meantime, know this. I work from within the castle. I work for you and for Kaye and for all of Pendrath. You will choose to feel for me whatever you must. I understand you perceive my previous actions as a betrayal—and one that must cut deep."

I took a breath. "Not as deep as Arthur's."

"You must have at least been expecting that one," he said shrewdly. "Whereas my own... Well, in time I hope you'll believe that it wasn't one. Not truly. I wish only the best for you, Morgan." He cleared his throat. "I cared for your mother. Very much. She was a dear friend. A trusted one."

And then he was gone.

CHAPTER 9 - MORGAN

I walked slowly back through the covered walkways and past the gardens of fruit trees in the open courtyard. It was evening now, and the moon was beginning to come out from beneath a patch of frosty, white clouds.

"He got me out, you know."

A woman's voice. Soft but clear.

I looked around.

Guinevere stood beneath a cherry blossom tree, the golden owl still perched on her shoulder.

The tree's slender, delicate, pink blossoms reached out like a dream, an unexpected beacon of beauty amidst the end-of-winter chill. The air was crisp where we stood in the open garden. A gentle breeze carried the scent of the blossoms over to me, whispering a promise of sweetness and warmth.

Short, chopped, brown curls framed a face lifted up to the darkening sky. The hues of her skin reminded me of warm amber and honey, telling the story of a lineage as rich and diverse as the fair land of Lyonesse from which she graced.

Guinevere took a step towards me, and the pale blue gown she wore rippled like a stream around her curving figure, a canvas of serenity that contrasted with the pink cascade of petals on the snow-tinged ground around her feet. Eyes like mahogany—warm and inviting, framed by dark, long lashes—looked back at me, reflecting the weight of countless trials and tribulations in their depths.

There was an air of quiet strength to Guinevere, but also an intensity that was disconcerting.

She licked her lips as if nervous. "I meant your uncle. Caspar."

"My uncle...? He helped you to escape?" I had thought that if anyone had done it, it would have been Merlin.

"He is a good man," she said simply.

I tried not to let any hint of skepticism show on my face.

"I hope you're right." I tried to smile at her.

I had wanted to speak to this strange girl, to learn more about her. But now that I was standing here, I had no idea where to begin. She owed me nothing. Yet I felt a weight of shame as I looked at her, as if I had harmed her myself.

"Merlin told me what happened to you at my brother's hands. Very briefly—" I added quickly, seeing her stricken expression. Merlin had spared me most of the details, but it had been easy to get the horrifying picture. What terrible words I had chosen to use. I cringed, averting my eyes from her face. "I wish to tell you how terribly sorry I am for how you were treated," I finished.

"You did nothing."

"No, but it was my brother. My family. I cannot help but feel responsible."

"Caspar Starweaver is your family, too, is he not? He helped me."

"That is true, I suppose," I admitted. They said two wrongs didn't make a right. What did one wrong and one right make? Balance? "I'm very glad he did."

"So am I." She looked at me in silence for a moment. "I cannot imagine how betrayed Caspar must have made you feel by what he did."

"Yes." I shifted awkwardly.

"I, too, was betrayed by my family. My father gave me to your brother." She looked away. "I was complicit in that part." As complicit as a princess of the realm could be. I knew something about that. What she spoke of was not a true choice. Girls like us were supposed to marry where we were told, for the good of our families, for the good of our realms. "But the rest... Well. He's dead now."

Her father and brother had taken a terrible risk and paid the price. I wondered if they had known what would become of the daughter and sister they left behind. Had they even thought about what their failure would mean for her?

"What has happened to your people is inexcusable, Guinevere."

"Yes." She stared off into the little grove of trees. "As a child, one believes monsters live only in the pages of books. Then one grows up."

"He... wasn't always like this," I stumbled, not sure why I was bothering to try to explain.

"But he's always frightened you, hasn't he?" she said, turning her head back towards me.

"Yes," I acknowledged. "He has."

"He frightened me, too. When I looked into his eyes... Nothing was holding him back. He was still a man. Flesh and blood. He has a soul. But nothing held him back."

I understood what she was saying. Something had snapped in Arthur. The part of him that cared about anyone outside of himself. It was fading. If it wasn't already gone completely.

"I see it in Lancelet, too," Guinevere said, so softly I wasn't sure I had heard her properly at first. "That void. Filling her with hate. It frightens me."

"Lancelet was very badly hurt. She must feel so terribly betrayed. She was alone. She must have been terrified. And no one came." I swallowed the lump in my throat. "I've thought about how she must have felt, what it must have been like, countless times since then."

"So have I," Guinevere said.

"She blames me, I suppose." I threw the words out into the cold air, hearing the desperate tone in my voice. "She won't hear me if I try to explain."

"Still, you must try. She's waiting."

I was stunned. "Is she?"

"Of course. She may not know she is, but she waits. She wants a reason. She doesn't want to feel this... this hate. So much hate. It eats her up inside. Worse than her scars is the hate. She feels so much of it already. For my sake. She hates your brother. She hates, simply hates. She cannot hate you, too, Morgan. Not her dearest friend."

"I hope you're right." I wavered for a moment, then asked, "How do you know all of this? Did she tell you?"

"Not in words. She doesn't need to. I can feel it."

She reached a hand up to the owl on her shoulder, gently stroking the bird's soft plumage along its neck, just beneath its sharp, curved beak. The owl tilted its head slightly as if savoring the touch, its eyes half-closed in contentment.

"I see." I hesitated. "She seems to care for you very much."

Guinevere looked away again. When she spoke, it was as if from a vast distance. "Yes. I don't know why."

"She is a good ally to have. A good friend."

"She wishes to protect me. To save me. I've tried to explain that it's too late for that."

"I doubt that went over well," I said wryly.

"It did not," Guinevere agreed. "She is... very persistent."

"Well, perhaps you should let her be," I suggested as gently as I could. "If it doesn't bother you. If you're the only thing she cares about. If believing she might be able to protect you helps her... Perhaps it's what she needs right now. And perhaps..." I knew I was probably overstepping. "Perhaps it's what you need, too."

"Perhaps. Yes." Guinevere nodded slowly. "I've wondered the same thing."

"Oh. Have you?" I felt oddly relieved. "Good."

"To be so bonded to another soul is a sacred weight, is it not? Do you feel it too?"

I was speechless. Did she mean Draven?

But when I looked at her, Guinevere's eyes were on the owl. She looked into its golden ones intently, as if it might also respond to her question.

"I am not sure I have," I lied. "Is that how you feel? Bonded to Lancelet?"

Guinevere was already turning, drifting away across the garden. "No," she said over her shoulder, her voice soft. "But I believe she feels that way about me. I... don't feel much of anything. Not anymore."

I watched her walk slowly across the courtyard and out into a covered corridor.

When she was gone, I crossed my arms across my chest and shivered.

A strange girl. She was strong, yes, but her strength had been hard-won and seemed as brittle as ice. Little wonder.

I walked back to my room with a heavy heart, wondering how many walking wounded there were in Pendrath tonight thanks to my brother and his devastating choices.

CHAPTER 10 - MORGAN

I woke up to a tongue the size of a dinner plate lapping enthusiastically at my face.

Opening my eyes, I found myself looking up into Nightclaw's yellow eyes. His massive, black and gold head towered over me. With a deep rumble of contentment, he lowered his face to mine and gave another slobbery lick.

My laughter bubbled forth even as I gently pushed him away and wiped at my face. It was not like being licked by a cat. No, not in the slightest. The exmoor's tongue was far too large for that. It *was* as rough and sandpapery as a cat's, however.

My fingers found their way upwards, stroking the dense fur between Nightclaw's ears. As the golden-brown behemoth nuzzled me with affection, I began to survey my surroundings.

Soft, dappled light filtered through tall, green trees around us.

I rose from a bed of soft moss and leaves. Around me, the forest whispered secrets in the rustling of leaves and the trilling of melodious birds.

As if realizing I was not about to disappear, Nightclaw strolled gracefully ahead into the trees, leading the way. I glimpsed the faint outline of his wings. Their presence could be seen beneath his fur if I looked carefully where the elongated bones and sinews added an extra layer of sinuous grace to his form.

All around us, towering trees reached skywards. A gentle breeze carried the faint fragrance of blooming wildflowers.

My feet sank into the cool, velvety carpet of leaves and moss as I walked forward, following the exmoor into an open glade filled with golden light.

He pranced forward eagerly.

Belatedly, I realized we were not alone.

A second battlecat stood in the glade as if she had been waiting for Nightclaw's return.

As she turned her head, I recognized her. Sunstrike. Draven's exmoor.

With a loud, happy rumble, I watched Nightclaw greet the female. The two approached one another, then rubbed their heads and cheeks together in a familiar and intimate gesture. Golden-brown fur mingled as they both began to purr.

Tears pricked the corners of my eyes. I couldn't have said why. Because Nightclaw was happy? Or simply because these creatures were such a breathtaking sight to behold? They awed me with their beauty and innocence.

And yet something was missing.

Watching them both, I saw the differences between them. Nightclaw was the darker of the two. Thick, dark stripes covered his frame, like the markings of a warrior forged in the crucible of battle. An intricate pattern of black markings stretched across his broad forehead and tapered down his powerful jaws.

Sunstrike's markings were just as resplendent, but her hues were lighter, resembling the purest strands of sun-kissed silk. Her stripes bore a more delicate pattern, like the brushstrokes of a master artist painted in every shade of brown. Around her liquid-gold eyes were faint ivory lines, giving her an air of wild beauty.

Suddenly, the two cats moved together, defying gravity as they pounced upon each other, leaping and playing.

The ground beneath my feet trembled, and I clutched a nearby tree for support as the two exmoors began a lively game of chase.

I watched in fascination. Nightclaw would crouch low to the ground, his powerful hind legs coiling with energy before he sprang forward in pursuit of his mate. Sunstrike would evade him with agile twists and turns before finally letting him pin her to the ground as they growled and wrestled.

"He's missed you."

I turned towards the familiar voice, hardly surprised that he was the next to appear here.

"Draven."

I had thought myself prepared. Even so, my breath caught in my throat as I took him in.

Dressed in attire befitting the lord of a realm, he looked every bit the enigmatic figure that had captured my heart and imagination from the first day we'd met.

His black trousers, tailored to perfection, clung to his long, lean legs, revealing the toned muscles beneath. They disappeared seamlessly into polished, black riding boots that he must have been using while training Sunstrike and added an air of authority to his stride.

His raven hair, glossy and dark as midnight, had been slicked back, accentuating the chiseled contours of his face. The horns he had sawed off during the Blood Rise looked the same as they had before the trial. Small and black, sleek and alluring, they adorned his brow, made of an ebony bone that seemed to soak up the very light around them.

My heart flip-flopped as I took in the familiar angles of his jawline and cheekbones, remembering the way his bronzed skin felt beneath my lips, under my tongue.

His mesmerizing green eyes held my own with an intensity that pierced my soul. I felt myself being beguiled as always, spellbound and intrigued by this man who always seemed to remain tantalizingly out of reach—full of secrets I doubted I'd ever fully be able to claim.

"Where are we?"

He ignored me, stepping past to watch the exmoors. "When you left, he was all alone."

The guilt came instantly.

"He was miserable without you. Hardly eating. Refusing to hunt. I couldn't leave him like that. We'd already tried introducing him to Sunstrike once before. But Hawl suggested we try again."

He stopped, watching as the exmoors' wrestling match came to an end and they lay down, basking side by side with their tufted tails entwined. Nightclaw lifted his head almost lazily before licking at Sunstrike's neck with a long, slow stroke. The battlecat's eyes met mine. There came a brief wink of gold. I smiled.

"And?" I prodded. "What then?"

He shrugged, rolling his broad shoulders with practiced arrogance. "You see the results."

"That easy, was it? This time?" I said, almost flippantly.

Why? Why was I being like this? He hadn't tried to make me feel guilty about leaving. He had only spoken of Nightclaw. But what did he feel?

Did he even miss me?

He turned to look at me, and the world around us came to a standstill. There was a raw, untamed power in his emerald eyes that was as intoxicating as it was formidable. His gaze held me captive. It was a look that spoke of a hunger for something deeper, of a fierceness that went beyond fury and passed into longing.

A longing I knew could consume us both.

I drew in a sharp breath and opened my mouth. But Draven was already saying something.

"The bond just snapped into place," he said. "For both of them."

And somehow I knew he wasn't just talking about the exmoors.

CHAPTER II - MORGAN

I woke up drenched in sweat, as if I had been running through the glade and not simply walking in it. As if I had been doing more than simply speaking to my Siabra husband. Much more.

But it hadn't been real.

Even now, my eyes were becoming accustomed to the dimness. I could make out the drab stone walls of my little room in the temple.

I sat up and swung my legs over the side of the cot.

It had just been a dream, I told myself. That place I had been in—the glade—hadn't been real. It was a fantasy. Not a vision like the ones I'd had before. Not a true dreaming.

I wiped my clammy hands on the bedsheets and kept trying to convince myself.

It was simply an indication of how much I missed Nightclaw, I told myself firmly. But my rational mind also knew that Draven would take care of him. And so I had dreamed the dream to put my mind at rest.

Perhaps parts of it were even true. Perhaps Draven really had decided to introduce Nightclaw and Sunstrike again. And perhaps this time, they hadn't tried to kill one another.

It was good to think that Nightclaw might have found companionship. Even if I couldn't be there to see it.

And Draven? Would he ever find companionship without me? Was it even possible after the way he'd bonded us?

The thought of Draven with some other woman was enough to make me rise restlessly from the bed.

Pulling a robe off a hook, I wrapped it over the thin tunic and trousers I'd worn to sleep, then pulled open the door to my room.

The temple was quiet at this time of night. Candles burned in stone sconces along the halls, providing some illumination for those who might have needed to rise from their beds.

I had no idea where I was going. Only that I didn't want to stay in my room or go back to sleep yet.

A cry of pain broke through the still, cool air.

I stepped out into the shadowy passage. A second cry came, echoing off the stone walls like a lament.

My footsteps made no discernible sound as I padded along the stone floor. A hushed murmur of distant voices reverberated through the narrow passage ahead of me.

Passing the closed doors of other sleeping acolytes and pupils, the sounds became more pronounced. A glint of light spilled onto the stone floor ahead of me. I approached a wooden door that had been left open a crack and pushed against it.

Sounds spilled forth into the hallway.

A soft cacophony of voices. The sound of rustling herbs. A muttered incantation to the Three.

I peeked inside.

A young man lay in the center of the room on a padded table. His pallor was a stark contrast to the rich crimson of the blood-soaked bandages that were strewn around him.

Merlin stood by the head of the table, dipping a cloth into a silver bowl of water and wiping it gently over the young man's forehead.

Across the room at a table along the wall, a young healer's face was a mask of concentration as she cradled a bundle of herbs in her hands, then dropped them into a marble bowl and began crushing them with mortar and pestle. The fragrant scent of rose and hemlock began to fill the room.

I had just stepped inside and pushed the door closed carefully when a choking sound made me wheel around.

Galahad sat in a wooden chair against the wall. His hands were cradled in his head. It took me a moment to register the fact that he was sobbing quietly.

"Galahad!" I stepped over to him, crouched down in front of him, and touched his face. "What's happening here?"

He raised his head, and I felt my heart plummet. Tear tracks traced a glistening path down his smooth, mahogany cheeks. His deep brown eyes held a profound despair.

I turned around. "Merlin, who is that man?"

"I thought we'd told Brooks to close the door," she muttered, wiping the back of her hand wearily across her forehead.

"It's closed now, Merlin. No one else heard but me," I reassured her, my heart filling with sympathy as I looked back and forth between the man on the bed, Merlin, and Galahad.

Merlin raised her eyes to mine. "His name is Christen. He's one of our spies."

"A spy?" Of course, I should have known she and Sir Ector would have already had something in place. There must have been a network of spies. Lancelet had mentioned something of the sort long ago. But just how far did it extend? The castle? The frontlines? And did they do more than simply observe?

"Tonight, Christen returned to us from the castle," she continued.

"Fenyx got to him on his way out." It was Galahad speaking from behind me. He had risen from his chair. "Christen told me he was to serve at a meeting tonight for the king's closest counsel."

"Christen worked in the castle kitchens," Merlin murmured.

I nodded.

Galahad went on. "He was excited about it. Thought he might hear news of the prince."

The prince. He meant Kaye. My heart sped up.

"I told him to be careful, that if this meeting seemed too good to be true, it probably was. He was bragging. Said he'd steal an updated map of the new frontlines for us if he saw it. I told him not to be an idiot. I thought he was half-joking. Offered to come along and stay in the background. To wait outside in case he needed help getting away quickly." He brushed a hand over his face. "He just laughed."

"Christen would do that," Merlin murmured. "He is very daring."

The young man on the table gave a gasping cough. Merlin leaned forward to wipe the blood trickling from his mouth.

The healer at the table was turning around. She held an earthenware tumbler in her hand. "I've prepared another tincture for the pain, Merlin. But I don't know if we'll be able to get him to keep it down..."

"Thank you, Kasie," Merlin said softly, looking down at the young man. "I don't think it will be necessary. He's slipping away from us. He's settled down. I don't think there will be too much pain now."

Still, I noticed she did not remove her hand from the young man's brow but, rather, smoothed Christen's hair back like a mother might.

I had an impulse.

Once, quite by accident, I had healed someone.

Slowly, I came over to the table.

Kasie, the young healer, was weeping. "The wounds were too deep for my skill, Merlin. I'm sorry."

"You've done your best," Merlin murmured. "That's all we can do. That's all Christen would expect. He knew the risks. He has been very brave."

"Arthur did this?" I had come to stand beside the young man. The blood-soaked bandages I now saw covered almost all of his chest.

I reached a hand out and gently touched Christen's arm.

"Sound is the last sense to go," Merlin said softly. "If you have anything you wish to say, Galahad, Kasie. Now is the time."

I looked between the three of them, suddenly wondering how long they had been working together. How many spies had Kasie treated in this room? How often had Galahad accompanied Christen or others on their missions, sneaking into the castle or other places to eavesdrop or steal materials and bring them back unnoticed?

Kasie gave a lurching sob and stumbled forward. "Oh, Christen, I'm so sorry. So very sorry."

She turned away, covering her face with her hands, and moved back to her worktable.

Galahad rose to his feet so swiftly, his chair toppled over behind him. His hands were tight fists as he strode over to the table. Had he always been so much taller than me? Larger? Or had I forgotten?

Gentle Galahad. Like a brother to me. Now he looked down at the young man on the table, his face grim.

"Christen..." I watched him close his eyes, then shake his head. "No, I can't. He... knows. He knows what I would wish to say. Christen..."

Leaning forward, he touched one of his hands to the young man's briefly.

Then, "Stay with him, Merlin," he begged.

I pushed the door gently closed once he had left the room, then came back to my place by the dying man's side and reached a hand out again indecisively.

"He'll linger a few more moments," Merlin said quietly, as if to reassure me it wouldn't be long. "Thank you. For staying with us, Morgan."

"I've done nothing," I whispered.

She didn't seem to hear me. "I'll pray now. Christen would like that."

Could anything be done?

Her voice rose, sweet and resonant as she chanted a liturgy I had heard many times before. Each word was a lifeline to a realm beyond. There was solace and there was hope in the words. I said a silent prayer of my own, to no goddess in particular, simply hoping that Christen could hear her.

Then I reached forward, feeling as if with tendrils of delicate thread, searching for something I had felt only once before.

In the chamber, time stood still. The world outside the room faded into oblivion.

Merlin continued her chant. Her heartfelt prayer was an offering to the Three that I could not match. An act of devotion in the face of the sanctity of life and the inevitability of death.

But I refused to accept the inevitable.

Beads of sweat formed on my brow as I tried to force the magic from me. I wiped at my forehead, hoping Merlin wouldn't notice. She was focused on Christen, her eyes on him.

It was a desperate effort to save one life. A life my brother had shattered. It made no difference if he had dealt the killing blow himself or if the one they called Fenyx had delivered it. He had done this, one way or another.

My fingers trembled. I could sense it now. There was magic in the room. Could Merlin feel it?

My mind's eye cast out tendril after tendril, seeking to connect with Christen's essence as I had so easily done with Draven's back in the inn that fateful night in Grimvale. The night I had made another desperate effort to save one life.

But as I pushed myself into the plane of the ethereal, a cold, disheartening truth settled over me.

There was no connection. No answer to my call. Only silence.

Christen's chest still rose and fell very weakly.

Frustration and helplessness washed over me. I tried again and again, but the result was the same. I was becoming exhausted. But nothing would flow out from me and into Christen. No power, no healing, no life.

The weight of my inadequacy threatened to crush me. The room seemed to close in around me.

A hand gripped my wrist.

I looked up into Merlin's cool gray eyes.

"He's gone, Morgan. We've done all we can."

I nodded. Unable to speak.

"He knew we were here. All of us. He knew you were here. He wasn't alone. He passed in love," she said gently, looking between me and Kasie.

I nodded again, numbly. Kasie gave a sharp jerk of her head, then turned back to her table and began to gather up her things.

"He seemed... important," I mumbled.

"Every life is important," Merlin agreed.

"No, I mean..."

She squeezed my wrist again. "I know what you mean." She sighed. "He was important. Not only because he was a very good spy but because he meant a great deal to Galahad. They were acolytes together. Then, when Arthur forbade their progression, well..." She gave me a significant look, and I nodded.

"After that, Christen found employment in the castle, working in the kitchens. But he was still well-known to everyone here. The perfect go-between. He was sharp-witted, funny, and fast..." She trailed off.

Not fast enough, was the implication.

Kasie was slipping towards the door. I waited until Merlin had gone and embraced the healer, said goodnight, and closed the door again.

"What happened, Merlin? How was he caught?"

"As Galahad said, he was trying to eavesdrop at the meeting tonight." She hesitated. "There is... a passage we use. Leading between the castle and the temple. Underground."

"The one my uncle used to get Guinevere out, I presume?"

"One of them. This city is ancient, Morgan. Not even your uncle or I presume to know all of its secrets."

I nodded.

"When Christen was late," the priestess continued, "Galahad went looking for him. He found him lying near the end of the passage. He'd managed to somehow get that far. He'd been attacked."

"By this Fenyx?"

"Fenyx is Arthur's Lord General. His most powerful commander and a court favorite." Her lips thinned. "For the moment at least. But Fenyx would not have attacked a mere spy alone. If he had his suspicions about Christen, he would simply have sent his men to look after it for him."

"Yet Christen got away…"

Merlin nodded. "He managed to tell Galahad he had killed the ones who attacked him. I only pray he was right."

I raised my brow. "If he's wrong?"

"We've been lucky so far. Our spies, though young, have been relatively discreet. They have been loyal." She rubbed her temples. "We must hope that Christen was right. That the men who attacked him died as well." She looked at me. "This is where your uncle comes in handy."

"How so?"

"We've sent him word about what's occurred. On his end, he'll be cleaning up the mess." She frowned. "Quite literally. Looking for loose ends, too. If he believes there is a threat, he'll warn us."

"In which case?" I said sharply. "Then what?"

"Then we flee," she said simply. "We have sustained a small resistance in Camelot for months, Morgan. The temple has been our base. But it may not last much longer. Arthur is convinced his greatest foes now lie close to home. His fury knows no bounds within Camelot. He holds nothing back."

I bit my lip. "And Galahad? He and Christen?"

"They might have been anything to one another. Anything at all. And before Arthur, they had the freedom to be," was all she said.

Acolytes were supposed to be celibate. That did not mean they did not still have hearts, did not fall in love.

"Why had they not been conscripted yet? I would have thought that Arthur would be taking every single young man that he could."

"Oh, he is," Merlin said bitterly. "Young women, too. Some have joined on their own, of course, believing the king's propaganda. Convinced this is somehow a just war—or at least a way to protect their families and their kingdom. But you're right. Many have been conscripted against their will. I'm sure it's just a matter of time before they come for Galahad. Sir Ector is no longer trusted in court. I've wondered…" She bit her lip.

"Yes?" I prodded.

"I've wondered if he is bribing officials," Merlin admitted. "To keep Galahad safe."

"He would know the right ones, I suppose," I said, thinking of Sir Ector reduced to paying bribes to keep his only son from the front lines. If that was what he was doing, I was shocked it had worked this long.

I shook my head. "Merlin, I'll do what you suggested. I'll spy on Arthur for you. For all of you. Just tell me what needs to be done. How to go about it." I hesitated, then gritted my teeth. "And if I have to take Caspar's potion again, so be it. I'll do it."

"I knew you'd say that," Merlin said softly. She touched my cheek. "My dear girl. If only things could have stayed the course. I would have been happy knowing you would have been High Priestess someday after me."

I grasped her hand with my own, and said, very gently, "But, Merlin, my brother would have still been king."

She lowered her eyes. "That is very true." She sighed. "I suppose it has always been coming. We cannot hide from our fate." She smiled slightly. "After all these years, I should know better than to even try."

She walked me back to my room, her hand on my arm.

CHAPTER 12 - DRAVEN

The cerulean waves stretched as far as the eye could see as the warship cut through the salty breeze. The rhythmic creaking of the ships' rigging and the shouts of sailors as they worked in tandem to adjust the sails had become a soothing background noise by this point in the voyage.

We were halfway across the Kastra Ocean.

But there was still a long way to go before I was back by my wife's side.

I leaned forward against the rails as a burst of spray splattered the deck around me. Licking my lips, I tasted the ocean brine.

Sea life agreed with me. I had made this voyage once before, but under very different circumstances.

A figure rushed past me as the ship heaved, reaching the rail just in time to heave up the contents of their stomach.

Unfortunately, sea life was not for everyone.

Gawain stepped back from the rails, his rugged, freckled face unusually pale for a moment. He wiped a handkerchief across his lips and forced a smile.

"Improving every day," he reassured me. "By the time we reach Eskira, this will have passed. It'll be a distant memory, nothing more."

I eyed him with skepticism as the ship rolled over the waves and he paled again.

At least he was right about one thing—the number of times he lost the contents of his stomach on a daily basis seemed to have been reduced from when we'd first left Myntra. But I suspected that was more because Gawain had cut back on his diet than that he was becoming truly accustomed to life at sea. Still, his stoic demeanor was impressive.

"All is well amongst our crew?" I asked, changing the subject. I had found that the worst thing for soldiers at sea was boredom. Everyone needed to feel useful.

Gawain straightened as if preparing to give an official report. "Crescent stitched onto each of the ships in our fleet this morning..."

I groaned. "I've told him he does not need to do that."

There were more than one hundred ships in the fleet that had set out for Eskira. At a bare minimum of two to three minutes on the deck of each ship, Crescent was looking at a time of at least three to four hours away every morning. Not to mention the sheer exhaustion of making so many stitches.

"He's pushing himself beyond his limits, Gawain. It isn't healthy," I warned Crescent's husband.

"Come on," the red-bearded man said, trying to shrug casually. "You know he likes to." He grinned. "If you really want to know the truth of it, he thinks he must make up for the fact that he decided to bring Taina along with us."

I cocked one eyebrow. "But you do not?"

"Oh, I told him not to bring her," Gawain said cheerfully. "And so since it was Crescent who caved, I now get to enjoy having her here with none of the guilt."

I shook my head. "Has anyone ever told you that you're a terrible husband?"

"Crescent tells me every day, but I don't believe him." Gawain winked. "You see how happy he is."

"He'll be passing out from exhaustion when he's back from checking in with all of the ships," I pointed out.

Gawain still looked remarkably unconcerned about his mate. "That's where Ulpheas will come in."

"Ulpheas?" I knew we'd brought the other stitcher. Not that Crescent had been letting him do much.

"Indeed. By my calculations, today's the day. Crescent could barely get out of bed this morning. He's reached his breaking point. As you've already rightly noted, it's completely excessive. He's going to snap."

I stared as Gawain rubbed his hands together gleefully. "You cruel man. You've been... what? Preparing for this?"

Gawain nodded and turned to point. "Ulpheas has, too. He's just over there. You see him?"

I looked across the deck and saw the blond-haired courtier lurking by the quarterdeck.

Ulpheas wore a tailored ensemble more suited to a ballroom than the deck of a warship. A doublet of rich, forest green hugged his slender form, fastened with a series of silver buttons. His honey-hued hair fell in loose waves around his face, and his sky blue eyes gleamed with an innocent curiosity as he watched the rugged sailors bustling about.

He looked absolutely out of place on the deck of my warship.

I swore under my breath. "Why the hell did we bring him again?"

"Well, that's not very nice," Gawain chided. "Because he's supposed to be back in your good graces again, remember? Be careful, I think he heard you."

Sure enough, Ulpheas had turned towards us with a distinctly crestfallen expression.

Sighing, I raised a hand gingerly. The courtier eagerly waved back.

"You do have his loyalty," Gawain said quietly by my side. "What happened to his cousin ensured there would be no doubt of that." Pearl. He meant Pearl. The Siabra woman who Avriel had put down like an animal in the training arena. Why? Just because he could. Because he'd been stronger than she'd been. And for many centuries, that had been the Siabra way. "Sephone lost his loyalty for good when she continued to support Avriel. And while I know you make no secret of despising him..."

"He broke into my bed chamber with Lyrastra when Morgan was—" I started to say angrily.

"I know," Gawain interrupted. "But you have forgiven Lyrastra for that intrusion. Kindly do the same for him. Besides, we need him. You've used him for stitching before. He's reliable."

Admittedly, Ulpheas had come in handy when I'd needed to reach Morgan in a hurry twice before. Once when Javer had been making a complete ass of himself.

A commotion across the deck drew our attention, and we looked over to see a wide-eyed Ulpheas with his hands up being berated by a barrel-chested sailor who seemed to think the courtier had stepped on some important pieces of rope.

"He's not suited for sea life, but he's a talented stitcher," Gawain observed, one corner of his mouth twitching. "And by this afternoon, Crescent will be begging him to share his duties."

"Oh, he will, will he? And how do you plan to arrange that?"

"Quite simple, really. If he doesn't do it of his own initiative, I'll tell Crescent I won't be sharing his bed any longer until he puts a stop to his mad morning stitching." Gawain grinned cockily.

I grimaced. "Lucky man to have someone to share his bed with at all."

Gawain tilted his head. "I know better than to remind you how easily you could fill your own if you wished to."

The fleet was full of the finest new recruits Myntra had to offer.

Well, the best we had been able to find on such short notice. A surprising number of both fae and mortals wished to join us. The prospect of warfare and adventure was still a draw for many, especially after a period of relative peace for over a century. And an intervention in a mortal-made war was a rare thing. Truly unheard of amongst the Siabra.

Now the ship I stood on and the ones around me were filled to the brim with men and women. I had caught some of their curious glances. In the galley that morning, a young mortal woman had "accidentally" stumbled and fallen against my chest when the ship had lurched. Even her tailored soldier's uniform could not hide pert curves.

But as she had grinned saucily up at me, I had simply stood her upright and stalked off. I had not wished to be rude, but I had hardly been able to hide my revulsion.

There was only one woman in Aercanum whose form I was interested in touching... or having in my bed again.

Now I scowled at Gawain. "Not interested."

"Not in the slightest, I know. I know," Gawain said soothingly. "I know that."

"They think that because my wife has run off I should, what? Tumble into bed with whoever I please? Where the hell do they think we're going? We're sailing across the bloody ocean to find her, for fuck's sake."

Gawain raised his hands.

I took a deep breath. "I'm sorry."

My friend shrugged. "It's all right. I understand. You're the most desirable man in a long line of royals who have a lengthy history of fucking whoever they please, but... that's not you. You're not your father."

I shook my head mutely.

"Neither am I," Gawain reminded me. "In case you'd forgotten." His father and my father had been much the same. Which was to say, not very fatherly at all. More interested in who they could bed next than in parenting their offspring with anything resembling affection.

"I'm bonded," I said through gritted teeth. "She's my mate, whether she understands that yet or not. It means something to me."

Gawain clapped a hand on my shoulder. "It certainly does. It means you're in hell, old friend." He grinned.

"Accurate." I took a deep steadying breath of sea air.

It felt like it had been years since I'd had Morgan by my side. Or in my bed.

Now, for a split second, I permitted myself to remember her sweet, curving body lying naked against mine. Her silver hair, loose and coiling down around her shoulders as her lovely rose-tinged lips parted and she lowered her mouth to mine. I closed my eyes, imagining her breasts brushing against my chest, her small, exquisite nipples hardening into berry-like buds as they touched my skin.

I forced my eyes open. "It's fucking hell, Gawain."

"You're on your way to her. You'll see her soon," he promised me convincingly.

I gritted my teeth. "Or she'll turn me away and I'll spend the rest of my life like a dog at her heels."

"Well, there's no other place you'd rather be, right? Barking behind her?" Gawain punched me in the shoulder playfully.

"Fuck, but it's true," I admitted. Lapping at those delicate little heels. I might even pop one of her toes into my mouth. And suck, long and hard. Would she let me do that much? Even if she hated me? For old time's sake?

I hid it well, but my body was as tense and hard as stone without her. Every second of every day.

"War and sex. There's no separating the two," Gawain said, stretching his arms over his head. "When people think they're going off to die, they want to... well."

They certainly did. The ship sometimes seemed to be rocking from more than just the waves.

Some of the soldiers in the fleet were old hands. Odessa had sent as many of those as she believed she could safely spare. But the majority were raw recruits. And as we spent weeks crossing the Kastra, the old were teaching the new everything they would need to know once we landed on foreign soil.

From the western coast of Eskira, the army would disembark, switching from navy to infantry, and beginning a lengthy trek through harsh and mountainous terrain. Crossing the Ellyria Mountains through Cerunnos and skirting Rheged, they would eventually reach the border of Pendrath and enter Arthur Pendragon's dominion.

Once we entered Pendrath, we had to be prepared to fight.

Of course, I planned to be far ahead of them by then.

It would take weeks, possibly even months, to make the crossing with thousands of soldiers through unpredictable terrain and weather. But if I went ahead on my own, well...

"You must wish you could simply stitch to her," Gawain said quietly, watching me.

That was exactly what I wished.

Every moment of every day. And certainly every time I saw Crescent or Ulpheas.

"It's an incredible distance. I know that. Crescent has told me of the dangers." I cleared my throat. "I want to get to her in one piece, Gawain. I can't take the risk of disintegrating halfway over Cerunnos. Or appearing on the wrong side of the continent."

"Still, if we find a gate..."

I shook my head. Even that was dubious. "We'd have to be completely certain it led to where I needed it to. And when we make landfall on this side of the Ellyria Mountains? I doubt we're likely to find one."

The fae were unlikely to have built many gates so far from Valtain or on the rocky coast along the wall of mountains. There was a slim chance, certainly. But I doubted it.

Furthermore, Morgan may not have realized it, but she had taken an incredible risk when she had leaped into the arch in the palace temple. If the one on the other side had been damaged, or worse, destroyed, she might have ceased to exist.

Thank the gods I could sense that had not been the case. I knew beyond a doubt she had made it through.

As for Javer...

Well, I hoped for his sake that Morgan hadn't simply killed the fool if he'd made it to the other side.

What the hell had made him think it would be a good idea to follow her? I supposed he had come to the temple to pray, and seeing Morgan go through the portal had caused something to simply... snap.

I often wished I'd been as quick as he had been. Many nights, I had lain awake, wishing I had just followed her through. Wondering why I had let her take a single step away from me.

But the truth was, some part of me had known to follow her then would have been wrong. She'd needed to go. I had let her.

That didn't mean I had to stay put forever.

Gawain looked as if he were opening his mouth to try to say something comforting when the deck erupted into chaos.

A brown-furred tempest exploded from the lower decks and hurtled towards us.

I knew better than to take a step back. Instead, I folded my arms over my chest and waited.

Hawl's dark brow was furrowed in anger, and a low growl rumbled from their throat as they pushed their way past terrified-looking crew members who scurried out of the Ursidaur's wake like startled mice.

The bear's choice of attire—a breastplate embossed with the insignia of the Umbral Throne and striped, silky, flowing fuschia pants that looked like something a pirate would have thrown out the nearest porthole—were more of a peace offering to the sailors than an actual gesture of modesty. Of course, no one would ever have dared to say a word against Hawl's absurd outfit.

Secretly, I was simply glad the stubborn Bearkin had conceded to wear any armor at all.

"Do you know what your ship's cook is called?" Hawl's burly voice boomed out.

I leaned back against the rails, trying as always not to be intimidated by the imposing presence of the massive, nearly seven-foot-high, burly brown bear glaring down at me.

"I can't say I do...Wait." I snapped my fingers. "A woman, I believe. Wemak? No, Vemak, isn't it? Something of the sort."

"Vemak. That is correct." Hawl leaned forward. I could see the whites of the Bearkin's eyes. "Vemak *Bear-Killer*."

Beside me, I heard Gawain make a stifling sound.

I managed to keep my own features impassive. "A very unusual surname. Though I suppose it might be common in some parts of Myntra. I take it the woman is mortal?"

"Mortal, yes. She seems unduly proud of her family name, vile though it is. Whereas to me, an Ursidaur, a Bearkin, a species nearly extinct thanks to the stupidity of mortal hunters, the name is exceedingly offensive."

"Indeed," I murmured. "I can see why you would find it so."

Hawl straightened their back, towering over me even higher than I had thought possible. "Hence, I demand that you instruct her to change it. Immediately. Furthermore, I will pay no damages for the pans which were thrown. Or the pots."

"Pots? Pans? Change it?" I glanced at Gawain. The bastard was hardly hiding his laughter. I decided I would throttle him later. "I'm not sure I—"

"Or better yet, why don't you simply ban the name from all of Myntra completely," Hawl demanded. "Yes, that would be most just and fitting. And while you are at it, there should be a ban on the hunting of any Ursus, intelligent or otherwise."

I cleared my throat. "You do realize, Hawl, that in some of the more rural parts of Myntra, common, non-speaking bears *are* a threat to some of the subsistence farmers and their families."

The Bearkin snorted. "Nonsense. Bears don't bother those who don't bother them."

"Lies!" a female voice shrieked from behind. A second figure was ascending to the deck, her face red and panting. "Oh, the dent you put in my pan! Cast-iron that was! I hadn't thought it possible, but for a brute like you, I suppose even the worst things are. You'll pay! Oh, yes, you'll pay."

"Oh, dear Vela, this is going to get even better," I heard Gawain mutter beside me.

"Clap your hand over your mouth if you can't contain yourself," I snapped at him as I eyed the woman I presumed must be the ship's official cook stomping up the wooden steps towards us.

In contrast to the towering Ursidaur, Vemak Bear-Killer was no more than five feet tall.

She had a mane of unruly, gray hair tied up under a ragged blue bandana, but it was her faded, stained, white apron which really got my attention, embroidered as it was with the title "Bear-Killer" in bold, red letters.

I wondered if the name was merely a family surname after all or pertained to an accomplishment she was personally proud of.

Sure enough, as she neared us, the cook yanked up on the leg of one of her pants, revealing a wooden peg leg.

"Do you know where *this* went, Ursidaur?" she shrieked like a crone caught by a cauldron in the woods.

Hawl stared down their nose at the woman, almost as if bored. "I presume you lost the limb in some tedious accident. Mortals are always tripping over their own body parts. Silly little creatures."

"A bear took it!" the cook screeched. "A bear, you fool!"

"Nonsense. Look at you. What bear in their right mind would wish to eat you?" Hawl shook their furry head in disgust. "You look as if you only bathe once a year."

"Hawl," I said warningly under my voice to the Bearkin. Stepping forward, I inclined my head to the woman. "Pardon me, Cook, but I don't believe we've been introduced formally."

The woman stopped and stared up at me, something like horror crossing her face. To my chagrin, she started to try to sink to her knees. "My Grace... I mean, Your Grace... Oh, Your Majesty..."

"There's no need for that," I said quickly. "Gawain."

The big man hurried forward and gently raised Vemak back up.

The little cook tried again. "Your... Highness. My prince... my emperor..."

"You may address him as Prince Kairos or Your Highness," Gawain said, not unkindly. Shockingly, he had managed to repress his laughter for a moment.

The woman squared her small shoulders. "Your Highness. Very well. Your Highness, I demand you get the Bearkin out of my kitchen."

She raised her arm and waved her wooden spoon like a scepter. "Either the bear goes or I do."

Clearly, my royal blood would only take me so far in settling this dispute.

Hawl growled in the back of their throat. "Considering there are mice in your kitchen and cockroaches in your larder, I hardly think the prince should see your threat as anything but a gift."

Vemak Bear-Killer made a tortured, gasping sound. "Mice! Cockroaches! In my kitchen? How dare you!"

"There are mice on many ships," I said soothingly to the cook.

"Not in my kitchen! The disrespect! The audacity! Why I ought to..." She took a step forward, waving the wooden spoon threateningly.

Hawl let out a snarl that sent most of the crew members on deck scurrying farther back. "Stand back, mortal. I dare you to slap me with that pitiful wooden instrument. It will be the last thing you ever do in your miserable life."

Hawl lunged forward before I could stop them, jaw snapping.

The woman shrieked and took a step backwards—right into Ulpheas's arms. The courtier was, surprisingly, the only one who had remained nearby.

Hawl made a noise I suspected was a laugh. Beside me, Gawain had been overcome by a fit of coughing.

The finely dressed courtier looked surprised for a moment, then gently eased the little cook upright. After not very covertly dusting off the front of his doublet, Ulpheas looked over at me. "If I may..."

"Yes?

"I believe I have a solution that may satisfy both parties."

"Please offer it," I said, secretly filled with relief.

"Well, Mistress..." He paused to cough delicately. "Mistress Bear-Killer"—Hawl let out another growl, but Ulpheas pressed onwards—"was obviously assigned to cook for the galleon and has been doing a wonderful job of it," Ulpheas said with the smoothness of a practiced courtier.

Vemak nodded her appreciation. Hawl snorted in derision.

"Hardly edible," the Bearkin muttered.

I was inclined to agree somewhat. But the crew had not complained. I did hope Hawl was wrong about the cockroaches.

"Hawl is accustomed to cooking for the prince back in the palace, however," Ulpheas went on. "Therefore, why not allow them to continue doing so if it is their wish, and permit them to use the kitchen facilities that are attached to the prince's cabin quarters?"

I clapped my hands. "An excellent idea. I'd forgotten those were there."

"They are... rather small," Hawl complained. "I would have to hunch. But they might suffice, I suppose."

Now it was Vemak's turn to snort. "Perhaps a creature of your size ought not to be cooking at all if you can't fit in a decent-sized kitchen."

"I fit in the ship's kitchen just fine," Hawl growled. "Perhaps we should swap. You're abnormally small even by mortal standards."

Vemak huffed. "If you are proposing I prepare meals for the entire crew in the prince's small—"

"No, not at all, not at all," I interjected. "I believe Ulpheas has the right idea. We'll make this work. Won't we Hawl?" I shot a pointed look at the Ursidaur.

Slowly, the Bearkin nodded. "And as for the absurd surname which this woman wears like a badge of honor on her apron, mocking me before the entire crew? What of that insult?"

I glanced at the cook. Her eyes were steely. Nevertheless...

"I must admit, I believe Hawl is correct, Mistress Bear-Killer. If the surname is your family's, you have every right to it. Offensive though it may be," I pointed out. The cook's eyes narrowed still more. "However, the apron must go. Hawl is an honored and valued member of this crew, and I would not want the other crew members to get the wrong idea." I paused. "Furthermore, I would ask you to keep in mind that the bear which tragically took your leg was unlikely an Ursidaur..."

At least, I certainly hoped it hadn't been.

Vemak tossed her head. "It was not."

"Very good. So perhaps parlay may be possible between you and, um, Hawl," I suggested as diplomatically as I could.

"Parlay! Ha!" Vemak spat.

"Never," growled Hawl. "Sooner jump overboard."

"Fine," I snapped, starting to lose my temper with them both. "Perhaps not today. But you *will* be cordial to one another, and there will be no further... pan throwing." I eyed the spoon. "Or spoon hitting." I saw Vemak start to open her mouth and swiftly added, "Or abusive behavior with kitchen utensils of any kind!"

For a moment, the little cook glared at me. Then she seemed to think better of whatever she had been about to say and, instead, whirled back towards the ladder to the lower decks.

Rubbing my temples, I turned to the Bearkin. "Well, Hawl. We've been aboard this ship for weeks, and yet, strangely, it's only now that you and Vemak have this violent encounter. How very odd."

"I've been sneaking into the kitchen at night to cook," Hawl admitted. "And to tidy up that woman's mess. Ate some of the mice, too. Figured it was the quickest way to get rid of them."

I pressed my lips together tightly to stifle a grin.

"So long as you didn't slip them into a pie," Gawain murmured.

I cleared my throat. "I must admit, Hawl, it'll be a pleasure to have you cooking for me again. I didn't want to set myself apart from the crew, but if you really have missed the task, well..."

"I'll provide treats for the crew on occasion as well," Hawl said thoughtfully, tilting their head to one side and looking as if they were already planning the upcoming menu. "To give them a taste of some real food."

"Ah, yes, out of sympathy, of course. Very kind of you."

"Cockroaches can be very nutritional," Hawl noted. "Ground down into a fine powder and put into a cake, why, I doubt the crew would even think twice..."

"No!" Gawain and I exclaimed at the same time while Ulpheas looked a little green.

"I believe we have the necessary provisions aboard not to have to resort to ground insect powder at this time," I said. "But should rations run low, it's truly heartening to know you could improvise, Hawl."

The Bearkin sniffed. "Mortals and their strange tastes. I suppose I've become accustomed to them, however. Fine. No cockroaches. Now, a nice mouse stew, on the other hand..."

Gawain groaned.

But I had already turned my back. As Hawl continued to speak about the culinary delights of mice, I looked out over the Kastra at the setting sun.

Something had begun gnawing at my mind. A persistent feeling of unease.

Thousands of miles away in Pendrath, something was wrong.

CHAPTER 13 - MORGAN

A fter the events of the night, I hadn't gotten much sleep. Even after returning to my room, I'd tossed and turned, my mind on Galahad and the young man I had watched die on the healer's table.

Over the course of the day, I was irritable and cranky. I spent a few hours in one of the temple reading rooms, searching the small library for mentions of Excalibur and the grail.

By evening, something had snapped in me.

Perhaps that was why I was now standing in the doorway to Lancelet's chamber, my arms crossed with carefully feigned arrogance over my chest as I looked in at her.

"If you want to duel, I'm ready when you are."

She glared back at me, her blue eyes filled, as they always seemed to be now, with cold fury.

"Duel you? I don't want to duel you. Close the fucking the door."

"No." Instead, I took a small step forward into the small room. "I see your bed is as tiny as mine." I kicked at a shirt lying on the floor, deliberately trying to provoke her. "And that you're as messy as always."

Clothes and pieces of armor were strewn around the floor. Her weapons she treated slightly better. I saw a sword in its scabbard laying on a wooden chest.

An unsheathed dagger sticking out of a pair of trousers caught my attention.

"You're going to trip on that and poke an eye out," I observed, seeing the furious gleam in her eyes.

I was poking a sleeping bear.

But then, politeness hadn't worked out for me so far.

And continuing to just ignore one another was not an acceptable solution to me. I wasn't ready to accept it as the status quo. To pretend we didn't know one another. To accept there would be no going back to what we used to be.

Lancelet bared her teeth and actually growled, reminding me a little of Hawl, though not quite so gracious. "So? Perhaps it would be an improvement."

"Is that what this is about? You think you're, what? Ugly now?" I laughed. "You couldn't be ugly even if you tried."

Maybe it was a slight exaggeration. But it was what I truly believed. Even with her scars, Lancelet was beautiful. She always would be to me.

"What are you? My mother? There's a fucking hole in my face. No one in their right mind would think I was anything but a..." She stopped, biting her lip.

"A what? A monster? Is that what you want us all to believe you are?" I shook my head. "Try harder."

She smiled coldly. "Not everyone, Morgan. Just you. And you do, don't you? You look at me and you see a reminder of the girl you left behind. Well, I'm not going anywhere."

I stared at her in shock. "That's not at all what I see. And I wouldn't want you to go anywhere. Don't you understand how glad I am that you're still *alive*?"

Had I even said the words once? I should have shouted them up and down the corridors of the temple. I realized that now.

"If seeing you reminds me of my guilt, it's only what I deserve. Don't think I don't know that. Vesper pulled me away. I know you won't believe it, but he overpowered me. I wish..." I paused, swallowing hard. "I wish I had stabbed the bastard then and there." The bastard I'd thought I was falling in love with. "But I didn't. And I know it doesn't matter. What I did was unforgivable. I left you behind. I left you for dead."

Lancelet sneered cruelly. But I knew I deserved it. And in the end, maybe this was why I was really here. To force her to punish me. "You went off with your boyfriend, Morgan, while I was being fucking *eaten alive*."

"I did. I also killed him. My *boyfriend*."

"You what?"

"I killed him," I said bluntly, enjoying the look of surprise on her face. "He poisoned me first. I haven't exactly had a chance to tell you. He dragged me away so he could poison me and use me to get Excalibur. He had a plan all arranged with Arthur. He..." I paused to exhale. "He didn't care about me at all. Not really. In the end, he stabbed me and basically left me for dead."

It stung. Even now. The memory of Vesper.

The memory of my stupidity.

But then who had shown up as I was bleeding out? Reliable as always?

That dark, monstrous, dangerous man who was now my mate.

Mate.

No. Not that word. It sounded even more permanent and intense than "husband." And I was ready for neither.

I cleared my throat. "So I think I know a little something about being left for dead. Though not, admittedly, by a friend who you trusted and who should have known better than to ever take one single step away from your side."

Lancelet was quiet.

"Draven went back for you," I said. "He tried. I wasn't even conscious when it was happening. But after he rescued me, that was the first thing he did. He went back for you. Brought an entire rescue crew to look for you."

Lancelet's eyes widened slightly. "He did what?"

"It's true. He led a group of Siabra to look for you." I thought back to what he had said. "He thinks he's the one responsible for your death. I mean, he still thinks you're dead."

Lancelet wrinkled her still-perfect nose. I tried not to smile, abruptly close to tears. "What? Why would he think that?"

"He saved Odelna instead of you. He made that choice, and it haunts him. Odelna who wasn't Odelna at all, it turns out." I could sense it. She was curious.

Lancelet crossed the room and picked up the dagger from the crumpled pair of trousers.

For a moment, I wondered if she was about to stab me with it. But she simply tossed it onto the wooden chest next to the sword, then turned back to face me.

"That's stupid. He wasn't responsible. He tried." She gave me a significant look that clearly said, *"Which was more than you did."*

I nodded. "That's what I tried to tell him."

"What do you mean Odelna wasn't... Odelna?"

"I mean that girl we found in the camp that day had died already." I savored the shockingness of the words. I had Lancelet's attention. I wasn't about to let it go. "She was being...inhabited. By something else. Some sort of spirit or creature. Something powerful."

To be honest, the entire thing unsettled me. Nor did I particularly like to think about how some *thing* in a dead child's body had been the only witness to the messed up rite Draven had performed that had led to us being bound in this fucked up form of marriage.

"And here I thought that monster children eating my face was the worst thing that could happen." Lancelet sat down on the little bed, looking a little green.

I resisted the urge to sit down beside her, as I would have done in the past.

She hadn't thrown me out. I had already made progress. But I had to tread carefully.

"I'm serious about the duel," I said, watching her. "You want to go, I'm ready. Anytime."

She rolled her eyes.

"I'm serious," I insisted. "I owe you that. If taking my life will somehow help you to reclaim yours. If it will settle things…"

"Oh, really? And what if you win, Morgan?" she shot back. "Did you think of that? Or what? You'll just let me win? Let me…what? Murder you for leaving me?"

I shrugged. "If I win, I'll let you live, obviously."

"But if I win, I can brutally kill you?" She shook her head. "How gracious of you. But no, thanks. I'm not going to let you assuage your guilt that easily."

"Easily?" I snapped. "How would… Oh, never mind. That's not what this is about."

"No? Then what is it about? Why are you really here?"

"Do you really need to even ask? I'm here because I miss you," I choked out. "I'm here because I want you back. Truly back. I'm here because I miss my best friend."

Lancelet gave me a strange look. "I'm not sure she's here anymore."

I clenched my jaw stubbornly. "You've changed. Fine. In more ways than one, sure. I can accept that. I've changed, too. But the old Lancelet is in there, too. I see her. I see you." Abruptly, I switched to a new tactic. "So, you're finally in love are you?"

Her head snapped up. "What are you talking about?"

But it was written all over her face. She'd flushed guiltily to the roots of her blonde hair.

I sighed, seeing I wasn't going to get anything out of her on the topic.

"It doesn't matter. If you don't want to talk about it, we can save it for another day." I lifted the heavy, black cloak I'd been holding over one arm all this time. My hair was already braided into a long plait that hung down my back. Simple and practical. "Look, I'm going out. Want to come?'

She curled her lips. "Are you mad? You can't go out. We're in hiding."

"Since when would that have ever stopped you?" I challenged her. "I'm going out into the city. I'll hide my hair and cover my face. You could do the same."

Lancelet shook her head as if I were being an idiot—which, to be fair, I was. Purposely. For her.

"For what? To get a drink in the tavern? To buy some sweets in the marketplace?" She threw herself back onto the bed and folded her arms behind her head. "Seems like a stupid reason to get arrested by your lunatic brother. No, thanks."

But I was ready with my rebuttal. "I won't be visiting the tavern. I want to see the state of *our* people. I want to see Camelot. I want to see what Arthur has done to it. You already know. But I've been away. I know you might not believe this, but I've been trying to get back here, to all of you, all of this time. I didn't... I didn't mean to stay away this long." My voice was shaky with emotion.

But one emotion was missing. Anger at Draven. He had held me back from Camelot. He had kept me by his side instead. I found I couldn't blame him for that now. He'd believed he was doing the right thing. He saw it as his duty to protect me.

Now here I was, alone, about to do something utterly stupid. Without him.

It was a surprisingly lonely feeling.

Lancelet was looking at me with something I hoped was affection. She shook her head. "Admirable. But still stupid."

"You're telling me you've never left the temple once since you got back? Not even to visit your family?" I demanded.

"No, I haven't." She turned her head to look at the wall. "I didn't want to put them in danger. Besides, I don't want them to see me like this. Merlin sent them word that I was... alive." She said the last word so resentfully. As if it were barely true.

"They must want to see you, Lancelet," I said gently. "You know that. They don't care what you look like. But I can understand not wishing to put them in danger." I hesitated. "So you haven't snuck out? Not even to see what's going on out there? Not once?"

"We get reports back all the time. We know what it's like. Food shortages. Riots in the marketplace. Beheadings. What's there to see?"

I shrugged. "Maybe you're right. Maybe it is a stupid idea. But I just... I need to see for myself. At least once." I bit my lip. "Before I do what Merlin asked and return to my brother."

Lancelet sat up slowly. "You're going to do it?"

"I'll do whatever you want me to do. Like I said in the meeting."

She snorted. "The Knights of the Round Table. What an utterly stupid name."

I tried to hide my smile and failed.

She glared at me. "What?"

"Well, it's just that you came up with it," I reminded her. "Or had you forgotten that?"

"It was a joke! I didn't think that Galahad was going to give a pretentious little speech and actually make us adopt it!" She looked at me and shook her head. "So, you came back. And now you're going to Arthur. Completely stupid. But brave, I suppose."

"I came back," I echoed.

She cocked her head and looked at me astutely. "Or perhaps you were just running away from something else?"

I flinched. The words hit too close to home.

But Lancelet was preoccupied. She was sitting up. "Fine. We'll go out. There's a way I know of. One of the tunnels beneath the temple. It leads into an alley near one of the city squares. We can walk around for a while. You can look your fill. We won't talk to anyone. Then we'll head back. Half an hour at the most."

She snapped out each word as if she were Sir Ector drilling us back in the training courtyard.

I couldn't hide my smile. I had won. I had gotten to her. She was actually going to go somewhere in my company. I could hardly believe it. "You're coming? Really?"

I just hoped I wasn't about to get us both killed. Or worse, arrested.

She scowled at me, and I tried to wipe the smile off my face. "I'm coming to make sure you come back in one piece. Merlin has been through enough. Besides, if you fuck up, then you'll be no good to us. I don't know how Merlin is planning to get you back into Arthur's good graces, but I doubt she would want you getting publicly executed before she can even make an attempt."

"Is it really that bad? You make it sound like executioners lurk on every corner."

She shrugged, then picked up a wrinkled tunic off the floor and sniffed it. "Depends on what you consider 'that bad.' After Meridium, well... I'm sure a few rotting corpses in the marketplace won't be enough to put you off your food, right?"

I thought of the Blood Rise competition in the Umbral Court. "Right."

She started to shake out the tunic, then glared at me. "Do you mind?"

"Oh. Right." I stepped out into the hallway just in time to narrowly avoid the door hitting me as it slammed shut.

When the door opened, Lancelet carried a dark cloak over one arm as well as a long scarf to wrap around her face.

I hesitated as I tugged my own scarf around my face and pulled up my hood. "Will we look... out of place?"

Lancelet shook her head and started walking. "I doubt it. Our spies say more and more people are choosing to go out in masks and cloaks. No one wants to be seen these days. Some of them are probably deserters who don't want to be sent back to the frontlines. Others just don't want to draw any attention to themselves, good or bad. The king's city guards patrol everywhere, day and night. We'll still have to keep our heads down."

She glanced back at me. "And I hope you aren't hungry. Because if you thought the food in the temple was bad..."

"It's been fine." Not the best food I'd ever had. But basic fare.

It was obvious from the way she moved that Lancelet had become very familiar with the temple. I followed her from corridor to corridor, almost losing track of where we were in the complex. Finally, she led us into a room with a set of stone stairs leading downwards.

At the bottom was a new maze of halls. Lancelet ushered me down a dark passage that had water dripping from the ceiling.

"We're eating like kings compared to most people in Camelot," Lancelet said bluntly, as she walked gingerly around a large, dark puddle that I hoped was only water. "Your brother has warehouses and stores of food, mostly grain. He allocates some each month to be sold in the markets, but it's nowhere near enough to meet demand. With the kingdom at war, farming is supposed to be a priority. But Arthur stripped many farms of their best workers when he conscripted them. So production plummeted. We can't import food from the other kingdoms even if we wanted to, obviously."

She glanced at me almost shyly. "Enough about Camelot. What was it like?"

"What was what like?"

"You went to another world. Another continent. You saw fae. You lived among them. You are fae now."

"I always was," I said.

There was so much I could tell her. So much I was choosing not to say. About my powers.

About Draven.

"The Siabra are cursed," I said instead.

"What?"

"There are two groups of fae." I'd already briefly told them this. "The Siabra and the Valtain. They used to be one. When the Siabra poisoned the Valtain children, the Valtain retaliated. Applied some sort of a curse so that the Siabra can't bear children at all. Or, well, hardly ever."

I thought of Draven's little daughter. Would she have lived if she had been allowed to?

"Seems like a fair curse to me," Lancelet commented.

I wasn't going to argue.

I thought of what my uncle had told me. That the Valtain king had been complicit. My father.

Did I tell Lancelet that part of things? I swallowed. Not yet.

"The Siabra court is underground. Their palace is built next to a volcano under the earth."

Lancelet gave me a look as if she wasn't sure if I was joking.

"Truly, it was. They have powerful magic. They can do incredible things. The palace was beautiful. Beyond anything Arthur could possibly fathom. And the people..." I searched for words. "They're so different. Not simply different-colored hair or eyes. They have claws and horns, even wings."

Now Lancelet looked repulsed.

"But they're beautiful," I said quickly. "They're different, yes, but incredible. Each one is so unique. And their abilities..."

Lancelet raised a hand. "Wait. Hush."

We'd traveled through the passage and up a narrow stone flight of stairs. Now I realized we had come to a dead end. A stone wall.

"Cloaks and coverings," Lancelet instructed. I checked my own as she pulled her scarf more tightly around her face, concealing all but her eyes.

"Your skin is glowing," she said accusingly, as she inspected me.

I had covered my hair completely with the scarf and hood, and now I pulled the scarf up over my mouth and nose.

"I can't help that," I said, my voice muffled slightly. "Is it very noticeable?"

She shook her head slowly. "But it'll be even darker out there. They don't light as many of the street lamps as they used to. We'll stick to the shadows. No one should notice. Unless they get close."

She touched her hand to the wall. "All right, let's go. Quickly. I don't want this door open longer than a second. We'll go back a different way, in case we're followed."

I nodded, standing as close to her as I dared.

She moved her hand to one side, slipping along the stone wall, and I heard a clicking sound. An opening appeared, narrower than a door but big enough for us to squeeze through one at a time.

"Go," she hissed, stepping back.

I moved quickly through the opening, then stepped to the side as Lancelet emerged behind me. Flicking a hidden lever in the wall, the opening slid shut.

"Do you think anyone saw?" she asked, her voice low.

"There's no one around us to see."

It was true. We were in a dark, covered alleyway.

It reminded me of the one I had once stood in with a knife at my throat. The night Draven had ridden up and slaughtered the men who threatened me, then tossed me onto his horse like a sack of hay.

Of course, it hadn't been all bad. Being pressed up against his warm, firm body on that horse hadn't been unbearable.

A lot had happened since that ride.

"Less and less people out," Lancelet said bitterly, looking down towards the end of the alley which opened into a market square. "They're afraid. This used to be a bustling market, even late into the evenings. Well, you remember. Now look at it. We're lucky we didn't step out into the midst of an encampment."

She started walking down the alley.

"Encampment?" I asked, hurrying after her.

She nodded to the square ahead of us. "You'll see."

Alfrida Market had once been a bustling market square full of small eateries and taverns with a festival always on the go. Now, the cobblestone plaza lay shrouded in desolation. Even the moon seemed to hang low in the sky, casting a mournful, gloomy light over the scene.

We reached the end of the alley and stepped out into the once-grand space. Marks of desecration were all around us.

A row of white stone pedestals—where noble sculptures of knights and queens and other historical figures from Pendrath's past had once stood—now lay empty. Some of the statues were crumbled at the feet of the pedestals, strewn in shattered pieces. Others had simply vanished.

Lancelet kicked at a broken piece of statue that had been part of a queen's crown. "Your brother's men mostly did this. The statues with gemstones were stolen when things started to get really bad. Some were smashed open, the perpetrators hoping to find gold inside. No such luck."

I looked beyond the ring of pedestals. Market stalls which had previously brimmed with food and handicrafts were now mostly empty. At least half were shuttered up completely. The stalls that were open had pitiful offerings. Sparse, withered produce and grains that looked mildewed and barely edible. The market vendors' faces were gaunt and weary, presenting their wares with airs of resignation, as if they had no other choice.

People shuffled through the square quickly, their voices cast in hushed whispers. I saw a mother, her face lined with hunger and exhaustion as she led her two small children by the hand, skirting around the edges of the stalls. Her children clung to her, eyes wide with confusion, faces marked with dirt and grime.

Nearer to where we stood, an elderly couple hovered forlornly before a stall, clutching a few small coins. With hungry eyes, they scanned the near-empty baskets of produce. I listened as they haggled with the vendor over a price that seemed exorbitant to me.

Instinctively, I took a step towards them. Lancelet's hand clapped down on my wrist. "Don't even think about it."

She pulled me slowly forward in an iron grip, her arm in mine as if we were two sisters coming to the market to buy food.

We walked past more stalls at a slow, measured pace. Here and there, Lancelet would pause and examine the food as if she was pondering a purchase.

Further down the square, I caught sight of a limping man with trembling hands approaching crates used for waste. Digging into the bins, he pulled out a handful of moldy bread crusts. As I watched, tears filled his eyes. But instead of putting the scraps back, he stuffed them into his pockets with an eagerness that could only be a sign of starvation.

I bit my lip and turned to Lancelet, hoping she would say she had a few coins in her purse.

But instead, she was looking past me, towards the other side of the square.

"There," she said bitterly. "An encampment."

I followed her gaze. Across from us, sprawled on the worn cobblestones, was a cluster of tattered tents and ragged, makeshift shelters. Stakes and branches anchored the flimsy shelters to the ground, though it was clear they offered little protection from the winter cold. Children, their cheeks hollow and eyes bright with hunger, wandered aimlessly between the tents. A small tot clutched at the frayed hem of a woman's dress as she stared past us with hollow eyes.

"Refugees from the borderlands," Lancelet said. "They have nowhere else to go. But does Arthur offer them proper shelter? No. Instead, he sees these camps as eyesores. An embarrassment to his proud capital. He has his soldiers come and tear them down almost as quickly as they can be set up."

"That's ridiculous," I said angrily. "Where does he expect people to go if not here?"

Lancelet shrugged. "I don't think your brother cares much. I've heard stories of some encampments vanishing completely, tents and people. Maybe the king forces them out onto the farms to work. Maybe he sends the men back to the frontlines. Or worse. Who knows."

The only spark of hope in the center of the little encampment was a small fire. Its feeble flames cast shadows across the faces of older refugees who sat huddled around it on broken crates and pieces of logs. The aroma of their scanty rations simmered in a large, battered pot. A meager respite from the gnawing hunger that seemed to be plaguing them all.

But the worst was yet to come. The refugees' stew was not the only scent being carried across the market square on the wind.

Looking past the encampment, I realized that a new point of focus had replaced the noble sculptures of stone that had fallen from their pedestals.

Arthur had replaced carved stone with flesh and blood.

A grisly spectacle of bodies hung suspended in eerie silence from makeshift gallows that sat like scars around the edges of the market. The lifeless forms swayed slightly in the chill breeze, a sinister dance of the damned.

Faces once animated in life were now locked in contortions of agony. Some eyes were wide with terror, staring out into the bleak night with haunting emptiness. Others had no eyes left with which to stare. Carrion birds had plucked them away.

Most of the bodies were bloated and putrid. Patches of skin had darkened and peeled away, revealing the gruesome spectacle beneath.

There was no dignity in death for Arthur's enemies. They were condemned to a slow perdition.

I raised a hand to my face, pressing the scarf more closely to my nose as the wind rose, carrying the fetid stench more strongly towards us.

"Seen enough?" Lancelet asked. She snorted in a way I knew was more from fury than amusement. "Or maybe that ought to be, *smelled* enough?" She eyed me. "You're not going to pass out, are you?"

"No." I was too sickened to be offended by her implication that I was a sheltered, hothouse flower. "I told you, I want to see it all. Everything. The worst." I turned to face her. "Is this it? The worst?"

"You want to know the worst?" Her beautiful blue eyes blazed back at me, remarkably unscathed by the tortures she had faced. "Sometimes, the bodies go missing."

I had a sinking feeling I knew what she meant, but still I asked, "Missing?"

"Oh, not these ones," she said, gesturing at the rotting corpses. "Not the ones the flies have already been at for days. Not the ones the birds have tasted. No, the freshest ones. The ones with the most meat on their bones. Soon after they're put up, they mysteriously vanish."

I stared up at the bodies, wondering if there was anyone I knew hanging from the ropes.

"If that's how someone feeds their family, who are we to judge," I said softly.

"I wouldn't dare to judge," Lancelet said, her eyes flashing. "But think about it. If things are this bad now, what will they be like when the inevitable happens?"

"The inevitable?"

"What will things be like when Tintagel and Lyonesse break through our frontlines once and for all and storm this city? Oh, Morgan, you didn't actually think your brother was *winning* this war, did you?"

She laughed so loudly, I looked around nervously. It was a brutal, desperate sound that told me she was closer to her breaking point than perhaps even she realized.

"Perhaps he's deluded himself into thinking we still have a chance. But from what Sir Ector and Dame Halyna say, it's simply a matter of time. Tell me, do you think our neighbors will be merciful when they come for Arthur? Or towards the rest of us?"

I thought of the village I had seen Arthur's soldiers burning in my dream. The screaming priestesses on the pyres.

"I don't know," I said honestly.

"We don't deserve their mercy," Lancelet snarled.

I eyed her with concern. "Perhaps we should go back now. Perhaps this was a bad idea. You seem... very upset."

"Upset? Am I a little upset?" She tugged down her scarf and spat on the pavement by my feet. "By the Three, I'm fucking furious. Do you know what your bastard of a brother has done to our people? Do you know what he did to Guinevere?"

That's what this was about.

Lancelet was being reminded with every step we took of how devoid of mercy my brother was.

"Merlin told me briefly," I said. "I'm so terribly sorry."

"Sorry? She was supposed to be his *wife*. His wife! Can you imagine? The things he did to her, Morgan."

"She's spoken to you about it?"

Lancelet turned away. "A little."

"You two seem very close," I said carefully. "I'm glad that you have... someone. Like Guinevere. She seems to need you."

Lancelet scoffed, "Need me? I wish she needed me. The truth is I need her." She looked at me, her eyes hollow and desperate. "She should have left Camelot. She should have gotten out of the city while she still could. He'll come for her, Morgan. And what will I do then? I can't keep her safe."

Was this love? Was this how I had left Draven? Desperately wondering if I was all right?

"You are keeping her safe," I said, trying my best to be comforting. "She's safe in the temple. You and Merlin and Sir Ector and Tyre and the rest of you have a secure arrangement. You've made it this far."

But Lancelet only stared back, her eyes wide and haunted. "But how long can it last? Really?"

I didn't know what to say to that. I touched her arm gently. "Come. Let's go back. Take me back."

We walked out of the square and into a narrow, winding street. From nearby, I could hear the sound of flowing water.

The Greenbriar River. In the distance, I could see the spires of the castle. We were closer to my brother than I had thought.

"We're walking towards the castle," I murmured to Lancelet. "Don't we want to go the opposite way?"

"This is the way back. I'm taking us to a different access point," Lancelet said shortly. "It's not far, don't worry. We won't be near the castle."

Not very near, she meant.

As we reached the next street corner and the river came into view, it was strange to see the Greenbriar. I remembered the last time I had stood on its banks, watching the straw figure of Marzanna being sacrificed to the waters.

I stumbled and nearly tripped on the foot of a beggar woman who lay up against one of the decrepit buildings. Her threadbare shawl was pulled tightly around her as she slept. Murmuring an apology, I crept around. She didn't wake.

Lancelet tugged at my cloak, pulling me around a corner and into another alley.

A makeshift shelter lay tucked away at one end.

She swore. Then, before I could stop her, she stomped down the alley towards it. Pulling back a flap of tattered blanket, she peered in and then stepped back just as quickly.

She came back towards me, her face very pale.

"What is it?"

"Nothing. It's fine," she snapped, refusing to meet my eyes. "Come. The door is this way."

I followed at her heels as she moved to the center of the left alley wall, then watched as she frowned and ran her hand over the wall.

"What now?"

"The passageway. It's been left open slightly. Just a crack, but still that's odd. It must have been one of the newest recruits. I'll speak to Merlin. We can't tolerate such slips. It's pure laziness." Still scowling, she slipped a hand into a crack in the wall and pulled. A patch of stone slid to one side and she stepped in. I hastened after her, then watched as she firmly sealed the opening, making sure all cracks had vanished.

When we were alone in the dark and quiet, I dared to ask again, "What was in the shelter?"

She had started to walk ahead of me. Now I watched her shadowy figure pause.

"Fine. You really want to know? Children."

"Children? What if they saw us?" I exclaimed.

"They didn't. They're dead." She turned to look at me slowly, tugging the scarf down off her face. Her lips were twisted in pain. "Frozen to death. Two little boys."

I covered my mouth with my hand.

"It happens all over the city. I shouldn't have been surprised." She shook her head angrily. "There's no food. There's no firewood. People are afraid to leave the city to hunt or chop wood. They see Camelot's walls as this impenetrable barrier when, really, they won't keep our enemies out for long if they want to get in. And maybe what's inside the walls is worse than what's outside them anyway."

"I wonder where their parents went. Perhaps they simply went to find food." My heart was aching. I imagined their mother returning, her arms finally full of food for her children, and being met instead with the sight of their stiff little bodies. "Perhaps you were wrong. Perhaps we should go back and look again..."

"No." Lancelet's voice was flat. "I know what I saw. You'd have been certain, too."

I stopped questioning her. I knew she must be right.

We walked through the darkness in silence for a long time, not bothering to light a lantern.

In the end, I wonder if that was what saved us.

CHAPTER 14 - MORGAN

L ancelet came to a halt. She stopped so quickly, I collided with her back, my face pressing against the wool cloak she wore, reminding me that she was a few inches taller.

"What is it?" I hissed softly.

"Don't move," she murmured, holding up a hand. "I heard something up ahead. We're not alone in here."

She pushed against me, prodding me backwards. Step by step, we moved carefully back the way we had come, trying not to let our booted feet clatter on loose pebbles.

When we came to the last junction we'd taken, Lancelet finally paused, keeping her eyes on the direction we'd just retreated from.

"Are you armed?" she asked bluntly. "There's someone up there."

"Someone from the temple?"

She shook her head. "I don't think so. They're just standing there. As if they're waiting for something. Our people wouldn't linger. We go in and out." She clenched her jaw. "I should have known something was wrong. No one's ever left a door open like that."

"Is it a soldier? One of Arthur's men?"

"If it is, they're not wearing a uniform." She slid a sheathed knife from her boot, then reached into her tunic and pulled out another.

I think I surprised her when I lifted my cloak and flashed her a glimpse of the rapier I carried on my belt. The hilt of the rapier was a work of art. A twisted metal rose. Part of the Flamebloom set of armor that Draven had crafted for me. Odessa had set aside the weapon in our chambers when she'd helped me dress for the last round of the Blood Rise.

I had taken it just before I'd left Myntra. A keepsake, if you will. Draven... Well, there was no denying he had excellent taste.

A silent understanding passed between us. With a subtle nod, Lancelet turned back the way we had just come, keeping her footsteps slow and steady.

The air was heavy with the musty scent of ancient stone and mildewy dampness. Torches flickered in sconces along the rough-hewn walls, casting wavering shadows that danced eerily in the cramped space and set my heart beating faster.

I had been in battle before, I reminded myself. You could not call what Draven and I had done over Noctasia anything but that.

This was merely one man. And Lancelet was ahead of me. If necessary, she was obviously more than prepared to dispatch him.

We turned the corner.

I could see the man now. He had his back to us. He wore no uniform, but it was clear that he wasn't a mere innocent civilian. He was dressed for violence in a patchwork of leather and chainmail that clung to his broad frame. One gloved hand rested firmly on the hilt of a sword.

My heart hammered. The man was just outside the door we had exited through only a few hours before, evidently guarding the way back inside. Which meant he wasn't alone.

Who else was with him? How many were there? And what were they doing in the temple? To our friends, to the people we loved?

As if in answer, a shout rang out from beyond the door where the man stood. The man tightened his hand on his weapon but did not move. Evidently he had been instructed to stay put.

I glanced at Lancelet. Her face was grim. She had tightened her grip on the daggers she carried in each hand.

"Wait here," she whispered.

She moved forward, her feet blessedly silent on the damp earth and pebbles, the sounds of the dripping water the only noise.

The man still stood with his back to us.

In seconds, Lancelet had nearly closed the gap. She was just a few feet away. Striking distance.

I watched, tense and waiting.

Her daggers were out. She was close enough to use them. But still, she hesitated.

She raised her right hand.

Even from where I stood a few meters behind her, I could see that it was trembling.

Oh, shit.

A pebble clattered. Lancelet misstepped.

Double shit.

Our foe turned. For a moment, his eyes widened with shock as he saw Lancelet behind him.

But as she remained frozen, making no move with the knives she held, the man's expression changed to a sneer, and he slid his sword from its sheath.

I didn't hesitate.

Darting forward, I briefly caught a glimpse of Lancelet's panic-filled face as I passed her. And then it didn't matter anymore.

I was lunging at the man, my blade slicing through the air.

The small rapier was no match for a longsword. Its reach was laughably limited in a close-quarter fight like this. And we had lost the element of surprise. Nevertheless, as the man's blade hit mine, I somehow held my ground, gritting my teeth and pushing back against the force of the heavy sword with everything I had.

He was larger than me. Stronger than me, most likely. I was probably going to lose. Unless Lancelet snapped out of it and did something to even the odds.

Instead, it was Draven who came to my aid.

The hilt of the rapier began to pulse with latent power as if responding to an unspoken command. A subtle tremor coursed through my hand, sending shivers of warmth up my arm.

Transfixed, I watched as a slender stream of fire snaked down my wrist and across the top of my hand, weaving its way through the steel of the rapier.

The blade's dull metal roared to life, shimmering with ethereal flames as its surface blazed with a fiery glow.

The heat began to cascade down the rapier's length, more and more intense.

I glanced up. The look in my enemy's eyes shattered my trance. Panic filled his face. I knew this was my opportunity, and it was bound to be brief.

Heat was pouring from the rapier now. The longsword the man held was beginning to gleam with a contaminating heat. Soon, the sword would be too hot for him to hold. From the look in his eyes, he knew it, too.

Clenching my jaw, I shoved forward before the man could rally himself and do the same to me. With a sudden desperate burst of sheer force, I sent the longsword pressing against his chest. The man let out a yelp, presumably from the heat of his sword, but he didn't let go of it.

That was all right. I leaned back swiftly, then arced my arm forward, quickly altering my grip on the rapier. As my blade sliced through the air, I targeted it towards a gap in the man's chainmail, just above the collar where a worn link had created a vulnerability.

I pierced downwards, shoving my flaming blade into that gap. The molten steel sliced through the weakened metal and into the man's throat.

A gurgling sound escaped his lips. I yanked the rapier out and stepped back, breathing hard.

The man clutched at his throat, desperately trying to stem the bleeding, but it was no use. He collapsed to the floor.

I turned to Lancelet.

My friend's eyes were focused on the blade in my hand. The gleaming heat was already dying down.

"What... was that?"

I opened my mouth to start to explain, but a scream coming from the gap in the door cut me off.

"They're under attack!" Lancelet moved forward as if she would pass me.

But I grasped her by the arm, holding her in place. "If we go in there, will you be all right?"

She met my gaze, her blue eyes filled with shame. "I froze."

"Yes. Will it happen again?"

"They need us." The words were a strained whisper.

"Guinevere needs you," I said firmly. "Will you freeze or will you fight for her?"

The words were cruel, but they did the trick.

Lancelet pulled out of my grip and squared her shoulders. "I'll fight. Let me go. I have to go to her."

I nodded tersely. "Carefully, then."

We pulled the door open, peering inside the temple corridor from our shadowy recess.

A long hall stretched out before us. Reliefs along the walls depicted scenes of peace and worship before the Three. But now, the tranquility of the temple had fallen into turmoil.

Torches that usually lined the corridor walls had been extinguished or knocked to the ground. The sputtering flames cast uncanny light.

The air was filled with the acrid scent of smoke and burning wood. Somewhere within the sanctuary, fires raged.

Off in the distance came the jarring sounds of battle. A clash of weapons. Frantic cries.

Just ahead of us, amidst the flickering torches, lay the fallen bodies of acolytes, priests, and priestesses sprawled across the cold, stone floor. Their tattered robes, symbols of purity and devotion, were now stained with blood and dirt.

I swallowed hard, filled with a sense of foreboding. I had not sheathed my rapier. Lancelet seemed to have had the same thought. Her daggers remained in her palms. I watched as she loosened her grip then tightened it again. Were her palms as clammy as mine? Quickly, I wiped mine on my cloak.

A clattering sound came from down the hall. A young priestess, her once-pristine white robes now torn, ran into the corridor, terror written across her face. She scanned the hall, obviously looking for shelter. Then her eyes took in the sight of her fallen friends. Before I could even call out to her, she darted away, disappearing back into the depths of the temple with a smothered scream and a sob.

"We need to find Merlin," I said aloud. I stepped out into the corridor.

"Guinevere." Lancelet's jaw was clenched.

"Her, too. Did they have a plan for this?"

She swallowed. "For the temple to be attacked by the king?"

I ground my teeth. There was no point in saying this wasn't Arthur's doing.

Who else would stoop to murdering innocent devotees? Who else would commit murder in the Three's own house, staining their walls with blood?

At least those who had fallen here had died believing they were going to the goddesses' embrace.

We moved forward into the corridor, quickly checking each fallen figure on the floor for signs of life before moving on. It was a grisly task. But even worse would have been leaving someone behind to slowly die alone.

We found no survivors. Not until we reached the end of the hall, turned a corner, and began to approach one of the courtyard gardens.

A group was hurrying towards us from the opposite end, making their way around the corner of the arched cloisters.

I saw a flash of steel, and for a moment, my heart lurched and my hand tightened on my rapier.

Then I recognized the man holding the sword. "Galahad!"

His face was flinty as he rounded the corner, but as he caught sight of Lancelet and me, it filled with relief. Beads of sweat glistened on his skin. One side of his face was streaked with blood.

Beside him, her face flushed with anxiety, marched a petite girl holding a torch in one hand. The warm light reflected off her dark brown curls and rosy cheeks.

"Guinevere!" Lancelet leaped forward. For a moment, I thought she might actually embrace the young woman. But she skidded to a halt a few steps from the group.

I had no such qualms. I had not embraced him since I'd returned from Myntra, but now, I flung myself into Galahad's arms, knocking him back slightly.

"It's good to see you," I said, my face muffled against his rough, wool tunic.

His free arm came tentatively around me, squeezing me tightly for a moment.

"And you, Morgan."

I let go of him and stepped back.

Behind Galahad and Guinevere was a small group of people, their faces haggard. Some were soot-stained, others bloody. I scanned their faces but saw no one I recognized.

"Where are the others? Merlin? Tyre?" And then I had a terrible thought. "Javer? Have you seen Javer?"

Lancelet shot me a strange look as if she couldn't believe I was concerned about the man.

Yes, I was concerned. But not for the reason she thought.

"We haven't seen Tyre," Guinevere said. "We saw Merlin briefly. She was with us, then she disappeared." She rubbed a hand across her forehead.

"What happened?" I asked.

"Isn't it obvious?" Lancelet said bitterly. "Someone sold us out."

"Some of them came in through the front gates," Galahad said quietly. "Brazenly. But other groups entered through at least two of the tunnels. They were informed. They knew their way around. They weren't trying to hide. They simply wanted to catch as many of us off guard as possible."

Thank the Three that the temple complex was relatively huge. Arthur's men were probably going around systematically. Based on the bodies lying behind us, they must have thought the corridor Lancelet and I had come through was already clear.

"Come back the way we came," I said. "There's no one behind us. We'll get these people out through the passageway into the city and then..."

"And then?" Guinevere looked up at me with wide, owlish eyes.

"Then I'm coming back to search for Merlin."

"I'll stay with them," Lancelet said swiftly.

She didn't want to leave Guinevere's side now that she had found her. I understood.

I nodded. "Fine. Galahad, are you badly hurt?"

He shook his head. "I'm armed, but none of the others are."

It was strange to see him with a sword in his hand. But thank the Three his father had insisted on training him despite his temple aspirations. It had come in handy tonight.

We hurried back the way Lancelet and I had just come, with Galahad and Guinevere leading and Lancelet and me taking up places at the rear of the little cluster.

Guinevere gasped as we turned a corner and she caught sight of the bodies lying in the darkened hall leading up to the passage entrance. A woman in the group moaned, evidently seeing someone she recognized.

"Was it this bad elsewhere?" I asked quietly.

"Some of the acolytes tried to fight," Guinevere said in her soft voice. "They were slaughtered. They were very young. But most were being herded together and rounded up."

"With luck, they'll be sent to the frontlines," Galahad said. "Never mind that most of them have never held a weapon in their lives."

I decided not to ask where he thought they'd be sent if they were unlucky. I could hazard a guess based on what I'd already seen.

I exchanged a glance with Lancelet. It went without saying that Arthur was looking for someone. Most likely Guinevere, considering he had no idea I was even there. Or even alive.

"We have to get her out," Lancelet murmured to me, pleading with her eyes.

"Morgan!" The familiar voice came from behind us.

I turned with relief to see Merlin hurrying down the corridor, her long, flowing, gray robes sweeping behind her. The owl, Tuva, was perched on her shoulder. The bird stared at all of us with wide, assessing eyes.

"Oh, Galahad, Guinevere. Thank Devina." Merlin looked around the little group. "You'll take them into the city? Guinevere, you know where to go?"

The gray-haired woman exchanged a knowing look with the girl from Lyonesse.

"Good." Merlin seemed to be put at ease. "Go now, quickly." She hesitated, then added, "The king is here."

There were gasps all around, and I saw Guinevere turn ashen.

"He's looking..." Merlin cleared her throat. "Guinevere, you know what you must do. Go. Go immediately."

The girl in blue gave a jerky nod.

Lancelet had gone as white as a sheet, making her scars stand out pink against her skin. I saw her grip her daggers tightly. I hoped she was ready to use them this time.

"Move out," Lancelet commanded Galahad. "Go down the passage first. Guinevere, Merlin, and the group will follow you. Morgan and I will come behind."

Galahad nodded, then stepped into the passage. Guinevere began ushering the others in after him.

Merlin touched my arm. "Morgan is coming with me, Lancelet. There is something I must show her."

Lancelet opened her mouth to protest, but Merlin cut her off.

"I've had word that your brother is moving Kaye from the frontlines. You must come with me at once, Morgan."

My ears rang. "Kaye? What do you mean? How do you know this?"

"You must come with me now, Morgan," Merlin insisted again. She began moving back down the hall, carefully stepping around the fallen bodies. "Now, Morgan. There's no time to waste."

I looked helplessly at Lancelet, then turned to follow Merlin.

"This is madness," I heard Lancelet mutter from behind us.

But as I stepped around the fallen bodies, I wasn't so sure.

As I thought of Arthur, I suddenly longed to meet him.

Preferably with my rapier at his throat.

He had done this. Committed this sacrilege.

Merlin must be in shock. She was behaving far too calmly, even by her standards.

"Merlin, have you seen Javer? The Siabra man?"

"I have not forgotten who he is," Merlin said ahead of me. "No, I have not seen him tonight. Why?"

"No matter. I'm sure he can take care of himself."

My sense of unease grew. Someone had sold us out to Arthur.

What if I was the one who had brought the traitor into their midst? Just why had Javer followed me to Pendrath? Had he really come to be my humble servant? Or had it been to find a new place at a new court that would suit him even better than the old one?

Merlin was skirting away from the center of the temple, back towards where I knew her own chambers lay.

"How did you learn about Kaye?" I demanded, catching up to her as the older woman continued to walk quickly down the corridors, displaying a remarkable lack of concern for the danger.

"He's to be taken from the frontlines and returned to the city," Merlin repeated. "We must get you into the castle tonight."

"Yes, but how? Do you have a plan?" I wrinkled my brow, confused by her demeanor.

"Of course I do. Here. In here, quickly. They'll be coming this way," Merlin said abruptly.

We'd reached her chambers. She pushed open the door to the room she used as a study. A lantern burned low on a dark wood desk in the center of the room. A censer of incense hung from the wood paneled ceiling, its calming scent filling the room as it swayed slightly. There was a chill breeze coming from a small square window set into the stone wall. I glanced out. The moon was still high in the sky above Camelot.

On the far wall of the chamber hung a beautiful, multicolored tapestry I could not recall ever seeing before. It depicted the Three Sisters standing side-by-side, hand-in-hand, smiling at one another in a grove of juniper trees. Behind the goddesses, rabbits, deer, and other wildlife stood in a half circle, looking on as if in awe of the divine siblings.

With a soft hoot, the owl lifted from Merlin's shoulder, flying to a tall perch on the other side of the desk.

To my surprise, Merlin raised her hand to her lips, as if saying farewell to the bird.

I suddenly heard the sound of tramping footsteps from further down the corridor, and my heart raced. "We've gone in the wrong direction, Merlin. We need to get out of here. What did you want to show me?"

Merlin stepped forward, lifting a wrinkled hand to touch my brow gently. She had been more free with her affection since I had returned. Now I wondered if this, too, was a sign of her advanced years. Was her mind becoming muddled?

"It's all right. It's fine, my dear girl," she murmured as she stroked my brow.

I looked at her, baffled, suddenly wondering if she had suffered some sort of injury after all. "Merlin, it's not fine. We need to get you out of here. We should have gone with Galahad and the others."

Her eyes were gentle. "I'm so sorry, my child. I didn't want it to be like this. But believe me, it was the only way."

I looked at her then. Really looked at her.

The High Priestess of the Temple of the Three Sisters. The Keeper of the Sacred Flame. My oracle, my guardian, my mentor, my friend. Dark shadows lingered beneath her eyes. Her pure white robes were stained with dust and soot. The gold and silver hem of her vestments were edged in blood from the path we had taken. Her small frame was as graceful as ever, but was now bent like a willow in the wind with exhaustion. Her once-lustrous, ebony hair was full of silver strands that flowed in the heavy, serpentine braid encircling her regal head.

As I gazed upon her, my heart ached to see the woman who had guided me through so much of my life now looking older and wearier than I had ever known her to be.

I squeezed her hand. "It's all right, Merlin. There's nothing to be sorry for. But we need to go now."

I put a hand on the hilt of my rapier and started to turn back to the door.

I would take care of Merlin. I would get us out. We'd find Galahad and the others. We'd find a new place, somewhere to rebuild the Round Table's resistance all over again.

And then a cocoon enveloped me. Invisible bonds held me. I opened my mouth and found I could not do so. I could not move an inch.

My body was being moved and manipulated like a puppet on a string. Slowly, I was lifted up from the floor and turned.

Merlin stood behind me with her hands raised. Her expression was sorrowful but focused.

I struggled to part my lips. It was a fruitless exercise.

With a deft wave of one hand, the High Priestess lifted the tapestry of the Three that I had been admiring, revealing a hidden recess. In a small alcove, a polished, wooden dais stood.

Suspended above the floor as if I weighed no more than a feather, I felt myself moving across the room and turned by an invisible current of energy until I hovered over the dais like a porcelain doll to be displayed in a shop for children to peer at.

With that horrifying thought, the room's tranquility was shattered.

The tramping had grown louder. The heavy chamber door swung open with a resounding crash, filling the room with the harsh clamor of armored boots striking the stone floor. The scent of leather and steel mixed with the flickering light and sweet smell of Merlin's incense.

In the doorway stood my brother, Arthur Pendragon, with a group of armored men behind him. He wore a fine set of armor made from deep, inky hues of polished metal.

A dark, maroon cape billowed around his shoulders. Dark-haired and handsome like our father, he might have passed for any fine prince of the realm or a wealthy nobleman's son. Only his eyes hinted at the malevolent power he had kindled within himself since he had taken his seat on the throne of the Rose Court of Camelot.

Arthur's eyes narrowed in confusion as he took in the scene before him. Me, hanging in the air like a rag doll about to be hidden behind the tapestry like some bizarre, treasured work of art. Merlin, her hands still poised in the air, brimming with unconcealed magic.

The High Priestess regarded my brother with surprising calm. "Greetings, High King."

"Merlin. I see you make no attempt to hide yourself." Arthur turned to the man at his side. "She did not run as you said she would, Fenyx."

The man by his side smiled slowly, never taking his eyes from Merlin.

This was my brother's new favorite.

Fenyx had golden hair which framed a ruggedly handsome face marked by piercing, steel-blue eyes. He surveyed the room with an air of quiet confidence. Strong, capable hands rested on the hilt of a broadsword. A flowing white cape cascaded around the Lord General's shoulders. He wore a cuirass of azure blue with an intricate pattern of silver and white.

Every plate, every buckle, every link of his chainmail was polished to a mirror-like sheen. He held his helmet under one arm, adorned with a rose and a silver crest. His own insignia blended with Arthur's Rose Court motif. Fenyx must have held a special place in my brother's cruel heart indeed.

But though his appearance was one of radiant beauty, I sensed a treacherous undertow beneath the calm seas. A malevolence that lay just beneath the surface.

"Your sister, I presume? You failed to tell me how lovely a creature she was."

I couldn't move, couldn't scream, couldn't do anything but *be* as the two men looked at me assessingly, Arthur with cold suspicion and Fenyx with a wolfish gleam in his eyes.

"She wasn't as comely before she left," Arthur observed as he looked at me. "She's... changed." His head snapped back to Merlin. "What have you done to her? She's different."

Merlin did not reply.

"You've been keeping her here, I suppose?" he pressed. "This is where she's been all of this time? Why? What is the meaning of this?"

"Weakening the king's morale, of course," Merlin said, her voice soft and controlled. "If you believed your beloved sister had betrayed you..."

Arthur's lips curled. "Ah, yes. You sought to weaken me by taking something you believed I loved."

He did not specifically deny he loved me, I noted. The implication was there.

"You must have moved her about quite a bit. She did not go willingly, I presume?" Fenyx asked, still looking at me with interest.

"No. I betrayed her. She hates me for it," Merlin said clearly. "She has been kept here all these long months. As my captive."

I understood now. Understood what Merlin was doing. Giving me an alibi. Buying me a story.

But did she understand the price this story was going to cost?

"She is not the only one I have stolen from you, King," Merlin said, her voice becoming crafty and boastful.

"What is that supposed to mean?" my brother demanded sharply.

"Why, Guinevere, of course," Merlin said with false innocence. "You have come to fetch her tonight, have you not? Is that not what this attack was all about?"

Merlin was baiting him. I could see Arthur's temper rising. Soon, it would explode like a spark in a barrel of kindling.

"Where is she?" he said through gritted teeth. "I want her. I want her back now."

"Do you not wish to know how I spirited her away from you in the first place? How I stole her out of the castle?"

"By some secret means, I suppose," Arthur said dismissively. "We know there are passages. We will find each one and root them out."

"I disguised her, and out the front door we went," Merlin said, blatantly lying. I knew it was my uncle, Caspar, who had helped Guinevere escape my brother. And that he had used one of the castle passages to do it, not the front door. Merlin was being very bold—and very deceptive.

I wondered if my brother would really fall for all of this.

"Poor Morgan," Merlin sighed. She looked at me, and only I could see the expression in her eyes. *Oh, Merlin.* "She longed to return to you. Her fury must have known no bounds."

"Release her," my brother said coldly. "I would speak with my sister."

"I'm afraid it is not so easy as that," Merlin said, her hands still raised as if to hold me in place. "I've bound her like this quite permanently."

Arthur's eyes narrowed. "How permanently?"

"I meant to kill her in the end," Merlin said, and there was a tinge of malice to her voice that made my blood run cold—even though I knew it for a lie. "You are not the only one who believes in the power of blood offerings, my lord. Would you have mourned your sister, I wonder, King Arthur?"

"This insolence has gone on long enough, my lord," Fenyx said, his voice a low snarl. "May I dispose of her?"

Something flickered in Merlin's eyes. A hint of fear? Or something else?

"Ah, yes, that frightens you, does it, Merlin? Is it because it is the only way to free the king's sister?" Fenyx demanded. "By ending your life?"

"Or we could simply take her back to the castle and torture her." Arthur's eyes were glacial. "Perhaps once she broke, the bonds holding Morgan would break, too."

Fenyx glanced at his king. "You do not wish to free Lady Morgan immediately?"

If I had been able to snort with laughter, I would have. Clearly, this general knew nothing about my family.

Yet something crossed Arthur's face. Hesitance?

"I want her back, of course. I wish to hear her tell us herself precisely where she has been."

Fenyx seemed genuinely surprised. "You do not believe the priestess then?"

"Morgan returned from Valtain through an ancient fae arch below the temple, which I have now since destroyed," Merlin declared. "You will find the evidence of it if you search."

The portal *I* had destroyed. Surely that was the one she must have meant. There must be more than one for Lancelet to have come back through another.

I prayed the others were hidden so well that my brother would never find them.

My brother exchanged a glance with his general. "A fae arch?"

"We have heard of such things," Fenyx murmured quietly.

"Yes, she was grievously wounded," Merlin continued. "She babbled incessantly about the sword you'd sent her after. Her guilt at failing to bring it back seemed overwhelming. Stupid girl."

She glanced at me with undisguised affection this time. Careful, Merlin, I pleaded silently. Be ever so careful.

Arthur was looking at Merlin as if she were a fool. "Is there anything else you wish to confess to, High Priestess? Besides kidnapping my sister and helping a valuable prisoner from Lyonesse to escape?"

Merlin tilted her head as if giving it serious consideration. "I believe that is everything. Of course, if you wish to find Guinevere…"

Arthur took a step forward. "Yes? Where is she?"

Fenyx put a hand on the king's arm, then quickly removed it as he noticed Arthur's furious expression. "Pardon me, Your Highness, but does the priestess care nothing for the safety of the former queen?"

"She's not to be called that," Arthur hissed.

"Of course," Fenyx said smoothly. "Guinevere then." He gazed at Merlin with suspicion. "You cared enough to help her escape. Why help us find her now?"

"I care about nothing but myself at this juncture," Merlin said clearly and distinctly. "The temple has fallen. Camelot will soon fall."

"Don't say that," my brother snapped. "Pendrath triumphs." He glanced back at the men behind him. "Step out into the corridor and wait for us there."

I caught Fenyx nodding to the soldiers as if to confirm the king's command. Then he pulled the chamber door shut behind them himself.

"You are a weak and pitiful king, Arthur," Merlin said disdainfully, ignoring my brother as he flushed with fury. "A weak man who surrounds himself with fools." I supposed that dig was meant for Fenyx. But the blond man remained serene. Evidently, he was not as easily riled as Arthur. "But I'm prepared to bargain for my comforts. I shan't submit to torture. A simple cell shall suffice. Preferably with some books."

The two men exchanged glances.

"She's gone mad," I caught Arthur murmur quietly. "The old hag."

"Yet you won't tell us how to free Lady Morgan, you say," Fenyx said, more loudly.

Merlin smiled cryptically. "Oh, in time, perhaps. When I have your word that I shan't be harmed in any way."

Fenyx smiled. The smile of a charming wolf preparing to devour a sheep. "Of course." He turned to my brother. "If I can free your sister, do we really need the priestess?"

"Her babbling bores me," Arthur said coolly. "What is your plan?"

Fenyx turned back to Merlin. "Where is Guinevere? Begin your bargain with that, and we shall honor the rest, good lady."

"She slipped out into the city, poor little doe. She's in a panic. She's out of place. I'm sure she won't be hard to find." Merlin's voice was infuriatingly untroubled, as if she were not just handing Guinevere's life over to a sadistic monster.

I prayed she knew what she was doing. That Guinevere and Galahad were long gone. That they were safe.

"We'll find her easily," Fenyx said in a low voice to my brother. "She'll tell us nothing more. Whereas who knows how long your sister has been kept in this miserable state."

My brother nodded, glancing at me briefly. I doubted he cared how long I had been held frozen. Fenyx was acting as if he cared, but I suspected it was simply another way he thought he could insinuate himself into my brother's favor.

Still...

"She truly is lovely," Fenyx murmured again, looking at me. This time, his eyes moved down my body in a way I found distinctly unnerving.

Arthur cleared his throat imperiously. "If you like her that much, perhaps an arrangement can be made. She is a king's daughter, after all. Though you should be warned, she's not as *simple* as she may look."

Fenyx grinned. It was a radiant smile that must have charmed many of the ladies in my brother's court. "Oh, I've heard Agravaine's blathering. She murdered his son and somehow hid the body without anyone the wiser, did she? I must say, she doesn't look the type."

My brother followed his general's gaze. "You may be right. It is a tall tale." His eyes lingered on my face. "Perhaps I misjudged her when I believed her capable of greater manipulation." I wondered if he was thinking of the hunters in the woods. "Perhaps stupidity was her only sin."

"For women it often is," Fenyx said so serenely that I wanted to punch the serenity right out of him.

"Can she hear us, Merlin?" Arthur suddenly demanded.

If I could have rolled my eyes, I would have. Finally, a halfway intelligent question.

But Merlin simply shrugged. "Who is to say? I've never released her to ask."

"You're crueler than you look," my brother observed. "So much for the mask of piety and kindness. Why, you're no better than—"

"A Pendragon king?" Merlin finished. "What a high compliment."

My brother flushed furiously. "That was not what I—"

"Do you wish to have your sister back now, Your Highness? Let this decrepit priestess cease to trouble you with her prattle any longer," Fenyx interrupted.

My brother nodded tightly. "Proceed."

"A cell with a window, mind you," Merlin said calmly, acting as if she really believed she was about to be arrested and carried off to the castle dungeons and then left in peace.

Fenyx smiled and nodded at the older woman.

A terrible feeling came over me.

The blond man stepped forward.

In one swift movement, his broadsword was unsheathed and in his hand.

In the next, he had crossed the room and, sliding the blade upwards, impaled the High Priestess upon it.

Merlin turned her face to me as she fell, her life blood pouring onto the stones.

Her eyes were knowing, and her lips were parted in a smile that would be marked on my memory for all time.

Fenyx gave the sword a savage twist like a corkscrew in a bottle of wine, and she was...gone.

As she died, I was released.

I *felt* again. I *moved* again.

I fell to the floor in a crumpled heap, my eyes never once leaving Merlin's body.

Blood. There was so much blood all over her beautiful, white robes.

My brother opened the door to the hallway and began calling for his guards.

Behind the desk, Tuva let out a violent screech. As the two men looked at her in surprise, the bird unfurled her talons and, swooping across the room, flew out the door into the hallway before anyone could stop her.

CHAPTER 15 - MORGAN

A man was carrying me in his arms.

It was not Draven.

I knew this simply from the sensation. I would have known my... husband's... touch anywhere.

I peeked my eyes open and glimpsed fair hair and silver metal.

Fenyx.

Merlin's spell had been more powerful than perhaps she had known. After I had begun to scream, the strength had gone out of me, and I had lain on the floor in a daze.

Now I could feel my body's power returning slowly.

I had my blade at my belt. It would be the work of a moment to slide that blade right into Fenyx's smooth, golden-tanned throat.

He had murdered her. He had murdered Merlin.

Merlin. The woman I belatedly understood was not simply my anchor, not simply the heartbeat of the Temple of the Three but the cornerstone of all of Camelot, perhaps even Pendrath.

She was dead.

And I could not avenge her. Yet.

She had planned for this. She had known it would happen. The look in her eyes as she had felt her life blood drain out of her had not been one of agony or regret but of peaceful acceptance. As if her time had come, and she had known it down to the very last second.

She had lured me to her rooms, used the magic she had hidden for so long, and then sacrificed herself to convince the king of the lies she had told. So that he would pity me. See me as nothing more than a weak victim of the High Priestess's manipulation.

And then have his most trusted general carry me straight back into the heart of the Rose Court.

Her plan was working to perfection.

Except that she was dead. And my heart was breaking.

I was breaking. She had given her life so that I could do what? Save the kingdom without her?

If that was the case, then the weight of what she believed I could accomplish was too much to bear.

First Beks. Then I had left Draven. Kaye was nowhere in sight. Now Merlin was gone forever.

There was a sound of a commotion from up ahead, and I opened my eyes.

We were still in the temple, walking down a corridor I recognized. We were nearing the main entrance.

Another group of Arthur's soldiers were coming towards us from the opposite direction down the stone hall.

My heart skipped a beat.

They were dragging someone between them.

A woman, tall and lanky with short, cropped, blonde hair.

She had been badly beaten.

Lancelet.

One of her eyes was swollen shut. Her lips were split and dripping blood.

As the armed men neared us, half-dragging, half-carrying her, one of the men in front stepped forward and grinned eagerly at my brother.

"Look what the cat dragged in."

"Lancelet de Troyes," my brother said coolly, eyeing my friend. "Merlin claimed to have no idea where she had gone. Even her own family pleaded ignorance. And I pressed her father. Hard."

Lancelet leaned forward suddenly, spewing blood on the floor at Arthur's feet.

"Bastard king," she snarled.

Silently, I groaned. So much for subtlety.

"She's a traitor," Arthur declared. "That's clear to see."

"She killed three of our men," the soldier leading the others said. "She was bludgeoning the fourth to death when we found her. Took five of us to pull her off him. Like a wild animal, she was," the soldier marveled, looking down at Lancelet with an expression of near admiration.

My heart surged with pride. I knew exactly what Lancelet had been doing when they found her. Covering Galahad and Guinevere's escape.

"Five of my men against one woman?" Arthur glared at the talkative soldier. "A humiliation, that's what it is. I shall have some thinking to do about the quality of my soldiers."

The soldier shifted uncomfortably. "Yes, my king."

"And Guinevere?" Arthur demanded. "Where is she? You bring me this hellcat, spitting and foaming, but where is the woman we came here to retrieve?"

I nearly snorted. Hellcat? I thought of Nightclaw. My brother hadn't seen a true hellcat yet.

Yes, Lancelet was fierce, but if Arthur could get a single glimpse of Nightclaw, he'd piss in his gleaming boots. I longed for the opportunity to show him an exmoor.

"But Merlin suggested—" Fenyx began.

Arthur raised a hand. "Who knows if anything that witch told us was true or not." But he seemed to relent a little. "Once you have searched the rest of the temple thoroughly, every nook and cranny, you will split the men into two groups. One will remain here to search the temple a second time. Who knows what rats may emerge when they think we have left."

"Excellent thinking, my liege," Fenyx murmured from beside Arthur.

Arthur ignored him. He was probably used to the fawning. "The second group will go into the city and turn it upside down until you have found Guinevere of Lyonesse and brought her back to me. Is that understood?"

Between the two soldiers, Lancelet started to growl.

"Oh, the hellcat is most displeased," Fenyx observed with amusement. He wrinkled his nose as he peered down at Lancelet. "God, what have you done to her face, man? Is that a hole?"

"Bite marks, my lord," the soldier replied. "And she had most of those to begin with. Ghastly, aren't they?"

"By Perun's blade." I thought Fenyx sounded gruesomely fascinated. "Just when I thought I had seen it all. No man will have her now. Who did that to you, girl?"

Lancelet bared her teeth and snapped.

"Truly a wild thing," Fenyx marveled. He hoisted me slightly in his arms, and for the first time, Lancelet seemed to realize I was there.

Her eyes widened.

I stared back at her in silence, not daring to say a word.

"We have not yet found the High Priestess," the soldier leading the other group said, pulling Lancelet back roughly. But as soon as we have discovered her hiding place, I will send a report at once."

"That won't be necessary, Captain," my brother said. He glanced at Fenyx. "You'll find the High Priestess's body in her chambers. Dispose of it."

There was total silence in the hall for a moment.

Then Lancelet let out a moan of agony so deep that it sent my heart splintering into even smaller pieces.

Even the soldier's face had paled a little. Was he a believer? Had he visited this temple as a child? Had he grown up watching Merlin lead the festivals and perform the rites?

My brother did not seem to notice the man's discomfort.

"Very good, my king," the soldier mumbled. "Of course. An honorable burial. We shall see it done."

My brother had begun to turn away. Now he stopped in his tracks. "Honorable? Nothing was said about *honor*. Do we honor traitors, Captain? Perhaps you believe we should give Merlin a royal funeral procession through the streets of Camelot?"

The soldier had gone white. "No, my king. Of course not, my king. I only meant..."

"What do we do with traitors, man?" Fenyx barked so loudly I nearly jumped.

The soldier straightened. "We hang them in the markets, Lord General."

"Then do it, Captain," Fenyx commanded. "Hang the witch. Strip her of her vestments, and hang her shriveled body from the first free gallows. Let the crows have her eyes. Let the ravens claw her wrinkled skin. Such is the fate of all who defy the Pendragon."

If I thought I'd hated Fenyx before, now my hatred deepened a thousandfold.

It burned in my heart like the heat of the sun until I thought I would implode.

But I said nothing. I did nothing. I simply looked. Looked at Lancelet as she bled between her captors. Looked at her bruised and broken face, full of such pain, and said *nothing*.

Did she realize I'd been there when they had killed Merlin?

Did she think that because I was now being carried in Arthur's general's arms that I had been complicit in it somehow?

She looked back at me, and I prayed she understood the reason for my silence. Or if she did not understand, then I hoped she would forgive. Some day.

Arthur's attention had returned to Lancelet. An unwanted gift. "You've been found in the temple, de Troyes, so clearly the High Priestess has been concealing you. She also has been hiding Guinevere, as well as keeping my sister under some sort of a spell. What do you know of all of this?"

Lancelet simply glared up at the king with hate-filled eyes. She made no attempt to conceal her disdain.

Like me, she said not a single word.

"Fine," Arthur said shortly. "For the sake of the friendship you once bore my sister, I will give you one day to speak of what you know. After that, if you fail to cooperate, you will be treated like any other prisoner."

"She's a noblewoman of Pendrath, my liege," the captain said nervously. "Her family is influential. Shall I put her in a tower cell?"

"Did you not hear what I just said?" The veins in my brother's neck were pulsing.

The soldier must have seen them, too. He shook his head swiftly. "Fatigue, my king. I pray you forgive me. She will be put in the dungeon with the other prisoners. No special treatment. I understand."

"Her 'special treatment' is being held in reserve," Fenyx said. I heard the smile in his voice. "Consider your king's offer carefully, de Troyes."

"Don't get your hopes up, Fenyx," my brother said, frowning. "And if you do get your hands on her, make sure you don't lose her before you can extract information."

He whirled, whipping his cloak behind him, and began marching towards the temple entrance.

"Very good, my king," Fenyx murmured.

He glanced down at me and seemed surprised to see my eyes were now open.

"My lady, I'm sorry you had to hear all of that."

So I was to be treated like a lady of the court, was I?

I had known men like Fenyx before. Men who would treat noblewomen with the greatest courtesy and then go out into the city and beat common whores for pleasure.

Fenyx was such a man. It was written all over his face.

The good thing about knowing what he was, however, was being able to use it to my advantage.

I fluttered my eyelashes and murmured, "Thank you, my lord."

Then, clutching the sleeve of his fluttering, pure blue cloak, I pretended to faint.

I heard Lancelet being dragged away.

But at least now I knew where they were taking her.

BOOK 2

BOOK 2 PROLOGUE

"The time approaches...Will you be ready?"

The voice was ancient. Male. Distinctly royal. The voice of a powerful being who did not ask questions he did not already know the answers to.

Nevertheless, there was a pause.

A disapproving awareness filled the room.

When the young man finally answered, his voice was rebelliously, dangerously sullen.

"Preparations continue. I have told you this already. I..."

"Silence."

The word was as heavy as a boulder slamming down on the wings of a bird.

"You will be ready. You have failed me once before."

"That was no failure, I..."

"Enough."

A gagging sound. The sullen young man grasped at his throat, clawing for a voice that had vanished and for breath that had fled.

"Yes. This suits you much better." The royal voice was tinged with amusement. "Panic does you no credit. I already know you for the measly worm that you are. Now listen, worm, and live." A pause. "You *shall* be ready. You know what needs to be done. I have waited long enough. A second failure on your part will not be tolerated."

The contact was broken.

The young man's hands slipped from his throat as breath suddenly swelled once again through his lungs and air flowed in through his mouth in a choked gasp.

He was still alive. For now.

The deal had been inked in blood and signed in regret.

Bargaining with a devil may grant one many things, but peace was never one of them.

CHAPTER 16 - MORGAN

I was back in the castle. Back in my old, little tower room.

I could almost pretend I had never left.

But I had.

Now Merlin had paid the price of my readmittance with her life.

How could anything be the same for me after that?

I lay on the bed, staring up at the ceiling.

Fenyx had carried me here before marching off with another tramping contingent of Arthur's brutish guards.

After Fenyx had left, Arthur had sent a healer to me. They had marveled over my relatively good health after my long period of magical confinement. I had refused to move or undress or speak, pretending to be too fatigued to do anything but lie there dully. It fit the narrative Merlin had crafted for me. But more importantly, I didn't trust myself to speak or to stand. And I had no will to do so.

All I wanted to do was lie on the bed. Preferably forever.

Eventually, they left. I heard the healers speaking to my brother in the corridor outside my room. It went better than Merlin could have hoped. They seemed entirely convinced I was the victim of the High Priestess's cruelty.

Arthur's voice had been quiet as he responded to them, and surprisingly gentle. Finally, the footsteps had faded away.

Arthur had not returned.

Tomorrow or the next day, I would have to look him in the face. Pretend he had not condoned the slaughter of one of the greatest women our kingdom had ever known. I would have to feign gratitude and relief.

Above all, I would have to take up my old role in his court—a smiling, cooperative member of the royal family. I would have to endorse his merciless war and pretend it was not killing our people.

And I would have to do so convincingly.

I wasn't sure I had it in me.

So I lay there, staring at the ceiling, pretending the night could last forever.

Until, finally, sleep came and took me away.

"There you are. You disappeared in a hurry the last time." The voice was deep and ironic. I would have known it anywhere.

My eyes popped open. "You again. I thought it was just a dream last time."

"So did I."

"I wanted to see Kaye. Not you. Kaye." But it was a lie.

The last thing I had thought about before falling asleep, I remembered, was not my brother Kaye. It was the look in Draven's eyes as he had cupped my face in his hands and tilted my lips up to his own.

That was what I had been thinking of as I had drifted off into sleep.

Not Kaye, but a kiss. Anything but a simple one.

While I may not have wanted to see Draven with my conscious mind, I had *needed* to see him. I needed him right now, most desperately. More than I could ever admit, even to myself.

I pushed myself up onto my elbows.

I was lying on a bench, looking up at a tree. Dappled sunlight streamed through. It seemed to be about midday. Wherever this was.

Draven was standing across from me, his arms folded over his chest. He was dressed more simply than he had been the last time, clad in a long-sleeved, black tunic that was tucked in at his waist with a narrow, silver belt. Slim-fitting trousers of deepest charcoal tailored to his lithe muscular form were tucked into knee-high, black leather boots. Small leaves of embossed silver were stamped onto the cuffs of the boots.

His sleek, black hair had been gathered into a small, oval-shaped knot at the back of his neck, as if he were a sailor.

Or a pirate.

I found I rather liked it.

He looked wicked. Well, more wicked than usual.

I tried to suppress the stirrings I was feeling at seeing him and knowing that, in some strange way, this was real.

And then the memory of what was all-too-real came flooding back, and I was choking with horror, leaning forward on the bench, my body hunching over with the pain of the recollection.

In an instant, Draven was beside me, crouching on the ground, his hands on my shoulders, rock-solid and strong.

"Morgan, what is it?" His voice was sharp and filled with concern.

I struggled to breath, unable to reassure him. I managed to lift my head slightly, looking at him as I gasped.

His face darkened. Did he know what I was about to say? Had he seen that a death was written in my eyes?

"Breathe easy. Slowly."

Rising to his feet, he settled his large frame onto the bench beside me. With a deliberate motion, he extended one of his legs along the bench's seat, creating a space for me to fit in. Gently, he reached out his arm and coaxed me into that inviting gap between his legs where I found myself cradled within his embrace.

Nestled against his chest, I felt his warmth and strength enveloping me. A sanctuary amid the storm.

In that moment, cocooned within his protective hold, I realized I was in the arms of the man who was not just my husband but also my refuge.

My breathing slowed as it attuned itself to his. Gradually, I felt my body beginning to relax.

I exhaled and inhaled, willing myself to calm.

Finally, I got the word out. "Merlin."

"Merlin? The High Priestess? What of her?"

I forced my lips to part again, my voice dry as dust. "She's dead. Arthur...and one of his men. They slaughtered her. I was there. I saw it all."

His grip around me tightened ever so slightly. I didn't protest.

"Tell me everything."

So I tried.

I told him how I had come through the portal and how Javer had followed me.

I told him of seeing Lancelet standing there at the top of the stairs.

I sensed rather than felt his shock, then his immense relief, but he asked no questions, merely continued listening as the words poured from my lips.

I told him of the meeting at the Round Table and of all we had discussed. I told him of Merlin's idea that I return to Arthur as a spy—and then his grip truly did tighten.

I shifted in his arms.

"I'm sorry," he said hastily, relaxing his arms without releasing them.

I put my hands over top of his. They looked so small and pale there above his large, brown ones. He held absolutely still, as if afraid any motion would cause me to remove them. But I kept them just where they were.

I kept speaking. I told him of how I had gone to Lancelet's room and made her speak to me, then of how we had gone out into the city. He made a slight disapproving sound at that but didn't interrupt. I told him of Camelot, how bleak and terrible the city had looked.

I told him about the two boys Lancelet had found frozen in their tent.

And then I came to the attack. I hesitated, then hurtled on, describing the way Lancelet and I had found the guard in the tunnel. Of how she had frozen, and I had stepped forward, marveling when my Flamebloom rapier had channeled my magic without any conscious thought.

I heard an approving sniff then. So he had known, perhaps had even had Laverna design it that way.

Then I reached the part where Lancelet and I had stepped out into the temple, and I stumbled over my words.

I could hardly describe what had happened next. How Merlin had led me away while the others fled. How she had taken me to her chambers and then demonstrated powers I had never known she possessed—and used them to imprison me.

A low growl rumbled through Draven's chest.

I hurried on, eager to explain the High Priestess's motives, squeezing his hands with mine.

I described Arthur and Fenyx's appearance. Their conversation with Merlin.

And finally, I reached the end. Merlin's end.

I told Draven how Fenyx had taken his sword and impaled the High Priestess with it, so savagely, so brutally.

"I saw the look in her eyes, Draven. She knew what was coming. She led me there. Everything she said to Arthur seemed to have been planned and rehearsed. Why?"

Draven was quiet for a spell. "Where are you now? Not here with me, but back in the waking world. Where are you?"

I shifted against him uneasily, knowing how he would react when I told him. "I'm back in the castle. Back in my own room in the tower. I must have fallen asleep." I cleared my throat. "Fenyx...he carried me there."

I felt Draven take a deep breath as if trying to calm himself.

"Well, there you have it." He spoke lightly, but I sensed the tenseness behind the words. He was terrified for me, but he didn't want to show it. Couldn't show it when he was hundreds of miles away back in Myntra... and when I had abandoned him.

"What do you mean?" I asked.

"You're right where she wanted you to be."

"But none of this is what she wanted. Merlin wanted me to spy for them, Draven. For the group. The Knights of the Round Table—" Then I had to explain the stupid name and listen to Draven's slow, deep chuckle. A sound that filled me with much-needed warmth, like a hot cup of tea on a cool, autumn day.

When the rumbles had subsided, I pressed on. "But how can I be a spy now? I have no one to report to. Merlin is gone. The fellowship she created is broken. I don't even know where Guinevere and Galahad have gone or if I'll be able to find them. And Lancelet... She was caught. Arthur has her in the castle dungeons. I don't even know if I can reach her there."

"But you'll try."

I nodded. "Yes. I'll try. Of course I will." It was heartening to know that he had no doubt I would.

"Not everyone was captured or fled," he reminded me. "You didn't see Javer. Or that other man. The priest."

"Tyre? No, you're right."

"And your uncle. He wasn't in the temple at all. So he's probably safe."

"You're right," I acknowledged. "He had no reason to be there. Hopefully Arthur still has no idea he's been involved."

"Guinevere and Galahad can't have gone far. They won't have left the city. And what of Sir Ector and Dame Halyna?"

"I have no idea. They seemed to come and go. But it was clear they believed Arthur no longer trusted them." The fact that they had gotten away with all that they had for so long was frankly miraculous. "I'll seek them out tomorrow. Perhaps I can make contact." I had a thought. "If anyone would know, my uncle would. I'll go to him first."

"Good. But be careful. Arthur is not as stupid as he seems, Morgan. If he brought you back to the castle, he may have had other reasons for doing so. He'll be watching you. If you go straight to Caspar, there's a chance he'll find out and wonder why."

"Good point." Perhaps I should wait until my uncle came to me. I decided I would wait at least a day and see how long it took.

"Meanwhile, Merlin was right," Draven continued. "There is much you could learn if you're careful. Excalibur must be somewhere close to Arthur. Where is it, and what does he plan to do with it? Oh, I don't mean go and ask him on your first day back. But play the game. You weren't too bad at it before."

"The game? The game of court, you mean?" I had grown up with the intrigue and the pretense. "I suppose the Rose Court will be child's play compared to the Court of Umbral Flames."

"My people might be more savage on the surface," Draven agreed. "But yours have subtle thorns. This Fenyx for instance... I don't like what you've told me about him."

And I had left out the parts I thought Draven would like even less. About how Fenyx had stared and stared. And what Arthur had seemed to offer.

"You look fae now, Morgan. You're sure to attract more attention than you did before, too," he reminded me.

"Most people will shun me, if they didn't already," I said. "Especially if they aren't sure whether Arthur truly has decided to favor me again."

"They won't know how to react. Use that to your advantage. Remember your strategy. The one Merlin..." He cleared his throat. "The one Merlin clearly wished you to use. You've done nothing wrong. Rather, you have been wronged by the High Priestess herself. Before she was justly executed"—I cringed, but knew he was right—"she confessed to everything, and you were witness to that. You are the victim here, only too happy to be back in the court where you belong." He paused. "Perhaps you can try to take credit for getting Excalibur back to Arthur, too."

"Sure. Once I find out exactly how he got it in the first place," I said grimly.

"Right. But you were the one who opened Orcades' prison and pulled the sword from the stone. Perhaps you can remind Arthur of that. Then give him a modified version of what happened afterwards."

"You mean don't mention how the half-fae rogue he sent to follow us became my lover and then tried to kill me? And how you had to save me and then take me back to your dark fae court? That part?"

"That part," he said, his lips twitching.

"Are we really married?" My voice was low.

"We are. I wouldn't tell your brother that either."

"You don't think Arthur would rejoice to have you as a brother-in-law?" I said sarcastically.

Draven moved his head, and when he spoke again, his breath was hot against my ear. "I'm confident that would be the quickest path to the dungeons, my little silver one."

He had never called me that before. I felt a tingling sensation as his lips brushed against my skin, reminding me of everything that had come before, all that had been between us.

"I'm not little," I protested.

"You're smaller than me." I heard the smile in his voice, and it was all I could do to keep from turning my head to look at that beautiful face.

"I left you," I said, my tone meek.

Silence. Then, "You did."

"And?"

"And I don't blame you. I probably would have left me, too."

I was shocked. "You would have?"

"It's your life, Morgan," he said mildly. "You're the one who has to live it. I made a choice for you. Two choices, actually."

"Two?"

"I chose life over death. I chose that for you. I didn't ask if it was what you wanted. I couldn't ask. I didn't have that luxury."

He was right. "Would you have asked me if you'd been able to? Either question?"

The answer came quickly. "One of them. Not both."

I was startled. "What do you mean?"

"If you'd said you didn't want to live, I don't know if I could have accepted that."

"Oh."

"You'd also just had to deal with that complete and utterly treacherous bastard. You'd been betrayed by someone you... loved. I don't think I could have trusted you to believe that, well, that you'd be happy again some day."

"I didn't love him," I said. It was important that he knew that. I half-turned to him, my hand sliding up to his wrist. "I thought I was going to. I mean, I might have... if that had never happened."

He was quiet for a moment. "I understand."

"No, that's not true either," I said, feeling frustrated with my own ability to say the words properly. "You were there. You were always *there*, Draven. Lurking. Watching." I pinched his wrist. "Literally following us into the woods."

"I had a bad feeling about Vesper," he said. "His appearance was too convenient right from the start."

"Even though Laverna vouched for him? But yes, you were right." I sighed. "Of course you were."

"I couldn't stand the thought of you going off with him. Of him touching you." He moved his hands up and down the plane of my stomach possessively, and I smothered a little gasp. "It was fucking torture, Morgan. But it was your body. Your life. You had the right to do what you pleased, and I had to tell myself that."

From the strained sound of his voice, it sounded like he'd had to tell himself over and over again.

"Right," I said. I hesitated. "And the other question?"

"The other?"

I elbowed him in the stomach, and he feigned a groan. "You know what I'm talking about."

"Would I have asked you to be my wife? Asked you to be my mate?"

"Yes. That question." I felt as if I were holding my breath.

"I didn't know that I was going to do that...until the way opened up and there was no other choice. The two things were really one and the same."

I swallowed. "And that's the problem, Draven."

"What do you mean?"

"My life and this...mating. One hinged on the other. You could only save me by creating this bond with me. Right? That's how it worked?"

"That's how it worked, roughly. It was a very old and very ancient ritual. Someone very powerful was present. She blessed us, in her way. I'm not sure it would have worked otherwise. It's not how Siabra usually marry, you know."

"And so you married me under compulsion." The words tumbled out. "You were forced into it as much as I was."

I felt him stiffen. "What do you mean?"

"You could only save me by doing what you did. And you refused to let me die. You were too...I don't know, too fucking honorable to do that, I guess. So you bound yourself to me. You bound us together."

"I never said that."

"Yes," I insisted. "You did. On the battlements, the day that Rychel left. When I came back from the Blood Rise. You said you had done what you did to save my life. Those were your words."

He was quiet for a moment. "Two things can be true, Morgan."

My heart sped up a little.

I felt him sigh. "I didn't save your life because it was honorable. If it had been someone else lying there... Well, I would have done all I could have. But the mating ritual? I'm not sure I would have, *could have* gone that far. But with you? I didn't hesitate."

"Why?" I whispered.

"Because I would not not let you go." His voice was as dark and forbidding as a starless night's sky. "And if giving you part of me—or hell, if giving you all of me would keep you in this world, then that's what I was prepared to do. You were lying there, dying, Morgan. And even before I'd spoken the words, I knew."

"Knew what?"

"Knew you were already my mate." He paused, as if his throat had closed up a little. "And I wasn't about to let you die. I was going to do whatever it took, give whatever I had to."

"And so you did."

There was silence.

"How could you have known?" I asked finally. "How could you have known I was your mate?"

His grip on me tightened again. "Do you really want me to say the words? Is that what this is about?"

I said nothing, simply waited.

His lips tickled my ear.

"There are no limits to my love for you, Morgan. When Myntra and Eskira and every place in Aercanum have crumbled into oblivion and the universe itself dissolves into nothing, my heart will still beat for you."

There was silence.

Then I let out a deep breath. "Draven Venator, you bought my life with your blood. You made me your mate."

I felt him tensing up as I spoke, already assuming the worst.

"You redeemed my life with your own, but you could never take my heart. Love... Love must be freely given."

Draven's body felt like a rock, a wall of armor around me.

A wall that would shatter with a single wrong word.

"But my heart was already yours. When I lay dying in Meridium, you were all I could think about. I knew you would come for me. I had no doubt."

I twisted slightly to see his eyes. They were deep and full of something I thought might be hope. "Did I ever tell you that?"

Mutely, he shook his head.

I turned back, looking off into the trees. "I know you would burn the world to the ground and lay it at my feet if I told you it would make me happy."

His lips brushed my neck. "It's true. I would."

"But you've never asked if I would do the same for you. My mate."

He froze with his lips still pressed against my skin.

"I fell..." I stopped, my voice choking. "I fell in love with you on that trip through the woods. I fell in love with you when you were burning up with fever and too stubborn and too stupid to stop for help until it was nearly too late. I fell in love with you when you were dying in the room at the inn while we were being ambushed and I..." I took a deep breath. "I saved your life."

He was holding absolutely still.

"I still don't know how I did it. I don't know if I'll ever be able to do it again." I thought of Christen. "I've tried, and it... it hasn't worked. I think that's because there was no bond. But between you and me, even then. There was. There was *already* a bond."

I took another breath. "When I was...dying, I lay there thinking of all that had happened in my life. With Vesper. With you. And only the memory of you was pure, Draven. You..." Now there were tears, stinging my eyes, catching in my throat. "You were the very best part of my life. You were never afraid of me. And I was never afraid of you. I can't... I can't imagine you not being with me. And yet, here I am, a thousand miles away, because I'm a fool and an idiot, and I love you and yet I left you."

And then the tears were flowing. For Merlin. For Draven. For my stupidity. For all of it. He was so close and so far away and it was all too much. I couldn't bear it.

Draven was moving me. Turning me to face him. His lips were on my face, kissing my eyelids, kissing my cheeks, kissing away each tear as it fell.

"Shhh," he murmured. "Shhh, silver one."

"I left you. Why did I leave you?" I sobbed. "And now Merlin is dead. If I had never come back, she wouldn't be dead, Draven. I should never have left."

"You did the right thing," he said firmly, wrapping his arms around me and pulling me against him. "You left for Kaye. I understood why, Morgan. I still do. You're in the very best place you could be. You did nothing wrong."

"But I love you, and you're so far away." I hiccuped, then wiped at my face. I was a mess. But he just smiled down at me with a smile so tender, it wrenched my heart.

"Do you know where I am right now?" he asked.

I shook my head.

"Well, if I haven't been assassinated in my sleep by a vindictive cook..."

I punched him. "Don't even say such a thing."

He grinned. "Or if we haven't been boarded by pirates or capsized..."

My eyes began to widen. "Pirates? What do you mean? Where are you?"

His grin deepened. "I'm on a ship. More than halfway across the Kastra by now. I'm on my way to you, Morgan. Did you really think in a million years and a million lifetimes that I'd ever be able to stay away?"

CHAPTER 17 - DRAVEN

S he looked so beautiful. Staring up at me half-bewildered, face still streaked with tears, a spark of hope beginning to fill her lovely eyes.

"Your eyes are golden now, you know," I said. "They remind me of Nightclaw's."

I watched her face flicker with confusion. "They are? They do?"

I nodded. "They used to be hazel. When I first met you."

"Dull brown, I would have said."

"There has never been anything dull about you," I said with conviction. "In any case, they've changed again."

She raised a hand to touch her face. "Changed how?"

"They're flecked with green now. I suspect if I looked at my own, very closely, in a mirror, I'd see something similar."

She leaned towards me. Her face was very close. She gazed into my eyes, and an expression of fascination came over her, making her glow with radiance. "You're right. There's gold there."

I couldn't wait any longer.

I kissed her.

I felt her eyelashes as they fluttered, small wings brushing against my cheeks.

Her lips were soft and sweet.

"I'm glad," I said as our lips pulled apart.

"Glad for what?" She sounded breathless and happy. It was a start.

"Glad we're not enemies anymore."

She smiled briefly. "When I next see you, who knows. The impulse to murder you might return."

I grinned. "I'll keep letter openers away from you, with that in mind." Leaning forward, I whispered in her ear, "You can kill me, but my soul will come back and find yours."

She leaned back slightly. "Is that a threat? Are you threatening to haunt me, Draven Venator?"

I grinned. "Simply saying that even death can't part us."

Let the world go up in flames around us. Let her brother sweep the world with his war. I'd let all of Aercanum burn before anything harmed her. That was my silent vow. The one I'd secretly been saying to myself since I'd met her that day in the training courtyard.

I pushed a strand of gleaming, silver hair off her face.

"We're all alone."

She rolled her eyes. "That seems fairly obvious." She frowned. "Is it a dream? Am I dreaming this alone? How do I know you're even really... here?"

"Do your dreams usually pick up where the last one left off? I remembered the last one, didn't I?"

"Well, if I'm dreaming you, you'd remember anything I told you to. Wouldn't you?"

I shook my head impatiently. "Have you ever had a dream this real before? So real it... hurts?"

"No," she admitted. Then she frowned. "Hurts?"

I leaned forward and sank my teeth gently into her neck. She let out a little moan of pleasure that made the hairs on my arms stand on end. "In a good way, of course," I said, slightly breathless as I released her. "Fuck, but you taste good."

I eyed her admiringly, imagining all the places I planned to taste.

"Stop looking at me like that," she ordered, squirming a little.

"Like what?"

"Like you're about to... you know. Devour me."

"Don't you want to be devoured?"

She couldn't hide a guilty smile. I growled.

Her eyes widened. "I've missed that sound."

"What?"

"Your growl. So bestial. So..."

"Charming?" I supplied.

She rolled her eyes again. "I suppose..."

I leaned forward and spun her all the way around to face me, then grasped her legs and rose from the bench, lifting her up into my arms.

She threw her arms around my neck but still complained, "Put me down."

I grinned as her grip on my neck tightened. "I'm not going to drop you."

"I know that, but..." She looked around. "Where are you taking me?"

I nodded. "To that cottage over there. With any luck, it'll have a bed."

Or a table.

A floor. A wall, even. We could make do.

"Cottage?"

She looked in the direction I was carrying her. Sure enough, a little thatched-roof cottage stood a short distance away in a clearing.

The little hut's walls were covered with pale green ivy. Square glass windows in a diamond-shaped lattice pattern caught the light of the setting sun in a playful dance of fractured rainbows. A cobblestone path led to the front door, winding through a colorful garden of wildflowers that filled the air with their sweet, earthy perfume.

Behind the house, chirping birds flew between the trees over a babbling brook that flowed softly under a little red stone bridge.

"Where did that come from?" Morgan demanded.

She wriggled in my arms, and I reluctantly set her down on the grass. Immediately, her hands went to her hips and she stood surveying the cottage with a stubborn set to her lips I was all too familiar with.

"It was there all along," I said.

"And you want to go inside? What if there's... I don't know..." She searched for words.

I smirked. "A wicked witch?"

"Well, it's a dream, isn't it? What makes you think everything will be safe and innocent?"

"We're shaping this dream. Well, you are," I clarified.

"Me?" She shook her head. "Oh, no, I'm not taking responsibility for this."

I frowned thoughtfully. "Perhaps we both are." I looked at the cottage closely. "Come to think of it, it does look... familiar."

"How so?"

I felt my cheeks heat slightly. "I used to imagine something along these lines."

"A cottage? You?" Morgan looked delighted. "Draven, do you have secret fairytale aspirations? Perhaps you wish to become a farmer and give up court life altogether?" Her eyes twinkled.

"There are worse things than becoming a farmer," I said, refusing to be embarrassed. "A simpler life wouldn't be so bad."

"So this cottage, it came from your imagination, did it? I wonder what's inside..." She gave me a playful look and began to stroll up the path.

Just the way I'd dreamed she would. My heart thundered in my chest like a drum as I watched her walk away.

Did she have any idea how bewitching she looked? Doubtful.

The runes along her arms glistened like stardust against her golden skin, while her long, silver hair fell in undulating waves down her back, catching the fading sunlight as if each strand were a ribbon of moonlight. Her gown, a rich, velvety crimson, clung to her in all the right places, the fabric caressing her hips in a way that set my pulse alight. Every delicate sway of her hips was emphasized by the soft, shimmering material, creating a captivating play of light and shadow that made my heart skip a beat.

I breathed deep. I could almost feel the warmth of her skin and the softness of that moonlight hair beneath my fingertips.

She was a feast for the eyes, leaving me hungry for more.

I followed her up the path and watched as she lifted her hand to the polished, bright blue door and gently pushed it open.

Inside, a tea tray was arranged by a crackling fire. Cups of a sweet-scented herbal brew sat steaming beside a squat teapot, accompanied by plates of warm, buttery scones still fresh from the oven.

It was as if Hawl had simply stepped out for a moment.

I grinned to myself. I had no wish to see the Bearkin in the fur, as it were, in this dream.

Over our heads, wooden beams stretched out across the ceiling, crisscrossed with strings of dried herbs and flowers that dangled like chandeliers. The walls were a soft, buttery cream color and had been covered with paintings and sketches, some showing landscape scenes and others portraits. One in particular caught my eye. I turned my head away quickly.

Sunlight filtered through lace curtains, casting gentle patterns on the wooden floor. Over the mantle hung a large, wood-framed mirror that reflected the room's light, making it feel bright and spacious.

Hand-painted dishes and brightly colored jars sat on open shelves over a large, wooden counter in the little, rustic kitchen, while in another corner of the cottage, prettily painted wooden screens bordered a bathing area with a copper clawfoot tub in the center.

At the far end of the cottage, a beautifully carved four-poster bed dominated the room. Flowing linen curtains in pastel shades of green and blue billowed in the breeze from an open window like ethereal clouds. A vase holding an arrangement of fresh wildflowers sat on the nightstand beneath a square glass window.

Morgan turned here and there, taking in everything. Then she looked back at me. "Who lives here?"

I cleared my throat. "I think we do. At least..."

Her eyes became wistful. "For tonight?"

"We might be able to bring ourselves back here if we try," I said. "Would you like that?"

The truth was, I had no idea what was or wasn't possible. I had never shared a dream with anyone before. Certainly not two in succession.

But I had no doubt whatsoever that this was real.

Oh, not the surroundings. But Morgan—her presence, all that she had told me. This was real. And it would become a very real memory for us both in the morning.

Until then...

Morgan was looking at me with a strange expression, biting her lip.

"I've missed you," I said directly, meeting her gaze and feeling the heat as her golden eyes turned scorching.

We stepped towards each other, two souls with one thought.

"Pretend." My voice was thick and muffled as I pressed my face against her hair, breathing in her scent. "Pretend this is our home."

I felt her nod against me.

I leaned down to kiss her lips lightly, then again, less lightly.

Everything went very quickly from there. Fabric slid from her shoulders, falling to the floor in a puddle of red. Morgan's fingers fumbled with my trousers while I pulled my shirt over my head and tossed it across the room.

And then there was nothing between us.

I looked down at her, drinking in her curves, silently worshiping her body with my every breath.

It was easy to tell how badly I wanted her, and I knew it. Her eyes had gone wider as I'd shucked off my trousers. Now her fingers played with the curling hairs on my chest as she stepped towards me.

"You're so damned beautiful," I breathed. "I've missed you so much."

She looked up at me, her gold and green eyes wide and open. "No more secrets. No more lies. Just us, like this, together. Truly mates."

"Always." I gently touched the shining strands of her hair . "All or nothing. In dreams as in life."

"In dreams as in life," she whispered back with understanding. There was wonderment in her eyes, as if she were finally starting to grasp just how incredible it all was. Us, here, together. Inside of a dream.

"Anything can happen," I teased. "Anything at all. It's your dream. What do you want?"

"You. I just want you." She bit her lip in a way I found enchanting... and that filled me with need. "The sooner the better."

I brushed my mouth against hers. "Beds are all well and good. But have you ever tried a wall?"

She took a small step back, and I glanced down at her naked body, my eyes trailing over full, beautiful breasts, the planes of her stomach, the swells of her curving hips, and then down, down, down to bare thighs and perfectly formed calves.

She took another step back, then another.

Until her back was against the wall.

Slowly, she pushed her hips out towards me.

"A wall like this, you mean?"

I let out a sound halfway between a groan and a growl, then prowled towards her.

One moment, I was on my knees. In the next, my hands were on her hips. In the third, my mouth was worshiping her body. Covering her stomach and hips with kisses before finally pushing her thighs apart and setting my mouth overtop the sweet, wet heat between them. Laying claim to what I had very, very much missed.

She made a soft whimpering sound that I took as a good sign, then leaned back against the wall, her hips relaxing against my mouth.

Her hands were in my hair, pulling the short ponytail loose and running her fingers through it. I closed my eyes for a moment, the sensation of her fingers caressing my scalp exquisite.

It had been too long. This time without her. Time without her touch, the scent of her skin, the feel of her body beneath my mouth.

Too long since I had given her pleasure, heard her soft sighs of contentment—and her louder cries as she shattered beneath me.

I ran my tongue over her, tasting her salty dampness. Wet. She was so wet for me.

I dipped down, delving into her, rubbing her clit with my tongue. Her thighs tightened between my grasp. Above me, she let out a gasp, her head falling back against the wall. I felt her thighs tightening against me and pressed my palm firmly against her hips.

Her eyes were on me. Watching me as I worked to make her come. Good. There was something incredibly arousing about knowing she was watching, knowing she was unable to look away.

I moved a hand, sliding two fingers inside her. The movement startled her, and she arched against me as I filled her, sliding long fingers in and out with excruciating slowness as I circled her clit with my tongue.

She moved her hips against my mouth, urging me on, harder, more.

I complied, moving one hand to cup the glorious curves of her ass as I pulled her against me, touching my tongue against the place she wanted it the most.

She gasped, cried out, hips bucking. Her hands slapped against the wall hard.

"Draven, please..." She was barely able to get the two words out.

I stole a glance upwards at her breasts thrust beautifully towards the ceiling, her rosy parted lips, her closed eyes as she moved against my fingers as I fucked her.

And then my mouth was on her clit again, nipping gently, licking softly, and her knees were trembling. Her hands tightened in my hair as a roaring surge of release came over her.

As the wave ebbed, I didn't take my fingers from her, just kept thrusting them in and out slowly as her wetness soaked them.

"Draven," she whispered. "That was..."

I thrust a little harder, not giving her any break, and she let out a low moan.

"Tell me what you want next," I urged her, my body still charged with desire. "We've been apart for weeks." I kissed her hip. "Surely once isn't enough for you." I kissed the other side of her hip and then trailed my mouth down the curve of her thigh. She shuddered beneath me.

"I don't want," she whispered.

I glanced up at her. Her eyes were blazing fiercely.

"I *need*."

I swallowed hard.

"I need you, Draven, now, here, inside me. I need my mate. And I need him to take me the way he wants me. Like a Siabra." She ran a hand down my cheek, tracing the angle of my jaw. "Gentleness can come later."

In a heartbeat, I had her turned around with her hands flat against the wall.

I moved my mouth to her neck, my teeth biting down on the curve where her neck met her shoulder. She gasped. I pushed my body against hers. I was panting, my chest rising and falling as I pressed along her back.

"Morgan," I murmured her name, the word a caress and a promise. I ground my hips against hers.

She moaned, her hips lifting slightly in anticipation, and I clamped down on her neck again, biting my way along it before replacing teeth with tongue and gently caressing the places I had just pierced. Intentionally, slowly, possessively. Leaving my marks on her.

I ran my hands down her smooth sides to her waist, then gripped her hips.

The time for playing was over. I needed to feel her now. All around me. Joined with me.

Her hips rolled out eagerly. I steadied them with a touch of my hands. And then I was pushing inside her, and she was crying my name, helplessly turning her head to and fro as I thrust again, deeper than before.

I slid my hands up her torso, feeling the softness of her skin. Her breasts were pendulous and heavy. I cupped them, rubbing the tips of her nipples as I thrust again and again inside her, filling her to the hilt. My lips were on her back, her shoulder, her neck. I swept her hair away and kissed the spot just below her nape, nibbling gently as I moved my hips, taking her deeper, harder, again and again.

I groaned, feeling myself on the edge of rapture, all of my senses beginning to dissolve.

Take her like a Siabra, she had said. I thrust into her hard and let out an uncontained growl of pleasure.

But I couldn't take her like a Siabra. I could take her only in the way I knew how. As my *mate*.

I slid a hand around her hips, circling the bud of her clit, and she moaned, pressing back hard against me.

"That's it, beauty," I said almost lazily as my fingers worked against her. "Fuck me back."

She shocked me, letting out a growl to match my own, then slamming against me so hard, I gasped.

I could feel the crescendo of desire peaking. Molten pleasure engulfed every one of my senses.

My silver one shattered beneath my hand as I erupted, filling her as a thunderous surge of bliss cascaded through me like lightning.

When it was over, we were both trembling. I stepped back, tugging her onto the bed, pulling her down on top of me. I stroked her silver hair, strands of silken moonlight flowing between my fingers.

She kissed my chest and then pushed herself up, propping her chin in the center of my ribs and wrapping her arms around my torso. "Tell me where you are. What you're doing."

"I'm probably sleeping in my bed in my cabin while Hawl bangs pots and pans around in the kitchen next door." I smiled. "It's amazing that I haven't woken up already, actually. Hawl usually begins around four in the morning."

"You brought Hawl with you?" Her eyes lit up with amusement.

"I had no choice, did I? Have you ever tried to stop a Bearkin from going to war?" I shook my head.

"War?" She looked stricken for a moment.

I rubbed her cheek with the back of my hand. "Of course. War is inevitable, isn't it? You live in a land at war."

"Just who else is with you?" she asked. "Besides Hawl."

I understood what she really meant. "I've brought you a fleet. One hundred Siabra war ships."

At first she seemed stunned. Then she shook her head. "One hundred ships won't do us much good on the other side of the continent."

I smiled. "We'll be leaving the ships behind and marching over to you. It would have been nice if Pendrath was a western country, preferably with a coastal capital," I teased. "But we'll make do."

I decided not to tell her I planned to go on ahead of the fleet and try to get to her as quickly as possible.

"And then what? When your soldiers finally get here, I mean."

"Then you'll tell your brother the truth," I said. "About who and what you are. You'll claim my soldiers as your own, and you'll tell Arthur to withdraw his forces from your neighbor's lands."

She nodded slowly. "He won't do so willingly."

"Then the time for asking will be over," I said. "Like it or not, you are an empress in your own right, Morgan. You'll use that to sway him. If he won't back down, you know what must be done."

I wasn't about to tell her to kill her own brother, but I didn't see any way this war would end without Arthur Pendragon's death. And to be honest, I was rather hoping to have that pleasure if it came down to it.

"And Tintagel and Lyonesse..."

"When they see that Pendrath seeks to withdraw, well, hopefully they'll decide to allow you to surrender and cease fighting. You'll have to make reparations, of course."

"Kaye will do so," she said. "With the help of the best advisors."

"Of course. You can see a council set up before you leave."

I'd spoken too quickly, without thinking. Now I felt her freeze.

"Leave?"

"It's a long ways away. You don't have to leave until you're ready, of course. But... eventually? I'm hoping you'll come back home with me."

"I have two homes, Draven," she said, her eyes sweeping over me. "I'm not sure that's a choice that's so simple to make."

"I understand." And I did. "I'll stay with you in Pendrath for as long as it takes."

"What about Myntra? Who have you left in charge?"

"In charge of that court of vipers? Why, the queen of vipers, of course." I grinned. "Lyrastra."

"Lyrastra! How is she?"

I scratched my chin. "She was not doing so well. Her injury... It's taking some getting used to. But I hope her role as regent will give her something new to dwell upon."

"It'll certainly be a lot of work."

"It will. But with Odessa by her side, I'm sure she'll make a success of it."

"You left Odessa?" she exclaimed.

"All is not well in Myntra. If anyone can help Lyrastra to keep order, it's her. You'll be happy to hear that Crescent chose to accompany me. And Gawain."

"How close are you?" Her face had become pinched. "Days? Weeks? Now that I'm in the castle... I'm not sure how long this situation can last, Draven. And with Lancelet captured..."

"Not days," I said reluctantly. "Weeks. At least weeks. Possibly months."

"Months." I watched her face fall.

"There is much you can still learn in the meantime. Just... please... be careful."

Something was happening. I felt my body shake. The sensation was happening not here in the cottage but elsewhere. Back on the ship.

"I think I'm waking up," I said quickly. I grabbed her arm and kissed a trail of kisses up and over the silver markings that covered her golden skin. "Meet me here again."

"How? How do we even... do this?"

"We'll figure it out. I know we will. We'll see each other here again. And until then, just know how badly I miss you, Morgan. How much I've missed this. Not just holding you, touching you, but talking to you. Being with you. Hearing your voice." I forced a breath. "You must... You must stay safe for me. Swear it."

"I'll try..." The little room was fading. Morgan's face was becoming blurred. "Draven..."

And then I was gone.

I opened my eyes.

I had been right. I was in my bed in the cabin where I recalled going to lie down hours before. A much-too-small bed that had been made for very short sailors.

I stretched out, hit my foot against the wall, and groaned.

The ship was shaking, yes. But these weren't the tremors of sea waves.

Something else.

Something hit the ship with a heavy thump. I was up and out of the bed in a flash, tugging a heavy linen shirt over my head and moving to the door.

My quarters were nestled in the aftcastle, the raised upper deck at the stern of the ship. As I stepped out of the small cabin, the scent of sea air mingled with the whiff of fresh baked bread and sizzling smoked meat.

The rhythmic sounds of simmering and chopping were coming from the small kitchen adjacent to the cabin.

I looked around the corner, intending nothing more than a quick peek inside. The kitchen felt like a magical hideaway, so fully had Hawl already made it their own. Jars of colorful spices lined the shelves, and an assortment of mismatched cookware dangled from hooks overhead. All brought by Hawl themself. The Bearkin must have vastly exceeded their luggage allowance.

Hawl stood with their back to me. The low ceiling forced the towering Ursidaur to hunch forward as they worked in the cramped space. Now I watched as the bear's massive paws moved with surprising dexterity and grace, their low, contented growls providing a rough melody to the culinary alchemy filling the little room.

The chopping ceased abruptly.

"We aren't being boarded," Hawl's voice boomed out at me without turning their back. "If that's what you're worried about."

"We aren't?"

A spring squall? I answered my own question by looking out the windows. A rosy-fingered dawn was peeking its head over the horizon. An indication of a beautiful coming day.

The rocking had stopped.

Hawl shook their grizzly head without turning. "Go and have a look. They're back."

I opened my mouth to ask whom, then understood.

I left the cabin and loped across the deck, my pulse quickening in anticipation. Across the deck, some of the crew were already gathered—standing in a nervous group, murmuring together.

I followed their gaze to the rail of the ship where Sunstrike sat, perched like an incredibly large bird, licking one of her paws delicately.

Overhead in the gray sky that was rapidly turning blue and purple with the rising sun, Nightclaw circled, flapping his massive wings and casting a dark shadow over the deck below.

I brushed past the crew and approached my exmoor.

Sunstrike looked at me from under long, brown lashes and continued to groom herself, but I could sense she was pleased to see me.

I ran a hand over part of her shoulder—the part I was tall enough to reach. Sitting on the three-and-a-half-foot ship's rail, she was at least nine feet high.

Her fur was soft and silky, a deeper texture than her mate's. As if reading my thoughts, she looked skywards. I felt her begin to purr as she watched Nightclaw with satisfaction as he soared and dove.

"Good hunt?" I asked.

She made a contented chirping sound and switched her attention to her left paw, flicking her large, batlike wings out briefly.

"Show-off." I smiled. Ever since Sunstrike's wings had developed, she had been trying to display them to me every chance she got. Only within the last few weeks had they finally grown large enough and strong enough for her to join Nightclaw in his hunting escapades.

The timing had been perfect for the sea voyage. The exmoors would leave the fleet, sometimes for days at a time, feed, and then return at their leisure.

I looked at Sunstrike's wings, then at Nighclaw high above me.

The answer, I realized, had been staring me in the face all along.

I had been planning a grueling journey over the Ellyria Mountains, one that involved a great deal of hiking, stumbling, and rocks in my boots.

But I didn't have to walk at all.

Not when I could simply fly to my wife on the back of an exmoor.

CHAPTER 18 - MORGAN

I woke up feeling happier than I had in a long time.

The sun was streaming in through the window over the desk, shining on my face and causing me to squint as I rolled over. I hadn't bothered to rise and draw the curtains during the night.

For a moment, all I could recall was Draven. The feel of his solid, strong body pressed along mine. His hands holding me, tender and possessive.

The words we had said echoed through my mind.

All harshness and bitterness was in the past. We had turned a new corner. From here on out, we would move on together.

Together but apart.

I wished he were here with me now.

And with that thought, I suddenly remembered Merlin and sat up in bed.

She was gone. In one night, she had been taken from me.

It was morning. I was back in the castle of Camelot.

And Merlin was never ever coming back.

Sorrow welled up like a fountain. I let it fill me, holding the pain in my heart.

If Merlin had died at some other time with some worthier monarch on our throne, the entire city of Camelot—nay, the entire *kingdom* would be mourning her loss. Bells would be ringing for days. There would be a funeral procession in her honor, attended by nobles and diplomats from not only Pendrath but other kingdoms as well.

But we were at war. And Merlin had died a seemingly ignoble death at the hands of a tyrant.

If what Arthur had threatened was true, then her body would hang in the marketplace—as if she were a traitor and not a hero.

So I would mourn her. I would let myself feel the pain. But I would remember I was not alone. As soon as word reached Sir Ector, Dame Halyna, Galahad, and all of the others, they would be mourning alongside me—stoically and silently, but with their whole hearts. I had no doubt of that.

A tapping came. At first I thought it was the door. Memories of Florian briefly flooded my mind. I pushed them away. That bastard had never knocked.

I rose to my feet. The tapping was not coming from the door, I realized.

My bed lay on one side of the narrow, rectangular chamber. The desk by the window in the center.

On the opposite side was my reading nook. Tall bookshelves lined the walls around a large stone fireplace.

I walked towards that side of the room, and the tapping came again, louder this time. Feeling incredibly foolish, I cleared my throat. "Enter?"

There was a squeaking noise, like a tired hinge in need of more grease.

Then a bookshelf swung open towards me.

"This is ridiculous," I complained, as I took in the sight of my Uncle Caspar standing in the shadows looking far too pleased with himself. "Does every castle in the world have a network of secret passages?"

"I couldn't possibly say." The white-bearded man stepped out, wheezing a little, and immediately took a seat in an armchair near the hearth. "I have not visited all of them."

"Well, I've been in two," I grumbled. "Not to mention the temple. And they all possessed them."

"Highly convenient for you, I presume. Not to mention for all the kings and queens and spies who needed to get around unobserved in the past."

"They have come in handy," I admitted. I remembered part of the discussion from the night before. "Arthur knows the castle has some now. He mentioned it in front of Fenyx when..." I stopped, remembering.

My uncle's expression turned sad. "Yes, word of Merlin's passing reached me in the night."

I raised my eyebrows. But I wasn't entirely surprised to hear it. Clearly, my uncle had his own network of power.

"You were forced to bear witness to it. I'm truly sorry for that. She was an incredible woman." His eyebrows furrowed. "The attack on the temple... I had no warning. Which means it was impulsive. That suggests someone brought information to Arthur, perhaps as late as yesterday evening. There is an informer amongst us."

"More than one," I said ironically.

I wondered if I should mention my suspicions concerning Javer.

My uncle nodded gravely. "We have our own spy now."

"Though I no longer know who to report to. With Merlin gone and everyone scattered..."

"For now, you and I will stick together." He tried to give me a reassuring smile. "I'm sure it won't be long before I have word of Galahad and the others. I'll let you know when I do."

I cleared my throat. "The passages. As I was saying, Arthur plans to conduct a search. He'll probably fill them in with bricks when he finds them. Or use them for his own completely horrible purposes."

My uncle did not look concerned. "He's welcome to try. He's gone this long without knowing they were here. In fact, I've deliberately left some purposely exposed. I figure it will do him good to find a few. He'll feel more secure afterwards."

I shook my head admiringly. "You really are an utter rascal, aren't you?"

"I prefer the term 'gifted spymaster,'" he said in a tone so unexpectedly prim that I couldn't help but laugh.

"Speaking of which, have you locked the door? I could easily make an excuse for being in your rooms this early in the morning, but going forward, I don't wish for you to take any chances."

I nodded. "I've locked it."

It had been the one and only thing I'd done once I was alone in the room. Right before falling back onto the bed and into sleep... And into my mate's arms.

"Good. Make sure it remains a habit." He shifted in the chair. "Arthur's lapdog has been praising your beauty to anyone who will listen."

"I assume you mean Fenyx. Does that mean Agravaine is out of Arthur's favor and Fenyx is in?" I wouldn't be sad not to have to see Florian's father again. Though part of me was curious about what he'd have had to say to me.

"You may see Agravaine in passing. But his obsession with finding his stray son quickly grated on Arthur's nerves and he lost favor, yes." Caspar's eyes were hawkish as he observed me. "Florian vanished the same night you left, in fact. I suppose it was sheer coincidence."

I tried to shrug casually. "Can't say I'll miss seeing Florian around these halls."

I also had absolutely no idea where his body was buried. Perhaps Draven had chopped it up into little pieces and fed it to the fishes in the Greenbriar. If so, I hoped it hadn't choked them.

Caspar smiled wanly. "Indeed. Well, with Agravaine out of favor, Fenyx rose to prominence when he led the force that caught the Lyonesse uprising. Oh, their forces have not given up, but killing their king and his eldest son dealt a significant blow to Lyonesse's morale."

"I remember. Guinevere's father and brother," I said hollowly. So Fenyx had been responsible for that.

"Fenyx believes you a rare prize," my uncle remarked. "He's praised you before half the court."

"Considering I only returned to this castle last night, he's had little time in which to do so." The thought of it made me uncomfortable.

"Arthur's already annoyed by it, but intrigued, too. Really, this obsession could work in our favor."

I frowned. "How so?"

"Arthur is evidently remembering that you once had your use."

"He was considering marrying me off to Florian instead of letting me go to the temple as Father had intended, if that's what you mean by 'useful.'"

"Precisely. There is no chance that you will be allowed to retreat to the temple and become a priestess of the Three now. None whatsoever. But a useful political marriage that would strengthen ties to his Lord General, a man who many of Arthur's most loyal soldiers look up to? That would be much more helpful to Arthur at the moment as he struggles to maintain control over his army and quash any trace of dissent."

"In case you'd forgotten, I'm not interested in being married off," I snapped.

Besides, I was already married. That made it rather complicated.

"Well, you wouldn't have to actually go through with it." My uncle stroked his long, white, braided beard thoughtfully. "This is why I wished to catch you as soon as you awoke."

"Have you been watching me sleep?" I exclaimed.

"Not at all." He looked offended. "In fact, I sealed up the peephole to this room long ago. Why do you think I bothered to knock? It was my second time trying this morning."

"Oh. I see." I took a breath. "Well, thank you for that, I suppose."

He nodded. "We should discuss the strategy you plan to adopt before you leave this room."

"Dutiful sister, obedient to her king in all things. Loyal subject, grateful to be back at court," I said in a flat, monotone voice. Weren't those the roles Merlin would have wished me to play?

"Excellent. Exactly." He cleared his throat. "But perhaps we could also add 'swooning maiden who is exceedingly grateful to Lord General Fenyx for rescuing her from treachery' to that list of roles you'll be playing."

"Be grateful to Merlin's murderer?" I gritted my teeth.

"Fenyx is a dangerous man, Morgan. He is much more observant than Arthur. Subtler, too. He'll be watching you closely. If one thing could put him at ease, it would be that which almost every mortal man is weak against."

"Flattery." I sighed. "Fine. I'll do my best not to vomit all over his feet while I sing his praises."

"A few sweet looks here and there," my uncle encouraged. "Wide eyes, a gentle manner. That should be enough to help lower his guard. And then your time in the castle will be... well, let us hope, much more pleasant."

"I *will* kill him in the end though, you know," I said, meeting my uncle's eyes.

He didn't dismiss my bold claim. "He's your kill to make when the time is right. I shan't try to stop you or take it from you."

"Thank you."

I already knew how I longed to do it, too. Slowly. And with fire.

There would be no letter openers to the throat for Fenyx.

But just in case.

"Guinevere was helpless before Arthur," I said before I could stop myself.

My uncle watched my face. "And that terrifies you now that you are back here. Of course, it would." He leaned forward, his face serious. "Believe me, Niece. I would never let it get that far. There will be no wedding night."

"But you didn't stop Arthur," I said, my voice low. "Not in time."

He leaned back, his face suddenly haggard. "I did not. Before I knew what was happening, it was too late. There were too many people around them. To save Guinevere from that wretched fate, I would have had to attempt to strike Arthur down myself. There was no time for poison or stealth." He looked at me beseechingly. "I am an old man, Morgan.

Older than you may even realize. I did not have the strength for it. If I had failed... Well, we might have been worse off than we are now."

He averted his gaze. "But yes, I failed the Lyonesse girl. I will never forgive myself for it. She was an innocent little dove, and I could not save her." He pressed his lips together. "But you. Should it come to it, I would stop at nothing. The time for waiting has passed."

I appreciated the words, even though I still wasn't sure I could count on him in a situation like that. As he'd said, he was a very old man.

No, I was on my own. I had to hone my strength and bide my time. Draven was coming. But for now, he felt very far away.

"Merlin displayed extraordinary power before she died," I said, changing the subject. My uncle seemed relieved. "I had no idea she possessed it."

"Yes, I've heard about what she did." My uncle stroked his beard thoughtfully. "I believe there must have been fae blood in her not-so-distant ancestry, yes. Though she never bore the physical signs. She showed power, you say, before she died? I admit, I suspected she had more than she ever liked to let on. If she held it back, I expect there was a good reason for it." He waved a hand. "Well, the temple has been reticent with its power for quite some time now."

"I think she knew she would die last night, Uncle," I said quietly. "She seemed to... well, almost welcome it."

"She was a clever woman of great foresight. It doesn't surprise me that she would have chosen the circumstances of her own death."

"She died for my sake. To smooth my way back into Arthur's inner circle. It seems..." I searched for the right words but in the end there were none. "It seems like such a stupid thing to die for. Such a waste. I mean, what did she think I would accomplish here, really?"

And how much more might I have been able to accomplish with her wisdom and discernment to aid me had she lived?

My uncle shook his head. "You can't think that way, Morgan. It's futile and sure to drive you mad. Merlin had her reasons, and if she believed her death was waiting for her and didn't fear it, well, then that's more than most of us get. Have faith. You must trust she knew what she was doing." My uncle rose to his feet. "Oh, I suppose you'll want news of Lancelet before I go."

My heart leaped. "Lancelet? You've found her? Of course I want news. Have you seen her? Is she well?"

His mouth twisted into a grimace. "As well as someone who has been badly beaten by a gang of grown men can be. She was not...otherwise harmed."

I understood what he meant and felt some relief.

"I visited her briefly this morning," he continued. "I left some herbs in her cell. With luck, she'll find them and know what to do. She was sleeping at the time."

"I want to see her," I said, lifting my chin. "Can you take me to her now?"

"I think we both know that there are more important places for you to be than visiting your friend this morning—a visit which could risk your life," he said gently. "But if you wish to visit her, I suggest you go at night."

He gestured to the passage behind him. "I've left chalk drawings in the passage here leading from your room. One shows the way to my chambers if you ever need to visit without being seen. I would prefer you visit openly, however. It would be safest for us both. If you follow the directions in the other drawing, it will lead you down into the dungeons. Bring a lantern. You'll see another tracing on the wall as you go. It will guide you to the cell I found her in."

I nodded. "Thank you."

"Now, if I were you," he went on. "I would dress and prepare for your presentation at court today. Things have changed since you left. There is a pattern to court life now. Every day begins in the Great Hall where the king and queen greet the court and listen to petitions and so on. Then they retire for a few hours. Arthur goes off to discuss the war with his council. The queen goes to her own chambers or to walk in the gardens. Sometimes she rides with a retinue of nobles or takes part in a hunt. In the evening, dinner is served in the dining hall, and the king and queen are usually present. I would make an effort to be there each night, at least at first. There will be a powerful symbolism to you taking your seat at the table alongside your brother. Use that to your advantage. Remind the court of exactly who you are."

"The fae-blooded daughter of a fae high king, you mean?" I reminded him sourly.

My uncle smiled slightly. "Remind them of who you're *supposed* to be, then. We both know life at court is about masking reality, not truth-telling."

"I suspect Arthur will wish to introduce you to the queen this morning. I'm not sure how much true feeling there is between them, but he's certainly very proud of her. Queen Belisent is much admired amongst the nobles for her grace and beauty." He paused. "Though not for much else. She's reticent and rather haughty. With any luck, you'll be able to break past that. If you can become the queen's confidante, there is much you may be able to find out about Arthur and his plans."

The idea of sidling up to a queen obsessed only with her own appearance while her people were at war was not especially appealing, but I would do my best.

"What about his plans for Kaye?" I demanded. "Before Merlin died, she claimed Arthur was bringing Kaye back to the city."

My uncle's bushy, white eyebrows went up. "Did she now?"

"But she may have simply said what she thought would get me to follow her," I admitted.

"If Arthur is bringing your younger brother back from the frontlines, I haven't heard of it. But he is certainly planning something. I've heard him and Fenyx discussing plans for some sort of tournament."

I scoffed, "Entertainment? While the people starve and war rages?"

"Arthur remains deluded to any chance of failure. He believes he'll win this war. I think he sees himself as a new kind of emperor, seizing the lands of Tintagel and Lyonesse and expanding Pendrath's reach across Eskira. In the meantime, like many grandiose men of the past, he sits in his palace watching it all—and becoming bored while he waits for the outcome. He and Fenyx plot and plan and direct others but..."

"But Fenyx is no longer actually fighting," I supplied. "And I suppose Arthur hasn't even visited the frontlines."

"Oh, he's visited them a few times," my uncle replied. "In gleaming armor, giving stirring speeches. But does he fight alongside his men like a true Pendragon king of old would have?" Caspar shook his head.

"My brother is not only cruel but cowardly," I said despondently.

"Arthur has had his chance. His time is coming to a close. We will see to it," my uncle said. He pushed himself out of his chair with a groan. "Well, I'll be on my way. There is much work to do. For both of us."

Sure enough, a lady-in-waiting arrived just a few moments after Caspar had departed. Behind her stood a maid holding an assortment of gowns.

"King Arthur has asked us to prepare you for court, milady," the noblewoman said. She was tall and dark haired with a milky complexion. I didn't recognize her.

It had been, I quickly realized, a statement rather than a question. Within moments, the lady-in-waiting, whose name I learned was Lady Eve, and her maidservant, Aliza, had bustled into my room.

Gowns were laid out on my bed, and the two women talked in hushed whispers about which one would suit me best, with rapid glances back at me.

Then I was pushed onto a stool and seated before the large mirror as Aliza unbraided my hair and worked her fingers through it to untangle and smooth the silvery locks. Small moonstone combs were threaded through my hair, and it was secured in a new, loose braid with delicate tendrils of curls left to frame my face.

Next, Lady Eve took a careful, but not particularly discreet, sniff of my person. Thanking the Three that I had bathed before going to see Lancelet the evening before, Lady Eve nodded and seemed to decide scrubbing me down would not be necessary.

It was on to clothes.

Apparently, showing up in the Great Hall in my training leathers was not going to be allowed, despite my attempts to persuade Lady Eve that this was how I would be most comfortable.

Ignoring me, she and Aliza selected a gown from the bed and proceeded to shove me into it.

It was a very pretty dress, though exceedingly different from the styles I had grown accustomed to in the Court of Umbral Flames. The new queen had apparently brought with her new fashions. Ones involving heavy, rich fabrics and formal styles. The bodice was a deep sapphire velvet decorated with gleaming pearls and silver stitching. Sleeves—fitted at the wrists and forming elegant points trimmed with silver lace—draped down to my fingertips.

The neckline was modest yet graceful, framing my collarbones.

But only the most high-necked dress would have hidden my scars.

I saw Lady Eve catch her breath as she belatedly noticed the marks. Leaning in for a closer look, her eyes widened. The scars had faded somewhat, but evidently she had managed to read and recognize the name. I wondered if she would mention what she had seen to anyone else.

Biting her lip, Lady Eve seemed to come to a decision and, clapping her hands, sent Aliza off to fetch a piece of white chiffon. This was carefully draped over the offensive scars and tucked into the velvet bodice of the gown.

Finally, my waist was cinched with a silver girdle and the flowing layers of pale blue silk skirts were smoothed down around my hips.

I looked at my reflection feeling dazed, and I wondered where Kaye was at that moment. Was he as finely dressed as this? Did he have servants to care for him? Or was he lonely, tired, and dirty? Perhaps even being treated roughly?

Lady Eve opened the door to my chamber and ushered Aliza out into the hall before turning to me expectantly.

It was time to meet the new queen.

CHAPTER 19 - MORGAN

It had been nearly a year since I had stood beneath the lofty, vaulted ceiling of the Great Hall.

I walked slowly past familiar tapestries that told tales of triumph and conquest, worthy battles fought by Pendragon kings and queens in times long past. A cloying aroma of roses enveloped me with each step I took. Arthur had not given up the silly pretension, even in wartime.

The buzzing of voices grew louder as I walked down the center of the hall.

Courtiers and nobles stood on either side, watching me as I walked and discussing me behind raised lace fans and polished monocles. Like the Great Hall, their appearance had not changed much either. They were still dressed in silks and velvets adorned with thorns and roses, and they carried posies of fresh flowers.

All while, outside the castle, the common people starved.

My brother's throne graced the raised dais. Dark wood adorned with gold leaf showcased the familiar thorn and rose pattern.

Kaye's smaller throne still stood off to one side. But the throne for the high priestess had been removed.

A new throne had been placed beside my brother's. The heavy, wooden frame bore intricate engravings of roses and thorns that seemed to burst forth from the throne's surface, petals and thorny tendrils creating a kind of sculpted halo. The throne seemed to bristle with life, as if the very roses and thorns themselves could reach out and ensnare any one who dared approach too closely.

Seated regally upon this new throne was a queen of extraordinary beauty. In an instant, I could see why she had held the court so spellbound.

After all, she had bewitched me just as easily the first time we had met.

Queen Belisent's rich brown hair had been left unbound and hung around her shoulders. Large, wide eyes that sparkled with a mystifying allure looked back at me, framed with long, dark lashes. Her skin looked as smooth and pale as the petals of a rare, exotic flower. A sweet, intoxicating fragrance I couldn't pinpoint trailed from her, mixing with the smell of the roses.

Small diamonds and amethysts covered the fine, plum-colored silk gown she wore, causing it to shimmer with a lustrous sheen. The gown's skirt pooled at her feet like a river of purple waves.

Beside the queen, my brother sat gazing at his wife with a look in his eyes I had never seen before. Pride. Perhaps even adoration.

As I watched Arthur, golden circlet resting on his brow, I might have almost managed to pretend his nature was different than what it was. My brother was a handsome young man, and he shared much in common with our younger brother, Kaye. His thick, chestnut hair was cropped shorter than Kaye's but was the identical shade. Their eyes were similar, and when Arthur smiled, truly smiled, which was extremely rare, he had Kaye's dimples.

But beneath the veneer of youth and fair looks, Arthur's presence was malevolent. A palpable undercurrent of malice filled the Great Hall, which even the new queen's beauty could not dissipate.

As I stepped closer, Queen Belisent lifted an alabaster hand and placed it to her midsection. It was a nurturing and protective gesture that spoke of the life stirring within her.

My heart sank as I took in the wide swell beneath her opulent gown.

Of course she was pregnant. With Arthur's child.

I lifted my eyes back to the queen's face and regarded my sister steadily.

Orcades, or Belisent as she was calling herself now, seemed to glow with a soft radiance. Was it because of the new life she carried? Or because she was secretly fae?

Haughty and reticent? Was that what Caspar had called her?

I nearly laughed to myself. Orcades had seemed even haughtier that day beneath the lake when I had set her free from her watery prison. The day she had encouraged me to pull Excalibur from its place in the stone.

And then left me for dead on the floor of the ruins of Meridium, taking the sword for herself.

She'd said she would bring the sword to Arthur. Until this moment, I supposed I hadn't fully believed her.

Nor had I expected her to marry my brother.

Yet here we were.

It was a strange moment of bittersweet understanding as she looked back at me.

Without a word passing between us, I understood she had no wish for me to reveal what I knew.

And so, together, we sisters shared something. A silent acknowledgement of a shared secret. A recognition of a connection that transcended the grandeur and falsities of Arthur's court, however unwanted and unwilling.

Standing there staring at my sister-in-law who was also my sister, I realized I didn't even know if Orcades and I were half-sisters or full-sisters. Had we shared the same mother as well as father? Somehow I doubted it. The dream I'd had of my mother Ygraine—or Idrisane, as she was called amongst the fae—had made it seem as if she and Orcades were contemporaries, not mother and daughter.

I recalled my mother had been tempted to go to Orcades for help before fleeing Gorlois. What did that mean, I wondered? Would Orcades have had sympathy for my mother's plight? Would she have helped her to escape—and me as well?

Back in Meridium, Orcades had not actually harmed me herself. Vesper had been the one who had thrown the knife. Orcades had simply... not intervened.

I supposed that made her slightly less despicable than Vesper had been.

But then, it wasn't as if she owed me anything.

The court was waiting. Arthur was rising to his feet to address us all.

He looked out upon the Great Hall, then let his eyes linger upon me.

I stood very still, suddenly remembering a day long before when Arthur had meted out his version of justice upon a young fae boy with brightly colored hair.

At any moment, I might meet a similar fate. My life hung in my brother's hands.

"Nobles of the Rose Court, courtiers of Camelot, loyal subjects of the Pendragon throne and of Pendrath," Arthur began. "For many months, my dear sister, Morgan, has been absent from our court, her absence a bleakness that has been felt by all."

He paused. This didn't seem like a terrible start. Though I doubted many present there today had actually missed me.

"Her return today is a cause for rejoicing, for it signals a reunion of the Pendragon bloodline, a reunion we have much longed for. With the expansion of our kingdom into new lands and horizons, the Pendragon throne must remain strong."

He looked down at Orcades, her hands still resting protectively on her belly.

"This line must endure for the good of our people, and I will see to it that it does. In these times of turmoil and uncertainty—"

Oh, was that what we were calling our brutal attacks on our neighbors? How fascinating.

"–unity within our family and within this court is paramount."

Another pause. Arthur's face turned flinty.

"I must acknowledge the ordeal that Morgan endured while she was lost to us these long months. An ordeal that was orchestrated by those who would seek to undermine our great kingdom and this throne. The former High Priestess Merlin, once a trusted guardian of our sacred temple, proved herself a traitor to Camelot. I thank Perun that I removed her from her position of power before her corruption could run its full course. Nevertheless, even I could not foresee every aspect of the insidiousness of this woman's treachery until it was too late. Merlin kept my sister unjustly imprisoned with her dark arts, and only through Morgan's resilience and the valiant efforts of our glorious Lord General does she stand here before you today."

Valiant efforts. I swallowed the bitter taste in my throat as Arthur lifted one of his arms and gestured to the front of the crowd where I caught sight of Fenyx.

The golden-haired man was a blatant showman. He grinned and raised both his arms over his head, eliciting a cheer from the normally subdued crowd of nobles.

Arthur smiled thinly down at the general.

It seemed Fenyx had his uses. Keeping the nobles happy must have been one of them. Arthur had never quite managed to play the hero. But together with Fenyx, he seemed to have stumbled upon a powerful partnership.

My brother raised his hands for silence, and immediately, the court fell quiet again. "Now, let us not dwell on the shadows of the past, for we are a court that looks towards the future."

He paused significantly, and I shifted awkwardly on my feet, feeling all eyes return once more to look at me. "With that in mind, I encourage each and every one of you to extend a hand of welcome to Morgan, to offer her your support and friendship. Loyalty and trust are the pillars upon which our realm is built, and we must ensure that they are unwavering."

I tried very hard to keep my face absolutely impassive.

Arthur's eyes met mine. "In unity, Camelot, we shall prevail against any threat that dares to darken our kingdom's doorstep."

Arthur turned to look at his queen. "Let this day mark not only Morgan Pendragon's return, but a renewed commitment to our shared destiny. As the sun rises on this new chapter, we stand together as guardians of Pendrath's legacy."

He held out a hand, and Orcades rose gracefully to her feet and took it.

Standing beside each other, I had to admit, they made a truly impressive-looking couple.

Orcades had obviously used some sort of glamor to hide her true fae features, but even so, she was resplendently beautiful. More so than any mortal ever had the right to be.

Beside her, Arthur made a picture-perfect king. One might easily imagine him to be a happy husband and a just ruler.

But the truth of his corruption burned within my breast.

"Now, come, Morgan," my brother commanded. "Step forward, Sister, and meet your new queen."

I moved towards the dais, praying I remembered how to curtsy properly.

When I reached the edge of the platform, I sank to my knees, my skirts swirling around me.

A small, white hand appeared before my face, reaching out for me.

I took it and let Orcades lead me up onto the dais.

"This is where you belong, dear sister," she murmured, tucking an arm around my waist as I stood between her and Arthur.

I looked out over the Great Hall as the crowd of nobles lifted their voices in another cheer.

Down below, Fenyx caught my eye and smiled, his polished armor gleaming like gold in the light of the hanging candelabras.

CHAPTER 20 - MORGAN

I had no further chance to speak to Orcades. The king and queen slipped away soon after, and I was left standing in the Great Hall—surrounded by people but alone.

Despite Arthur's fine words, no one offered the hand of friendship to me, though some nobles did deign to give me a tight-lipped smile or a nod before quickly moving away.

It was fine. I had been persona-non-grata before I'd left.

To them, I must appear even stranger now. Worse, I had the taint of a traitor on me. For there had been a shadow behind Arthur's words, despite their welcoming tone. That emphasis on loyalty and unity...

"Morgan, my dear." A portly man in white robes trimmed with gold touched my arm.

"Tyre!" I stared at him, hardly able to believe he was real.

The priest forced a smile. Of course he was in mourning for Merlin, yet here he was, compelled to pretend along with me that all was better than ever. "I was here all along, my dear lady. I have no intention of ever sitting on that dais. I prefer to stand behind a pillar and hope not to be noticed."

I smiled a little, remembering how Galahad and I used to do much the same.

Tyre gestured towards a quiet space near one of the pillars, and I followed him over. He looked around carefully before speaking again. "I was not in the temple last night when the attack came. To my deep regret, I had gone out into the city and was helping an encampment of refugees move their tents and possessions before the king's soldiers could tear them down."

"Why should you be sorry for that?" I said, remembering the encampments. "That sounds like a worthy task. I'm glad you remained safe."

"Yes. The king tolerates my charitable works, even if he does not encourage them. I've managed to assure the king that Merlin and the others were acting entirely alone. It's cowardly, I know, but—"

"But this way, you can continue to oversee the temple," I interrupted. "No, it's an excellent idea, Tyre. The people left behind... Well, they need someone to care for them. Were many of the acolytes harmed?" I remembered the fallen bodies, the pools of blood.

Tyre's lips thinned. "The soldiers were careless. The king had given them free reign for their violence. I believe they were misled into thinking we would be armed in turn, that they'd be facing a group of violent rebels rather than unarmed priests and priestesses. Sadly, we lost at least a dozen people. Many young men and women who had just begun their devotional journeys. Innocent lives, all of them." He lowered his head, his face full of sorrow.

"Merlin is gone," I said softly, reaching a hand out to touch his arm. It was warm and solid. "But at least they still have you. The temple needs you. Those who remain need reassurance."

"Reassurance?" Tyre smiled briefly. It was not his usual jovial expression. "Reassurance that I can protect them? Or reassurance that I will cooperate with the king no matter the price to my conscience?"

"For now, perhaps both." I was quiet for a moment. "We need to find out who betrayed us. Arthur knew Guinevere was there. Could it have simply been a frightened acolyte who told him?"

"I've considered it. Merlin placed a great deal of trust in her people, not just the ones working within our network but in all who resided in the temple complex. It is terrible to say, but perhaps her trust was misplaced."

I hesitated. "The Siabra man who was with me. The court mage, Javer."

"Yes, I recall him."

"I didn't see him that night. In fact, the last time I saw him was at the meeting."

I met Tyre's eyes, and he nodded slowly. "You think he may be the traitor?"

"I honestly don't know," I said. "But I'd like to find out what's become of him if we can."

"I'll see what I can dig up," Tyre said quietly.

"Of course, the traitor may have already lost their lives that night," I said. "I can't imagine my brother leaving an informer alive, unless he believed they could provide more value to him down the line."

Or, maybe the traitor was still out there. And worse, they would continue to infiltrate the group and send Arthur more information.

"You'll be relieved to know," Tyre murmured, after glancing around again to reassure himself we were still unobserved, "that we've managed to secure Merlin's body."

My eyes widened. "How?"

A look of distaste came over his face. "The bodies the king hangs in the market gallows go missing at times."

"Yes, Lancelet told me. Some people have been forced to resort to, well, cannibalism."

Tyre shuddered. "It's a terrible aspect of war. Especially for the refugees who are unemployed and looked down upon by the city residents. They do what they must." He glanced around, then lowered his voice still more. "Merlin made many friends among the refugees. She and I would frequently go out and bring them food and other supplies that the temple could spare. Her kindness has now been repaid. Some of the refugees managed to steal her body away. They made contact with Galahad and passed it along to us. Merlin will have a decent burial, Morgan. I thought you would like to know."

I nodded. "Thank you for telling me. What I've been imagining was far worse."

The refugees could have kept the body after all.

Tyre shook his head. "It could be any one of us up on those gallows next. But to lose the High Priestess... Well, it is a devastating blow."

"Is the rebellion continuing without her? What exactly is being done?" I had been in the temple too briefly to learn much about what they had planned. And now, here I was, isolated at court.

"Galahad and Guinevere have stepped into Merlin's place. They're taking the lead quite admirably. Mostly, they're maintaining the networks we had already established. Sending our people out to discreetly collect information about military movements but also corruption within the court. You never know when it will be useful to know who's ready to accept a bribe to look the other way. Of course, there's also the safe house to run and monitor..."

"Safe house?" I interrupted.

He nodded. "Lancelet's family has been providing shelter for those who need a place to hide before they can be smuggled out of the city. Her father was badly wounded by the king's guards, but he's since recovered. A brave man. So far, the king has not targeted the de Troyes family again. Pray that it stays that way for all our sakes."

I thought of Christen, the spy I had seen die. If he had lived, perhaps he would have been sent to the de Troyes safe house.

"That sounds incredibly dangerous," I couldn't help remarking. "The de Troyes have small children to think of."

Tyre sighed. "They do, but they have brave and loyal hearts like their eldest daughter, and they wish to do their part."

"What else is being done?" I prodded, knowing our tête-à-tête would soon have to break up.

"Propaganda posters are being printed and will be placed around the city. Small things, but we try to bolster the people's spirits and tear down Arthur's resolve in any way we can, small or otherwise. And then, of course, there is sabotage."

"Sabotage?" I hissed.

Tyre smiled broadly. "Of course. We've been collecting weapons among other items. Anything we can use to weaken the king's control."

I thought of what Lancelet had said about Camelot eventually facing invasion.

Tyre's face brightened. "And then, of course, there are our infiltrators. First and foremost of which is you."

"I haven't exactly learned anything useful yet," I said dubiously.

"Not yet, but I have no doubt you will. And you'll be reporting to me when you do. I visit the castle almost daily, you know. Arthur likes to make a show of going to the small temple attached to his chambers and making a display of devotion to Perun. Cavan, the priest of Perun's temple, mostly takes the lead. But out of acknowledgement to the people, Arthur often concedes to offer a small prayer to the Three." Tyre smiled ruefully. "It is not so easy to sway an entire kingdom to give up their worship of the goddesses in a matter of months, no matter how hard the king tries."

I frowned. "I should hope not. Zorya, Marzanna, and Devina are part of our culture. They have been for centuries."

Tyre shot me a curious look. "Is that all they are to you?"

I felt uncomfortable. "I wouldn't really describe myself as a true believer. Not like you or Galahad. But I do believe the goddesses deserve the utmost respect," I added quickly.

Tyre nodded, then glanced around us again. "Someone is approaching," he said softly. "We'll end things here. Remember what I've said: you report to me with anything you believe would be useful to the cause."

I nodded, though I honestly was surprised to hear Tyre demand I report to him. My uncle had made it sound as if the Round Table no longer had a clear leader. But I supposed it made sense for Tyre to step up, especially if he was traveling between the temple, the rebels' location, and the castle so regularly.

That reminded me that I had not actually asked where Galahad and Guinevere were. Or if Tyre knew anything about Sir Ector.

But it was too late.

A golden-haired man in gleaming armor was striding purposefully towards us. His face broke into a broad smile as he approached, revealing shining, white teeth.

"How good to see you, Lord General," Tyre said, dipping into a low bow.

I was not about to bow to Fenyx. Though I could understand the reasons for Tyre's false humility towards the despicable man.

"And you, High Priest," Fenyx said smoothly without breaking his gaze. "I know the king appreciates your presence in the Great Hall. Especially on such a fortuitous day as he welcomes back his dear sister."

Fenyx made a low bow to me. "Lady Morgan, how good it is to see you. I wonder if I could interest you in a walk with me in the gardens. They are lovely at this hour."

This was the start of it then. My charade.

I took a deep breath, then smiled prettily. "What a kind thought."

The Lord General held out his arm, and I took it, keeping my touch as light as I could.

Tyre was already moving off to speak to a group of nobles.

Fenyx led us from the Great Hall and out into the formal gardens. My small tower window overlooked these spaces from above. My mother had loved to walk in the gardens before she died and had passed her love for them on to me, which I had then passed to Kaye.

I tried to remember the last time I had been in the gardens with Kaye.

For as long as I could remember, the formal gardens had been the same. Whoever had designed them was long dead and gone. Some previous king or queen, I supposed. Their design may have been old-fashioned but remained beautiful. Neatly trimmed hedges surrounded lavish flowerbeds stretched out in spiraling geographic patterns, each one aligned to a specific color and flower. Some burst with vivid hues of crimson roses, others royal purple irises, and others golden marigolds. Statues of ancient heroes and mythical creatures—carved from marble and now dripping with moss—stood sentinel along the meandering pathways.

The gentle rustle of new leaves in the cool, spring breeze provided a calming backdrop to the singing of birds as they flit from tree to tree. In the center of the garden, a large fountain gurgled a watery melody which mingled with the omnipresent hum of bees and butterflies, busy at work among the blossoms on this sunny, spring day.

I glanced over at my companion. With his tousled, blond locks and chiseled features, his polished silver armor and ocean-blue eyes, he was a dashing man who seemed every inch the embodiment of a gallant, chivalrous knight.

Indeed, as we passed a group of young, giggling noble girls, my heart sank. They looked at Fenyx with adoration in their eyes, then cast jealous glances at me.

All while Fenyx smiled charmingly. He seemed more than capable of winning loyalty—not just the hearts of naive, young maidens but even of the king, my brother.

"Have you recovered from your ordeal at the hands of that white-haired witch, Lady Morgan?" Fenyx asked, breaking the silence.

"Indeed, I have. Thank you, Lord General." I tried to strike the right tone.

After all, I, too, was just another maiden in the eyes of most of the court. Young, naive, and just the type of neglected girl who would be most susceptible to someone exactly like Fenyx.

Little did Arthur's Lord General know, I was already married—and that my husband was crossing continents and seas to be by my side and help me put down my kingdom's tormentors.

It was this thought, the thought of Draven, that filled my heart with the courage to play my part.

"Please. There is no need for formal titles. Call me Fenyx."

"Very well. Have you lived in Camelot long, Fenyx? I can't recall meeting you before I left."

"I spent my youth in Rheged. My family fostered me with a noble family there."

I was surprised, but this helped me put my finger on the distinctive sound in his voice. His words were always very clipped and precise.

"You must be wondering how a man from Rheged becomes your brother's most trusted advisor, Lady Morgan," Fenyx said.

His voice was a deep baritone, edged with authority like Draven's. But with none of Draven's richness of speech or his sincerity.

"I wasn't about to ask such a prying question, but it is a good one," I admitted.

He laughed. "My family sent me to Rheged to learn all I could about their ways. They have a distinct warrior culture, you know. One which died out in soft Pendrath decades ago."

I thought of Dame Halyna and Sir Ector and all of our fine, strong knights but said nothing.

"Rheged prides itself on strength," Fenyx continued. "Their ways may be brutal, but they are effective. And my loyalty has always been to Pendrath—my family ensured that this was so. So, when your brother began his campaign of battle, I was eager to return from my family's country seat and join him."

"Considering Rheged offered Arthur their aid and then withdrew it, I'm surprised my brother did not turn his fury towards that nation," I said carefully, "rather than expending our forces upon peaceful Lyonesse and Tintagel."

"Tintagel and Lyonesse were peaceful," Fenyx agreed. "And thus, ripe for the plucking. Once we have them under our belt, we'll be in a position to go after Rheged. A much more challenging foe."

"I can imagine," I murmured.

"You need not be afraid any longer, Lady Morgan," he said, mistaking my reticence for nervousness. "The witch is dead, and soon all of her followers will be, too. Some like to speak of an uprising in Camelot, but the truth is that the traitors are few and far between. We will keep order in this city, I assure you of that."

"That's a great relief," I lied. Immensely relieved to know Fenyx thought my rebel friends would be so easily put down.

"In fact, most of the time, there is so little to occupy the residents of Camelot that your brother and I have been considering some new forms of amusement. To rally the people and give them a little taste of the excitement that takes place on the faraway front lines," Fenyx went on.

I couldn't hide my frown. "Camelot seems to be in a precarious state, does it not? I have heard some in the court speak of food shortages—"

"Nonsense." Fenyx brushed my question away. "Those rumors are greatly exaggerated. Amongst those who have nothing to do but sit in the markets refusing to seek the work of good, honest soldiers, perhaps there the lack is felt. But most of the citizens receive grain rations. All who have family fighting for the king do. They are small, yes, but more than adequate to maintain good health."

I thought of the children I had seen. Wide-eyed and emaciated. I thought of the refugees and the missing bodies. But I said nothing.

I removed my hand from Fenyx's arm and wandered a little ways ahead.

"Tell me more about this entertainment you and my brother have planned," I said over my shoulder. I clasped my hands behind my back carefully so that he would not be tempted to try to take one.

Fenyx moved to follow me, trailing so closely, I could smell the scent he had drenched himself in. A musky fragrance with a sickeningly sweet undertone of vanilla.

I thought of Draven's scent. Leather and woodsmoke. Sandalwood and cinnamon. Warm and earthy. There was an ache in my chest as I remembered it.

"It will be a grand tournament," Fenyx boasted. "Like nothing this kingdom has ever seen."

I followed the pathway towards the fountain, and bending over, trailed my hand in the water. "How marvelous."

"Of course, you and the queen will be at the center of it all. Seated up in the royal pavilion so all of the city may gaze upon your beauty."

"How wonderful," I murmured, trying to conceal the disgust I was feeling at being at the center of such a thing.

A hand shot out and gripped my wrist, yanking me to a halt.

I gasped as I was spun about. I found myself facing Fenyx very closely, my chest pressed against his breastplate. I tilted my head up to look at him.

"Pardon me, Lady Morgan, but am I boring you?" His blue eyes were cool. No hint of the fury he might be feeling there.

I longed to tell him what I really thought. Or better yet, to shove him backwards onto his ass into the fountain.

Instead, I took a shaky breath and looked up at him from under my eyelashes, a ploy I had seen some noblewomen use to their advantage.

"Not at all, Fenyx. To be honest, I'm simply... overwhelmed."

He frowned slightly. "Overwhelmed?"

"By all of this. Being back in the castle. By my presentation in court. And now, this, being here with you." I bit my lip in a way I hoped would look enchanting and not simply vapid. Though I suspected Fenyx wouldn't mind either one. "I see the looks the court gives you."

"Oh?"

"Yes. You're a very..." I searched for the word that would please him best. "Powerful man. Immensely powerful."

"And having the attention of such a powerful man is overwhelming to you, is it, Lady Morgan?"

It was easy to allow a blush to creep over my cheeks.

"Well, yes, truly. I did not have many suitors before Arthur sent me on his quest." That was mostly true.

"And now? Now that you have returned and are no longer promised to the temple? Would you *like* more suitors?" There was a gleam of amusement in Fenyx's eyes. I decided letting him think I was stupid was better than letting him think I was bored and deceitful.

"I should have to wait for my brother's word on the matter," I said cautiously while trying to hide a shy smile.

Fenyx smiled. "Oh, I don't think you need fear ever having to step foot in that decrepit, old temple again. Arthur has no plans to send you back there. Not when you could be useful in other ways."

"Other ways?" I made my voice as sweet as I could. "Of course, I should like to do anything I could to help Arthur."

"Excellent. The best way for a woman like you to help our king would be to marry," Fenyx said smoothly. "A strong alliance between the king and one of his closest allies."

He had never let go of my wrist, and now his grip tightened, almost painfully.

"You're hurting me, Fenyx," I said breathlessly, trying to pull away. I forced a smile. "I suppose you don't know your own strength."

"I know how I like to touch a woman. And I've found most women enjoy being touched roughly, even if they deny it's true." I felt a sick feeling in the pit of my stomach.

He moved even closer towards me, pushing himself up against the bodice of my dress as his gaze moved hungrily downwards over my breasts. "You certainly didn't mind my touch last night when I carried you through the temple."

I tried to stay very still. To hide my revulsion. "You rescued me. I am forever in your debt."

"Indeed. You are." Fenyx sounded overly pleased with himself. "Be sure to tell your brother of your gratitude. I should like to spend more time in your company, with his approval. Who knows what a powerful alliance we might form together, Lady Morgan."

"You have no qualms about spending time in the company of a fae woman, Fenyx?" I dared to ask.

His smile deepened as his eyes roamed over my body. My skin crawled with disgust. "Not at all. I find the fae... most fascinating. A highly overlooked people. And with such unique beauty, too."

"Some fear the fae," I hedged.

"Fools." He chuckled. "Oh, your brother despises them, yes. But what is there to fear? Their time is long gone. Now is the time for mortal power."

I highly hoped he was wrong. An incoming fleet of Siabra ships might certainly suggest otherwise, but I said nothing, merely smiled as if he had flattered me.

"Truly a high compliment, Lord General," I murmured.

I had hoped he would release me then, but to my horror, he instead moved his hands to my waist.

I didn't have to feign the sharp intake of breath. But what Fenyx mistook for maidenly shyness was in fact cold rage.

He leaned down, his lips inches from mine.

"I see in you a rare beauty, Lady Morgan. It's not often that a woman catches my eye, though many have tried."

Egotistical prick.

"I mean to claim you. Last night... Well, fate brought you to me. Right into my hands." He gave my waist a squeeze, then dipped his hands lower. Much lower, cupping my ass and almost lifting me from the ground.

I let out an outraged gasp and tried to squirm away, but he held me tight.

"I've lingered over picking a wife, but now I'll be pleased to tell your brother I've made my selection. With any luck he'll consent, and we shall be wed by the time of the tournament."

I knew I was supposed to be playing a role, but this had gone too far, even for that.

I raised my hands and pushed firmly against Fenyx's chest, breaking his grip. Breathing hard, I stepped back.

"It takes two to make such an arrangement, my lord," I said, trying to keep my voice steady. "We have known each other only a very short time."

Fenyx smiled at me. The slow smile of a man who was used to getting his own way and was rarely told no.

"The way I see it, Lady Morgan, you owe me much more than marriage. You owe me a life debt."

"That doesn't sound like any sort of chivalric code I've ever heard of," I said, lifting my chin.

"Rheged has a unique code of its own. And in this, I honor it."

"What if I do not?" I challenged him.

Fenyx laughed. "I like a woman with spirit. It speaks well of what you'll bring to our offspring."

Our offspring? Stomach churning, I tried not to clench my hands into fists and reveal just how much he was upsetting me with this talk of marriage and my becoming his grateful broodmare.

He took a step forward. "I had not given you leave to be released, Lady Morgan."

"I am not accustomed to asking for permission," I said, letting a little anger flash in my eyes. "I believe this walk has gone on long enough, my lord. I am grateful for all that you have done for me by freeing me from the High Priestess's wiles, but I believe you are presuming far too much."

But all Fenyx did was continue to smile. "Do not make the mistake of becoming my enemy, fair fae lady. Your brother has learned I make a much better ally."

He crossed his arms over his armored chest and looked around the garden. "I like this court. I like this kingdom. I've risen high here and plan to stay that way. With the king's sister by my side, well... I could do much more."

Not *we* could do much. No, this was all about Fenyx and his solo ambitions.

"You have a most pleasing form and person, Lady Morgan," he said as his eyes continued to freely roam over my body. "You should be grateful to be singled out. I am not accustomed to begging women for attention."

"I have no wish to make you or anyone else beg, my lord," I said softly, trying to return to my previous attitude of humility and calm.

"Indeed. Yet you have just all but refused my marriage proposal." Now his blue eyes seemed frosty.

"I'm simply not used to being touched so freely, by you or anyone else."

Instead of apologizing, he took a step towards me. I felt myself flinch.

"I plan to do much more than simply caress you through your gown, Lady Morgan. Much more." He reached out a hand and traced one finger down my cheek to my throat. Then, to my shock, he flicked aside the piece of chiffon that Lady Eve had so studiously used to cover Florian's name and smirked. "Ah, yes. I had heard of this."

He'd heard I was marked? I longed to ask from whom.

"Some might say you were used goods, Lady Morgan," Fenyx said softly, his eyes lingering on my chest. "Marked by another man. It would be off-putting to many suitors."

But not to him. From the look in his eyes, something about me fascinated him. Right down to my scars.

"Whatever happened to the Emrys lad?" Fenyx asked, his gaze sharp. "For a while there, his father would not stop blathering about the stupid boy's disappearance. Muttering to anyone who would listen about conspiracies afoot and a certain girl who was much more than she seemed."

I was quiet for a moment. "And you believed Lord Agravaine's rantings? The ramblings of a mad man who had tragically lost his son?"

"I did not say I believed him. The rantings were vague and, as you say, could be a sign of madness. But the fact remains that Florian Emrys did disappear." Fenryx smiled down at me. "Very strange timing, coinciding with the night you left."

"I left with two men that night, my lord," I said calmly. "Ragnar Whitehorn, Agravaine's own man, and Kairos Draven, the king's captain of the Royal Guard. Neither of them have returned either."

He whistled. "Are you saying you disposed of them, too?"

"Not at all. I am saying there are explanations for everything. I left with a dangerous assassin who my brother had assigned to me. Perhaps he had some trouble with Florian and disposed of him himself. As for Whitehorn, if you must know, I watched Kairos Draven butcher him on our trek to Valtain." That was not a lie, though Draven had had his reasons.

Fenyx raised his eyebrows. "Now there's a theory Agravaine might be able to get behind. The bloodthirsty and barbarous Kairos Draven had it out for the Emrys family, did he?"

"I have no idea. He may have. It's true that Captain Draven insisted we leave earlier than we were supposed to. The decision was not mine, you know. Either way, I cared nothing for Florian Emrys. He was cruel to me. And if he is dead, I am glad. We need men of strength and goodness in Pendrath, not weak-hearted, fiendish louts. Which one are you, Lord General?"

"One of strength. Goodness is far too close to weakness for my liking, Lady Morgan." He grinned in a way that hinted at subtle depravities. "I have been called fiendish before by some. I can't say I despise the term."

I tried not to let him rattle me. "I believe I'll retire to my room now. Thank you again for the walk."

"You'll dream of me tonight," he promised.

I had begun to walk away. Now I half-turned, sorely tempted to issue a rebuttal.

"And I, Lady Morgan, will most certainly be thinking of you while I'm in my bed-chambers this evening," he called mockingly as I continued to walk away.

CHAPTER 21 - MORGAN

I didn't want to dream of Fenyx, and unless it was a nightmare, I knew there was no chance of that happening.

The person I longed to see above all was Kaye. And failing that, Draven. I felt choked with how much I missed my mate, and it had been less than twenty-four hours since I'd seen him in our shared dream.

But Kaye—I was past desperate to know how he fared. The guilt of not knowing was overwhelming. If only I could get a glimpse of where he was, of his surroundings. To know if he was safe.

I determined I would try to conjure a true dreaming of him tonight. After all, I had caught a glimpse of Arthur's soldiers once. Admittedly, without trying. But still, perhaps I would be able to do so again.

However, it wasn't nightfall. It wasn't even dinnertime. So instead of making my way to bed, I made my way to the castle library.

It had been a long time since I'd visited. The library had not improved in my absence. If anything, it had fallen into even dustier neglect. There did not even seem to be a librarian anymore. Instead, the curtains were drawn and the large, cavernous room with its high, stone walls and wooden shelves was empty. The only light came from candles on tall, iron stands.

I was saddened to see evidence of dampness on the stone walls and mildew on many of the books.

Still, it was the largest library in all of Camelot. It was no rival for the one in the Court of Umbral Flames, but I had to start somewhere.

"Beware the dread curse of Three..."

My uncle's words hung in my mind. He may have downplayed their significance, but to me, they now seemed full of meaning.

As he had said, it all came back to the three objects. The objects of power.

I looked around. Many of the books in the castle library were hundreds of years old. They predated what had happened to the Valtain fae children. They predated what Rychel had done with the grail. They couldn't help me with current matters. But perhaps they held some wisdom from the past.

After all, the grail, the sword, and the spear—the item I knew the least about—had all been forged long before I was born. Millennia ago.

Surely they must have come up in the history of Eskira before now. Surely someone must have recorded something about them.

I needed more insight into each of the items—what they were exactly, how they could be used, when they already *had* been used and by whom. Not just legends about Vela and Perun, but solid truth.

For within the castle walls, one of the objects surely lay. It could not be a coincidence that Orcades had taken Excalibur and brought it to Arthur.

Excalibur lay somewhere nearby, and besides spying and avoiding Fenyx's disgusting hands, my plan was now to get a hold of it. Doing so would surely weaken Arthur.

It might even be able to stop this entire war.

But hours later, as I sat in a hard chair by a dusty table covered with dusty and tattered old books and sneezed for the umpteenth time, I started to wonder if the castle library contained what I needed.

From what I could discern, all of the books that had seemed promising had been written by mortal historians. Very few mentioned the fae. The ones that spoke of magical objects were mostly fairytales.

There was another possibility, of course.

Gaps on the shelves and gaps in Pendrath's history. It spoke to someone carefully curating the collection and removing books which had made too much mention of the fae. Or which had been written by fae.

Even before leaving on the quest to Valtain, I'd wondered about this strange gap of knowledge. After all, my uncle had said the fae had *more* power in the past, not less.

Perhaps when fae power had seemed to be waning, mortal monarchs had wished to have that part of our past forgotten as quickly as possible.

Tiredly, I packed up the books, promising myself I would return another day and try again. I reshelved each tome where I had found it, determined not to leave the library in greater shambles, then started to make the lengthy walk back up to my tower room.

I passed guards at their stations as well as groups of chattering nobles bustling through the corridors. All of the nobles seemed to be heading in the same direction.

And then I remembered my uncle's decree and groaned.

Dinnertime. Everyone was heading to the dining hall. And so that was where I should have been heading, too.

I looked down at myself. My beautiful, sapphire gown was rumpled and covered with dust, not to mention a few cobwebs that had been hanging off the books.

I gritted my teeth. I could go like this and try to avoid Lady Eve's disappointed stares, or I could return to my room and change into something that better suited me.

I ran up the tower stairs, suddenly eager to remove the gown that contained not only dust but the memory of Fenyx's groping paws.

Shucking it off into a heap on the floor, I yanked open my wardrobe and pulled out an outfit that was the sort of thing I had worn before leaving the Rose Court. A creamy, wool, long-sleeved tunic that covered my hips and thighs and a pair of dark brown, fitted leather pants that tucked perfectly into soft, ankle-length doeskin boots.

I ran my hands over my hair, swatting away the worst of the dust balls and cobwebs, then yanked the door open and went down to the dining hall.

The hall was already full. I must have been late. I made my way between packed rows of benches. Ahead of me, on the raised dais, was the Pendragon royal table.

As I approached, I realized Arthur was seated there almost alone. Queen Belisent—my sister, Orcades—was not beside him.

I had wondered if Fenyx might have been honored with a place at the head table, but instead, I spotted him seated with a group of soldiers and noblemen near the front of the room.

The only family member besides Arthur was my uncle. The Master of Potions was just rising to his feet. With a small smirk, he gestured to the large candle clock mounted on the far side of the dining hall. As the candles burned, etched markings tracked the passage of time.

I observed that it was nearly half-past seven o'clock. Apparently dinner had begun at seven.

I gave a tight nod and mounted the dais, then paused, unsure where to sit.

Arthur was looking at me. Before I could choose a seat at the end, he pointed to the vacant one right beside him.

I hurried over to it.

"I see you've returned to your old wardrobe, Morgan," my brother said, looking at me with amusement. "I must say, my queen will probably be relieved to know you're not interested in competing with her in terms of fashion."

"Not in the slightest," I said. "I would never bother to compete with such a lovely woman in any case. Where is Queen Belisent this evening?"

"Apparently, carrying a child is more work than we know. Her stomach troubles her, and so she sometimes misses these dinners. However, I am pleased to see you join us. I hope it will become a habit. In the past, you often hid off on your own."

"I didn't hide. I simply didn't know if... Well, if I was wanted," I said.

"It has been strange being here for so long without you and without Kaye," Arthur said, almost echoing my thoughts.

"But you have a new family now," I pointed out. "A new wife."

I thought of Guinevere. I knew mentioning her would send Arthur into a fury.

I watched as he ate his meal, lifting his fork to his mouth as if he were just an ordinary man. A man who really had missed his sister. Who missed his younger brother.

He could be so deceptively charming when he chose. And part of me desperately wished to believe that there was still something good in him.

But all I had to do was remind myself that he'd sent our brother to the frontlines and that wish went up in a puff of smoke.

"You must be very excited about the forthcoming birth of your child," I said, trying to change my focus. I pulled platters towards me, filling my plate with food I wasn't sure I'd actually be able to eat. Fluffy chicken pastries, roast pears drizzled with honey, and cheese studded with dried fruits and nuts.

Arthur was dipping his spoon into a lemon syllabub, stirring it thoughtfully.

"Yes. It will be good to have a son," he said. "There are a few things I thought we should discuss. As you're here now, I suppose you've saved me the trouble of summoning you to my chambers tomorrow morning."

"Yes?"

He took a small bite of syllabub. Arthur, I suddenly remembered, was quite fastidious about his own appearance and hated to be perceived as overly-indulgent. At least, with food. I remembered our last meeting in his chambers a year ago and the noble girl who had nearly run past me.

Suddenly, I wondered just when Orcades had made her first appearance at court. It must have been after Guinevere had already fallen from favor. Did my fae sister know how Arthur had treated his last, mortal bride-to-be? Did she care?

"Two things," Arthur said. "First, I've summoned Kaye back to court. I think it's time, don't you?"

I stared at him, hardly believing my ears. "Time?"

"Yes, I suppose you wouldn't really know. But Kaye was at the frontlines. Has been for some time now. He wished to rally the men. He's something of a little soldier now, you see. Very brave. You can be proud of our Kaye."

"I always was," I said softly.

He nodded. "He's been on the border of Pendrath and Tintagel."

"Is he well? Has he fought in any battles?" I asked, my heart beating fast.

"No, he's far too valuable for that," Arthur said, shaking his head.

Not too young. Simply too valuable. Well, if it had kept Kaye safe...

"There have been some attempts on his life, from what I understand. Limited, amateurish ones. Arrows shot towards him from the opposing lines, that sort of thing."

My hands gripped the edge of the table. "Amateurish, I see."

"He's never begged to return home, if that's what you're worried about. He understands his duty."

"So why are you bringing him back now?" I asked.

Arthur's eyebrows went up. "Well, I thought you'd wish to see him."

"I do. Of course, I do," I said hastily.

But it was difficult to believe Arthur was doing this simply for my own pleasure.

"I think it's time the family was all back together again. And with the queen preparing to deliver in a few weeks... Well, I thought it would be best to make sure Kaye knows where he stands."

Ah. I understood now.

"I wish for you to understand that, too, Morgan," Arthur said, looking at me carefully. "Kaye is no longer heir to the throne of Pendrath. As soon as my child is born, he will be the Crown Prince."

"Or Crown Princess," I suggested.

He frowned but conceded, "Or princess."

"I'm glad to hear that your child will inherit even if she is female," I said.

"Of course she shall. Why wouldn't she?"

"No reason," I murmured, deciding not to bring up Arthur's removal of Merlin as High Priestess. This was definitely not the time to discuss my brother's horrible pattern of behavior towards women.

"Truthfully," Arthur said, leaning towards me and lowering his voice, "Belisent would murder me if I should dare to suggest otherwise."

And then he shot me a conspiratorial grin that left my mouth hanging open.

Could it be possible? Did Arthur actually care for Orcades?

"She's a brilliant woman as well as beautiful," my brother continued. "She'll make a wonderful mother."

I remembered what I had read about Orcades being one of our father's foremost generals and cleared my throat. "She certainly seems to be... very versatile."

"Oh, you've seen nothing yet," Arthur said. "She's brought something to this court that's been missing for a long time. Beauty, yes. But something else that's hard to pinpoint. Glamor is perhaps the best word for it."

I had taken a bite of my chicken tart and now nearly choked on it.

Arthur slid a pitcher of water towards me, and I gratefully filled my cup.

Glamor.

By the Three, was that how Orcades had done this? Had she glamored Arthur as my mother had done to Uther Pendragon?

It would certainly explain his slightly improved countenance. I wondered how often the glamor had to be reapplied.

"I shall be very, very happy to see Kaye, Arthur. Thank you, truly, for bringing him home," I said, as soon as I had swallowed my food.

Arthur looked gratified. "Of course, Sister. It will be good to have this table full again."

I felt a pang in my heart. Was my brother trying to bring his family back together, to be a true head of our family as he might have been? If so, it was too terribly late. Oh, for what might have been.

Arthur's expression shifted into a darker one. "It pains me to tell you this, Sister, but I fear I must."

I felt a prickle of fear. "What is it?"

"Sir Ector will be named a traitor to the crown tomorrow in the public square. My men are already searching for him."

"He has fled Camelot then?" I tried not to sound too hopeful.

"Perhaps. He's left his residence. His son, Galahad, is a known traitor. You must know this already."

I nodded seriously.

"It would seem that many of your former friends are now our enemies, Morgan," my brother said, studying my face. "I meant what I said earlier about unity. We must stand together against treachery."

"Of course," I murmured fervently. "How did you discover that Sir Ector was a traitor? May I ask?"

"There have been suspicions concerning him and Dame Halyna for some time," Arthur replied.

My heart plummeted. Not Dame Halyna as well.

"But in the end," Arthur continued, "Dame Halyna assisted us in uprooting the true traitor. She worked with us to locate Sir Ector, but unfortunately, we were too late. He had already slipped away."

Dame Halyna had implicated Sir Ector. I couldn't believe it. If it was true, I would destroy the woman myself.

"When Kaye returns," Arthur said, his eyes still fixed on me, "I hope you will help me to guide him."

Guide him in remaining loyal to Arthur, he meant. Kaye would be devastated by the news that Lancelet was imprisoned and Galahad and Sir Ector were being hunted.

"I do what I must, Morgan," Arthur went on, "to protect our family, this throne, and our kingdom. I hope you know that. Under my reign, Pendrath will grow mightier than it has ever been. Empires are not spun from the silk of virtue but from the threads of ambition."

I nearly choked again. "Did you read that line in a book, Arthur?"

Arthur seemed amused at the question. "No, I heard it from our uncle once."

"He probably got it from a book," I muttered, tapping a finger against the rim of my glass.

"War is difficult," Arthur said. I tried not to scoff. What did he know about any of it? Sitting here decked in velvet with heaping platters of food before him? "But perhaps it is true that the darkest of threads can weave the most enduring of legacies. I want my empire to last. Now I must build the foundation."

"And what of Excalibur?" I dared to ask. "The weapon you sent me to retrieve? I failed you, Arthur."

I was fishing. Perhaps very dangerously but I couldn't resist.

Arthur shook his head. "You didn't fail me, Morgan. You still don't have the full picture. I keep forgetting your absence and the reason for it. Excalibur is exactly where it should be. Right here in this castle."

I drew in a sharp breath.

"The sword was brought to me by my queen. One of the reasons she holds my affections." He pushed back his chair and rose from the table. "Perhaps you'll visit her tomorrow. I believe she would like that. She accepts few visitors, preferring to hold a small court of her own for her ladies-in-waiting. A very select few, you understand. But I believe, for my sister, she would make an exception. I'm sure you'll have much to talk about."

"Yes. I'm sure we will. I'll make sure to do that."

I could not wait to find out what Orcades had told my brother about how she had found the sword. Had she claimed to be a treasure seeker like Vesper who had stumbled upon it in Meridium that day?

Or perhaps she'd told Arthur the truth—that she was a secret fae princess warrior whose incredibly powerful and evil father had imprisoned her in an underwater dungeon for countless years surrounded by dangerous treasures, and only with the power of my blood had she been able to finally escape, after which she'd left me essentially for dead, and brought Arthur his precious sword.

Somehow I doubted it.

I was alone at the table. I scanned the room. Thankfully, Fenyx was gone.

I finished my plate, then rose and returned to my room.

I needed a bath. A hot one. The day had been long, and now that it was drawing to a close, I felt as if I had been drenched in not just dust but a toxic grime.

Welcome back to the Rose Court, Morgan, I told myself grimly as I pushed open the door to my room and pulled the bell for a servant to bring hot water.

CHAPTER 22 - MORGAN

I slipped into sleep, and when I opened my eyes, I knew I was back in the same idyllic place where I had last encountered Draven.

This time, it was long past twilight. The stars were already bright overhead.

Candles in tin lanterns glimmered in the windows of the little cottage ahead of me. Woodsmoke streamed upwards through the red brick chimney.

I walked up the cobblestone path and pushed open the door, expecting to see Draven lounging in a chair by the fire.

Instead, the cottage was empty.

But a fire burned in the hearth. Someone had kindled it not long ago.

I looked around. There were other signs of recent habitation. Walking towards one of the armchairs by the fireside, I reached out a hand and touched a black, linen shirt that had been carelessly tossed over its back. It was still warm.

Taking another step forward, I saw a pair of familiar, dark trousers pooled on the floor beside a set of leather boots.

Draven had clearly been here. And he had discarded most or all of his clothes.

I had to admit, the idea of him walking around the small cottage stark-naked was highly appealing.

I imagined the lean lines of his naked back. The bronze of his skin glowing in the firelight.

But where was he now?

I stepped towards one of the walls near the bed. Like the others, it was covered with an eclectic mish-mash of paintings. I hadn't taken a good look at them the other day, but now I examined them with interest, looking from one frame to another. There were a vast range of styles, from charcoal sketches to watercolor pastels. Even a few oil paintings.

One of the paintings depicted a tranquil orchard bathed in the soft, golden light of the setting sun. The air seemed to ripple with serenity as if capturing a moment suspended in time. And at the heart of the scene stood a young woman.

I let out a little gasp.

A woman with long, silver hair trailing down her back.

She had been caught in the act of reaching upwards, her fingers poised to pluck a ripe apple from a tree. Silver markings gleamed softly along her golden skin, juxtaposed with the warm, earthy tones of the orchard. A small, secretive smile played on her lips.

Every detail had been carefully rendered. From the delicate curve of the woman's fingers to the leaves dancing in the gentle breeze.

The woman in the painting was me.

I stood frozen before the frame, struck with the surreality of it all. A painting that hung within a dream.

Still, something told me it was a real reflection of a painting that existed outside of the cottage. A painting that could only have been made by one man.

Goosebumps rose on my skin. The painting was a work of art that told a story and revealed something about the artist along the way. I looked at the expression on the girl's face. My face. My gaze was directed at the apple with a mix of curiosity and longing, as if the apple represented my thirst for knowledge—and something subtler, even more enigmatic that was harder to pinpoint.

Once again, Draven had seen me in a way no one else ever had. He had looked into my soul, captured the essence of my spirit, my desires, and then presented them on canvas with a profound depth of understanding.

Then another realization struck me with equal force.

If Draven had the talent to paint such a depiction of me without my ever guessing, what else had he concealed beneath the surface of his maddeningly oblique persona? What other secrets and hidden talents lay in this man, waiting for me to uncover them?

Better yet, would he even allow me to do so? A part of me was fearful of the answer.

Another part of me said I would never know until I had truly tried.

A newfound determination welled up within me. I longed to unravel the mysteries of Draven's soul just as he had already begun to do with mine.

As I gazed at the painting, my love for him grew.

My husband had painted me. My husband, my mate.

"Morgan, is that you?"

Draven's voice called out to me from a distance. I turned in a full circle. The cottage was still empty. His voice hadn't seemed to come from outside.

"Where are you?" I called back, my eyes once again returning to the pile of clothes he had left behind. "And why did you leave your clothes?"

I thought I caught a muffled snickering sound.

Then, "Come and find out."

I frowned impatiently. "I would if I knew where you were."

I waited.

"See the trap door? Follow the stairs."

I looked around the room, this time more slowly.

There. In the far corner, half-hidden behind the screen. A worn rug had been tossed back to reveal a square embedded in the floor. A wooden panel stood open on its hinges revealing a gap below where the faint scent of damp earth wafted upwards.

Descending a creaking wooden ladder, I found myself in a subterranean cave.

The cave's walls were slick and cool to the touch. They held the scent of ancient stone and mineral-rich earth.

I walked slowly across the uneven floor, uncertain of what to expect, until... There.

A hint of sulfur.

A hot spring, its steamy tendrils mingling with the cave's natural scents, filled the air with warmth. The soft trickling of water echoed gently, the sound peaceful and hypnotic as it mixed with the occasional drip from the stalactites above.

Lanterns dotted the cavern's walls, illuminating the space in an inviting radiance. Their flickering lights danced over the rippling surface of the pool.

And there, on the far side of the water, lounging on a ledge with a wicked grin on his face that sent my heart racing, was Draven himself.

He reclined with an air of profound ease, his bronzed torso bare like some god of desire made into flesh. Ebony strands of hair, as dark and inviting as the secrets of eternity, framed his chiseled face. A face I could not imagine any other rivaling for masculine beauty.

Glistening droplets of moisture clung to his skin. Every ripple of his muscled form seemed as if it had been carved by the hands of deities, as if the essence of temptation had been given earthly shape.

I stepped closer, like a moth drawn to a flame, and Draven turned towards me, his emerald eyes as green and as deep as a forest.

The water around him undulated as he shifted, rising to his full, imposing height within the spring. Beads of water fell from his glinting horns as he shook droplets from his ink-black hair.

With a sinuous grace, he stretched out one arm along the pool's edge. A slow, seductive smile curved upon his lips. His gaze, intense and filled with desire, traveled from my eyes down my form, lingering hungrily on every curve and contour.

His admiration was palpable, and I felt a heat rise within my core, triggered by the wordless invitation that stirred my senses and ignited a longing that mirrored his own.

And then I understood.

He was the apple.

He was my irresistible temptation waiting to be explored. The one creature in this world I was most curious about—and terrified of truly knowing. For looking into Draven's soul meant looking into my own reflection. And who had ever dared to look into oneself so honestly as I knew my mate had done with me?

My skin was already damp with the humidity of the cave. I could smell the scent of Draven's skin from here, mingled with the faint musk of the spring waters.

Without breaking my gaze from his, I began tugging my own clothes off. They had suddenly become an unwanted, heavy burden.

I unfastened the ties of my front-lacing gown, spreading the bodice open to reveal my breasts. I let the moment linger, reveling in the hungry expression in Draven's eyes as he looked at me. Then I slid the dress from my shoulders and pushed it down my body to the ground. My underthings were next. I slid them from my hips and to the cavern floor, then stood, naked and waiting, drinking in the sight of my husband's body as he stood in the pool thirsting for mine.

His lips had parted slightly as he'd watched me undress.

Now I raised my hands to my breasts and provocatively lifted them, feeling their weight and heft, feeling the familiar strained sensation of my nipples as they puckered in the air. I ran my fingers lightly over them, rubbing their tips, and was gratified to hear Draven elicit a strangled groan.

He took one step out of the water, then another, and suddenly I found myself quite distracted.

He was a very pleasing man. In all ways. But he had been endowed with one gift in particular which now stood out.

His cock had risen, full and hard, pulsing with desire. I stared at it in fascination. Seeing my gaze, he lowered his hand and began stroking himself expertly, teasingly.

"Can't get enough of caves, can you?" I tried to joke, my knees already threatening to become jelly.

"Can't get enough of you." His eyes blazed with a heat that made me feel weak from head to toe. "Come here. Come to me."

I had hardly taken more than two steps forward when he lunged out of the pool and seized me, grabbing me like a wild animal and lifting me towards him.

He set me down on the ledge he had been sitting on, then roughly pushed my shoulders back.

My breasts swayed upwards, nipples dancing tantalizingly towards his mouth. I held my breath.

My body was weak with need. I felt as if I'd do anything, say anything. Draven was pure carnality as he stood over me, easily twice my weight in muscle, broad and nude and masculine. My gaze flicked over his damp, black hair, dripping chest, and then lingered, long and hard, on his groin. He was all Siabra beast. All raw strength. All mine.

And I wanted him in any way, every way.

Everything but him, but here, was completely forgotten.

There was only this moment. Our bodies, here, naked, and together.

I conjured up a vivid memory of the last time. My hands pressed to the wall of the cottage. Draven filling me from behind. I let out a little moan of longing.

Draven smirked, drawing my eyes back to his wicked, wicked mouth, and I knew I had given too much away. Shown too clearly that I liked what I saw and wanted more of it.

He moved in upon me then, his mouth hungrily descending to kiss my belly, then up to my breasts. He sucked on one nipple, then the other, before biting hard enough to make me gasp.

And then he was moving downwards, down to the space between my thighs. I knew just what he'd find. I was wet and dripping with heat.

He started to lick between my legs, lapping slow and deep. His tongue pressed against my clit, and I let out a gasp. The pressure was building rapidly. I wasn't sure how much more I could take. I closed my eyes, leaning backwards, and felt his hands rubbing my nipples as he worked his mouth on me below.

I was going to explode.

"Draven," I said, my voice hoarse. "Draven, please."

"That's it," he said, lapping at my pussy as if it were an oasis in the desert and he a dying man. "That's it. Come for me, Morgan."

I took one last good look at his cock. At how hard he was for me. At what I was doing to him.

And then my body heaved and waves of pleasure flooded through me as bliss took over.

His hands ran up and down my thighs as I turned into a hot, liquid, quivering mess, my body throbbing as I broke into a million pieces under his hands, his lips, his tongue.

And then it was over. I was drenched in sweat and steaming water, and Draven was there, looking down at me as if I was the most beautiful thing he'd seen in his life.

I looked up at him, wondering if he could see the very same thing reflected in my eyes.

I let my gaze trail down his body, lingering on his hips, his groin, then finally his cock.

He groaned as if my eyes were touching him viscerally.

"Your turn," I said, my voice low.

His hand shot out, gripping my neck, and I gasped. The touch wasn't gentle, yet it wasn't rough either. Simply... firm. Firm and utterly dominating. I looked up and saw the need in his face. His hand cupped the back of my neck, pulling me towards him, and I understood.

I grinned. He growled.

"I know what you want," I whispered.

He growled again, low and desperate, a sound that could send me over the edge.

I raised my hands, skimming them over the contours of his chest, then tracing the thin line of curling hairs down the center of his stomach to his groin.

I moved my hands downwards, palming his length, and Draven groaned in appreciation, his eyes rolling upwards.

"Take it, Morgan. Please."

There was nothing like hearing a massive, monster of a man beg me to take him in my mouth.

I felt filled with flames of lust, my hands on fire as I skimmed his thighs, stroked his cock once more, then enveloped his length with my mouth. My soft tongue licked down his shaft, caressing the tip, teasing him until he was almost pulling away.

And then I sucked, hard and deep, so deep that a sound ripped out of Draven, guttural and bestial.

"Don't stop," he commanded.

I could feel the heat coming off of him in waves. Steam was rising from all around us in the pool, a curtain of mist surrounding us and drenching us in fresh moisture. I thrust forward, sucking him like he was a fine wine, all while my hand stroked careful, steady circles over his thighs, over the planes of his muscular stomach.

Draven's hands reached out. One wrapped itself in my hair, holding me so tight it almost hurt, but I didn't protest. He reached his other free hand down, cupping my breasts, squeezing my nipples so hard, I thought I would scream.

Then I felt him arching, his cock thrusting hard into my mouth. And all the tension in his body, all the hardness—just for a moment—dissipated as the spasms of climax racked his body and convulsions came through his entire core. His release drenched my mouth, filling it with his seed. I swallowed it hungrily, then pulled back reluctantly, licking my lips clean of the last drop.

"Fuck, Morgan."

I looked up to see Draven's eyes wide as he looked down at me like he'd never seen me before.

"That was—"

"Tell me what to do next," I said.

Lightning flashed in his eyes. He didn't have to be asked twice.

"Come sit on my cock."

"Is that what a good Siabra girl would do?" I teased, running a hand down his chest.

He shot me a surly grin. "I have absolutely no idea. I don't know any. I only know wicked fae Valtain girls with hair like moonbeams and breasts like golden orbs."

Suddenly, his hands were on my waist and he was lifting me up again, switching our positions on the low ledge and pulling me onto his lap until I was straddling his thighs.

His hands were in my hair. His lips against my ear.

I felt time slowing down again.

"But what I do know," he whispered, his breath hot against my skin, "is that you deserve to be worshiped as a fucking goddess, as the warrior princess that you are. You deserve to have every inch of your body adored all night long. You deserve to be fucked until you scream."

I felt my heart beginning to pound.

Draven moved my hands behind my back, holding my wrists in place with one of his strong hands while his other dipped between my thighs, lazily stroking my clit.

"Let me dominate you here, let me command you. Let me tell you to sit on my cock, let me tell you to take me in your mouth, but always know that outside of here, you're not just my equal, you're my fucking superior, and I'd follow you to the ends of the world if you told me to." He gave a shaky laugh. "Hell, I'm already doing it, Morgan, and you haven't even told me to."

"Stop," I whispered, my eyes holding his. I didn't bother to struggle against his grip. He was right, after all. Some part of me wanted this man to hold me down and take me like an animal.

But another part...

I slanted my mouth against his, and he moved his lips on mine without reserve. His jaw brushed my chin—harsh, unshaved stubble scraping against soft skin. Time slowed as I tilted my mouth up to him, flicking my tongue along his lip, then sucking hard. He felt so good. His hand continued to play between my legs. I spread them wider, feeling how hard his cock had again become.

His tongue penetrated my mouth, a pulse of slow strokes, then fast ones. I lost myself in the rhythm.

He moved his hand, lifting his cock to stroke my clit with the tip. He was all hot girth, all masculine hardness, and I could hardly breathe.

I wiggled my hips, and he let go of my wrists, cupping my ass with his hands as I lowered myself onto his cock inch by inch.

He filled me up, filled me so perfectly. I felt myself tightening, stretching. It was so good.

I braced my hands on his shoulders, rubbing my breasts against his chest as he slid further inside me, burying himself deep.

And then he rocked into me, hitting a place deep in my core. My head rolled back as a moan tore through me.

I met him with a thrust of my own, letting him slide almost all the way out, then pushing myself over him, bringing his cock plunging back inside me. I screamed as he gripped my hips, thrusting harder and deeper until I felt him beginning to reach his release.

How could it be this good, I wondered? How could we lose ourselves in each other so easily?

Draven slipped a hand between my legs again, finding the sweet spot that would take me over the edge just as he slammed into me one last time. Our pleasure crashed over us like a tidal wave.

I felt Draven's shoulders relax then tighten beneath my hands.

"My mate," he breathed against my ear. "Say it, Morgan."

"You're my mate," I whispered back. "My husband. I wouldn't have it any other way."

I felt him tense up, freeze, then take a deep breath.

"The moment I met you, I knew what would happen." His voice was the promise of darkness...and the start of something dangerous.

"What?" I whispered, hardly daring to breathe.

"You were the fire right from the start. And I could feel myself wanting to run straight towards your flame. I'm not a good man, Morgan. I'm not sure I've ever been one."

"I'm not sure I'm one to judge," I said, my throat tightening as I thought of the things I'd done, the lives I'd taken. Starting with the man I'd known as my father.

"Nothing you do could ever scare me or make me love you less."

"You used to scare me, Draven," I whispered, skimming my fingers over the back of his neck.

He was quiet for a moment. "I know. But I was never your prison. Never your captor. All I've ever wanted was to be your protector. Your sanctuary."

My heart flipped over in my chest.

Draven reached out a hand and caressed my hair. "I saw you, and I wanted to consume you. Like a fire that would only burn for me."

"I think you've succeeded all too well," I murmured, tilting my forehead gently against his.

"Yours is the only kingdom I'll pay fealty to. Yours are the only feet at which I'll willingly kneel." He leaned back and touched my chin, lifting it. "I'd rather be a villain by your side than play the hero for anyone else. The world is dark and vile, but I'd willingly follow you into the depths of hell itself. All I want to do is shield you. Do you understand, Morgan? You're my redemption, good or bad, right or wrong."

I looked into his eyes and understood. He may not have been a knight in shining armor, but he was the one I was meant to be with. There was no scaring him away. He had looked into the depths of my shadows and seen the light. He'd looked past every twisted fragment and loved me anyway.

"So consume me," I whispered. "I see your shadows, too, Draven. And I'll only burn for you."

He touched my lips with his and then he did. Again and again.

CHAPTER 23 - MORGAN

L ater, we lay in the bed upstairs in the cottage, naked in each other's arms. We'd stoked the fire to a roaring blaze, and a wonderful warmth flowed from it.

"I wish this were real," I said sleepily.

Draven was silent. I'd told him of the events of my day, catching him up on all that I'd learned.

But I'd downplayed my walk in the garden with Fenyx, leaving out the touches, the full ferocity of the demands that had been made.

Even so, I suspected that Draven had read between the lines.

"I do, too," he said darkly, stroking my hair as if he found it just as soothing as I did. "It would mean you were safe."

"I'm not... unsafe."

He snorted. "Please, Morgan. I can't think of a worse place in Aercanum for you to be right now. And to be there without me..."

I felt his body tense.

"This Fenyx. Be wary of him, Morgan. I don't like what you've told me."

"I thought you'd be more curious about Orcades," I said lightly, trying to draw him away from a subject I found equally troubling.

"She's a subtle woman with her own plans. Arthur has clearly played right into them, like a stupid boy."

"Do you think she's cast a glamor over him?"

He shrugged. "Perhaps. Does it matter? Would you care?"

I thought for a moment. "No. If anything, I'm more concerned for her than for Arthur. Is that odd?"

"She's your sister. She didn't harm you directly. She simply... didn't help you. I suppose you'll have to figure out whether she means you harm or not now."

"My only sister, and it's already so complicated." I sighed.

Draven laughed. "I doubt she's the only one, Morgan. Gorlois was prolific with his offspring."

Now it was my turn to tense. Gorlois. I disliked even hearing the name.

"What is it?" Draven looked curious.

"I still can't believe he's my father," I said carefully. "Everything I've learned so far suggests he's an even worse man than Uther was."

Draven touched my cheek. "I can see how that must be unsettling."

"He wanted me for something. And my mother wouldn't allow it. Do you think Orcades can tell me more about it all?"

"Perhaps. All you can do is ask. She'll keep her secrets, I have no doubt. She probably has enough to fill an armada of ships. But maybe she'll let a few slip. You are her little sister after all."

"Maybe I can convince her I mean her no harm. That I'm willing to be an ally."

"Just be careful of how much you reveal, Morgan. Your powers... Well, even among fae, they are rather unique."

I wasn't sure if he meant my abilities with fire or the new ones I'd gained from our mating. But either way, I nodded.

"I have to go." Reluctantly, I sat up in the bed.

"Go?" Draven tilted his head. "Go where? You're sleeping back in Camelot."

"I know. And now I need to wake up." I glanced around. "Um, how do I do that exactly?"

Draven seemed amused. "Pinch yourself. Or, here, I can do it." He leaned forward and pinched me in a particularly soft spot and I squeaked.

"I'm still here," I complained.

"Maybe I should have pinched harder." He leaned forward and I moved away. "Or bit." He grinned ferally and I felt my heartbeat speed up.

"I don't have time for that," I said, trying to retain a measure of dignity as my nipples puckered in the firelight at the thought of Draven's teeth on me.

I slid out of the bed. "I'll simply will myself to wake," I decided.

"This should be interesting," Draven muttered, folding his hands back behind his head and watching as I stretched out my arms and closed my eyes.

"Wake up," I said out loud.

Then in my head, I added, "I need to wake up now. Morgan, *wake up*." I said the last phrase as sharply as I could, willing my body to comply back in the waking world.

And then I was gone.

CHAPTER 24 - MORGAN

I pulled my cloak tighter around my shoulders as I followed my uncle's directions and tread through the passageways that lined the interior of the ancient castle walls down to the dungeons.

Dawn was a few hours away. I had two visits to pay before then.

Lifting my lantern a little higher, I caught sight of a chalk drawing on the stone wall ahead.

Lancelet's cell was indicated with an X. It was around the next bend.

As I turned the corner, it was as I'd suspected.

I wasn't going to be able to get close to Lancelet, even if there were a lack of guards at this time of night. The passage I was coming through bordered the back wall of the row of cells. My only access point was through a small square in the stone where a piece of wood had been painted to blend in with the wall of the cell.

I stepped up to the wooden block and slid it to the side as quietly as I could, making certain to rest my lantern on the floor lest the light cast a gleam that gave me away to any guard passing by on the opposite side.

"Lancelet," I whispered, softly at first.

I listened. The soft snoring of prisoners was all I could hear.

A pair of eyes popped into view, filling the square space in front of my face. I nearly yelped.

"Lancelet! You nearly scared me out of my skin."

Her blue eyes flickered over me. "What are you doing here?"

"What do you think I'm doing?" So it was going to be like that again, was it? "My uncle said he left you some healing herbs. Did you get them?"

There was a slow blink. "I got them. They helped. Thank him for me. Now get out of here."

"Stop trying to get rid of me. I just got here. I wanted to see if you were all right."

"Well, you've seen. I'm fine. Now go."

I narrowed my eyes. "All I can see are your eyes."

"Well, then you've seen the best part of me." She suddenly broke into a fit of coughing that sent her doubling back.

As she drew away from the little square window to catch her breath, I glimpsed her face. It was covered with bruises. Dried blood caked her lips.

"You're not fucking *fine*," I hissed. "What are they doing to you?"

"Oh, you know," Lancelet said airily. "Daily beatings. A few lashes. Maggoty bread. The usual sort of thing."

She gave another hacking cough, and I watched in agony.

"This isn't right. I'm up in my old room while you're suffering down here."

"It's a dungeon, Morgan. What did you expect? Life's not exactly fair. And you're in no position to do anything about it. Now forget about me and go and do what you're supposed to be doing. Spying. And not on me."

"Don't you want to hear about Guinevere?"

Her eyes gleamed. "Guinevere? What do you know?"

"I know that she's safe," I said, wishing I had more to offer. "She and Galahad got away. They're reorganizing. And Merlin... Her body was stolen by some refugees and brought to the rebels. She'll have a proper burial now."

"But have you actually seen her?" Her voice was low and desperate. I knew she hadn't meant Merlin.

I shook my head. "I've only spoken with Tyre and my uncle. I'm sorry. I haven't seen her myself. But I can try to find out more." I hesitated, then added, "Arthur told me that Sir Ector is on the run. They think he's a traitor. Dame Halyna implicated him."

"Dame Halyna? That's ridiculous." Lancelet narrowed her eyes. "She'd never do such a thing."

"It does seem unbelievable," I agreed.

"Well, go and find out the truth," Lancelet demanded. "Stop wasting your time here with me."

She looked at me with wild eyes. I half-expected her to start shaking the bars of the cage. I was suddenly sure she spent half her day doing so just to annoy the guards who would, more than likely, be happy to retaliate.

"Can't you try to keep your head down in there?" I pleaded. "Blend in, stay low, that sort of thing?"

"You mean while they beat and rape the other prisoners and take them off to be hanged every day?" Lancelet gave an unpleasant little laugh. "What's the point? My days are numbered. I can practically feel the noose around my neck."

"Don't say that. It's not true. I'm going to get you out of there."

"Really? How? By telling Arthur you're a traitor, too? Or simply by begging for a favor? You think he pardons traitors easily, even for his own sister?"

"I don't know, but I swear I will get you out, Lancelet. Please, believe me. Don't make things worse for yourself." I closed my eyes. "I can't imagine how horrible things are in there. I'm sorry we can't trade places."

Once again, she had the worst of it. But this time would be different.

"I swear to the Three, I will break you out of this cell with my own bare hands if I think you're truly to be executed," I vowed, determined to convince her.

For a moment, she simply looked at me. Then, "Really? You and what army?" She slunk back from the window as if my words had momentarily filled her with false hope then sent her plummeting downwards again.

"Get back over here," I whispered furiously. "Me and what army? Come and look at the fucking army I've brought, Lancelet."

I saw her reluctantly move her face back to the small square.

Before I could change my mind, I stretched out my hands and poured out my will.

Instantly, balls of flames erupted from my fingertips, their tendrils shooting upwards towards the stone ceiling.

I let them burn for a second, then clapped my hands together, throwing the passageway back into darkness.

I stepped towards the window—so close, my nose almost touched my friend's.

"What the fuck was that?" Lancelet breathed. "You did something like that back in the temple with your blade when it touched that soldier's."

I nodded. "I can do much more." I wasn't one for pointless boasting, but I wanted her convinced. "When I say I will burn the walls of this castle down around us to get you out, I will do it, Lancelet. Do not doubt me."

She studied me in silence, her eyes in shadow, then said at last, "Don't waste your powers on me."

"Waste?" I said sharply. "Waste? It would be no waste."

"You'd free me and perhaps some of the others, but then what?" She shook her head. "You'd be captured, tortured, and it would all have been for nothing. My beatings. Your lies and spying. No, we need to think beyond ourselves, Morgan. When you use that power you have, it has to be for something great. Something more important than simply saving one person."

I looked at her steadily. "I'll decide how and when to use my abilities. If I think you're worthy, you're worthy, and I won't regret what I do."

"Well, then you're an idiot," she snapped. "I don't need saving."

"No," I said, shaking my head in disbelief. "It's not that at all. It's that you want to die in there, don't you? This is exactly what you've been hoping would happen all along."

"You're mad."

"I'm not. It's true. You saved Guinevere. You must feel very satisfied with that. You can die knowing she got away. You'll be a martyr in your own mind. Dying for both causes. But you've never told her you love her, Lancelet."

"Shut up."

"And she could still die. She's still not safe," I pressed on. "She still needs you."

"Shut up, Morgan. I'm warning you."

"What are you going to do? Stop talking to me? I'll shout into your cell until I wake the guards."

"They already think I'm mad. I shout to myself half the night just to piss them off." Lancelet grinned demonically at me from the shadows.

I bared my teeth, not about to back down. "You stay the fuck alive in there. Do you hear me? Don't lose hope, and don't resign yourself to an easy death."

"Easy?"

"Yes, easy. You don't get off this easy. I don't care what's happened to you. I don't care if you have a shitty friend like me who let you get half-eaten by fucking rabid children, you still have to stay alive. Guinevere needs you. *I* need you!"

Lancelet said nothing, she simply glared at me with hostility. I glared back at her.

"Fine," she said at last.

"Fine?"

"Fine. I'll do my best. Now will you get out of here?"

I whipped my cloak around myself. "Fine! But I'll be back."

"It's your funeral," she whispered as she backed away. "Now close that stupid window."

Muttering under my breath, I did as she'd suggested.

"Well, that went well," I whispered to myself as I walked back down the passage.

And there was still another visit to be made.

I had no chalk directions to follow for this one, but I thought I could find my own way.

The barracks attached to the main keep of the castle were a sturdy stone structure built within the inner bailey walls. They provided lodging for the knights and soldiers of the king. Functional but basic, most consisted of rows of bunk beds with simple straw mattresses, wooden footlockers for storing a few personal belongings, and a central hearth.

Sir Ector and Dame Halyna had their own residences in the city, but I knew that most of the time, they'd preferred to remain in the private chambers they had been assigned in the barracks. The chambers of the knight captains had a degree of privacy and comfort that the ordinary soldiers and knights did not usually enjoy.

I doubted Fenyx would be sleeping in the barracks, even in a private chamber. No, I suspected my brother had given him rooms in a wing of the main keep.

At least that meant I wouldn't risk running into him tonight.

I moved through the passageways leading out of the dungeon and emerged from a concealed doorway hidden behind a tapestry in a dimly lit corridor. After taking a moment to get my bearings, I moved down the hallway as silently as I could, my soft, leather boots quietly scuffing across the stone floor.

All was still and silent.

I reached the chamber that had been Dame Halyna's the last time I'd visited and said a silent prayer that she hadn't been assigned to a new, grander one.

With a sad glance at the door next to hers which had housed Sir Ector, I pushed on the wooden frame.

It didn't budge. Of course Dame Halyna would lock her door at night. Lancelet had been right, I truly was an idiot.

I cursed silently but wasn't about to retreat.

Instead, making sure the corridor was still completely abandoned, I raised my hand to the lock, focusing my energy and calling upon the force within me. For a moment, my hand shook, then it steadied, and a slender, searing stream of flame emerged from my palm.

Glowing like a bright ribbon, the flame flowed into the keyhole and began to work, slowly but surely.

The lock's iron grew red-hot and pliable under the focused fire, and I felt a surge of gratitude for Draven's precision training back in Myntra, though I knew I hadn't come anywhere close to true mastery yet. I maintained my focus, the narrow stream of flame unyielding. Sweat beaded on my brow. The only sound was the faint hiss of the metal lock as it melted.

Finally, after what felt like an eternity, the iron components gave way. I pushed on the wood, and the door creaked open with a soft groan. I stepped inside the dark room, pushing the door closed behind me and leaving only the faded scent of charred metal in my wake.

Or so I hoped.

For a moment, I stood still in the blackness, letting my eyes grow accustomed to the dark.

As they did, I caught a flash of steel across the room.

"I wondered if you'd come, Morgan," Dame Halyna said. "Why don't you tell me what you're doing here."

Dame Halyna was not lying peacefully in her bed. She was standing across from me with her sword drawn.

She stepped across the room and pulled the hood from the lantern resting on a small, wooden table. I lifted my hand to cover my eyes, blinking in the unexpectedly bright light.

"It should be obvious. I'm here to find out if you're the traitor in our midst."

"And if I am, then what?"

I hadn't prepared for this, but still, the answer came easily. "Then I'll kill you here and now, before you can spill another secret to my brother."

Dame Halyna remained unruffled. "That was impressive work with the lock just now. It simply melted away. Some kind of fae power, I suppose?" She shook her head. "Not sure how I'll explain that in the morning, but I'll think of something."

I swallowed. I hadn't thought of that.

"If I'm alive in the morning, that is." Dame Halyna smiled at me, then set down her sword on a nearby table. "I'm not the traitor, Morgan."

"You told Arthur that Sir Ector was one," I said quietly.

"I did," she agreed. "Because he and I had decided one of us had to take the fall."

I lifted my chin. "And he insisted he would go on the run? Am I really supposed to believe that?" Though, in fact, it did seem exactly like something the stubborn old man would do.

Dame Halyna looked at me calmly. "Believe it, because it's the truth. You've known me since you were a child, Morgan."

"I've known Sir Ector that long, too," I said.

She nodded. "That's true. And therefore, you know exactly how bullheaded he can be. I wanted to be the one to go so he could stay near Galahad. But what do you think he had to say to that?"

I could easily imagine. Dame Halyna had no family in Camelot to worry about, so she would have been the logical choice.

"He didn't want to say goodbye? To tell me any of this himself?" I asked.

"Of course he did. But he didn't have that luxury. Neither of us did. It all happened very fast. The night of the attack on the temple."

"That's why neither of you were there."

She nodded. "I was in a holding cell waiting for your brother to make up his mind about what to do with me. And Sir Ector had, thankfully, already fled."

"Where is he now?"

"Far from Camelot by now, I hope. He knew Arthur's men would be searching for him here. One of our supporters has a residence not far from the border of Tintagel. Ector planned to ride there and then try to make contact with the Tintagel forces."

I stared. "He's going to make contact with Arthur's enemies?"

"Yes. Arthur's enemies, not ours," she pointed out. "Before all of this, they were our neighbors. They still could be."

"He's going to help them break through the frontlines and into Pendrath," I said slowly.

She nodded. "If he can."

It was a desperate act. One of high treason. If he accompanied the forces from Tintagel, then Sir Ector would be forced to fight against his own people. But I supposed it was a price he was ready to pay. Anything for a chance at peace.

"If they succeed, they'll ride for Camelot. Kill Arthur," I said.

"We can hope." Dame Halyna met my eyes. "We all know there will be a price to pay."

"It's not Arthur I'm thinking of but the people of this city." If the city was breached, there might be a slaughter.

"Soldiers will die," she agreed. "Civilians, too, yes. But soldiers are dying every day, far from home, fighting for your brother and his aspirations of an empire. What else can we do if we ever want this war to end?"

I thought of Draven and his army. But they were weeks or months away, he'd said. If an army from Tintagel could get here faster...

Everything was chaotic. Arthur had made a horrible mess of things. Now here we were, actually hoping the kingdom we had attacked might be able to help get us out.

I let out a breath. "I hope it works."

Dame Halyna seemed relieved. "I hope so, too. Anything could happen on the road to Tintagel. We won't know if he's made it through for quite some time."

I nodded, then turned to go. "I'm sorry about your lock."

"Wait, Morgan."

I looked back at the older knight, her faded, light brown hair criss-crossed with gray. Like an older Lancelet. Older and wiser, I hoped. "Yes?"

"May the Three be with you," she said. "In all you do for Pendrath. We all stand behind you. Know that, and may it give you hope."

I cleared my throat. "May the Three be with you, too."

It had been a long time since I had said the familiar phrase to anyone. I prayed it would have weight.

CHAPTER 25 - MORGAN

T he Mistress of the Robes was just leaving my sister's chambers as I arrived early the next afternoon. She looked irritated, her lips pursed in a sour line. She curtsied to me briefly, then marched down the hall. I assumed a fitting had not gone as she had hoped. I doubted Orcades was an easy queen to please.

A guard held the door of the antechamber for me as I went inside.

The rooms had once been my mother's. It was strange to see them being used again now. Somewhat to my relief, Orcades had exercised her own taste and redone the decor entirely, replacing old tapestries of hunting scenes and flower gardens with bright, richly colored ones in geometric patterns. Faded carpets had been removed and thick, plush rugs put in their place, so soft that my feet practically sank into them as I walked. The draperies had been altered and all of the furniture exchanged for a new style in a pale wood accented with silver rather than the traditional royal gold.

Orcades' color preference seemed to be firmly in the imperial purple spectrum. Violet and plum and amethyst shades permeated the room. Even the flowers seemed to have been picked with their colors in mind. Fresh lilacs and bouquets of lavender filled towering vases; their sweet, heady fragrance wafting over me as I walked through the lavish receiving room.

Beyond the antechamber lay the queen's inner chambers.

The door was slightly ajar. I could hear the sound of someone playing the harp from the room beyond.

I stepped closer, then hesitated.

"Come," called a female voice, regal and melodic. "I've been expecting you, Sister."

Pushing the door open, I entered the room. Orcades sat at a large, golden harp, strumming it softly. She wore a long silk robe in a deep shade of mauve, and beneath it, something very lacy. I glanced across the room at the large bed. The sheets were still rumpled. I tried and failed not to think of the implications, my stomach heaving slightly.

"Don't you mean sister-in-law, Your Majesty?" I asked sweetly, turning to face her.

Instead of responding, Orcades raised her hand, snapped her fingers, and the door slammed shut behind me.

Orcades smiled. "There. That's better."

I looked at her and remembered the first time we'd met. Her ethereal beauty had seemed so exotic to me then. Her wild tangle of amethyst hair. Her magnificent violet eyes.

Even now, with her fae features purposely muted, she was quite possibly the most beautiful woman I had ever laid eyes on. She also seemed to radiate magic. The door had been but the snapping of fingers to her.

She had been extremely powerful once—and valuable to our father.

Orcades sniffed delicately, and I knew she sensed it, too. The magic I had grown accustomed to, simmering off me in turn.

Strange how our positions had almost reversed. Here I was, looking more distinctly fae than ever. While she masqueraded as a mortal woman.

My queenly sister rose from the stool by the harp and crossed over to me, looking me up and down. "You've changed. Grown up somewhat."

"Yes, much has changed since we last met," I said. "Queen Belisent, is it?"

She smiled briefly. "One of many names I've used from time to time. Not my only one. But then, you know something about changing names yourself, don't you?"

For a moment I was afraid she meant my marriage. My heart hammered. Could she have found out where I had really been?

I carefully took a few steps back from her, remembering the trick she had used the last time.

"Morgan Pendragon. Morgan le Fay," she pointed out, waving a hand.

My shoulders relaxed in relief. "We're both Pendragons for now, I suppose."

She laughed. "For now. Well put."

"So this arrangement you have with Arthur, it's temporary?" I asked cautiously.

She shrugged. "For now, we both gain from it. I've brought him the sword. He provides me with a shield." She smiled as if she had said something funny. "I suppose you're angry with me."

"For leaving me that day, you mean?"

She ran her hand along the top of the harp. "I suppose I might have helped. But I was... a little muddled. I had been in that prison for so very long." She snuck another look at me. "Honestly I could hardly believe you were truly my sister at all."

"But when you peered into my head—without my permission, might I add—that's what my memories told you?"

She nodded slowly. "I saw you as a child. And Idrisane." My mother's fae name.

"Were you friends with her?"

"Of a sort." She smiled to herself. "I'm older."

I should have suspected that. "Oh."

She shook her head as she looked at me. "You don't remember me at all from that time, I suppose?"

"You mean before Meridium?"

She turned back to the harp. "You were just a child in Numenos. None of us knew exactly what Father had planned. I thought the war was almost a game to him."

"What do all men play at war for?" I said. "But to accrue more power for themselves."

Orcades nodded. "True enough. Men and their toys. Men and their swords."

"Speaking of which, do you really think giving Excalibur to Arthur was the best idea?" I asked carefully. "I thought you planned to use it to slay your enemies." Her *Siabra* enemies.

She smiled, revealing gleaming white teeth. "Before I was imprisoned, the Siabra had been my foes. Once I was released, I spent some time reflecting and reconsidered who my true enemies really were."

I swallowed. "That sounds ominous. What conclusion did you come to?"

"There is one man at the heart of all that has ever gone wrong in this world."

"That is... quite the blame you're placing."

Her eyes narrowed. "But quite true."

"And this man is?"

"Hardly a man at all."

My heart skipped a beat, hearing an echo of my uncle's words.

"Do you mean our father?"

She nodded. "The High King. Higher than all. He lurks out there, desperately trying to accrue power again even now." She gestured vaguely out the window. I glimpsed white clouds floating past. "We cannot allow that, Morgan."

"How can we stop him?" Pendrath was already at war. Did we really need to worry about a High Fae King now, too?

"For the moment, I have matters well in hand," Orcades replied. "There is a prophecy..." She paused. "But no, you don't need to know about that for now."

"Do you mean the prophecy written on the stone I pulled Excalibur from?" I asked quickly. "The sword, the grail, the spear. All of that? I remember it."

Orcades rolled her eyes. "The pieces of power. Thank Vela your brother will never actually wield one."

My heart soared. "He won't?"

"He and his Lord General are playing at things they know nothing about. Did they tell you of their silly tournament?"

"I've heard it mentioned, yes."

"The entire thing is a pathetic attempt to use the sword. Your brother has no idea how to wield it." She shrugged innocently. "Since I'm a mere mortal woman who chanced to find it and bring it to him, I can be of no help, of course. So instead, he'll conduct these ridiculous experiments."

"Experiments?"

"Oh, undoubtedly they'll be called entertainments. You and I will be expected to watch them and yawn and clap."

"And then what will happen exactly?"

"Mortals will try to wield the sword. They will fail and they will die." Orcades shrugged. "What happens in any tournament?"

I stared at her. "Knights on horseback charge one another with lances made of wood. Sometimes they fall off."

"Off the horses?" Orcades looked disgusted. "How utterly ridiculous."

"Perhaps less foolish than letting Arthur play around with an incredibly powerful weapon and getting innocent people killed," I snapped back.

"Death is unavoidable for us all in the end, mortal and fae. Many men do not avoid death but run towards it eagerly." She tilted her beautiful head. "Women, too, some of the time. If they are brave."

"Is that what you did?" I burst out. "Weren't you our father's best warrior? Yet now you wish to destroy him. Just what did you do for him to imprison you, anyhow? And why the sudden change of heart? You sound just like Arthur. What's the point of another war?"

Orcades' expression became glacial. "Like Arthur, you have no conception of what you speak. Either I must destroy Gorlois le Fay or he will destroy us all. You really have no idea what he's done, do you?"

"Why don't you tell me?" I challenged her.

She sniffed disdainfully. "Honestly, Sister, you've forgotten so much. It's as if you aren't really fae at all."

I flinched but forced myself to say, "Pardon me if I don't consider that much of an insult. Neither race seems to have much to offer over the other."

"That may be true," she said thoughtfully. "Though there is something to be said for being vastly more powerful and longer-lived." She walked over to a purple velvet chaise and sank down onto it, then patted the spot beside her. "Come, sit here beside me. We need not be enemies. I left, but you lived. It all worked out in the end. Let us not fight."

"Has it? Worked out?" Gingerly, I took a seat on the chaise a few feet away from her, eyeing her protruding belly.

"Why didn't you just take the sword and kill your—our—father with it if you want to do it this badly?" I asked once she had settled herself.

I watched as she placed her hands once again over the swell of her stomach. Could she feel Arthur's child moving inside?

"The sword would not have been enough. Not for me, in any case." Orcades looked down at her belly. "So I thought of something much better to wield."

I froze. "Please tell me you aren't talking about your baby. Are you speaking of your unborn child as... what? Some sort of a *weapon*?"

"Why do you think *you* were conceived?" Orcades asked cuttingly, her violet eyes slicing over me like a knife. "Why do you think you were born into this world again at all?"

I swallowed. "I still don't quite... understand... that part."

"Yes, your mother made sure of that. Stealing you away. Fogging your memories. Hiding who you really were. Perhaps she expected you to have an ordinary mortal life." Orcades sounded contemptuous of the prospect.

"Yet she left these markings on me." I pulled up the sleeves of the gown I wore. "They're not exactly ordinary. And they are magical, aren't they?"

Orcades eyed them. "They are. She gave you all she had. How fascinating. Is that what motherhood is? Giving all for one's offspring?" She sounded skeptical.

"I suppose it was, in my mother's case," I said. "I've been told it was because she was trying to protect me." That was Draven's theory.

"She hid you quite well, for a time," Orcades said consideringly. "Father's fury was unsurpassable. You truly did seem to simply vanish."

I wasn't sure if she was fishing for where I had been. I decided not to offer the answer. "Is Arthur in on your plans?"

Orcades threw back her head and laughed. "A mortal king? Part of my plans to destroy the High King of the fae? I doubt Arthur has any inkling the High King even exists. You think your brother would be *useful*?" She snorted. It was actually rather adorable. Despite my best efforts, I found myself somewhat liking this strange older sister of mine. "He is a weak pawn providing me with concealment, nothing more."

"He seems to care for you," I observed. "Admires you."

Her rose-colored lips formed a sneer. "He is proud to possess me. There is a difference between that and true affection. He has his uses. For now. But in the grand scheme of things? I tell you he is no one. Even you, well…"

The implication seemed to be that even *I* was of more significance to her than her husband ultimately was. I wasn't sure how to take that.

"Why did you choose him then?" I pressed her.

"I saw within your mind that he was young, ambitious, and greedy for might and power. He seemed an obvious choice."

I thought of the prophecy she had mentioned. Did it concern the three objects of power? Was it the same one my uncle had recited? Or was there something else guiding her plans?

"Your brother has a heart stained with darkness, you know," Orcades observed. "It made things much easier."

Made him easier for her to manipulate, she meant.

"He does. I've known that for quite some time." I hesitated, then ventured, "You've looked into his mind. Is it entirely dark? Is there no hope for him at all?"

She looked at me in disbelief. "I looked as far as I needed to, and believe me, it was not a pretty sight. You think to, what? Try to redeem him? Women always believe they can redeem the worst sorts of men. Do you know what he did to the girl who was almost queen before me? Poor pathetic mortal. No, I wouldn't waste your time."

I swallowed my pride, knowing she was right. I felt like a fool for having asked the question.

Still, at least I hadn't married the asshole.

Orcades rose to her feet, pulling her silk robe around herself. "The tournament is to start soon. I suppose that will be a diversion of sorts." She glanced at me curiously. "Knights falling off their horses. Fae entertainments were much bloodier. You really do have a soft heart, don't you?"

I lifted my chin. "I've seen my share of blood."

She laughed a tinkling laugh. "I'm sure you think so, Sister."

How many battles had this fae general seen? Over how many centuries?

"I might have gone to him, you know," Orcades said softly. She had moved to look out of the window. "Returned to his court. The most powerful place in Aercanum."

It had been her home.

"Why didn't you go then?" I asked. "I suppose he would have been angry that you had escaped. He was the one who put you in that prison, wasn't he?"

She turned back to look at me. "But then I would have had to tell him I'd seen you."

"And left me," I pointed out. "Or you could have lied."

She shook her head. "It's very difficult to lie to Father. If you remembered him clearly, you would know this."

"So, he would have been angry that you left me?" I asked cautiously. "Sounds like he has some sense of family loyalty."

Orcades tipped her head back and laughed, her amethyst curls dancing, as if I had said something hysterical.

"Oh, Morgan. Oh, Sister. Is that what you'd call it? Family loyalty?" She chortled.

I scowled. "What is it?"

Her expression sobered. "He loved you once. At least, so he swears. Since then, he has searched for you across time and realms."

My heart began to hammer. "Why?"

Orcades gave a dry chuckle. "Why does anyone claim to love anyone else? So they can use them."

"That's a very cynical view of love," I said gently.

"Is it? Well, know this at least, Little Sister. When my child and I destroy our father, it will save you from a far worse fate."

I shook my head in frustration. "You truly plan to use this baby as some sort of a weapon? How is that possible? They haven't even been born yet."

She smiled cryptically. "What? You think I would become a mother out of the goodness of my heart?"

"That's one reason I've been told people have babies."

She gave me a look that said I was unbelievably naive. "And Arthur, do you think he's bringing your younger brother back out of the goodness of his heart?"

"What do you mean?" I demanded.

She smiled thinly. "Be cautious, Morgan. Don't say I didn't warn you."

"A cryptic warning is no warning at all," I protested.

There was a tentative knocking at the door.

"Send them away. Whoever it is. We have more to say to one another."

But Orcades was already rising and gliding back to her harp. "Time for my music lesson. We can speak more at the tournament."

I knew I had been dismissed.

CHAPTER 26 - MORGAN

I 'd had enough competitions to the death for one lifetime.

But no one had asked me what I wanted.

Arthur and Fenyx's tournament began a few days after my talk with Orcades.

There was an old stone arena outside the city walls which had been used for such purposes in times past. Now it had been awakened from hibernation for Arthur's new purpose.

Around the ancient stone core, additional tiers of wooden seats had been added, spiraling upwards in a sweeping amphitheater.

At one end of the arena, a raised pavilion on a platform had been constructed, jutting out to provide Arthur and his elite entourage with the best possible view of the proceedings below. At each corner of the platform streamed banners of red and gold fluttering with the Pendragon crest. Inside the half-enclosed pavilion, velvet drapes hung around the edges while sumptuous cushions in rich hues of purple and crimson covered seats of polished wood.

Originally, I had wondered who might attend such a spectacle. After all, the kingdom was at war. The city was dejected and starving. Was Arthur planning to sell tickets? Or perhaps demand that his citizenry show up?

But as it turned out, when you offered people free bread, ale, and entertainment—especially the chance to potentially see a slaughter—they rallied quite impressively.

The tiers of seats were filled to the brim with laughing, talking, jostling people.

I followed the king's procession as we walked towards the royal pavilion, watching the people in the stands with fascination. As Arthur passed by, there was a low cheer from the crowd as well as a few boos and hisses. The latter were quickly suppressed when my brother's guards made a threatening move towards the crowd. Arthur raised a hand briefly in acknowledgement, ignoring the sounds of contempt.

The vast majority must have hated him. But apparently many were willing to put their hatred on hold for the sake of a diversion.

I tugged at the sleeve of my gown. Lady Eve had arrived early that morning with her helper Aliza to deck me out in a dress of royal blue silk. The skirt, voluminous and regal, featured layers of white silk and organza. From beneath the layers, embroidered dragons, their eyes aflame with tiny rubies, peeked out as I walked. Long, billowing sleeves lined with silvery brocade fell down to my wrist and were fastened with sapphire-studded clasps.

A long train, embroidered with silver thread and covered with crystal beads, followed behind me like a river and had to be held up by two small page boys.

The entire ensemble was ridiculous.

I understood that Arthur wished to have me dressed as a princess, as a symbol of Pendragon power—his power—but this was more pretentious and ceremonial than anything I had worn in Myntra. I hated it.

Furthermore, I hated the fact that my hand was presently resting on Fenyx's blue-velvet-covered forearm. A shade of blue that perfectly matched my gown, as if he had planned it himself, which, on further thought, I realized he likely had.

As far as I was concerned, it was as if Arthur had gifted me to his warlord general already.

Fenyx certainly appeared to think so.

After our walk in the garden, I could not seem to escape him. Whenever I'd appeared in public, he had been by my side in an instant. That first dinner with Arthur had been the only private moment we'd had. Every night thereafter, Fenyx arrived at the Pendragon table—apparently with Arthur's permission—and had seated himself beside me.

"Smile, princess," he murmured now. "The people are watching."

"And? How exactly will my smile help them?" I snapped.

"Arthur wishes for you to smile. And *I* wish for you to smile. That should be an ample reason." He grasped my wrist and squeezed. Slowly at first. Then more tightly.

Then with so much pressure, I had to suppress a gasp of pain.

I could melt him like a candle, I reminded myself.

I was *tolerating* this. He did not have the upper hand. I was allowing him to believe he did. I silently chanted the words like a prayer, trying to ignore the pain in my wrist.

Still, the memories of Florian would not stop pouring back into my mind.

I forced a smile, gritting my teeth.

"There," Fenyx said approvingly. "Much better." As usual, his eyes slipped from my face to the rest of my body, lingering on my bodice. "You look stunning in that gown. Practically ethereal."

I said nothing. Refusing to accept the compliment. There was only one man who I wished to hear such words from.

I wondered if Fenyx would berate me or try to punish me for not playing along politely. We were nearing the steps to the royal pavilion, and he was almost out of time.

But then, sure enough, he moved, slipping his arm around my waist and turning me so that I was forced to look out over the edge of the arena and down at the people below—many of whom were looking back up at us.

"Smile and wave at them, Princess," Fenyx ordered me, leaning closer to my ear in a horrible reminder of Draven.

I tried to tilt my face away, but he pulled me tighter against him, his hand slipping down my thigh, caressing me through the silk.

"Let go of me, Fenyx," I said, still smiling. "Or I'll call for one of my brother's guards."

His handsome face crinkled into a smile so perfect that, by rights, it ought to have been beautiful. But on Fenyx's face, it only served as a reminder of how corrupted this golden knight really was. "Go right ahead. Who exactly do you think they serve?"

His fingers were fiddling with the fabric of my gown, twisting and pulling as he lifted the layers. And then he was viciously pinching me through the dress—so hard, I knew I would have bruises later.

I willed myself not to react.

I had been through the fucking Blood Rise. What was a pinch from an overgrown bully?

Still, the feel of his hands on my skin, even through the layers of fabric, had me breaking out in a cold sweat.

I was a spy, yes, but was I really supposed to tolerate everything Fenyx dealt? It was taking everything I had not to strike him down in a torrent of flames.

I was doing this for Kaye. For Camelot. I didn't need flames. I needed restraint.

"We'll be married soon, sweetling," Fenyx promised, moving his hands to my ass and giving me another vicious pinch. "Then your body will be entirely at my disposal."

I hadn't tried to talk to Arthur about Fenyx's maniacal marriage proposal yet. Mostly because I was afraid Fenyx was correct and that Arthur had already given his full approval for the marriage. After all, my brother hadn't cared about my opinion before when he'd been planning to let Florian have me.

"Once the tournament ends, I've asked your brother if we can begin plans for the next celebration," Fenyx murmured.

Suddenly, I understood there was a time limit on my mission. For I had no plans to be present at any marriage ceremony to Fenyx.

In the last week, I had done my best to gather all of the information I could, delivering it to my uncle but also to Tyre—whenever I'd had the opportunity to speak with the High Priest without Fenyx lurking nearby.

Most of what I'd gleaned was probably useless. Changes in the guard rotation schedule. A few overheard comments about troop movements from some of the nobles in the Great Hall. Observations about Arthur's daily routine.

But I had also passed on what Orcades had mentioned about Kaye—that Arthur was bringing him back for some other purpose. And not necessarily a benevolent one.

The problem was, what could Galahad and the others really do about that? They were in no position to protect Kaye. All I could do was keep my eyes and ears open and plan to protect him myself with everything I had, as soon as he arrived.

And if Fenyx dared to go near my little brother... Well, then I really wouldn't hesitate to turn him into a puddle of melted flesh.

Unsnapping the clasps holding my train, it fell to the ground as I yanked myself away. I glimpsed a look of surprise in Fenyx's eyes. Evidently he had underestimated my strength. I knew I had made that mistake myself in the past. I wasn't planning to make it again.

Hoping Fenyx wouldn't turn his annoyance upon the little page boys who were now standing there open-mouthed, I marched up the steps of the pavilion swiftly and took in the scene at the top.

Arthur was already seated. His head rested on one hand as he looked out with boredom over the crowd below.

Orcades sat serenely beside him, her hands resting over her belly. She hadn't noticed me yet.

I could hear Fenyx's footsteps pounding up the steps behind me. Before he could reach the top and try to dictate where I sat, I quickly slid into the empty seat next to Orcades. Conveniently it was also the last one in the row on that side of the pavilion.

As Fenyx clambered up the last step, his face red and angry, I shot him a look of triumph. He glared, then stomped to the open seat on Arthur's other side.

Beside me, Orcades was not paying the slightest bit of attention to either of us. Instead, her face had turned pained. She arched back in her chair a little and groaned, her hand caressing her swollen stomach.

I watched in fascination as her belly shifted beneath her hand. Something was moving inside of her. The child.

"Does it hurt?" I leaned over to whisper. "Do you need anything?"

She looked at me as if registering my presence for the first time, then shook her head and forced a smile. "False labor, it's called. I'm told it will happen more frequently as my time nears." She looked down at her pulsing stomach. "The babe is very active."

"Can you sense anything about it?" I asked, keeping my voice low so Arthur wouldn't hear.

"I sense it is in good health. That is all. I do not pry into its mind, and it does not do so with mine."

This was a strange statement to make about an unborn child, but before I could ask her any more questions, there was a flourish of trumpets and a herald stepped up to the front of the pavilion.

I glanced around. Nobles and knights in opulent attire sat and stood around us. Down in the tiered seats that encircled the arena below, the people had quieted. Most were looking up at the royal pavilion as the herald announced the tournament's commencement.

From down below, drums began to beat.

All eyes turned towards one of the heavy, iron-gated entrances to the arena which was slowly lifting.

Two men were led forth by a group of soldiers. Their gaunt countenances and tattered uniforms revealed them as prisoners of war. One was dressed in the gold and purple colors of Lyonesse and the other in the blue and silver armor of Tintagel.

I gripped the arms of my chair and stole a glance at Arthur. Was I really surprised he was going to use surrendered soldiers in such a way?

I could only hope one of the men would make it out today with his life. Perhaps it would be a simple duel. In which case, they would have a fifty-fifty fighting chance. Which was more than most had in the Blood Rise.

One of Arthur's soldiers stepped forward. He was carrying two swords. Looking between the two men, he lifted one of the swords, still sheathed, and passed it to the soldier from Tintagel. In its plain leather case, it looked like an ordinary blade.

Then, stepping up to the soldier from Lyonesse, he passed him the other sword.

My breath caught in my throat. Even from this distance, I recognized the scabbard that held Excalibur.

The prisoner of war from Lyonesse pulled Excalibur from the scabbard. I glimpsed metal so dark, it seemed to absorb the light around it. The hilt the soldier held twined around his hand in a pattern of vines with a red rose carved from a gleaming ruby at the top.

The soldier from Tintagel eyed the other sword his comrade carried a little enviously.

A shout came up from Arthur's men, and they quickly cleared the arena, leaving only the two prisoners of war behind.

For a moment, there was almost complete silence as the crowd's roar faded into an expectant hush.

The two prisoners stood looking up at us in the royal pavilion, their expressions wavering between defiance and confusion.

Silently, I wished them well, hoping their fates had not been sealed by my brother's cruel decree.

A howl broke the silence.

It had come from the other side of one of the gates.

As if drawn by an unseen force, the two captives moved to stand back-to-back with one another, forming a bond of strength against the unknown.

With a creak of hinges, four of the gates lining the perimeter of the arena began to creak open, the whine of rusty iron slicing through the hush.

The baying howls of wolves cut through the air.

But wolves like none I had ever seen. I leaned forward in my seat and felt Orcades doing the same beside me.

Once noble hunters of the wild, the wolves that prowled out of the gates had been reduced to specters of their former selves. They had been starved. Their fur clung to them in gaunt patches. Skeletal and emaciated, they still moved with an eerie, sinuous grace, their eyes gleaming with a manic fervor as they looked upon the two men and saw fresh meat.

Flecks of froth glistened at their slavering maws. A pungent stench of rot hung heavy in the air, and I caught some of the people in the stands below covering their mouths and noses.

I counted quickly. There were at least a dozen wolves.

Then, as if the wolves were not enough, a whistling sound filled the air as an arrow soared overhead.

The two prisoners below, who had remained standing back-to-back, let out shouts of panic and moved apart, running swiftly in opposite directions.

The arrow landed harmlessly in the sand, but that was all it took.

The men's solidarity was broken. They were on their own.

The wolves were off in both directions, some racing towards the Tintagel soldier and the others towards the one from Lyonesse.

The soldier from Tintagel already had his blade unsheathed. It was a plain, worn sword, but he held it well. Keeping it steady in both hands, he moved in a circle, trying to remain with his back to the wolves.

As one of the beasts ran forward, he shouted and darted towards it, slicing its shoulder with his blade. It yelped and slunk back, letting the next beast try.

I looked at the other soldier. The man holding Excalibur was not doing nearly so well.

Instead, he seemed almost ensnared by his own weapon. As the wolves ran forward, the prisoner from Lyonesse tried to strike, but the blade seemed to pivot backwards when he wished it to go forwards. The wolves around him were still hesitating, but only because he was shouting fiercely at them, not because his blade had actually made contact.

I watched in horror as a bold wolf crept closer. The man seemed to be thrusting Excalibur forward with everything he had, but the sword would not go. It was as if the very essence of Excalibur rebelled against him.

I glanced down the row of seats to my right at where Arthur sat. He and Fenyx were hunched forward intently, watching the scene below while speaking to one another in low voices. I wondered what they were saying.

Shouts rang out from the crowd.

The soldier from Tintagel had bravely taken down one of the wolves, thrusting his weapon through its gaunt ribs. He plunged his blade towards a second wolf creeping up on him, but as he did so, another of the beasts leaped on him from behind.

With a panicked cry, he fell to his knees.

And that was all it took. In an instant, the rest of the wolves were on him.

Across the arena, the man bearing Excalibur had held the wolves off so far by simply holding the blade out in front of him.

Around and around he went, holding the blade thrust forward. But as the wolves grew bolder and one finally raced towards him, he could do nothing. We watched as he tried to strike the wolf and was again met with inexplicable resistance. It was a bizarre dance, the sword moving back when it should have moved forward, retreating when it should have struck true.

A ripple of horrified realization went through the crowd.

As the man with Excalibur flailed in vain, the starving wolves seemed to sense his impotence. Worse, they caught the scent of blood, their eyes darting across the arena to where their comrades slurped and sucked at the body of the Tintagel prisoner who lay prone in the sand.

The prisoner from Lyonesse cursed fruitlessly, lifting his voice to the sky. His face became more and more panicked.

And then, the wolves surged forward, a wave of fangs and fur.

The prisoner let out a bone-chilling cry, futilely raising his arms to shield his face as the frenzied wolves descended.

The shouts of the crowd quieted as the sickening sounds of tearing flesh filled the arena accompanied by the sickly-sweet scent of fresh blood.

I stole another look at my brother. His face was a mask of frustration. Clearly, he had been hoping for something more. Lifting his hand, he gestured to someone. Instantly, the air filled with the whistling of arrows again.

Before they could even finish their gruesome feast, the wolves were dispatched, dying with pitiful gasps and howls.

The crowd was displeased. A murmur of dissent filled the air. Whether the people had pitied the two prisoners or the wolves more, I could not have said, but certainly the spectacle had been disappointing.

Arthur and Fenyx seemed disappointed, too. They conferred in low voices. Then Fenyx stood up and gestured.

Immediately, Arthur's soldiers ran out from the arena gates, dragging away the dead men and dead wolves. A few more soldiers carrying brooms and rakes ran out and cleared the blood from the sand until no trace of the "entertainment" remained.

All was still for a moment. The crowd seemed tense and expectant. So was I.

Then the drums began to play again.

The arena, bathed in the hazy light of the setting sun, seemed to hold its breath as a long procession of prisoners was ushered onto the sand, the clinking of their heavy chains filling the air. The prisoners' bodies bore the marks of beatings and deprivations. Some were older than Sir Ector. Others looked only a few years older than Kaye.

The herald who had played the trumpet earlier stepped forward again, his voice booming out over the crowd.

"People of Camelot, these prisoners of war are your enemies." His voice cut through the air like a chilling wind. "Do not pity them, good people of Pendrath. Hold no compassion within your hearts for our foes. Our noble and gracious king, Arthur Pendragon, in his unceasing wellspring of benevolence has hereby decreed a singular chance. Whosoever wields the blade Excalibur and metes out the fate of death upon their fellow captives shall, in turn, be gifted with a rich boon. Life!"

Cheers and boos erupted from the crowd. Pity for the prisoners? Or did they think Arthur was being too lenient?

I watched the faces in the crowd. Many were as hollow-cheeked and haggard as the wolves had been. Our citizens were desperate. They wanted to see others pay because they had been made to pay themselves. They could not take out their wrath and fury upon the one who deserved it—my brother, their king. So instead, they would punish those who they had been told had done them wrong. People of the neighboring kingdoms, no less innocent than they.

I understood this. That did not mean I had to like it.

Though at the same time, I knew my silence spoke volumes. My mere presence was a sign of my complicity. I sat in the royal pavilion, a Pendragon princess draped in jewels and silks. And I felt sickened with guilt.

I could not brandish my rebellion like a sword. Instead, I had to quietly suffocate it lest it be spotted like a spark in the dark.

The herald's declaration hung in the air as the crowd watched in morbid fascination. The prisoners, linked together by those unforgiving chains, stood in a solemn row.

The younger ones' eyes were wide with fear. One by one, they shared furtive glances.

The first prisoner, a boy who could not have seen more than sixteen summers, was unshackled and stepped forward onto the sand. His trembling was obvious as a soldier handed him Excalibur.

I watched as the boy's gaze darted up towards our pavilion and looked to my right. Arthur's face twisted in a cruel smile as he looked down at the boy.

Something in me twisted, too. The part of me that had held out some ridiculous hope that there could be any good residing somewhere in my brother.

A dark heart, Orcades had said? Yes, truly dark. And growing more shadowed by the day.

I leaned back in my seat as the boy looked at his victim, a man with a long, gray beard. The older man's eyes were calm and steady as he looked up at the youngster.

Then, his hands shaking, the boy raised the sword and prepared to strike.

I closed my eyes.

A gasp went through the crowd.

But when I opened my eyes, the boy was still standing there, the sword raised to strike. He had not moved. He could not move, I realized. The sword would not yield.

For a few drawn out moments, we watched as he struggled and pulled at the blade, twisting and turning his body this way and that.

But the sword would not aid him.

An arrow whistled through the air, and the boy fell to the ground with the dart in his throat, Excalibur dropping with a clunking sound beside him.

The next prisoner was unchained. The man with the gray beard.

A soldier tried to pass the man Excalibur, but the man held up his hands and refused it.

Turning to the pavilion, he lifted his voice before the soldier could move to stop him.

"Your king is a tyrant. You have all been deceived. Tintagel and Lyonesse wish you no harm, people of Pendrath. You have invaded our lands, destroyed our homes, burned our fields, and killed our children. May the Three have mercy upon..."

An arrow entered the man's throat, ending his tirade.

A ripple of discontentment went through the crowd. I prayed that at least some of the people down below comprehended the truth of what the man had just shouted.

A third prisoner was hastily unshackled. A girl this time, perhaps seventeen or eighteen. She drew a deep breath then took the sword, her expression grim. She looked at the next prisoner beside her, a middle-aged woman with close-cropped black hair. The woman nodded stoutly and lifted her head as if ready to embrace her fate.

But the entire twisted spectacle simply repeated itself. The sword would not yield to the girl as it had not yielded to any other.

She fell like the boy, dead from a soldier's arrow.

Then, the black-haired woman was unchained. Short and squat with a strong build, she stepped forward with surprising confidence and hefted Excalibur out of the soldier's hands.

For a moment, she simply looked at the blade. Then she muttered something none in the crowd could catch.

The blade began to gleam. Faintly, but unmistakably.

The woman's eyes widened in awe. Raising the sword above her head, she held it aloft with both hands, and turning to the royal pavilion, looked up at Arthur.

"For you, great Arthur! For your god, Perun of the mighty oak, Perun of the mighty thunder!"

Excalibur began to gleam more strongly, its light intensifying like the sun breaking through stormy clouds.

Gasps came up from the crowd as a searing brilliance scorched through the air.

With sharp cries, the crowd below raised their hands to shield their eyes.

The light grew more blinding. I didn't even have time to look at Orcades before the brightness swept over us, an unstoppable force.

My hand fumbled, reaching out for my sister's.

I wondered if she would pull away, but to my surprise, Orcades froze, then very carefully squeezed my hand in response, not letting go.

The luminance finally began to wane like a blinding sun going behind a cloud.

Around us, there was chaos. Men and women shouting, others crying in panic. Arthur was saying something to Fenyx I couldn't make out.

The light faded.

We looked down at the arena, finally able to see more than a few feet beyond our faces again.

The prisoners were gone.

Only shadowy outlines of their forms were left, scorched traces in the sand. Their chains remained. The metal hissed and steamed in the sand.

The soldiers were gone, too.

As were the spectators in the first two tiers of arena seats.

Sharp cries and screams broke out from those in the rows behind as they realized those ahead of them had been turned to ash, victims of Excalibur's unimaginable power.

The crowd began to rise, splintering into a frenzy.

Next to me, Orcades was already rising from her seat, her hand slipping from mine.

"We must go," she said sharply, looking towards Arthur. It was clear she was worried a mob might soon form. Her hands were protective over her stomach.

Arthur did not reprimand her for her insistence. Instead, he looked at Orcades' protruding belly and nodded. Shouting at the soldiers around us to form a ring, he led Orcades down the steps of the pavilion.

I watched them as they went. It was the only time I could recall ever seeing my brother care for someone else. But then, Orcades was carrying his heir. A child he hoped would be a son, a future Pendragon king. She carried his legacy.

To my brother and sister both, the baby was a symbol of coming power. Not a child to be desired simply for itself.

I turned away, looking around at Fenyx and the other nobles.

The Lord General was standing near me by the rail of the pavilion, staring down at the arena. Below, the soldiers were directing the crowd back to the main road and away from the route my brother and Orcades were taking in their gilded carriage.

I watched as the Lord General's eyes passed over the crowd and then lingered on the scorch marks where the prisoners had been moments before.

For a moment, I hesitated, not wanting to risk another encounter with Fenyx. But I couldn't help being curious.

"Is this what you expected to happen? Is this what you wanted?"

"Wanted?" He looked over at me. There was no fear on his face. Simply excitement. "To be honest, I had no idea what to expect."

I studied him. "I don't think Arthur did either."

"I'm sure once things have settled down, your brother will be highly pleased with the results of our first test."

"Test? That's all this was to you? Why not test Excalibur some other way?" I said furiously. "Preferably without threatening the lives of Camelot's people."

His eyes grew shrewd. "You mean like you did? I'm told the blade nearly killed you when you first touched it, and this was why you could not carry it back to your brother."

My eyes narrowed. "What were you told exactly?"

He smirked. "Queen Belisent told Arthur that she found you with the sword in Meridium. She picked up the blade believing you were dead, but when she turned back, you were simply gone."

I tried to keep my face clear. It was close enough to the truth from Orcades' perspective, I supposed. I wondered if she had really gone back to see if I was dead.

"The blade has great power," Fenyx continued. "Once we've shown the sword who its true master is, we'll end this war."

"Oh, yes? It'll be that easy, will it?"

"Certainly. Ideally, we'll learn to do precisely what that prisoner did just now."

I felt myself pale. "Level entire battlefields, you mean."

Fenyx smiled. "Or cities. Oh, it may take some sacrifice. Evidently, the ones who wield the blade will face some... resistance."

"That's certainly one way of putting it."

Fenyx's eyes were fixed on the scorch marks in the sand. "But there are many who would willingly give up their lives for Pendrath. Or for the sake of their families."

I swallowed. Trying not to let the disgust show on my face. Trying to remember who and what I was supposed to be.

"I eagerly await my brother's triumph," I said with as much sincerity as I could feign. "What a blessing it will be to have this war finally over."

"Of course, in the meantime, we must rid ourselves of the filth that has corrupted our fair land," Fenyx said. "Purging the court and Camelot of all traitors."

"Is that what you consider prisoners of war to be?" I couldn't help but ask.

He shrugged. "This was just another battlefield on which they gave their lives for their homelands. If we'd freed them and sent them back to their lands, they'd soon have returned once more to face us."

His cruel logic went against all the rules of wartime that I knew, but I forced myself to remain silent.

"But no, Lady Morgan, the true traitorous filth are the ones like your former friend," he continued.

My heart sped up. "Lancelet de Troyes, you mean?"

"The very one." He looked at me with a glint in his eyes. "Since you're such a true supporter of the king, you'll be pleased to know that he has a mass execution planned for a few days from now in Bevitt Square."

He listed the largest square in the city, named for Dame Danielle Bevitt, a famous knight who had married a Pendragon king.

I stared at him in disbelief. "You're saying Lancelet will be executed then?"

Fenyx nodded. "The dungeons overflow with her and her ilk. She cannot fester there forever. We need the room. After her betrayal, you must be eager to see her gone." His eyes glowed as he watched me, evidently hoping to spot signs of bloodlust that would match his own.

I forced a cruel smile to form on my lips. "Of course I am. But so soon? I'm simply surprised." I shook my head. "It seems too easy."

Fenyx raised his golden brows. "Easy?"

"Yes, to simply execute her with all the other common traitors." I shrugged. "I'm surprised my brother is giving her such a merciful death."

"How exactly would *you* have us kill her?" Fenyx sounded morbidly curious.

"Let her be part of the spectacle." I turned my face up to his and hoped it reflected something of his own dark and twisted soul to him. "Let her die for my brother's cause at least. Use her like you used these prisoners. Give her a chance to wield Excalibur and serve her king."

"You would have us draw out her pain? Perhaps even give her false hope?" Fenyx looked delighted with the idea. "Truly, you surprise me, Lady Morgan."

"Then I'll beseech my brother to do as I've suggested. If you agree, Lord General. You see? It seems we can agree on some things."

I was too honest to be a good spy. Because all I really wanted to do was kill Fenyx, destroy Excalibur, and free Lancelet.

Instead, here I was, trying to outplay my brother's general. I wasn't sure if I was succeeding or making things much worse—for Lancelet and myself.

Fenyx's blue eyes gleamed as he looked down at me. "You're more like your brother than you've let on, Morgan Pendragon."

"I suppose that is meant to be a compliment."

"I knew there was more to you than a simple maiden, and I'm glad to have been right. Like all women, you enjoy sparring with me." My stomach turned. "But in the end," Fenyx continued, "we're more alike than you care to admit."

Before I could move or turn away, his mouth was on mine.

His tongue was sweet and heavy, thrusting between my lips, plunging into me again and again. His hands gripped my waist, tugging me against him as I struggled, my hands pushing against his armor.

When pushing did nothing, I lost my temper. In a fury, I bit down hard on his tongue until I tasted blood.

I tried not to gag as he slowly removed his tongue and stepped back.

"Yes, fight me," he said, panting and licking blood from his lips. "It's so much sweeter that way."

"You're sick," I spat.

"Am I? I think you like it, you little bitch."

I glanced around to see if anyone had heard him, but Arthur's remaining guards were on the other side of the pavilion, and the nobles had all dispersed.

The memory of Fenyx's tongue in my mouth made me feel like retching out all of my horror and disgust.

"What about a deal?" Fenyx held up his hands. A small line of blood trickled from his lower lip.

Good. The only thing I liked about him was seeing him bleed.

"What deal?"

"I'll convince Arthur to put Lancelet in the arena next time. And in return..."

"No deal," I snapped, already guessing where this was going. "Whatever you want from me, you can't have it. Not from me."

I would get Arthur's agreement myself.

His lips thinned. "Fine. But as your brother has all but approved our betrothal, there's no point in continuing this little ploy. Enjoy your freedom while you can. It will be short-lived. When I am your husband, your every waking moment will be accounted for."

I moved to the stairs, ignoring his threats, and made my way down to the main road where another carriage was waiting to take me back to the castle.

Things were happening too fast. Fenyx and his obsession with me was a complication not even Merlin could have predicted.

I had to warn Lancelet and get her out of the castle before she could be executed, in the town square or in the arena. The latter might buy her a little more time, but it was infinitely more dangerous.

One way or another, Lancelet had to leave Camelot.

CHAPTER 27 - MORGAN

T
he sanctuary of sleep beckoned to me that night, but at first, I would not surrender.

Earlier in the evening, I had gone to Arthur and requested an audience but had been turned away. Perhaps, I'd been told, the king would agree to see me in the morning.

From there, I'd gone to my uncle's chambers in the undercroft of the castle. Surely he would be able to help me form a plan to spirit Lancelet out of the castle so that I wouldn't have to resort to what I had threatened to do—burning the place down around us all to save her.

There had to be a less conspicuous way to smuggle someone out, and if there was, Caspar Starweaver was certain to know of it. If we could free a few extra prisoners—or even all of them—while we were at it, so much the better. Hopefully, Galahad and Guinevere could spare enough resources to help Lancelet and some of my brother's former captives.

But when I entered the Master of Potions' laboratory, he was nowhere to be seen. An elixir brewing in a black cauldron had cooled down to a brown sludge. The fire was nothing but warm coals.

I scrawled a note on a piece of parchment, asking my uncle to come and find me as soon as I could, and left it pinned to the brick wall over his tea kettle full of very cold tea.

My next visit was to the library.

To my surprise, the musty, vaulted rooms were not empty this time.

A man was leaning over a table in the center of the library, rows of towering shelves to either side.

A man with golden hair.

I caught my breath. Fenyx.

I had seen enough of the bastard in close quarters for one day. Quickly, I crept into one of the high rows of books and then peered around the corner.

The table Fenyx stood at was covered with books. Books he was scanning intently. He was looking for something.

I watched as he flipped through the book in front of him, then paused, reading closely. He pulled another book towards him, flipped a page, then traced his finger over a column.

What was he looking for?

With a cold chill, I knew what it must be. Evidently, I was not alone in my search for more information about the three objects of power. Fenyx must be looking for anything he could find about Excalibur as well.

There was a clattering of boots. A soldier marched into the room from the opposite entrance and saluted.

"Lord General, pardon the interruption, but the king has asked to see you."

Fenyx made a sound of frustration but stepped away from the table and followed the soldier out into the hall on the far side of the library.

I listened until their footsteps had faded away, then emerged from my place of conceal-ment.

Fenyx had left the books he'd been reading open on the table. Clearly, like me, he'd incorrectly assumed the library had few to no visitors.

I crept towards the table, my eyes peeled and my ears open for any indication of his return.

My eyes honed in on one of the open books. Words jumped out at me.

Child, blood, spring, kingdom.

I read the passage, then read it again.

By the time I finished my third reading, my hands were trembling.

I picked up the second book Fenyx had been looking at. The same text was written here with slightly different wording. The language was more archaic, but with much the same meaning, as far as I could tell.

I read it carefully, all the while telling myself I must be misinterpreting.

But just in case, I pulled a piece of parchment from my pocket and hastily scribbled copies of the lines.

I was just folding the parchment and tucking it back into my pocket when I heard the pounding of soldier's boots.

Cursing silently, I jumped away from the table and ducked into one of the stacks.

But no one materialized.

I heard the boots fading back down the hall and let out a breath of relief.

After a few more minutes of quiet, I stepped carefully out from between the rows.

The library was still empty.

Stopping for a moment, I put the books on the table back into exactly the same arrangement in which I had found them.

Then I made my way out the opposite side of the library and into the corridor.

Where I ran straight into Lord General Fenyx.

As if he had been waiting for me.

He stood by an arrow-slit window with his arms crossed over his chest. "Going somewhere?"

I raised my eyebrows. "Yes. Back to my room. Is there a problem?"

"What were you doing in there?" His voice was hard and suspicious.

"If you wanted to know, you could have entered at any time," I said calmly. "The library, as you know, is open to all." I pointed to the book I had tucked under one arm. "But I should think the answer was obvious. I went to get a book."

He scowled. "I'm told you have many books in your room."

"I've read all of those," I said sweetly.

Abruptly, he leaned forward and smacked the book out from under my arm. It fell with a thud to the floor, and he glanced at the title with a bored expression. "*Extinct Beasts of Eskira*. Animals? You wish to read about animals?"

"Why not? I'm surrounded by them after all." I could feel my blood rising. "It's been a long day. Do you always harass women as to their reading tastes?"

"Why don't you pick it up?" It was more of a command than a suggestion.

I narrowed my eyes. But I wasn't about to leave a library book on the floor.

Candle wax, I told myself, willing my body into tranquility. He's candle wax.

It didn't work. My blood was still boiling as I leaned over to pick up the book, making sure to keep my back to the wall.

"When you're my wife, you can pick up after me every day," he said with a sneer as he watched me. "Milady."

"No, thank you." I stood upright, clutching my poor book, and began to turn away from him.

Before I could take a step, a hand wound through my hair, wrapping the tendrils around it and holding me in place.

I refused to show how much it hurt. Fenyx gave another sharp tug, yanking me backwards against him.

Then the Lord General's voice was in my ear again, sending waves of revulsion over my skin.

"Arthur rewards those who are loyal. He rewards them with gifts. You, Morgan, are nothing more than gift. A gift that will be granted to me. Never for one second forget that. From today forward, you are mine."

"Over my dead body," I breathed.

He chuckled. "Dead would be no fun. You'll live in the manner I choose, in the way I see fit."

"You're truly charming. But you're completely delusional if you think I'd ever marry you."

He seemed unimpressed by my words. "You're a woman. Mere chattel. Especially as the king's sister. Beautiful chattel, yes, but a pawn. To be given or taken away from the man your brother deems worthy."

I longed to tell him to his face how unworthy I thought he and Arthur were. But once again, I said nothing.

My defiance, he clearly expected.

Outright treasonous words, on the other hand, could get me killed.

So I swallowed them down.

Fenyx released me. My scalp ached, but I didn't lift a hand to touch it. I simply turned and walked away as slowly as I could manage, feeling his eyes on me the entire time.

I'd hoped my uncle would be waiting for me in my bed chamber. But when I entered, the room was quiet.

I tossed my library book onto the bed. It had an interesting-looking chapter on exmoors I'd planned to read later, but after the encounter in the corridor, I suddenly couldn't stand the sight of it.

Curling my hands into fists, I moved towards the entrance to the passage by the hearth.

I couldn't leave Lancelet to Arthur's whims. With or without my uncle, I had to do something now.

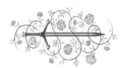

But when I reached the dungeons, Lancelet's cell was already empty.

The cells on either side of hers were vacant, too.

I prowled back and forth in the narrow passageway behind the rows of cells, unable to believe my eyes.

What now? I couldn't exactly go and demand to know Lancelet's whereabouts from Arthur or Fenyx.

Perhaps Orcades would know... But I dismissed the thought. I didn't think she and Arthur exactly shared plans.

But if I told her what Fenyx had said, if I told her what I had found in the library...

No, I decided. I needed to think it over first, at least overnight. Orcades might be my sister, but I still had no real idea just how far I could trust her.

I needed to talk to my uncle.

But barring that, I needed to talk to my mate.

CHAPTER 28 - MORGAN

I watched as Draven paced back and forth across the floor of the little cottage.

He loomed like a massive bear beneath the wood rafters of the low ceiling, his dark head hunched over, his handsome face shaded by a scowl.

I sat curled up in one of the armchairs by the hearth with a blanket tucked over my legs. Draven had built up the fire just before I'd arrived. Now it crackled cozily.

Perhaps I should have felt guilty, I thought as I watched him steadily pace and glower.

But I was simply exhausted. Telling him all that had occurred over the last few days—including the parts to do with Fenyx—had lifted a weight from my shoulders.

Now, Draven carried my invisible burdens on his own back, and I could see that it was killing him.

He let out an animalistic sound, half-howl, half-growl, as he moved past me, and instinctively, I reached out a hand and grasped his arm.

"Draven."

He didn't pull away, simply stopped in his tracks.

For a moment, he was silent. Then he turned his beautiful, dark head and looked down at me.

"This is intolerable."

What was intolerable, I thought, was the pain I saw there in his eyes. Worse than pain—the terror.

The man I loved was terrified for me because he was hundreds of miles from where I was... all because I had left him there.

"Everything is going to be fine," I said softly. "I'll be all right until you get here."

He ran his hands through his hair. "We're set to make landfall in the morning. Even if I leave as soon as the ships reach shore and push the exmoors hard..." He rubbed his temples. "I can't push them too hard. I don't want to break them. Sunstrike's wings are new and..."

I still couldn't believe the exmoors were really with him. That they had come all this way. And above all, that our exmoors had become a mated pair.

The idea of Draven riding on their backs to Camelot? Well, that was something I truly couldn't wrap my head around.

"Of course you don't want to push her too hard," I agreed. "They've already traveled so far. Maybe all three of you should remain with the fleet. You're their leader, after all, Draven. I can wait."

"Absolutely fucking not." The answer was instantaneous. "I'm coming to you, Morgan. As fast as I can."

He looked down at me, and I saw the darkness in his eyes. "We're going to fucking kill him. That bastard who dared to lay a hand on you."

I ran my hand over his forearm, trying to calm him but knowing it was probably no use. "I know. I believe you. You know I do. But..."

I took a deep breath. "Even if something happens to me"—I had to tell him. He had to know. Nodori hadn't had this luxury. But I did—"it won't be your fault," I blurted out. "It would be mine. I left you. I chose this. I know that. Anything that happens to me now is my responsibility, Draven. The choice was mine, and I made it."

His face was as still as stone. His arm was like a rock under my hand.

"I need you to know that," I finished.

He turned his head finally, his green eyes flecked with gold staring down into mine. My gold. His green. Even our bodies reflected one another now.

"Would you make the same choice again?"

I swallowed. "No. I wouldn't. We should never have been apart. I know that now. I need you, but more than that... we're stronger together."

He nodded as if I had said something he had known for a very long time.

He leaned down and gently kissed my forehead. "Good. Move over."

He came around the chair, scooped me up like I weighed no more than a rag doll, and settled me on top of him. I leaned my head against his chest, felt his head settle on top of mine, and let out a sigh of contentment.

"At least we're here, together now," I murmured.

He stroked my hair silently.

My eyes popped open. "What about what I saw in the library? Should I try to speak to Arthur about it?"

"I wouldn't. You said Fenyx was there. I'm sure Arthur already knows. Or will soon. You need to stay on the sidelines as much as you can. He wouldn't welcome the news coming from you, Morgan."

No, he certainly wouldn't.

"What about Orcades? Should I tell her? Warn her?"

"She might already be aware. Have you considered that?"

I was quiet for a moment. "She might. She might not." I made my decision. "I'm going to tell her."

"Very well. Just be careful."

I nodded against his chest, then slipped a hand inside his tunic, feeling the warmth and solidity of his flesh, the feel of his muscles, tense and hard.

"With any luck," he said softly, "I'll be there within a week. With Nightclaw and Sunstrike by my side."

"And then?"

"Kaye will be back by then, hopefully. You and I will take him with us to some place safe, somewhere outside the city. We'll wait for our forces to arrive."

Our. Such a simple word, but a thrill went through me as I heard it.

"We'll surround Camelot, send word to Lyonesse and Tintagel, and negotiate a peace treaty between the kingdoms." He paused his stroking of my hair. "Arthur will have to surrender. Unconditionally. Tintagel and Lyonesse will demand we give him up."

Even kings could be executed when they had committed crimes against entire continents.

"Then we will."

I felt him let out a breath of relief. "Good. You can't shield him forever, Morgan."

I felt offended. "I wouldn't try to."

"I know, but I think part of you secretly still wants to. Even after everything he's done. Even after what you told me he did to the Lyonesse girl."

"Horrible things. Terrible things. He's a monster." I repeated the words as if by rote.

"Yes. He is. You say the words, and yet I wonder if you really accept that they're true."

I didn't reply.

"He's your brother," Draven said, his deep voice gentle. "I know what that means. Believe me, Morgan, I know that better than anyone. But there is nothing you or anyone else can do for him now. He is too far gone."

"I could kill Fenyx in a heartbeat. Melt him into the ground," I said slowly. "I wouldn't hesitate if I had the chance."

"I know."

"But I can't imagine doing the same to Arthur." I tilted my head up, feeling unwanted wetness in the corners of my eyes. "I know he's a monster. I know he doesn't love me, doesn't care about me, is probably making plans to manipulate me at this very moment. But he's my brother. My *little* brother, Draven. Just like Kaye."

"I know," he said even more gently. "You don't have to kill him, Morgan. Simply try to accept that he doesn't deserve to live."

That was what it came down to.

I took a deep breath. "I've never told you this before but..." Was I really going to say the words?

Draven was quiet. He folded his arms around me, holding me closer and waiting patiently.

When I didn't go on, he spoke. "You can tell me anything, Morgan. You know that. But you can also tell me nothing at all. You don't owe me all your secrets. I only want the ones you choose to give."

I nodded. And just like that, I felt release, as if those words were precisely the permission I needed.

"I killed our father. I killed Uther Pendragon." I had never told anyone. Enid. I thought she might have understood. But she had died by then, died in childbirth with Kaye.

"No one knows this?" Draven's voice was very soft. There was no judgment in it.

I shook my head. "My uncle... Caspar. He may suspect. He was the first to find us."

"Us?"

"Arthur and I."

It hurt. Even now. It hurt so much to remember. I had wanted nothing but my father's love. Arthur, too. How different things might have been if he had received it. How desperate we both were.

"He found you and Arthur? So Arthur knows?"

"Arthur..." I felt myself shaking. Draven ran his hands over my back.

"Steady now, love. I'm here. You don't need to go on if you don't wish to."

I tilted my head up again, but it was no use. I felt the wetness flowing down my cheeks. "Arthur knows. He's only mentioned it to me once. He threatened to tell Merlin." I swiped at my cheeks. "He won't have the chance now."

"How did it happen? Do you want to tell me?"

"That's just it." I gave a shaky laugh. "I killed him for Arthur."

Draven went very still.

"Our father beat us, Draven," I said dully. "But he always hurt Arthur more than me. That day, he went after him like he had never done before. Perhaps Arthur had made a mistake in his lesson with our tutor or not performed up to our father's expectations in his swordplay. I honestly can't remember now. But something set him off. He started hitting Arthur." I winced, remembering how much blood there had been. "I thought he would kill him. I threw myself at him. First I begged. Then I hit and kicked."

I could feel Draven trying not to breathe, trying not to ask what had happened next. I sensed his suppressed anger.

"He threw me to the ground like I was nothing. Which, I suppose to him, was true. I was just a child. He saw me as no threat."

"But as Arthur lay on the floor, his eyes glazed, I'd believed he was dead—or close to it. And I was filled with so much pain, so much emotion. Empathy for my brother and rage towards my father for hurting us when he should have been protecting us."

"I'm still not sure what happened exactly. From the time my father threw me to the floor... I've blocked it out. I remember Caspar coming in and finding us. He looked so shocked."

"What do you think happened?" Draven asked very carefully.

"I think that must have been the first time my magic surfaced. Despite the potion. Despite my having no idea how to use it. It's the only thing it could have been. But there were no scorch marks. Nothing was burned. I still have no idea how it happened. But he was dead."

Draven rubbed his cheek gently against mine. "You should never have had to endure that, Morgan. Nor should Arthur. No parent should ever treat a child that way."

"I know. I know that. But..." I searched for words. "It's not that I feel guilt for what I did to Uther Pendragon. All of my guilt, Draven... It's for Arthur."

He was quiet. "It makes sense, I suppose."

"Does it? How? Shouldn't I hate him? Everyone else does."

He sighed. "The bonds of blood are so strong, Morgan. They transcend our rational minds. You were children. You know what he is, but you also know what he endured. Part of you must desperately long for it to have been otherwise."

"It could have been," I said bitterly. "If we'd had a different father."

"Perhaps. Or maybe Arthur would still have turned out this way. There is no way to know. But whatever happens, Morgan, you must understand something. It was *not* your fault."

I sobbed then. Sobbed like a child in his arms while he held me. It all flowed out. The tears I had never allowed myself to shed for the brother I had lost so long ago.

Finally, I tried to pull myself together.

But there was one thing left to say.

"I cannot lose Kaye, Draven. I just... can't." I sniffled and he pulled a linen handkerchief from his pocket and dabbed at my nose.

"I swear by Aercanum itself that you will not lose him, Morgan," Draven said quietly. The words were a vow. And I believed him.

He was Kairos Draven Venator, after all. Prince of Claws. And my mate.

I tried to smile. "Let's talk about something else." I had an idea. "Like those paintings on the wall over there."

I slid off his lap.

"The paintings?" Draven croaked. He seemed reluctant to follow me.

"Yes," I said, tilting my head consideringly. "They're lovely, aren't they? Such a wonderful mix of styles."

"Amazing what the mind can conjure," he agreed.

"But some stand out. They have a distinctive style all their own." I eyed him. Yes, he was looking uncomfortable. I pointed to the one of me plucking the apple. "This one, for instance. It looks downright familiar. And yet I can't quite put my finger on it." I mimicked the posture I had been painted in, right down to my hand lifted to pluck the apple. "Can you?"

He groaned. "Fine. So you recognized yourself."

"You painted it, didn't you?" I demanded, delighted at his discomfort. "Admit it, Draven."

"It is a dream rendition of a painting that is back in the palace," he said carefully. "I confess nothing beyond that."

"Oh, you certainly painted it," I crowed. "Now, which of the others here did you paint? That's the question." I started to scan the wall, tapping my finger to my chin.

Most were landscapes in very different styles than the one with the apple tree. I ruled those out.

A charcoal sketch stood out to me. It looked like a study that had been started but then left unfinished.

"Now this one," I started to say. Then I stopped.

It was of a small girl with chubby cheeks and chin-length black hair. She was no more than three or four. A joyful expression was on her face as she raced down a pebbled path towards someone, her little arms outstretched.

There was silence in the cottage.

Finally, Draven spoke. "Nimue. Or how I imagined she might have looked at that age."

Tears filled my eyes for a second time that night.

"Oh, Draven. I'm so sorry. I shouldn't have teased."

He rose out of the chair and came over to me. "No. It's all right. I'm glad you recognized it." He leaned over me and kissed the top of my head. "It says something, the fact that you knew, doesn't it?"

I felt as if I were looking at something infinitely private and precious as I stared at the drawing of the little girl.

Draven's dream daughter.

"She should have lived. Both of them should have."

"But then I wouldn't have you," he said quietly. With a sigh, he wrapped his arms around my waist from behind me. "Don't you think I've thought of that?"

"I... don't know." My voice sounded very small. "I could understand if you wished things could be different. If you wished you could have them back."

I felt him shake his head slightly. "I wish they were both alive, yes. But... Maybe it's terrible to say, but Nodori and I were never suited, Morgan. She would have made a wonderful mother. I cherished her as a friend. But we were never going to be... mates."

"I wish I could have met her. Is that strange? If she was your true friend."

"You would have liked her. She would have liked you. She hadn't a jealous bone in her body." He tensed. "And Nimue. Sometimes I wish I could hold her, just for a moment."

"You were cheated. Horribly cheated of being a father. Your brother..." I felt my throat closing up. "What sort of man could harm a baby?"

"One past all sense of right and wrong," Draven replied.

"Do you think..." I hesitated. "Do you think you'll ever see them again?"

Beliefs about the afterlife were radically different across Eskira. I assumed the same was true in Myntra.

"If the gods are real. If such things exist." Draven leaned his head against mine. "In Myntra, some say there is a glade. Others a forest. Either way, it's a beautiful place. Peaceful, full of trees and green meadows. Souls arrive there, but then they create what they wish to see. Time is a distant memory, and there is no pain. Others say the world beyond is a celestial court, where the gods of this world rule over a starry palace and the souls of the dead attend feasts and celebrations alongside the divine."

"I prefer the forest," I said with a shiver. I'd had enough of courts for one lifetime. I certainly didn't want to spend my afterlife there. Then I had a thought. "A glade of trees where the departed can conjure up anything they wish to see? You mean, like this place? The place we are now?"

Draven sounded curious when he spoke. "Are you saying you think...what? That we're in the world of the dead right now?"

"I don't know. But we have to be *somewhere*, right? Somewhere real. Somewhere our minds go to find each other when we sleep." I paused. "Or our... souls."

"Sounds like a question for the temple, not for me," Draven said mildly. "Does it matter?"

"I suppose not. But I've wondered..."

"Yes?"

"Well, are we the only ones in this place?"

I felt Draven stiffen. "You mean you think we're not alone here?"

"I'm not saying that for certain. I have no idea. I just... wondered. We haven't exactly explored very much," I said. I turned to him and pressed a kiss to his jaw. "We've been...busy."

"Yes, very busy." He kissed my lips, then my throat, nuzzling my neck, then nipping lightly with his teeth. "There are few true dreamers, Morgan. If this plane holds all of us somehow, well, then I'm sure they're off having dreams of their own. I doubt they're interested in us or this little cottage. For all we know, this place is infinite."

"That's true," I admitted. And I wanted him to be right. The thought of stumbling across another person in this place—our place—was vastly unsettling.

Draven's mouth was back on my neck, hungry and demanding. He kissed his way down my shoulders.

In a few moments, we were lying on the carpet in front of the fire, our bodies entwined as the flames writhed beside us.

And then there was bliss. Then quiet. Then sleep.

I woke a little while later, still in the dream. Draven was snoring softly.

I smiled to myself and gently traced the coating of dark stubble along the edge of his jaw. He looked so peaceful, so handsome. And he was mine.

It was hard to imagine anything dark or terrible while I was in this place. What could be darker or more terrible than my own mate when he was full of wrath and sworn to protect me and mine?

There was only Draven and our cottage. Our perfect retreat. Our sanctuary.

We were safe here. We were in love. And it was wonderful and ours alone.

I rose to my feet and pulled on a soft, white sleeping gown, then draped a wool shawl around my shoulders and stood by the window in the little kitchen looking out.

The stars were still glowing brightly up in the sky. I caught sight of streaks of green, then purple, and let out a little gasp of delight.

I hadn't seen the Aurora Noctis since I was a child. I still vividly remembered my mother shaking me awake one night and tucking a warm robe around me before bringing me out into the garden in the middle of winter to show me the dancing lights as snowflakes fell around us.

Pulling the door of the cottage closed behind me, I stood on the path staring up at the heavens as they were painted with an otherworldly brush. Ribbons of color wove and twisted, resembling sparkling silk scarves flowing across the sky.

I walked down the path and out into the open meadow in front of the cottage, away from the glow of the lamplights burning in the windows.

As I stood there looking up at the shifting colors, I felt a moment of pure transcendence. This beauty was a gift. A reminder of the goodness and the loveliness that existed in the world.

I cast a look back at the cottage that held my sleeping love and touched a finger to my well-kissed lips with a small smile.

These dreams were gifts, too. Profound moments that I would always cherish.

Draven and I had found each other here, truly found each other, in these dreams. Our mating bond had grown stronger with each dream we had shared until I could sense my mate, always in the back of my mind, even in my waking hours.

I turned, startled by a flicker of movement from the grove of trees ahead of me.

A man stepped out.

For a moment, I was too shocked to do anything but stare.

Wild tendrils of gray hair framed a face chiseled with the strength of storms. The man exuded a dark majesty that chilled me to the bones. Tall and commanding, he moved with the air of a king who had seen ages pass like fleeting moments. Eyes fierce and forbidding looked into my own, and as they did, I felt filled with dread. Red rimmed the corners of his lips. The color of blood.

The man was the embodiment of something intrinsically primeval, vast and terrifying.

I looked at him and felt my own essence hanging precariously in the balance.

I took one step back and then another, my hands reaching out to clutch for something that was not there.

Draven.

The man stared at me eagerly, something starved and hungry in his expression. As I moved back, he moved forward, prowling towards me.

I couldn't bear to look at him any longer or to have him look at me in that way, with his eyes so stark and knowing.

I was terrified to turn my back on him but more terrified of what would happen if I didn't.

And so I turned and ran. Ran with everything I had towards the cottage, towards Draven, towards home.

The man called from behind me, his voice deep and hoarse. He summoned me with an ancient name, a name I had no wish to remember.

The name he called me sent me trembling, but still, I did not stop.

I reached the cottage door, breathlessly pushed it open, and...

CHAPTER 29 - MORGAN

I awoke in my bed in the castle with Draven nowhere to be seen.

Someone was shaking me by the shoulder. For a single confused moment, I thought it was my mother and that I was a child again.

Then the person's face came into view.

"Uncle!" I pushed the hand away and sat upright, rubbing sleep from my eyes. "What is it? What are you doing here?"

Caspar Starweaver's white hair was a wild cloud around his head as he sank down onto the side of my bed.

"Do you know where Lancelet is?" I demanded, sitting up and starting to braid back my disheveled hair. "She wasn't in her cell when I checked last night. I was looking for you. Did you get my note?"

"Yes, that's why I've come. They've taken her. They've taken Lancelet."

"Taken her where?" My heart began to pound. I didn't have to ask who had taken her.

"The second round of the tournament. She was brought to the arena."

My hand flew to my mouth. "Oh, by the Three. This is all my fault."

My uncle looked confused. "Your fault?"

"Fenyx told me yesterday that Lancelet was to be executed," I said, speaking as quickly as I could. "I suggested that execution by hanging was too easy for her." My uncle's white brows raised. "I'm supposed to be one of them, remember? Besides, I was simply trying to buy her more time. So I suggested—"

"Yes, I see." Caspar Starweaver sighed. "The tournament."

"I thought it would mean a delay, not the other way around. The next round wasn't supposed to be for another week or more," I said desperately.

"Well, apparently, Arthur believes things went very well yesterday, and so he wants to move up the timeline. You were there, yes? You saw the sword?"

I clenched my jaw. "I saw everything. Much more than I wanted to. Arthur has no idea how to wield it and neither does anyone else. But he'll just keep killing people until something happens. Even if the sword's power kills half of Camelot next time."

"And now it falls to your friend," Caspar said quietly.

"She is not going to die in the arena. I'll get her out even if it means... well, making some enemies," I finished lamely, not knowing how much to disclose even at this point.

My uncle's eyes were shrewd. "A bold vow. If you think you can take on Arthur, his general, and his men in such a public setting."

I swallowed. "Excalibur will kill her."

"Will it?" My uncle's expression turned pensive. "Tell me about the sword."

"Tell you?"

"I know you were the one who freed the blade. How did you do it?"

"Vesper," I began. "One of the people traveling in our party. He cut me, spilled my blood into the lake. Then he pushed me in."

"Sounds like a charming fellow," my uncle observed.

I made a face. "Almost as charming as my dear old uncle who poisoned me."

"Touche." The old man sighed. "And then?"

"Then I went through—I don't know—some sort of a portal. I found myself in a room filled with treasures." I hesitated. Did I mention my sister now? I pressed on. "Excalibur was there. I took it and then... I got out somehow."

"Your blood opened the chamber."

"I suppose. Yes, it did."

"Excalibur was resting in a stone, you say? Yet you were able to pull it out."

I nodded. The blade had slid easily. Like a knife through butter.

My uncle looked pleased. "It's as I thought."

"What?" I asked impatiently.

"The sword," he said, with equal impatience. "It's attuned to you."

I stared. "So Arthur can't use it? Ever?"

"Perhaps if, as you say, he experiments enough, sacrifices enough, he may eventually find someone who can bear it and utilize it without doing so being immediately fatal. But I doubt he'll ever be able to fully access Excalibur's powers or, more importantly, be able to control it in the way that such a weapon has the potential to be used."

"And how is that?"

He shrugged. "A question for historians and academics. A fascinating topic."

"But here, now? Do we have any answer?"

"It won wars, Morgan. Clearly the weapon has incredible might."

"It won wars for mortals and for fae."

"Wielded by Vela herself, so it's said." My uncle's voice was soft. "And now it fights for you."

"I don't have it. It doesn't fight for me," I snapped.

His gaze turned hawkish. "Try to make it."

"Make it? What is that supposed to mean exactly?"

His gaze darted to the timepiece on the wall over my desk. "The tournament begins at noon. Dress and prepare yourself. I have no doubt someone will be coming to fetch you. In the meantime, I have much to do." He rose from the bed. "Do not lose hope for your friend. I've a trick or two up my sleeve yet, Niece. In the meantime, you have at least one cause for rejoicing. Your youngest brother returns today."

I was out of the bed in a flash, nightclothes and all. "Kaye? When? How do you know?"

He grinned at me, and suddenly, I saw the youth inside the old man. He tapped his nose, winked, and then stepped into the passageway he had left open behind him.

I stared at the bookshelves. My uncle was very sure of himself. But I was equally sure there was one thing he didn't know. At least, not yet.

Rising, I dressed quickly. I had a visit to the queen to pay.

Orcades was in the midst of dressing for the tournament when I arrived. The guard had announced me, and thankfully, my sister did not turn me away as my brother had the night before.

Clothes were scattered all over the luxurious bed chamber. Silks on one chair. Bright brocades on another. Satins spilled all over the floor. And Orcades stepped over them as if they were litter on a path.

Of course, purple ruled triumphant. Though I did spot a few pieces in a rose pink and one fluffy, silvery concoction that had been tossed over the chaise.

"Dressing for the tournament?" I asked pointedly. "I suppose, for you, it's simply another fashion display."

She eyed me with amusement. "Have you come here to criticize me? Few would dare be so bold."

"Few are your sister," I retorted. "But no, that's not why I've come."

"Good." She selected a dark plum satin undergown with gold laces at the back and, peeling out of her robe, slipped into it, groaning slightly as she did so. "Come lace me up."

I rolled my eyes but did as she asked. "Is this what sisters do? Help to dress one another?"

"I wouldn't know."

"Don't you have more than just me?"

"We have many sisters and brothers," she said. It was strange to think of. "But no, we did not dress one another. It was never like that."

I wasn't sure how tightly to do the laces considering her condition. Eyeing her protruding stomach, I gave a careful but gentle tug on the laces one last time, somehow knowing if I hadn't, she would have demanded I tie them even tighter. Then I started to tie a knot at the bottom of the fastenings.

"I suppose it is rather sweet," she conceded. "Having a sister to help rather than a maid, I mean."

"I'm better company than your maid? How very flattering."

She shrugged. "My maids are all frightened of me. You are not."

I laughed. "Oh, Orcades. Is that what makes a sister?"

"A good one, perhaps."

I was startled at the compliment. "None of our other sisters are... nice, then?"

"Most are dead."

"Oh."

"I rarely saw the others. Sarrasine sometimes. I was always fond of Tempest. No one has seen her in years though."

"A strange family," I observed.

She snorted. "You would know."

"Will you be wearing anything besides this?" I asked, stepping back as I finished and eyeing the very clingy ensemble.

"The violet tulle will do nicely, I think, overtop." She crossed over to the bed and picked up a cloud-like skirt with many layers of gauze. "Help me step into it, will you?" She leaned against the bedpost, a look of pain crossing her face, and groaned. "I cannot wait until this is over."

"That bad?" I asked sympathetically. I came over to her and held the skirt out for her to step into.

"The greatest sacrifice I have ever made was bearing this child," she muttered. "How mortal women do it over and over again, I will never know. The number of times I've regretted the decision..."

I finished tugging the skirt around her and fastened the clasp at the back.

Stepping back, I looked at her. Only Orcades could have gotten away with such a combination of styles and materials, I decided. She looked incredibly lovely.

"Of course, you need the child," I said quietly. "For your revenge. Arthur believes he is gaining an heir. But then, he doesn't know, does he?"

"Your brother is a man I am using for a purpose," she said bluntly. "Nothing more. When he has finished serving that purpose, he will be nothing to me."

I nodded. "I understand. Perhaps more than you know."

I fished in the pocket of my trousers, then pulled out the piece of folded parchment and held it out to her.

She took it and unfolded the paper.

I watched as she read silently to herself. Her calm expression did not change.

When she finished, she looked over at me and raised her brows.

"Does it mean what I think it does?" I asked.

"I suppose that depends on what you think," she responded, gliding over to a large mirror that hung over a dressing table where she began to fish through a jewelry box.

"I think that you may be doing something incredibly dangerous."

She turned to me with a smile on her lips and began fastening a diamond earring. "Oh, Sister. You really do care."

"I don't know why, but yes, it seems I do," I snapped. "What's more, Orcades, Fenyx found the book this text was written in. I'm sure he'll have brought it to Arthur's attention by now."

Orcades went very still. "Well, that does complicate things."

"I came to you because I don't want you to get hurt." I looked at her belly. "Or your child."

"Your niece or nephew."

"I hadn't thought of that. But yes, I suppose they will be."

She turned back to the table. "Arthur did not come to me last night."

I had no wish to know when Arthur did or did not visit her bed, but still, I was relieved. "Perhaps Fenyx hasn't told him yet."

"Or perhaps the man is too stupid to understand what he read," she suggested, fastening a string of amethysts and pearls around her lovely neck. "I'm actually surprised he can read at all."

I snorted. "Oh, I think he knew the significance of what he'd found, Orcades. Especially since the text was written in at least two of the books he had pulled out in the library."

She turned to me looking a little impressed. "You followed him? For me?"

"I had no idea it was going to involve you at all. I was simply visiting the library."

"Still, you came here to tell me."

"I did," I acknowledged.

She looked at me carefully. "You tried to warn me. I thank you for that, Sister. But never fear. Your pathetic brother could not harm me even if he tried. Still, there is something I will tell you now. It concerns your brother Kaye..."

There were hammering footsteps outside in the hall. I heard the guard's voice, then a much louder one.

Orcades and I looked at one another.

"Arthur," she said. "He's angry. Get behind the tapestry."

She pointed to a large hanging embroidery that was wafting gently in the breeze from the open window.

I sprinted. Pulling the heavy fabric back, I stood behind it.

Through small holes in the material, I could still make some things out, though my view of parts of the room was obstructed.

Orcades moved over to me, discreetly tugging a large armchair in front to hide my feet.

The double doors slammed open. My brother had arrived.

He was breathing hard. He held a piece of parchment in his hand.

"'In the heart of spring, a child shall rise. From royal blood, a king's demise,'" he quoted. "Do you recognize these words, Belisent?"

"What a strange poem," Orcades mused. She melted into the armchair she had placed in front of the tapestry and leaned her head on her hand. "Is this what's gotten you all upset, my lord? A piece of verse? I had not taken you for a poetry lover."

My brother shook the piece of parchment. "Not just a piece of verse. A prophecy."

Orcades yawned, delicately putting her hand to her mouth. "Many prophecies exist, my lord. Most are absolute rubbish."

"'In the heart of spring, a child shall rise,'" my brother repeated, his jaw clenched. "'From royal blood, a king's demise. Born of sister, born that day. Kings shall fall, in disarray.'"

"Yes, I believe you've read that part already."

Arthur took a step towards his queen. Behind the tapestry, I felt afraid for my sister. But she sat quite calmly.

"Is it our child the prophecy speaks of? Did you arrange this somehow?"

"Goodness me, there are many babes born in the spring, are there not?"

"Not of royal blood," my brother said, gritting his teeth.

"Born of a sister, though? I am *not* your sister, Arthur, or need I remind you?" She gave a tinkling laugh.

He stared at her then as if he had never seen her before in his life. "No. You are not. But are you Morgan's?"

Behind the curtain, I paled.

"Morgan's? Your *sister's* sister? What a very odd question. Of course not."

"What's odd, Belisent," Arthur said coldly, "is how you came into my life in the first place."

I swallowed hard. Was Orcades glamor somehow waning? Something in Arthur seemed to be... slipping. What did he know? What had Fenyx fed into his mind?

Orcades rose to her feet. "I came to you with the greatest tribute any woman has ever given a man. I might have brought that sword to anyone in the world. I brought it to you."

"Yes. To me. A sword you found that just happened to be lying beside my sister. Who then, you claim, disappeared. And from her side, you came straight to mine."

"The greatest king in Aercanum," Orcades said smoothly. "It shouldn't be very hard to understand why a woman would be filled with a desire to see the great Arthur Pendragon, monarch of a mighty empire, conqueror of realms."

She stepped towards him fearlessly. "I brought you that sword so you could win your wars. Isn't that what you desired?" She trailed a finger over his velvet cloak. "I did not *ask* to be your queen. Need I remind you that you begged?"

He slapped her hand away. "Begged as if I had been bewitched."

Orcades stepped back, her expression becoming annoyed. "Men always say that about women after the fact. Very convenient when the women have given them all, borne their children, made their meals, sacrificed their bodies." Now anger inflected her voice. "You have come here today to do what, exactly? I am carrying your child, Arthur. Your heir."

"Is it my heir you are carrying, Belisent? Or my doom?" Arthur eyed my sister's rounded belly. "Did you bear this child to destroy me?"

"To destroy you?" Orcades sounded derisive. "Our child could destroy many kings. I should think that would make you very happy. What makes you think the prophecy concerns you in particular?"

Arthur shook his head. "It's all too convenient."

"Is it? Or has that fool of a Lord General been filling your head with nonsense? Where did he find this prophecy, anyway? In some musty old book that no one has read in centuries, no doubt."

Orcades waved a hand and turned back to her armchair. "You've upset me. You've upset the child." She sank back into the chair with her hands resting on top of her belly. "Is the tournament not today? I would have thought you would be preparing."

"Yes, it begins in an hour. You will be there. By my side."

"Am I not always? I live to serve, my lord. I am your humble queen," Orcades said, her voice saccharine.

I watched Arthur stare at his wife, filled with suspense. Something was still not right. She had not convinced him.

No, more than that. Arthur's face was not simply angry. My brother was afraid.

He stepped towards Orcades until he was very close, then leaned over her with his hands on the arms of the chair.

"There is more at play here than you could ever know, Belisent. You are meddling in things beyond your ken."

Orcades, to her credit, merely laughed again. "By having a child? I assure you, it happens every day. Why, there must be hundreds of women across Pendrath about to have children in the spring, just as I am. Fifty tonight alone."

"'The death of kings, the birth awaits.'" Arthur stood back and crumpled the parchment in one hand. "That's what it says. The second stanza. Do you have any idea what my allies would do if they learned of this?"

I glimpsed shock on my sister's face. Orcades leaned forward, slowly forcing Arthur back. "Your allies? What allies, husband? You have never spoken of allies before."

Arthur turned away from the chair, hiding his face. "There are many things you do not know. Do men tell their wives everything?"

Orcades studied his back. "You truly do fear. For yourself or for another?"

Arthur whirled back around. "I do not fear."

"There is fear in your heart. I see it there. Or you would not have come here, accusing me of wishing to kill you with our child."

Arthur's face grew white. "It is not our child any longer."

"What are you saying? What madness is this?"

"You will attend the tournament." He began to walk towards the door. "Then you will return here to these chambers where you will remain. Guards will surround you at all times. When the time for your labor comes, the babe will not live a single hour once it is born."

Orcades rose to her feet. "I was right. You are mad."

"The tournament. In one hour. You will sit beside me. You will smile. Then you will return here." Arthur hesitated in the doorway. "Pray that the child dies at birth. Many do. There will be other children."

Orcades said nothing.

And then he was gone.

I watched as she pulled the panels of the doors closed, then I stepped out from behind the tapestry.

For a moment, we simply looked at one another.

"He has no idea who he's dealing with, does he?" I said finally.

Orcades smiled slightly. "The same might be said of you."

"I'll go now. But I am here for you, Orcades. You know that." I leaned forward and squeezed her hand. "Nothing will happen to your child. We'll get you out of here. After the tournament."

She nodded, not a hint of fear in her face. "I have no doubt of that. Arthur shall not touch a hair on my child's head."

Following an impulse, I moved towards her and embraced her swiftly.

"Soft-hearted Morgan," she whispered.

"I'll see you soon," I said.

BOOK 3

BOOK 3 PROLOGUE

In the heart of spring, a child shall rise,
From royal blood, a king's demise.
Born of sister, born that day,
Kings shall fall in disarray.

When springtime blooms, the babe is blessed,
Born of kin from the king's own nest,
A sister's child, the kingdom shakes,
The death of kings, the birth awaits.

Born of power in endless night,
To cast down realms, a dark birthright.
Both fae and mortals, their thrones shall swirl,
In the child's hands, lies the end of the world.

CHAPTER 30 - MORGAN

High up in the royal pavilion, I sat beside Orcades, waiting for the tournament to begin. Neither of us dared to say anything to one another. Not with Arthur and Fenyx so close by.

My brother and his general were conferring in whispers. When their conversation ended, Arthur clapped his hands and the herald stepped forward to officially begin the event.

The familiar drums sounded.

My stomach was filled with dread. I leaned forward, gripping the edge of the wooden rail in front of me.

Down below, the gate was opening. I glimpsed a group of people waiting with soldiers standing behind them.

As soon as the gate was fully open, the soldiers began to shout, pushing the people before them out and hitting them with spears, as if they were too afraid to escort them all the way into the arena.

I scanned the group, searching for Lancelet.

When my eyes finally landed on her, I hardly recognized her at first.

New bruises were layered over the painful scars on her face. She'd been beaten worse than the last time I had seen her.

Some part of me had held out hope that the participants in today's tournament would be equipped with armor. But not only did none of them wear anything protective, I couldn't spot a single weapon amongst them. Lancelet's clothing was basically rags.

Lancelet moved into the arena slowly, her left arm dangling by her side. Her face was lined with pain. A broken arm? Or a dislocated shoulder? I clenched my jaw, wondering how by the Three she would be able to fight, let alone hold a sword.

The soldiers had disappeared. The gate clanged shut.

The prisoners began to spread out, looking around in confusion. I wondered if they were all captives of war like the last group or if some were citizens who, like Lancelet, were accused of traitorous activity towards the king.

A shout rang out. One of the prisoners was pointing at something.

In the center of the arena, lying flat in the sand and gleaming with an unnatural light, was Excalibur.

A single blade.

I scanned the group. There were fifteen, no, eighteen prisoners.

The vast majority of them raced towards the blade with not a little pushing and shoving. I saw one woman go flying into the dirt as a burly man pushed past her in his haste to reach the sword.

Lancelet was not among the mob. She remained near the gate, her face apathetic as she watched the prisoners fight and clamor. A few others stood nearby with bewildered expressions as if they had no idea what they were supposed to be doing or why they were even there.

There was a creaking sound.

At the opposite end of the arena, another gate was opening.

Cynically, I wondered if it would be wolves again.

Or perhaps starving lions.

Instead, something very different emerged.

A creature from the realm of nightmares.

The beast which prowled forward was an uncanny fusion of the terrifying and the grotesque.

Yet as I took in the creature's appearance, I quickly recognized what it was.

The beast's body was an eerie aberration with the sinewy grace of a leopard and the cloven hooves of a goat. Its onyx-spotted hide gleamed with spectral patterns, while its malevolent, crimson eyes shone with an unsettling intelligence, unblinking and unfeeling.

Its elongated, serpentine head was crowned with jagged ridges of horns, and stretched upwards on a sinuous neck that was covered in iridescent, black, reptilian scales. The creature's maw was lined with dagger-like fangs, and gaped open gruesomely, revealing a yawning cavity devoid of tongue or palate.

The beast looked like nothing from this world. It was a creature that should not have existed.

I had only read about it in books.

Enough to know it was a legendary glatisant.

Where in Aercanum had my brother managed to locate such a creature?

As the glatisant prowled forward, it let out an uncanny baying sound that pierced across the arena, making some in the stands cover their ears and others cry out in fear. The creature's vocalizations sounded like an eerie human whine, as if the glatisant's past victims were somehow still alive within it and calling out to be saved.

The glatisant rumbled towards the group of prisoners who had converged around the sword.

One man, the largest looking of them, held Excalibur aloft. Shoving the other prisoners aside, he took up a fighting stance as the glatisant charged.

I held my breath. The man seemed like a confident and experienced fighter.

But as the glatisant bore down on its prey, Excalibur once more proved to be a cruel and unyielding accomplice.

As the man moved to strike, the sword remained lifeless and unbending, moving backwards when clearly he wished it to go forwards, and sideways when he wished it the other direction.

There was a single shout. Then the glatisant descended.

As the man was lifted into the air and into the glatisant's mouth, the only sounds in the arena became those of crunching bones and tearing flesh.

Excalibur dropped harmlessly back into the sand. Immediately, another prisoner rushed to pick it up, though she looked far less optimistic about her prospects than the man who had come before her.

Sure enough, moments later, she followed the first man into the glatisant's maw.

After five more had fallen trying to make Excalibur yield to them, the others began to scatter, deciding to take their chances running rather than fighting.

The sword lay in the sand untouched.

I looked at Lancelet. She still hovered near the gate. The glatisant had not approached that part of the arena.

Yet.

The arena began to turn into a nightmarish labyrinth as a desperate game of cat and mouse played out. The prisoners were easily cornered prey. They darted in frantic and disjointed patterns, trying to evade the relentless advances of the glatisant.

Amidst it all, Lancelet stood motionless at the periphery of the arena, watching the unfolding chaos. She had been lucky so far, but I knew it would not last.

Why wasn't she moving? Was it because of her arm? Or had she been consumed by despair?

My hands dug into the wood of the railing as my heart pounded. I was paralyzed with indecision. I had sworn I would get her out of my brother's clutches. Now she was in even more danger. Should I act? Should I strike?

But if I did, I would be exposing myself and possibly Orcades as well. And Kaye... He arrived today. If I had to flee, what would become of him?

I thought of what my uncle had said to me that morning, then glanced at my brother and Fenyx. Their eyes were eagerly fixed on the horrific game they had set in motion below.

As I looked back down at where Lancelet stood, the glatisant suddenly noticed the two prisoners standing by the gate and began to race towards them, lumbering along on its huge legs.

For torturous moments, Lancelet did nothing. Merely stood and watched the creature as it charged.

Finally, in the face of impending doom and with my hands itching to burn, she moved.

With a lightning-quick motion almost too fast to believe, especially for one so wounded, she rolled, somersaulted, then pivoted with the grace of a dancer as the glatisant skidded across the sand, its jaw already open in anticipation.

As Lancelet nimbly evaded, the beast shook its head and let out an ear-splitting bay, then turned to the cowering prisoner who still remained shaking by the gates, evidently too petrified to run away.

The prisoner's fate was sealed.

There were only a handful of them left now.

Lancelet's face was a portrait of agony as she leaned against the opposite wall of the arena. But I caught the glint in her eyes, the hard set line of her jaw. No, she had not given up.

My eyes fell upon Excalibur. It still lay untouched in the sand. No prisoner seemed willing to pick it up. As if it had become a cursed thing.

The glatisant was on the move again, easily picking off an older woman who could not run away quickly enough to escape it.

Little wonder. Few had Lancelet's dexterity or her incredible stamina. And the arena was a desert. There was nowhere for the prisoners to hide. All they could do was scatter and run, scatter and run, and see which of them the glatisant would catch up with first.

The torture went on.

Only Lancelet had managed to dodge the gnashing jaws and talon-like claws of the creature not once but three times in succession, moving her lithe form through the arena with a speed that left my heart lurching in both pride and terror.

But soon, the inevitable occurred. The contestants in the deadly dance of survival were down to a mere two.

Lancelet stood on one side of the arena, while the other remaining prisoner lingered on the other side as the glatisant finished feasting on the prisoner it had just slaughtered in the center.

I watched Lancelet clutch her shoulder. Sweat poured down her face. Each dodge and roll she'd made must have wracked her with pain, but she'd persisted.

The seconds stretched into eternity. Finally, the glatisant looked up from its meal. The creature's eyes fixed upon the other prisoner first, a young man.

Slowly, the beast began to move forwards, watching the man like a snake with a mouse.

In a desperate gambit, the young man sprinted not away from the glatisant but towards it, sliding across the sand and grabbing the gleaming hilt of Excalibur.

It was a bold and brave move, and from the murmurs of the crowd below, they thought so too.

I held my breath, hoping the young man would succeed, but knowing it was doubtful.

The prisoner swung the sword upwards with all his might as the glatisant charged forward, its monstrous form towering over him.

The blade made contact with the beast's body, just where its heart should have been.

But the crowd around us shuddered with despair when the sword bounced off the glatisant's hide, as if the sword were a piece of driftwood and not a sharp-edged blade at all.

Excalibur flew through the air.

And landed unceremoniously at Lancelet's feet.

For a moment, the blade merely lay where it had fallen.

Then Lancelet looked up at the royal pavilion.

Our eyes met.

Pick it up, I silently begged her. Pick. It. Up.

And then to Excalibur, I began to silently plead. *She is worthy.* She is worthy of you. More than I ever was. Please, help her. Aid her now. She is worthy, she is worthy.

Over and over again, more and more forcefully I soundlessly begged.

Excalibur, if it is truly I who you are bound to, then yield to me now and listen to my command. Let Lancelet wield you, this I command you. Let her strike, and let her fight. She is worthy of you, Excalibur, she is worthy.

Lancelet picked up the sword. From where I sat, I could see her complexion was ashen. Her lips were pursed tightly together as if trying to hold back her pain.

Still, her arms did not tremble. Her grip was sure. Her hold was steady as she lifted the sword upwards and assumed the position Sir Ector and Dame Halyna had drilled into us countless times.

Feet shoulder width apart, left foot forward, right foot back, knees bent, hips level, bracing hard.

The glatisant had finished crunching on the last prisoner.

It turned towards Lancelet and began to charge.

Shouts of excitement went up from the crowd as Excalibur began to shimmer in Lancelet's hands.

The people in the front rows of the arena got to their feet and quickly moved back, as if anticipating a repeat of the sword's previous devastation.

But the sword did not light up like the sun as it had the last time.

Instead, it began to envelop Lancelet in a radiant glow, weaving around her a golden cocoon of light.

I leaned forward even further, my chest pressed hard against the rail, hope blooming in my heart.

Well done, Excalibur, I silently sent out. Fight for her. Fight for this worthy knight. Fight for her and you fight for me. Please, I beseech you.

The glatisant was almost on top of Lancelet now. With a brutal battle cry that sent shivers down my spine, she lunged forward, striking out.

Her strike missed.

For a terrible moment, I thought it was over and I had lost my chance to even save her myself.

Then she ducked, rolled, and threw herself out of the beast's path just in the nick of time.

Picking herself up from the sand, she resumed her position just as the glatisant turned back towards her, tossing its foul head in rage.

My breath was caught in my throat. I kept up my torrent of silent pleas.

The golden aura around Lancelet grew a little brighter.

She launched herself forward as the glatisant bore down.

This time, her strike found its target.

Excalibur's gleaming edge sliced through the glatisant's hide, blood rushing down to the sand.

The arena erupted in screams and shouts. I saw many in the stands rising to their feet and clapping.

From the corner of my eye, something gold and brown caught my attention.

A bird soared high above the arena, its wings spread wide. A large raptor with golden eyes and tawny, dappled feathers.

The owl on Merlin's shoulder. Had Tuva roamed free ever since she had flown from Merlin's chamber in the temple that terrible night?

I wrenched my attention away from the owl and turned back to the scene below.

Lancelet was sprinting forward as the glatisant, wounded and enraged, emitted a deafening sound that reverberated through the very stones of the arena.

Excalibur's edge found its mark again, rending the glatisant's flesh and splattering the ground with crimson.

The creature's lifeblood was flowing freely now.

I tried to contain my glee, not daring to look to my right.

The glatisant was turning. Lancelet seemed just out of reach. She lifted the sword above her.

The glatisant made a monstrous swipe, sending her tumbling down onto the sand.

Lancelet lay stunned, her back to the ground, her expression dazed.

The glatisant's gaping maw began to descend.

The crowd in the tiers was going wild now, screaming and shouting, some calling suggestions, others breaking down into wails as if already anticipating my friend's demise.

Lancelet gripped the sword so tightly, I saw the whites of her knuckles. Screaming her defiance, she thrust it upwards, just as the beast's mouth lowered.

Flames exploded from the blade as it slid effortlessly through the roof of the glatisant's mouth. As the beast's lifeblood poured out, the glatisant let out a gruesome wail.

An intense and blinding light spread outwards from Excalibur as Lancelet pulled the blade free. A massive wave of incandescence engulfed the arena. Screams went up from the stands, but it was too late. The wave of brilliant energy passed over us all.

But this time, the light subsided as quickly as it had shot out, shrinking until it only encompassed Lancelet. Then only the sword itself.

Lancelet had shakily risen to her feet. She was drenched in the creature's blood. Wiping a hand briefly over her face, she dropped the sword, her expression weary.

The arena was silent.

Then the crowd began to murmur.

The murmur became a roar. From the teeming throng of people below, a resounding cheer erupted like the crash of ocean waves against a cliffside. It was an outcry like nothing I had ever heard, and the emotion pulsing through it all was pure triumph. Lancelet had vanquished Arthur's monster, and the people revered her for it.

Just as she began to turn her head towards the crowd, a whistling sound came from over my head.

I leaped to my feet, already knowing it was too late. The arrow was descending as fast as it had flown.

CHAPTER 31 - MORGAN

T he cheers of the crowd were shattered as the arrow found its mark, piercing sharp as a serpent's fang into Lancelet's left shoulder. Disbelief filled her face. Then she crumpled to the sand.

Horror was written across the faces of those who had witnessed her triumph mere moments ago as the tableau below them turned to tragedy before their eyes.

Then hope took root.

Among the sea of faces, a familiar figure caught my eye. A young woman with short, curly, brown hair had stood up and thrown back her hood defiantly.

She turned to her left, and a few rows down, I saw a tall, resolute young man with ebony skin stand tall.

In a chorus that carried above the tumult of the crowd, Guinevere and Galahad raised their voices.

I was too far away to hear just what they'd said, but around them, others began to quickly come forward. Rebels emerged from among the crowd like hidden stars revealing themselves in a dark night, tossing back hoods and cloaks to expose the knives, bows and quivers they carried.

Around me, those in the royal pavilion began to stir with faint alarm.

But it was far too late. The rebels pointed their bows upwards towards the pavilion.

Arrows soared through the air.

I was still standing motionless when Orcades yanked me down onto the floor beside her.

Our eyes met. "Hide your happiness, Sister, or it will be the last thing you feel," she hissed at me. I nodded mutely.

Chaos was spreading out around us. Screams went up as arrows hit some of the nobles in the seats towards the back.

Arthur's guards were shouting, "Protect the king! To the king! To the queen!"

As more guards stormed into the pavilion, Orcades was swiftly lifted up and pulled away.

I glanced up from my hiding place to see Fenyx standing over me. Pulling me impatiently to my feet, he paused to look out at the arena, then let out a roar of anger.

I followed his gaze and my heart soared. Rebels were pulling Lancelet's body away.

Excalibur, however, they left behind in the sand.

Bolting down the steps, Fenyx dragged me through the pandemonium. The king's carriage had already departed. Around us, the panicked crowd was fleeing. I caught sight of soldiers engaging with some of the rebels as they retreated.

Fenyx threw me into the next waiting carriage and slapped it on its side.

The carriage rolled off, taking me with it, as, behind me, Arthur's veneer of invincibility crumbled like a fragile facade.

As the carriage came to a halt in the bailey of the castle, the door was pulled open from the outside. I was only slightly surprised to see Tyre standing there, a worried expression on his round face.

"My dear, I've heard the news." He helped me step down from the carriage.

As my feet hit the cobblestones, I nearly keeled forward.

Tyre gripped my arm gently.

"I'm sorry." I shook my head, suddenly aware of how dizzy and weak I had become.

Something had been taken from me back at the tournament as Lancelet fought—energy or power. But it was something I was only too willing to have given.

Still, I had enough energy to grin. "That was amazing. Should we go back to help?"

Tyre glanced around surreptitiously. "Be careful, Morgan. The walls have ears."

I nodded, wiping the grin from my face as Tyre tugged me towards the keep and then down a stone corridor. The hall was empty.

Standing near a window, he turned to me, keeping his voice low. "No, I don't think we should go back to help. What could we do in any case?" To my surprise, he was frowning. "I had no idea they had such a foolish spectacle planned. What a ridiculous risk to take."

"But this could be it, Tyre. An uprising in the city. Guinevere and Galahad, they've truly done it. They rescued Lancelet as well." I found myself shaking with relief and excitement. "Arthur's men hit her with an arrow, but I don't think she's dead."

"She's not, I can assure you of that much," Tyre said curtly.

I raised my brows.

"The king and the Lord General were prepared to incapacitate any prisoner who was found able to wield the sword. The arrow was laced with something that would put her into a deep sleep, but not, presumably, kill her."

"I see." Evidently, Arthur had taken Tyre into his confidence more than I'd realized.

"It's incredible that she survived," Tyre murmured. "Absolutely incredible." He looked at me with a measured expression. "I'm to send a missive to Guinevere and the others shortly. Is there anything you'd like me to add?"

He had never bothered to ask me that before.

"Perhaps something to explain how Lancelet succeeded so spectacularly with the sword when all others failed?" He smiled so knowingly that I blushed. "Aha, my dear, I suspected you had something to do with it."

"Only a little," I admitted. Now it was my turn to furtively glance about before continuing. "My uncle believes the sword is attuned to me somehow."

"Because you were the first to touch it? How fascinating. But of course, that makes sense."

"Does it? I'm not sure any of it really does. All I know is that I tried to, well, speak to the sword. I begged it to help Lancelet."

Tyre's eyes were sharp and astute. "And the blade responded. You have power over it."

"Maybe a little. I have never tried to use it myself. But if what I did worked, then yes, please tell Guinevere." I thought of Orcades. "And tell her something else. Tell her..." I looked at Tyre and hesitated.

"Yes?"

If Orcades needed refuge, I wasn't sure she'd accept it from the rebels.

"Never mind," I said hastily.

He nodded. "Very well. In any case there is one thing I've been meaning to mention to you."

I tilted my head questioningly.

"The Siabra man who you wished me to try to find."

"Javer? What of him? Did you locate him?"

"Traces of him. He's disappeared quite thoroughly, but…" Tyre hesitated. "Well, there seems to be no doubt he was the traitor in our midst."

My heart sank. "Oh, no." I had a thought. "And yet, Arthur was expecting to find Guinevere, but he clearly was not expecting to find me that night."

I remembered what my uncle had told me. If anyone tried to divulge anything about me to Arthur, he had said, they would find themselves unable to utter or even inscribe the words. Perhaps Javer had been unable to betray me, even if he had wanted to.

"That is strange indeed," Tyre murmured. He shook his head. "Well, now that Lancelet is relatively safe and you're back from that bloody competition, I think it's time to tell you the good news. If you'll follow me."

I did as he asked, trailing behind him as he led the way down the corridor and into a small sitting room that bordered the Great Hall.

There, in a seat by the window, looking a little bored and much, much older than I remembered him…

CHAPTER 32 - MORGAN

"**K**aye!"

I swooped towards him as he rose from his seat with a grin that was, thankfully, exactly as I remembered it.

"Morgan!"

I was used to looking down on my little brother and wrapping him in my arms.

But now we collided, my head hitting his. At twelve, he was nearly as tall as I was.

I stepped back to look at him, then shook my head in wonder. "You've grown so much."

Kaye had sprouted like a sapling. Tall and slender, his light brown hair was just as shaggy as ever, falling around his face. Shyness wrapped around him as it always had, but there was still the same ceaseless curiosity in his soft, inquisitive, brown eyes. I felt a lump in my throat when I saw the familiar gentleness and warmth as he looked at me with a smile sweet as honey.

Yes, he had grown, and I was sure he had changed. But he was still my little brother.

I touched a hand to his cheek. "Oh, Kaye. How I've missed you."

Behind us in the doorway, Tyre cleared his throat. "I'll leave you two now, shall I? Warmest felicitations on your homecoming, Prince Kaye." With a smile and nod, he was gone.

Kaye and I looked at each other.

"I don't think I shall ever let you out of my sight again," I said finally. "I don't even want to let go of you."

Kaye squeezed my hand gently. "I've missed you, too, Sister."

"I've thought of you so often. I had the most terrible dreams about you, Kaye," I said softly.

"Well, I'm here." He stood up a little straighter. "I'm fine, as you can see."

"How was it? The frontlines, I mean."

His smile faded. "They weren't pleasant. But compared to the soldiers, what I saw was nothing. One of the men, a captain, took a liking to me. He and his men helped make my days more bearable. Less boring."

"Boring! How could being on the frontlines of a battlefield ever be boring?"

He shrugged awkwardly. "After months, it does become so. And I wasn't allowed to fight or to do much. I was just... kept there." He met my eyes. "So, Arthur has married."

"Yes." I kept my voice light. "Queen Belisent."

"She's with child, I've heard."

I sighed. "She is. However—"

There was a clattering noise in the hall. Kaye and I both turned towards the door to see a unit of soldiers marching past.

I ran to the doorway and peered out. A skittish-looking maidservant stood in the hall, pressed up against a wall, evidently so as not to be flattened by the soldiers when they stormed past.

"What's happening?" I asked her.

The woman's eyes widened as she recognized me, then widened still more as she caught sight of Kaye standing behind me.

"Queen Belisent," she said, a little breathlessly. "She's vanished. The king's guards are searching for her."

"I see. Thank you." I stepped back into the room and pushed the door shut behind me.

Kaye's eyes were wide. "Vanished? That's rather odd."

"Not as odd as you may think," I said grimly. "Nor as surprising."

Quickly, I gave him the bare details of Arthur's new fear—the unborn child and the prophecy.

"Sounds ridiculous to me," Kaye said with a frown when I had finished.

I opened and closed my mouth. I still had so much to tell him. Most of it would probably sound equally ridiculous at first.

"Well," I said lamely, "I'm sure Arthur has everything well in hand." A thought occurred to me. "Has our brother welcomed you?"

Kaye shook his head. "I haven't seen him since I returned a few hours ago. I understand there was a tournament."

Arthur had been attacked by rebels and lost his queen in one day. It was, apparently, a very bad day to be king.

"Well," I said, feeling distinctly cheerful, "there's nothing we can do for now." Tyre was taking my message to Guinevere. Lancelet was safe. Hopefully all of the rebels were, too. Soon Kaye and I would leave the Rose Court. As soon as Draven arrived. We would reunite with the rebels, find a safe place for Kaye, and then finish what had begun today.

And as for tonight...

"Sleep in my room tonight," I suggested to Kaye. "We'll have food brought up to us there. We can talk and read..." I wasn't sure if the same things that had once appealed to my younger brother would still hold true. But I needn't have feared.

"And snack?" Kaye finished with a grin. "Sounds perfect."

"Before we go upstairs," I said, "there is something I want to show you."

The outer bailey was very quiet as we passed through it and walked towards the stables. All of Arthur's soldiers must have been searching for Orcades or out dealing with the rebels. I had no doubt my sister knew what she was doing and would not resurface again until she was good and ready.

As for Guinevere and Galahad—I told myself they were well-organized, even better than I had hoped, and would have had a plan to swiftly go underground again as quickly as they had arisen.

I also knew that once Kaye was asleep that night, I would be able to go and seek out my uncle and ask for news. Clearly he had gotten word to Guinevere and the rebels so that they knew to be at the tournament. But what baffled me was why he seemed to have left Tyre out of his confidence.

I forced myself to walk calmly at Kaye's side and simply enjoy his company.

We had been apart for so long. Didn't we deserve a few hours of happiness? Of time to ourselves before Arthur remembered Kaye's existence and the wheels of rebellion and revolt turned once more?

Stepping inside the stable, we were met with the earthy scent of hay and the soothing whinnies and snorts of its equine inhabitants.

I led the way to a quiet corner and stood back, as if showing off some masterpiece I had created. Nothing could have been further from the truth.

The masterpiece was all nature's.

A calico cat stared up at us calmly from where she reclined, her soft fur a pretty patchwork of colors. Alongside her, a brood of kittens played amidst the hay-strewn floor, pouncing and tumbling and swatting at one another with their tiny paws.

Kaye let out a little cry of delight and immediately crouched down in the hay. One of the kittens, a sandy-furred little lady, immediately rubbed up against him, mewling with her small voice.

I watched as my brother gently picked up the kitten, cupping her in his hands, then cradling her gently beneath his chin, and smiled.

Had I really dreamed Kaye was in danger? That he might be dead?

It was the stuff of nightmares. A true dreamer I might be, but evidently, even true dreamers could have false dreams.

Kaye was here. He was safe. And looking at him, I saw he had not lost the capacity to be happy.

I felt filled to the brim with love.

And I longed to tell him about Draven.

Soon, I decided. Perhaps even later that night.

I crouched down beside him, my boots softly rustling the straw, and picked up a plump, black kitten. The small fellow began to purr instantly, cozying up against me as I ran a finger gently over his sleek fur.

"I wish I could keep one," Kaye murmured from beside me. "There were no cats in the war camp."

"We could bring it back to my room," I suggested. I looked down at the mother cat and the rest of the kittens and my lips turned upwards. "What's to stop us from bringing them all up? We could find a basket to carry them and—"

Kaye was already on his feet, cupping the orange kitten in one hand while searching for a basket for the others.

I grinned. "We can have the kitchen send up some supper for their mother, too. I'm sure she'd like some nice fish. Wouldn't you, milady?" I eyed the mother cat who was now cleaning herself.

"I wouldn't mind fish for supper either," Kaye said, coming back over. He was carrying a wooden crate in his free hand. I grabbed it and started lining it with straw, then added a horse blanket on top for good measure.

My brother beamed down at me. "Kittens and fish. What an excellent homecoming."

Kaye was truly the sweetest Pendragon of us all.

Much later, we lay side by side on my bed, stuffed with fried fish, dill and cream scalloped potatoes, and a sinfully delicious chocolate cake.

"I'd forgotten how good food tastes," I said with a sigh and a groan.

"Haven't you been eating?" Kaye asked, sounding a little concerned.

"I've been eating. I suppose I just haven't really been tasting." I had been more consumed with worry than I'd known until that night. Now I realized food had been nothing but ash in my mouth for the most part.

But with Kaye here, it felt as if I were floating on a cloud. I could breathe again. Easier than I had without Draven in weeks.

Kaye smirked at me. "I can't believe you're an empress."

I swatted his arm. "Hush. Don't call me that." I was quiet for a moment. "I still can't believe I am either."

"Well, you deserve to be one," Kaye said generously. "You should have been queen of Pendrath."

I looked nervously around my room. But I needn't have worried. The door was closed and locked. We were alone. We were safe.

"I don't know if I'm cut out to be a ruler," I said with a sigh. "Draven would be much better at it."

"From what you've told me about him, he's not going to let you get out of it that easily." Kaye turned on his side and propped his head on his hand. "Does he really have horns, Morgan?"

"He does. Small, black ones." I remembered how Draven had sawed them off during the Blood Rise. And then cut out a piece of his own heart. "You'll like him, Kaye. He's very..." I searched for the right word. "Well, he's impressive."

"He loves my sister, so that's good enough for me," Kaye said loyally. "But if he hurts you, I won't stand for it."

I tried to hold back a laugh. Kaye sounded so grown up. "Thank you, Brother. I don't think it will come to that."

I'd decided to leave out the unnecessary parts of my story with Draven. Such as how he had lied about my being his mistress back at the Court of Umbral Flames. No, Kaye did not need to hear that bit.

I snuck a look at my little brother. "How bad was it at the war camp, really? Don't hold back, Kaye."

He went very still. "The worst part was feeling so alone."

"Oh, Kaye," I murmured. I turned over and leaned my head against his. "You were never alone. Not really. I was always with you in my heart. In my dreams."

"I dreamed of you, too. I had some terrible dreams while I was there, Morgan," he confessed. "Some of them were to be expected, I guess. At times, we could hear the battlefield. And I saw the wounded and the dead brought back."

I gritted my teeth. He should never have seen any of that. He was a prince, yes, but still hardly more than a child. It would have been different at least if Arthur or I had been with him. But Kaye had been all alone, without even someone like Sir Ector accompanying him.

"But my dreams, they were the worst. You were never in them. But Arthur was. And... sometimes he was hurting me."

I froze. "What do you mean?"

"I could never remember them clearly when I woke up," Kaye said slowly. "But in the dreams, I could swear it was like I was dying. Arthur was there. And there was another voice, too. A man's."

I thought of the strange man I had seen in my dream the other night and felt a chill go through me. "Whose voice? What man? Did you recognize him?"

Kaye looked at me with amusement. "It was just a dream, Morgan. It wasn't real."

"Of course, it wasn't," I agreed quickly. "Just a dream."

I felt a prick of guilt. I hadn't told Kaye everything.

Like about how I wasn't his real sister, not flesh and blood. Telling him that truth would mean telling him about my real father, too. And that was something I hated to dwell upon.

Kaye had commented on my changed appearance, but only to compliment it. He hadn't seemed overly interested in why I had changed, so I hadn't elaborated.

Now he let out a huge yawn, obviously not put off from sleep by all of this talk of horrid dreams.

"Tired?" I asked. I smoothed his hair back from his forehead like I'd done when he had been a much younger boy. "You've traveled so far."

"Mmm," was all he said. His eyes were already starting to close.

I got up and fetched a blanket to drape over him, not wanting to make him move to get under the covers. By the foot of the bed, the mother cat had taken up a new position. Now she lay there, looking very content with her eyes slanted in the firelight, purring as her little brood rested around her.

I lay back down beside Kaye and curled up on my side.

I watched his peaceful, sleeping face for a long time before I, too, finally fell into a deep slumber.

CHAPTER 33 - DRAVEN

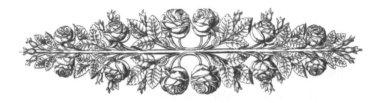

When the god Perun fought with his sisters and split the sky with his blade, legend says dark creatures came through. Beings not of Aercanum.

When we made landfall, creatures of the dark were waiting for us.

We reached Eskira as night was descending, the sails of the ships billowing like vast wings against the sky. Above us, the towering peaks of the majestic Ellyria Mountains came into view. Draped in emerald forest and crowned with snow, they seemed to almost touch the sky itself. The air was filled with the fresh scent of wildflowers and pine, a stark contrast to the saltiness we had gotten used to all these long weeks at sea.

As the first ships in the fleet neared the shoreline, anchors were dropped into the shallows and sturdy rowboats were lowered from the sides of the ships.

I stood watching from the deck of the first ship in the royal galleon, with Crescent and Gawain by my side, as groups of soldiers were ferried to the shore. One by one, young soldiers stepped down onto the sand with relief in their eyes as their feet touched solid ground once more.

Their moment of respite was short-lived.

A shadowy horde emerged, surging towards our forces in a nightmarish onslaught. The attackers had been lurking in the caves along the beaches, hiding in the shadows.

The clash of steel against unnatural flesh filled the air as the soldiers on the beach engaged their assailants.

Throughout the fleet, more rowboats were swiftly lowered and more groups of Siabra joined the fight on the beach.

The metallic tang of blood mingled with the scent of sand and sweat. The roar of battle and the screams of the fallen began to reverberate off the mountains.

Amidst the turmoil, the forces from Myntra fought with fierce determination. But the ambush had been swift and brutal. The coast was supposed to be uninhabited, a serene and untouched landscape. We had not anticipated resistance here. I cursed our folly. For we had been anticipated.

The shock of the attack rippled through the ranks as creatures born of corrupted fae and twisted humanity came in wave after wave from the shadows, their eyes burning with an eerie, malevolent light.

The new, untested soldiers struggled to find their footing. One after one, many went down, never to rise again.

At first, I flew above it all, riding on Nightclaw with Sunstrike beside me, raining down power upon the twisted creatures pouring out from the cliffs.

But as the battle raged on, fierce and unrelenting, I could not fight from the skies while my soldiers died on the sand.

Plunging off Nightclaw's back as he dove low, I rolled into the fray, thrusting my sword through the dark horde over and over.

When the dawn came and the dust finally settled, the price of victory was evident.

The dark creatures had been slaughtered. Those that were not had slunk away.

But we had faced losses. Especially amongst the newer recruits who had never faced such horrors before.

I had been wounded. Bruised ribs, a slice along my side. But I had been dealt far worse before. Blood coated my face, some of it mine, some of it not.

Amidst it all, I saw the faces of our soldiers. Shocked and horrified as the day dawned and they realized what they had been fighting. Shocked and horrified as they realized that may have been only the first fight of many.

I stood by Crescent, Gawain, and Hawl in a small cluster as we paused to take stock. All along the beach, the captains were reforming their units. Soon we would clean up from the devastation. The bodies of our people would be buried. Those of our attackers, burned.

"They were untried, untested, unprepared," Hawl said, their normally booming voice surprisingly soft. The Bearkin had a huge ax slung over their shoulders as they stared out at the beach.

"Yet they fought well and bravely," Crescent said stoutly. His eyes kept darting back to the ships. I knew Taina was safely waiting in one of them. Was he regretting bringing her now?

"We can send two of the ships back to Myntra," I said, my voice low. "They'll see Taina home."

We wouldn't be needing all of the ships for the return voyage, that much was clear. And once we reached Pendrath, our casualties would likely extend.

A strong hand clapped down on my shoulder.

"Let us worry about Taina. It's time for you to go." Gawain's voice was gentle but firm.

"Go?"

"Crescent, Hawl, and I have things in hand here. It's time you were on your way to Camelot."

I looked at the soldiers dragging bodies from the beach. "I can't leave you now. Not after this."

"I told you he'd say that," Hawl growled loudly.

A soldier passing by carrying a pile of driftwood nearly dropped it as Hawl's voice echoed over the cliffs, and I grimaced.

"This will take time," Crescent said softly. "Time to see to the wounded. Time to bury the dead. We'll lose half the day."

"You were never going to travel through the mountains with us," Gawain pointed out. "Morgan is waiting for you. It's time you got to her, as quickly as you can."

I looked between their three solemn faces and then had to clear my throat.

A little ways behind us down the beach, Sunstrike and Nightclaw splashed in the waves, catching leaping fish between their paws. They had fought bravely and well. But I could sense Nightclaw's growing impatience. He longed to be by Morgan's side almost as much as I did.

"You can alternate between the two of them," Gawain suggested. "We have no idea how fast they can truly go over long distances, but if they're anything like birds or bats, they should be able to cover more than a hundred miles an hour at their best."

"You might be in Pendrath by morning," Crescent agreed. "From the maps we have, it's less than a thousand miles, give or take, from here. You'll save days flying over the mountains. Even weeks."

Hawl cleared their throat. "Sunstrike is younger. Her wings are not as fully developed. Be careful with her."

I nodded. "I will. Of course. But—"

"Nightclaw is eager to get to her," Hawl added. "I can see it in his eyes. Their bond is strong, but he's loyal to you, too. He knows you are her mate."

"Two mated pairs," Crescent said with pride. "Our empress, our prince, and their exmoors."

I shook my head. "I appreciate the sentiment. But this is madness. We've just been ambushed. We don't even know who our enemy truly is or where they're coming from. I can't leave you like this. What if you're attacked while going through the mountain pass?"

Gawain, Crescent, and Hawl exchanged a glance.

"We fully expect to be," Gawain said bluntly. "But so what? We never expected this to be easy. That doesn't mean you should stay."

"Is she your mate or not? Is she our empress or not?" Crescent demanded, surprising me with his forcefulness.

"She is both. Of course, she is."

"Then your duty is not to us but to her. Go and get our empress back. Or at the very least, simply keep her safe. And tell her... Tell her we're coming to her as quickly as we can," Crescent said.

The lump in my throat was back. "I'll tell her."

And then I finally did as they'd insisted.

I left.

Mounted Nightclaw with a pack on my back and a small one strapped to Sunstrike and not much else.

This was it. I was going home to her. I was flying home to my mate.

CHAPTER 34 - MORGAN

"*M*organ, I see you. Can you see me? What is this place?"

    I struggled to open my eyes. A trickle of light filtered in, blinding me.

"You have to stop him. Morgan, he's going to kill us all…"

I sat up in my bed, then looked to my side.

Instantly, my heart was in my throat. Kaye was gone.

I flung back the blanket.

Starlight was pouring in through the window.

I slid out of bed. There was a sound coming from the passageway. I moved towards it, but before I could even reach for the concealed compartment, it burst open.

My uncle stood there, his beard wild and disheveled. He scanned the room frantically.

"Kaye? Where is Kaye?" He moved inside my room and his eyes widened. "No, no. It can't be. I'm too late. They've already taken him."

"Taken him where? Where is Kaye? Where is my brother? Who has taken him, Caspar?"

"Arthur. Arthur has taken him. Arthur and his cronies. I had no idea. This is what they were planning. I suspected. Yes, I suspected the traitor was amongst us all along."

I felt my pulse pounding in my ears. "What do you mean?"

"I should have warned you," he babbled, ignoring me. "But there was no time. No time at all. Now the children are being slaughtered… Oh, the children."

My uncle began wringing his hands, twisting them together. He stared wide-eyed at the empty bed where Kaye had been just hours ago.

My panic rose. This was not like my uncle. He was the calm voice of reason in the storm. Something truly terrible must have been happening for him to be acting in this way.

"What children?" I raised my voice. "What children are being slaughtered? Do you mean Kaye?"

He turned to look at me, his eyes glimmering with moisture. "Oh, Morgan, the babies. All the little babes."

A shadow broke away from the wall on the far side of my bed and moved towards us. I gasped.

The shadow took on the shape of a man as it crossed under the moonlight.

Fenyx.

He was not wearing his usual silver armor. Instead, he was garbed in a suit of a dark metal material. Pieces of small, strange stones, like gems, shone with a dull light on his breastplate, arranged in rows.

"You," I spat. "What have you done with Kaye?"

The blond man smiled cruelly.

I flexed my hands by my sides, preparing myself.

"Your uncle is quite right. Your brothers are together now, or will be. Kaye is helping the king with an important task."

"A dangerous one?"

Fenyx's smile widened. "You might say that. In the meantime, Arthur has left you in my care."

"I'm not going anywhere with you. Get the fuck out of my room."

"Tsk, such language for a princess."

I raised my hands, feeling the power running through my veins, in my blood, stronger than it had ever been.

"That's where you're mistaken, Fenyx. I'm no princess. You're addressing the wife of Prince Kairos Draven Venator and the Empress of the Court of Umbral Flames and the empire of Myntra."

And then I conjured my flames.

I had caught him off guard. A moment later, I might not have been able to touch him at all.

Orbs of flame appeared in each of my hands, and I threw them straight at Fenyx's pretty, pretty face.

He turned to one side and raised his arm to try to shield himself. One orb hit his strange, black armor. The other hit the side of his face.

I had never heard a man scream so very loudly. The fire must have been of a very high heat.

I watched the flesh burn from the right side of his face, melting like a candle. The sickening smell of roasting flesh filled the air.

"I've been waiting a long time to do that. Now, shall I do more, or will you take me to Kaye?"

At my side, my uncle's eyes were wide. "Oh, glorious. Glorious, Morgan. I had hoped, but never dared to ask. You lovely girl. My darling niece."

They were the last words he drew.

Fenyx turned to us, his eyes filled with rage. He touched a hand to his breastplate, and a small blue square began to gleam more brightly.

Beside me, my uncle began to gasp, clutching at his throat. I turned to him in time to see blood pouring from his eyes.

He sank to the ground and I sank down with him, trying to hold him up. As if from a distance, I heard myself scream, "Uncle! Stop! What have you done?"

But in my heart, I knew it was too late. The life force had left Caspar Starweaver. And as I looked up at Fenyx with hate in my eyes, I knew what I had to do.

Slowly lowering my uncle's body to the ground, I began to lift my hands.

There was a pricking at my neck and then pain. Incredible pain.

From behind me, I heard Tyre's voice echoing in my ears. "I'm so sorry, my dear, but you really have been asking for this."

The room went black.

I woke up bound to an iron throne, my wrists and ankles cuffed in manacles. The metal of the huge chair went all the way up, encompassing my head in its casing and holding it in place.

My neck was sore and aching. In my mouth, I could taste something bitter and acrid.

"Bloodwraith. It's fatal to most people, you know."

I looked across the room to see Fenyx standing at a table with his back to me.

There was a body on the table. It was my uncle's.

I knew exactly what bloodwraith was. It had almost killed Draven once, and it explained why I currently felt like I was more dead than alive.

I moved my eyes around as much as I could manage, trying to make sense of where I was.

Some sort of dungeon. Windowless. Stone walls. Candelabras hung from the ceiling, but the candles had burned low, leaving the room mostly in shadow.

Huge, cylindrical, glass containers stood in rows along the edges of the room.

My skin crawled with horror as I took in their contents.

Within the macabre sarcophagi floated the lifeless forms of fae. Their once vibrant and ethereal beauty was now frozen and faded in death. The transparent containers held them in a ghastly limbo.

I tried to weigh whether this was worse than Rychel doing experiments on the monstrous fae children and decided it was. Fenyx was clearly keeping these bodies for some gruesome, self-centered purpose. He wasn't trying to restore fae children to life. I had no doubt he had murdered those fae himself.

Arthur's Lord General turned away from the table, holding a vial of something dark and foul-looking. As he studied the contents, I snuck another look at the dark suit he wore. The breastplate bore rows of square gemstones, and as I stared at them, I knew they were no mere ornaments, but conduits of power.

Fenyx had somehow siphoned the very essence of the fae prisoners he had murdered in this vile laboratory. That was how he had been able to do what he had done to my uncle.

I looked at the Lord General's face. I'd burned him on the right side. The flesh had melted. I had seen it with my own eyes.

But when I looked at his visage now, it had already begun to heal at a rapid rate. He seemed no more bothered by the burn than he would have a scratch on his arm.

"Does your brother know that your uncle was part fae?" Fenyx asked conversationally, still examining the vial he held.

I looked past him at my uncle's body on the table and said nothing.

Fenyx set down the vial carefully in a wooden holder, then turned back to look at me. "Bloodwraith has wonderful properties. While it's immediately fatal to mortals, of course, it has quite different effects upon those with fae blood."

"How fascinating," I snarled. I rattled my chains. The throne in which I sat and the chains that bound me were of iron. But iron had never had this effect on me before—except when I had inadvertently ingested the pure shavings in my uncle's potion.

Yet, with a sinking feeling, I realized something had changed.

I could not feel my magic. Could not sense my power.

Worse, I could not sense Draven. It was as if the bond between us had been severed completely.

He was not even a dark space in my mind. He was simply... not there at all.

I swallowed, trying not to let my panic show.

Fortunately for me, Fenyx enjoyed hearing the sound of his own voice. Mad men often did.

"Bloodwraith, it will not kill a fae. At least, not outright and not in small, measured doses," Fenyx continued. "Instead, it has another effect. If administered at frequent intervals, it suppresses any unusual abilities the fae might possess, keeping them relatively subdued."

He gestured. "Like so."

There was a stinging sensation like a needle piercing through the flesh of my neck.

I twisted my head as far to the left as I could and saw it. A tube made of glass filled with a blood-red liquid. At the end of the tube was a needle-like thorn. Some sort of injector. The tip had just pierced through my skin.

"Another infusion. The first time you were injected, I had an assistant. Now it shall be much easier to keep you appropriately docile."

I remembered the sound of the High Priest's voice in my ear.

"Tyre," I said between gritted teeth as pain washed over me and the bitter taste filled my mouth once more. "The fucking traitor."

"The tube will deliver a continuous infusion of bloodwraith directly into your bloodstream every thirty minutes," Fenyx went on as if I hadn't spoken. "All automated, of course. It's an ingenious contraption, really. I didn't build it myself. No, I had a quite clever fae boy in here at one point. He helped me turn my idea into a reality."

The fae boy had helped craft the tool of his own destruction, Fenyx meant. I tried to imagine the fae boy being forced to build the torture device I now sat in, then having to eventually sit within its confines himself as he'd been poisoned, tortured, then had his powers stripped away.

"You speak of the High Priest as a traitor, Lady Morgan, and yet what of you? Did you not come as a snake into your brother's court to spy and to steal?" He paused. "I wasn't certain about you. At first, I really did wonder if you were not simply another young, naive girl, despite all of Tyre's fantastical claims. Then you suggested having Lancelet de Troyes brought to the arena. And when I saw her wield the sword, I knew you were more than you had pretended to be. You imbued her with the power to use Excalibur, did you not?

All along, you have known only you could use the sword. You played your brother for a fool."

In truth, I'd had no idea. Excalibur had been meaningless to me. But I wasn't about to tell Fenyx that.

I moved my eyes around the room. There. On a table near the back between two of the grotesque cylinders that held fae bodies, I spotted the sword.

Fenyx followed my gaze. "Yes, it's here now. Arthur wished for me to... discuss certain things with you first."

"Oh, a discussion? Is that what this is? Here I thought you'd brought me to some kind of torture chamber."

Fenyx smiled thinly. "Your brother tried to place limits on what I could do to you. It's very odd to me that there are yet some boundaries he will not cross. At least, not when it comes to you. I've never met a man with such darkness in him, and yet he has a remarkable soft spot when it comes to you. I wonder why. It was all Tyre and I could do to convince him of the traitor you truly are. But finally, he conceded that we needed you in order to do what had to be done. And so, here you are."

"And Kaye?" I dared to ask. "Where is he?"

"Oh, off with Tyre. You both have very separate purposes."

"What," I said very slowly through clenched teeth, "is Kaye's purpose?"

Fenyx leaned back against the table as casually as if he were at a banquet rather than standing in a dungeon. "Why don't I tell you yours first?"

"Fine. Enlighten me."

"You control the sword. Thus Arthur intends for you to be his weapon. Under the power of my compulsion"—Fenyx touched a hand very lightly to one of the stones on his breastplate. It was a subdued yellow color—"you will be very, very easy to control."

I felt myself beginning to tremble.

"And if you fail us or weaken, well, perhaps your friend, Lancelet, can be located and brought into our service. Our soldiers are searching for her and those rebel friends of yours as we speak. Clearly the sword is now familiar with her. How did you manage to get it to serve her? Not many would wish for such a weapon to work for anyone but themselves."

"I'm not a selfish bastard like you, I suppose," I spat. "That made it easier."

Fenyx laughed. "That's certainly true. If I had the power of Excalibur, I doubt I would ever give it up." His eyes narrowed. "And that's where Arthur and I diverge."

"Oh?"

"Yes, he wishes to keep you alive. He believes controlling you carefully will be enough. It's true that compulsion can be very effective." He tapped a finger to the cleft in his chin. "Here, perhaps a demonstration is in order. You look as if you have doubts." He touched his hand to the yellow stone, and this time, kept it there for a moment. "Pain, Morgan. I wish for you to feel pain. Feel immense pain."

The world around me seemed to warp and twist. And then an agonizing jolt surged through my body, a pain so excruciating it felt as if my very bones were being crushed by an unseen force. My muscles contorted in torment.

The pain was relentless. Unyielding. Liquid agony flowed through my veins like molten lead. Every nerve in my body seemed to scream out in anguish.

As if from a distance, I heard the sound of my own voice screaming.

And then, like a door slamming shut, the pain was suddenly gone.

My breath came in ragged gasps.

Across the room, Fenyx's eyes were filled with a complacent satisfaction.

A flare of defiance burned within me. I would get out of this chair. I would get out of this room. Wax. He would be wax beneath my hands in the end, and I would feel no regret as his flesh flowed in melted rivelets.

My hands twisted in the manacles. They seemed unyielding, but still I continued to move and rotate my wrists, pressing against the cuffs until my skin rubbed raw.

Fenyx had turned his attention back to the table on which my uncle's body lay. Now he picked up a set of gleaming, serrated knives. Taking out a small blade, he made an incision, cutting through skin and muscle with the ease of someone who had done this countless times before.

"Now, your brother believes that sort of compulsion will be enough to keep you subdued," he continued as if there had been no interruption. "The *threat* of pain, you understand. Not pain itself. He seems strangely averse to causing you pain outright. Odd that he feels no such loyalty towards your youngest brother."

I sat up straighter. "Kaye? What do you mean? What is Arthur doing to him?"

Fenyx ignored me. "But I, on the other hand, do not share your brother's confidence." He looked over at me. "Clearly, you are his weakness. And while I concede I find you a desirable woman, I believe trying to control you in order to control Excalibur would be more trouble than it is worth."

"It would be," I snarled.

His blue eyes sparkled as if I had said something amusing. "I'm glad we're in agreement then. Arthur wishes for me to bring you and Excalibur to him a short time from now. Thanks to dear Queen Belisent's flight, our timeline has been moved up."

He made another incision and began peeling open my uncle's chest cavity. "How saddened Arthur will be when I must tell him of how you unexpectedly died here instead. A terrible complication of the bloodwraith Tyre and I were forced to use in order to subdue you."

He ripped back another segment of flesh, and I shuddered. "But before you faded away from this world, I managed to extract from your essence the power you possessed over Excalibur." He gestured to a blank spot in one of the rows on his breastplate. "Once I have it equipped, I'll be the one and only wielder of the blade. The most powerful general Arthur has at his command."

I laughed, and Fenyx raised his brows.

"Oh, yes," I said sarcastically. "I'm sure you do all you do for Arthur and his great cause."

There was a momentary gleam in his eyes. "For now. Your brother is liberal-minded when it comes to my... experiments. He gives me great freedom. The freedom I need to pursue my research. But you're right, of course. With Excalibur in my hands, I could do much more than win your brother's war for him. I could cut him down where he stood if I wished. You'll be dead and gone by then, however, so it's a moot point where you're concerned."

He turned his back to me while he made another cut, then began to write notes onto a piece of parchment.

My body was still shivering from the ordeal it had been through moments before. Yet when I pressed against my manacles again, the harsh iron cutting into my skin, this time, I felt something shift.

The cuff on my left wrist was not as secure as it had been a few minutes ago. Glancing down carefully as Fenyx continued writing, I noticed a hint of rust beneath it where the bolts screwed into the throne.

Reaching my hand carefully downwards, I fished about under the arm of the chair.

My fingers touched it. A rusted screw. Moving my fingers nimbly, I tried to twist.

The screw began to move ever so slowly.

I held my breath. My eyes on Fenyx all the while, I slid my fingers back and forth. Each rotation was painstaking. I felt my skin split and begin to bleed as my wrists pulled against the edge of the cuff.

Still, I would not give up wiggling the screw, twisting it back and forth.

"Thirty minutes."

I froze.

Fenyx was looking back at me. "That's how long we'll have when I remove you from the chair."

"To dissect me, I suppose?" I said flatly, trying not to give him a glimpse of my fear.

"No, to fuck you." He was paying no attention to my hand. "You didn't think I was going to let your beauty simply go to waste, did you? I said I'd make you my wife. Well, that's what Arthur was expecting. But a wife I'd have to continually compel would be exhausting."

"And yet you have no qualms compelling me to, what...?"

"Oh, to whatever I please. Have no doubt of that. You'll be on your knees for me. Then on your back."

The disgusting threats sent a sheen of sweat breaking out all over my body and the bile rising up my throat.

"But in the end, sharing power with you?" Fenyx shook his handsome head. "No, I don't think I'd like that very much. Compelling you in our bed would have been my greatest pleasure. But having to compel my wife on the battlefield when I'm certain you'd fight me every step of the way, well, that would simply be a chore."

"Poor Fenyx." My voice was deadpan. "Pardon me if I can't find it in myself to pity you, you sick, monstrous bastard."

He waved a hand. "They all say that right about now."

"All of the fae you've kept in this fucking torture chamber, you mean? Did you rape every one of them?" I shook my wrists against the manacles.

To my gratification, I felt the left one loosen. The screw was giving away. I stopped my pulling. It wouldn't do to have the screw fall out completely before I could catch it.

"Not all of them. Merely the females." Fenyx turned back to the table as if bored with the turn of our conversation.

His timing was impeccable.

I slid my left hand under the arm of the chair again and fiddled with the screw. The rusted piece of metal fell into my hand. I cupped it carefully.

Now for the trickier part.

Gently, twisting my fingers until my hand was as small as I could make it, I began to pull it through the loose manacle.

"If you're going to kill me tonight anyway, why not tell me what's happening out there? Where is Kaye?"

"What's happening out there?" Fenyx turned around, blood dripping from the serrated knife in his hand. "Your brother's gone mad, that's what's happening." He waved the blade. "Or depending on how you look at it, he's doing exactly what needs to be done."

A sense of foreboding washed over me as I recalled my uncle's words just before he was killed. "What do you mean?"

"The queen was in labor when she ran from the palace earlier this evening. Did you know that? Were you aware of her plans?"

When I didn't respond, he shrugged. "The bitch has proven to be rather untamed. More feral than anyone would have expected for such a woman. She somehow managed to slay the regiment of guards Arthur had outside her chambers and disappeared without a trace. She can't have gone far, however. A woman in childbirth?" He chuckled. "Rather conspicuous."

A woman in childbirth who had just slain a contingent of guards. I wasn't going to panic over Orcades' safety just yet. "So they're searching for her?"

"Oh, they're doing more than searching for her. The king is furious. With the queen, but also with this entire festering, disloyal city. That spectacle at the tournament today? All of Camelot clapping for that hideous scarred girl, your friend? And then the appearance of those rebels?" Fenyx shook his head. "It was humiliating for your brother."

I replayed in my head the moment Guinevere and Galahad had risen to their feet in the stands. The moment Lancelet had plunged the sword up and into the glatisant's cavernous mouth.

Hope. The three of them represented hope to me. As long as I lived, I would not give up hope. Not when they hadn't.

"So, he's doing what? Searching for the queen, the rebels, and Lancelet? Seems like my brother has a lot on his plate."

"He's doing more than searching. He's delivering judgment."

A knot of anxiety tightened in my chest. "What do you mean?"

"There is a prophecy. It says that a child born to a king in the spring could spell the downfall of its father. It says other things as well, some more cryptic. A silly superstition, but the king immediately took it for infallible truth when I presented him with my findings."

It was finally my turn to smile. "Yes, I've read the prophecy Fenyx. You left it on the fucking library table after all. It's not as cryptic as you seem to think."

He looked at me, unsettled slightly. "You read it? That day in the hall, I knew you had been nosing about where you didn't belong. Tell me, did you take it to the queen?"

"I did. But she was already well aware of its existence. Now, shall I tell you the lines I like the best?" I cleared my throat and recited clearly,

"Born of kin, from the king's own nest,
A sister's child, the kingdom shakes,
The death of kings, the birth awaits.'"

I smiled serenely. "A sister's child. Now what could that possibly mean?"

Fenyx's blue eyes looked annoyed. "The queen is not Arthur's sister."

"No," I agreed. "But she is mine."

I'd never seen Fenyx gape before. It was a good look for him.

"But that's impossible," he stammered.

"Not as impossible as you'd think." I wasn't about to explain my family tree to my torturer. "A baby that can bring down kings. I can't say the idea isn't appealing at the moment."

Fenyx's look of concern was clearing away. "Some bastard from your mother's side, no doubt. It doesn't matter. Arthur's taken steps. Belisent's child will never see the light of day."

"You don't know Orcades. That's my sister's true name," I clarified. "I wouldn't be too sure if I were you."

But Fenyx's smile was returning. I felt a sense of looming dread. "It doesn't matter what her name is. Not a single infant in this fair city will live come dawn. Your brother has decided to take no chances."

My throat went dry. "What are you talking about?"

"Arthur's soldiers are, at this very moment, out in the city butchering every child born since the winter's solstice."

"What...? Why? Why would Arthur do such a thing?"

But the answer was already at my fingertips.

Fenyx gave a disinterested shrug. "Because he can? Because he's king? Because the prophecy went straight into his brain and filled him with fear and suspicion. He's reasoned that if he can't find his queen, he'll annihilate all potential threats. I suppose once he's finished with Camelot, he'll go through all of Pendrath if he has to. After all, the queen could have exchanged her infant for any one of the babies out there."

"They're infants," I raged. "Innocent children!"

"And he's a madman. I did try to tell you."

"You did this. You put him up to it. Planted the seed in his mind."

Fenyx tipped his head back and laughed. "Oh, no, that seed was planted long ago, and not by me. How I would love to take credit, but he came up with this plan entirely on his own. The priest was a little nervous. Tried to talk him out of it. Said if anything would make the people revolt, this would be it." Fenyx shrugged. "He may be right. But one does not stand up to a king when he is in such a foul mood as that."

At least, not until Fenyx had his hands firmly around Excalibur's hilt. Then I had no doubt there would be open mutiny.

"And Kaye? Will he be murdered tonight, too?"

"Not for the same reason, but yes," Fenyx said with infuriating calm. "Your brother is in an awkward position."

"Oh? The man with unlimited power who can murder so freely?" I seethed. "How so?"

"He does not serve himself alone. He is sworn to another. He's High King of Pendrath, yes... and yet not. If you see what I mean."

I went very still. "What are you talking about?"

"There is another High King. One you and I have never seen. One Arthur claims to have made a vow to long ago. He has been paying him fealty ever since."

My blood ran cold. "Who is this High King you speak of?"

"I doubt you'd recognize the name. Not many do. It's been a very long time since he made an appearance in Pendrath. No, he prefers to rule from afar."

"Does this king," I said, speaking very carefully. "Know that Arthur was to have a child? Does he know who Arthur's queen is?"

Fenyx gave me a strange look. "Why in Aercanum would he care?" Then he seemed to think he understood. "I suppose you have the prophecy in mind. The death of kings, plural, and all that. Arthur seems convinced that he alone is in danger, though I suppose you might be right." He shrugged. "Considering this man's power, I'm sure he can take care of himself."

A child born to Orcades. Arthur's sister's sister. The kin in his nest.

Fenyx turned back to the table to make another slice in my poor uncle's corpse.

Now was my chance.

With a careful but swift movement, I manipulated my left hand through the manacle. The metal creaked in protest, and I froze. But Fenyx did not turn around.

The skin around my wrist was slick with blood as I finally slipped my hand free.

My senses heightened, I raised my liberated left hand towards the needle-like injector positioned at my neck. Brushing my fingers against the cold, sharp edge of the device, I pushed, altering the injector's course just enough so that the next delivery of bloodwraith infusion would splatter harmlessly behind my shoulders.

Then, sticky with blood and perspiration, I returned my hand to its original place within the manacle, concealing my newfound freedom.

My pulse raced as I finished sliding my wrist through just as Fenyx began to turn back to me.

He held up a slice of something that looked like raw meat, and to my disgust, I realized he was chewing something.

"Fae heart. Legends say it's a source of great power. Care for a sample?"

I glared at him in revulsion but said nothing.

He swallowed, blood coating his lips. "Of course, it's not the true source of fae power. That's much more complex. It's in the blood, you see. These"—He tapped his breastplate briefly—"required careful distillation. Not to mention considerable willpower to wield."

"I don't care," I snapped, absolutely sickened. "I'm not interested in the fucked up ways you stole power from innocent fae-bloods, Fenyx. I don't care, because you're going to lose all of that power in a short while."

Fenyx popped another piece of heart into his mouth. "Oh?" he said, chewing. "And how is that?"

"Because," I fumed. "I'm going to kill you."

The Lord General smirked. "So optimistic for one in chains. I like that about you, Morgan. Sweetly, naively optimistic, despite all you've been through to teach you otherwise." His eyes roamed my body, practically peeling the clothes off my form. I cringed. "I think I'll finish up here and then we can get started. Your uncle can wait. After all, he's not going anywhere. And there is a Pendragon princess in our midst." He smiled in a way that made my skin crawl. "I'll enjoy what you have to offer. Then, we'll start your own... distillation."

He turned his back to me once more and began collecting instruments on the table. "We have at least an hour or two before I need to be at the temple."

"The temple? Is that where Kaye is?" I guessed.

"Very good. Yes, the High Priest has taken the sacrificial little lamb there. Your other brother should be joining us later tonight."

Once Arthur's massacre of innocents was ended.

"The king was supposed to use his own child for the ritual," Fenyx continued. I watched as he wiped the blood from his hands, then began putting his knife set away. "And he was fully prepared to do so. But the queen has put rather a damper on that plan."

"What ritual? If I'm not going to live through the night, you may as well tell me."

Something flared up in the back of my mind.

Draven. He was reaching out to me, desperately. I tried to reach back, but it was no use. My bond to him flickered like a dying star and faded away from me.

Still, it was a faint reminder that hope lived. The bloodwraith was already beginning to fade.

But it wasn't fading fast enough.

Fenyx was approaching me, a heavy ring of keys in his hand. He carried nothing else. Clearly, he thought the bloodwraith would keep me tractable enough for him and his breastplate to handle easily.

I took a measured breath, my pulse quickening. My gaze darted across the chamber to where Excalibur lay.

My senses heightening, I sent a plea towards it, willing the ancient sword to aid me in my time of dire need.

Fenyx's hands were moving to unlock my restraints. He was uncuffing me on the right.

I curled my left hand around the small, rusty screw I had discreetly concealed. It was a meager weapon, but for now, it was all I had.

My right hand was free.

As Fenyx moved to unlock my left, I brought the screw into play.

Sliding my left hand swiftly from the loose manacle, I drove the sharp piece of metal into the bastard's wrist, then dove forward and past him as he shouted behind me, staggering and clutching at the wound.

I glanced back. Fenyx was already fumbling at his breastplate, probably searching for the stone that had healed his face so rapidly earlier that evening.

I ran.

Past the table holding my uncle's defiled body.

Past the gruesome containers holding the bodies of dead fae that Fenyx had pillaged.

I ran straight towards the sword, straight towards Excalibur, straight towards my destiny.

My hand gripped the hilt, wrapping around the twisting metal vines. The feel of the metal was cool and reassuring in my grasp, and as my skin met the surface, a golden light began to glow.

I whirled around, holding the sword.

Fenyx was storming towards me. There was still blood dripping from the hole in his wrist, but I could see the skin already beginning to come together.

That fucking breastplate.

Raising his uninjured hand, Fenyx touched the yellow stone on his chest.

Compulsion. Of course the bastard would go for that first.

"Drop the sword," he snarled, his eyes gleaming.

I waited for my body to do just as he had said.

"I said, drop the sword," Fenyx snapped again.

Instead, I felt myself gripping Excalibur more tightly. The golden light was dancing now, casting beautiful shadows on the walls of the cursed chamber.

The light from the sword reflected in Fenyx's blue eyes as he glared at me with uncertainty.

"I don't think Excalibur likes you very much, Fenyx," I said levelly.

And then I lunged, slashing the greatsword across the Lord General's shoulder. Excalibur's edge sliced through fabric and flesh. With pleasure, I watched the blood well up and begin to spill from the wound.

I danced backwards, separating myself from the Lord General by keeping a long, narrow, metal table between us.

Fenyx gnashed his teeth and touched the yellow stone on his chest once more. Sweat was beading on his brow.

"It takes something from you, doesn't it?" I was starting to understand. "Each time you use one, you give up something, too."

I watched the wound in fascination. It was not closing as quickly as the one on his wrist had. Fenyx had already used the yellow stone's power twice that evening. How many times could he depend on it to help him before it stopped working?

"I give up nothing," he declared.

With a swift motion, he touched a black stone on his chest.

Instantly, the chamber was plunged into an otherworldly darkness, extinguishing Excalibur's golden glow.

I heard Fenyx laugh in the dark.

"Where are you, Princess?" His voice was closer now.

I lifted Excalibur then brought it down in a sweeping stroke. There was a crashing sound as one of the glass containers near me shattered, its contents spilling out onto the floor below.

I stepped backwards, hoping Fenyx would trip and fall in the disgusting mess.

Then I lifted Excalibur over my head and willed, Let the light come back. Don't let Fenyx's shadows win.

The blade's golden light swept over me in a heartbeat, then out over the chamber. I heard Fenyx cry out as the light blinded him, and I laughed in glee.

He was ahead of me and to the left. I jumped around the pieces of broken glass, trying not to look directly at the body of a fae woman that had been swept out of the container, and moved towards the Lord General.

Growling with frustration, Fenyx touched his hand to his chest again, this time touching a red gemstone.

Duplicates of himself appeared around the room. Mirages surrounding me.

The mirages began to run, to and fro, confusing me as to which was the real Fenyx.

I swept Excalibur in a graceful arc again and again, passing the blade through the mirages until each one dissipated in smoke.

Finally, only Fenyx remained. He was standing at the foot of the iron throne he had chained me to.

"Hasn't this gone on long enough?" he demanded.

"Funny, I was about to say the same thing." Breathing hard, I moved closer towards him.

Feinting with the sword, I watched him jump backwards, then darted forwards, slashing my blade across his other shoulder, then again across his arm.

He was bleeding freely now.

I spun around the throne, watching as his fingers, slick with blood, clutched desperately at the gleaming gemstones on his chest.

He touched one, then another, but nothing happened. Evidently, Excalibur was shielding me from their effects somehow.

I watched him tap the yellow stone again and again, his expression becoming more and more desperate and frustrated.

"What's the matter, Fenyx? Your stolen powers not working for you? What a terrible shame."

I sliced Excalibur forward like a needle, darting it into the center of Fenyx's chest, then out.

"You're a fucking knight. What kind of a knight doesn't carry his sword?"

Fenyx snarled like a rabid dog, pain finally starting to show on his handsome face.

"You look good like this. Bleeding out," I said. "You're going to look even better melted to the floor like wax. And when I'm through with you, I'm going to turn this place into a fireball. There will be nothing left of this horror you've created. Nothing of your legacy but ash."

But I'd spoken too soon.

With a flare of his nostrils, Fenyx brushed a blood-streaked hand against the blue stone embedded in the breastplate.

As his touch connected with the stone, my senses were immediately assaulted, as if a chilling void had descended upon me.

A pervasive numbness crept through my body, leaving my limbs heavy and unresponsive.

Each breath I took was suddenly a struggle.

I felt myself sinking to my knees.

Excalibur fell to the floor at my side with a metallic clang.

The very air had grown thick and oppressive.

My skin prickled as if unseen tendrils were wrapping around me, sapping my vitality.

Gasping, I reached out my hands to clutch at my throat.

There were stars in my vision. The world was starting to spin.

Weakness washed over me like a wave. I fell backwards, my head hitting the floor with a nauseating thud.

Fenyx stood over me. Even covered in blood, his gaze was hungry and predatory.

"What's wrong, Morgan? No more words for me? That's all right. I think we can still have a lot of fun this way. Of course, you won't be there for any of it. Just let me get cleaned up." I heard his footsteps begin to fade. "Say hello to the gods for me."

The siphon he had used wasn't letting up.

Fenyx was killing me, draining me of everything I had. I wondered if my lifeforce was filling him as quickly as I drained, healing the wounds I had given him. I hoped not.

I couldn't move my head. With trembling fingers, I reached out for Excalibur.

All I touched was air.

I pushed myself to extend my arm farther, then still more.

There. I felt it. The blade. My fingers brushed against a thin line of metal. So sharp. There was a stinging sensation. I had cut myself on Excalibur.

But what was a little more blood?

Draven. I felt tears prick the corners of my eyes. I wanted him. Needed him. Was I really going to die here in this horrible place without him? So far away?

A few minutes more, and my powers would have returned. I might have sensed him one last time.

My eyelids were closing. My body was surrendering to the encroaching darkness.

I tried to think of all of the good we had shared. But it wasn't enough. We hadn't had enough time.

Maybe I was selfish. But I wanted more.

And Kaye. Oh, my little Kaye.

From the corner of my eyes, there came a soft golden light.

CHAPTER 35 - DRAVEN

I was a thousand feet up in the air, flying over a snow-capped mountain range, when I lost my mate.

The exmoors had soared over the beach, leaving the fleet far below. Sunstrike had chirped once, a sharp and sweet farewell. Then we'd glided over the cliffs, and in moments, the ocean was gone from view.

Rosy-fingered dawn broke as we flew, casting its gentle glow over the landscape below. Around me, Nightclaw's powerful wings stretched out like the canopy of a dark forest. To one side and slightly behind, flying in the updraft of Nightclaw's wake, came Sunstrike, smaller but no less graceful, the rhythmic beats of her wings harmonizing with the rushing wind.

The world below us had completely transformed. From the swirling blue sea, we now flew over a sea of stone and snow. The air this high was crisp and invigorating. My fingers clung to the reins, my body leaning against the exmoor's sleek furred form.

We flew at a symphony of speed, slicing through the air at at least a hundred miles per hour by my estimation. The world around us blurred into ice, a kaleidoscope of wind and white as we hurtled forward.

After a few hours, my body was numb, and it was all I could do to burrow forward, tucking my head against the neck of the massive battlecat.

The day passed by. Nightclaw led our pack. There had been no need to give him direction or to ask him if he knew the way.

He flew towards Morgan with utter assuredness, as if a compass needle lay within his heart, his aim sure and true.

When twilight came, I estimated we were halfway there. By dawn, I could be in Camelot. By dawn, Morgan could be wrapped in my arms.

By noon, we could have her brother's head on a pike. Or, failing that, his ass in a prison cell.

Perhaps I was moving too fast. We'd get Morgan and Kaye out first. Find Morgan's rebel friends. Set up a base, if they didn't have one already. Sir Ector would be good for that. We'd draw in reinforcements and by the time our Myntra forces arrived, we'd be ready.

I was lost in these daydreams when a sickening sensation gripped me like a knife to the gut and I heard Nightclaw call out in sharp distress.

For a moment, the exmoor's wings faltered.

We plummeted.

Straight downwards over the fang-tipped rocky mountains below.

From above, Sunstrike let out a shriek of fear and dove down after us.

We free fell for what seemed like minutes but was probably no more than a few seconds.

And then it was over.

Nightclaw beat his wings rapidly and plateaued, soaring upwards again, though less assuredly than before. I could feel him trembling beneath me. My own body was shaking. Panic coursed through my veins.

I couldn't connect with Nightclaw the way Morgan was able to–or the way I could feel Sunstrike–but I could guess at what the big cat was feeling because I was feeling it too.

Emptiness. A horrible, haunting emptiness as I strained my senses, searching desperately for the lost connection that bound me to her.

But all I found was silence.

A terrifying blankness worse than the freefall had been.

High above the snow-covered peaks of the Ellyria Mountains, my mate's absence was an abyss that echoed in my soul.

We were alone, because Morgan was gone.

We spun through the air like this in disarray and confusion for what felt like hours. Behind us followed Sunstrike, desperately chirping her concern. The smaller exmoor, wings kissed in hues of gold and brown, hovered close by, her eyes wide with uncertainty as she witnessed our anxiety.

Finally, we leveled out and ascended again, Nightclaw's wings slicing swiftly and majestically back through the atmosphere. Yet, as I gripped the saddle pommel and leaned into the wind, the world was nothing but a fog of dread. The void still gnawed at my very soul.

We had not been severed, nor torn asunder.

Our bond had simply been *extinguished*, as if Morgan had become nothing but a blankness in this world. A silence where her presence should have resonated.

Beneath me, Nighclaw shivered in response to my anguish. The battlecat's easy confidence had been replaced by one of palpable unease.

But what else could we do but go on?

Hours passed. Each moment an eternity of torment.

Snow-capped mountains and craggy valleys stretched out below. The wind howled in my ears.

We hurtled through the sky at an unforgiving speed, the battlecat's muscles flexing and coiling beneath my thighs.

The world was reduced to a blur of sensations. Windswept hair, chilled skin, the roar of the wind, the heavy thud of a heartbeat.

And yet through it all the absence of one presence rang louder than all else.

And then, abruptly, a lightning bolt pierced through the fog of my despair.

A veil was lifted.

I was inside.

Looking down at Morgan as she lay in a nightmarish-dungeon, waning candles casting shadows on her exhausted, blood-streaked face. Her eyes were dulled with pain and locked onto her tormentor. A man stood over her, looking down at her with a sinister smile that left me cold with rage. The armored breastplate that covered his chest was lined with a strange array of gemstones, each one pulsating with ominous power.

A touch of his hand and one of the stones responded. I watched as Morgan's life force began to wane, the frail tendril of her essence slowly drifting away.

My eyes landed on the sword. As she dropped to the floor, it fell by her side with a clatter, slipping from her grasp.

Excalibur.

The metal of the blade was leaden and dark.

The man stepped away, satisfaction gleaming in his eyes. I heard the words he said and something my heart twisted and compressed.

But my silver one was not yet defeated.

I watched as her trembling fingers reached out, brushing against the sharp edge of the sword.

Blood slid, slick and crimson, from her fingertips down the steel.

Excalibur began to shine with a radiant, golden light–a beacon of defiance in the suffocating dark.

She was broken and bleeding. She was fading away. I felt myself begin to break, bleed, and fade, too.

Beneath me, Nightclaw let out a mournful howl, just out of sight.

The golden light was all I could see. It spilled before my eyes, stretching out over the mountains.

It blazed with the power of a thousand suns.

And then the light *pulled*.

I was wrenched from my seat. Spinning over snow-dusted peaks, twisting and turning as the air rushed past me, my stomach lurching as I fell through an abyss.

I landed.

Hitting the ground hard, my feet connecting.

Slowly I stood upright, flexing my fists.

A few meters away, the man in the strange black armor was turning, his blond hair glinting in the light.

His blue eyes widened as I punched him squarely in the jaw. I had just enough time to register the shock within them before the sound of knuckles hitting bone echoed through the chamber.

CHAPTER 36 - DRAVEN

T he impact resonated through my arm with a satisfying tingle, a bone-rattling shock that sent the other man sprawling backwards.

Briefly, I looked around the grim surroundings. I had arrived in a nightmarish tableau.

Across the room a partially dissected man lay spread on a nearby table. He was elderly, his long white beard hanging to one side.

Towering glass cylinders lined the room's periphery.

I had believed myself to be inured to horror. I had seen much more than most. But even I could be shocked, I now found. For each cylinder housed the preserved remains of a fae, their lifeless forms suspended in a thick, viscous fluid.

The sight of these tall, transparent tombs told me all I needed to know about the man at my feet and his unholy experiments.

This pitiful mortal male had been feeding off the powerful and vibrant fae who now hung in spectral suspension, their stolen vitality drained to feed his insatiable hunger and to power the armor he now clung to as if it were life itself.

"She's dead, you know." The man by my feet dared to sneer up at me. "You're too late."

He was wrong but he would learn that for himself soon enough.

I leaned down over him, my lips curling back in disgust, and delivered a second, resounding blow to the man's visage. The cracking sound rang through the chamber and the bastard's face contorted in agony, his arrogance temporarily obliterated by the raw force of the blow.

Then, smiling, I stepped deliberately onto the blond man's hand before he could finish reaching it up to touch it to one of the gemstones on his chest, and ground the heel of my boot until I felt the satisfying crunch of bones, one after another.

The man screamed.

It was not enough. It was nowhere near enough. It might never be enough.

She would have to decide.

My eyes flew back to where she lay on the unforgiving floor and a potent, primal force surged within me.

An ancient darkness, a tempestuous power. One I had long kept shackled and concealed, even from her. Especially from her.

Once it had threatened to consume me. Now I knew it had found its true purpose at this moment.

Swift as thought itself, I untied a knot I had kept in place.

A sinuous tapestry of air and shadow began to weave forth from my fingertips.

Coils of darkness spiraled through the chamber, sliding towards the blond man on the floor.

With amusement, I watched him try to scuttle backwards, his broken useless hand dragging behind him. Looking at me with his jaw clenched in agony, he raised his unharmed hand in a last attempt to thwart me and thrust it towards his chest.

In an instant, a tendril of my darkness wrapped around his wrist, yanking it upwards.

I looked down at the man where he lay on the stones, my gaze steely. The strange breastplate he wore clung to him precariously. Its straps had been reduced to fragile threads that threatened to yield at any moment.

Morgan's doing.

She had cut him. She had made him bleed. But when faced with all his stolen treasures, the powers he had murdered fae like her to possess, it had not been enough.

Excalibur had not been enough.

Yet the sword, I reminded myself, had gotten me here.

With a swift motion, I wrenched the accursed breastplate off the man's body and cast it aside. It hurtled through the chamber and landed with a thud.

In the opposite direction from where I had thrown it.

Turning slowly, I looked towards where the piece of armor had come down.

Atop the ancient blade coated in the thin veneer of Morgan's blood.

An ethereal glow began to rise, spreading outwards from the sword, encompassing the breastplate, then Morgan herself.

I heard the man at my feet make a frightened gurgling sound and turned to see his blue eyes wide with terror.

I followed his gaze. Around the edges of the room, within the glass cylinders, the lifeless eyes of the murdered fae were sparkling with a newfound luminosity.

"How did you kill them?" I asked the maggot, not really expecting him to answer.

His eyes slid to the breastplate across the room. To one of the stones in its center that gleamed blue.

I understood. He had killed someone like me, then used their power to kill the others. Siphoning their energy like a ladle from a pail of water.

But he had not fully comprehended how limited the work of his hands was. Nor fully perceived the extent of the lifeforce of those he stole from.

I moved my hands through the air. Shadowy coils shot out, encircling the maggot and lifting him from the cold, stone floor. His attempts to escape were rendered useless as ropes of darkness tightened their grip.

I flattened him against one of the walls and bound him there. He could wait.

I stepped towards Morgan.

She lay in the golden pool of light, her silver hair streaming around her like a thousand stars.

Her eyes were closed. Blood trickled from her mouth.

I looked past her and saw an iron throne.

The rest of the story.

Our fates were entwined in bonds of blood and destiny. I had saved her with my own blood once.

There were no limits to what I would do for her now.

Around us, within the glass chambers, the souls of the fae stirred and waited. I stretched out my senses, feeling their liminal power.

Something resided. Something lingered.

The man hanging on the wall behind me knew nothing of the true powers of life or death.

Or love.

He simply took and once he had taken his fill, he assumed there was nothing left but husks.

But something remained. Something close to darkness.

What remained was *mine*.

I reached out my arms and blackness spiraled again from my fingertips. Every thread of shadow found its mark, feeding into the glass cases that held the remains of my brethren.

Like whips wrought from the abyss itself, I lashed out. With precision, I struck. Thunderous cracks fractured the crystalline prisons. Shattered remnants rained down, bringing with them their long dormant inhabitants.

The fae bodies were muted now, tarnished in the grip of death. Yet still I saw beauty. Their once brightly-colored hair had faded into soft shades of pastel, like the many shades of a rising dawn. Some bore horns and claws, vestiges of their supernatural beauty which had waned in the throes of one mortal man's greedy power-stripping.

Now I, too, would strip their power. But not for myself.

Slowly but surely, my shadowy coils encircled each body in a dark embrace. The fragile forms trembled, surrendering the remnants of life they'd clung to.

The room filled with a spectral aura as one by one the fae heeded my command, returning to give the last seed of themselves before finally leaving the realm of the living for the one of the dead.

Across the room, my mate's body began to rise, the runes on her arms shining like liquid silver.

CHAPTER 37 - MORGAN

T hey were calling to me.

Their voices were a haunting chorus, tinged with an undying kinship.

"Avenge us," some cried as they faded past the veil. "Vengeance for us all. We beseech you."

Still others did not beseech, but rather furiously demanded. It was their right, they said.

And I could not fault them for it.

"Go in peace, lady," murmured one as she swept a kiss onto my brow without a backwards glance at the man who had killed her.

"Tell my mother," another begged. "Find her and let her have peace."

The last was only a child. "Hold on," he pleaded, his boyish voice soft. "Don't give up. Don't give in to him. Oh, please, hold on."

"Kaye!" I cried, remembering. "Oh, Kaye. Wait for me. I'm coming."

The boy smiled sadly and was gone.

One by one, they passed over me, through me, and out of me. Each one recognizing me and calling me by my true name.

"Only for you," a few murmured. "We would grant no one else this gift, lady. Only for you. For the gift you brought us is eternal peace."

Lady of night. Daughter of darkness. And then the last and most powerful of all.

The name I had first been given upon my creation.

No matter how I may have wished to, I could not shrug off the weight of their words.

"*Ferrum deae,*" they whispered, and I sensed them looking at Excalibur then back at me with reverence. "*Ferrum deae.*"

I passed out of darkness as they left me and back into the light where a man was whispering the only name I ever wanted to hear in the most cherished voice I had ever known.

"Morgan," my mate whispered. "Return to me now."

CHAPTER 38 - DRAVEN

T he light faded from the eyes of every dead fae as Morgan's body sank back to the floor and she drew a quavering breath.

I rushed to her, scooping her into my arms, breathing in the scent of her hair.

The smell of blood upon her reminded me of why we were here and my eyes went unbidden to the man on the wall who was watching us with undisguised loathing and anticipation.

My mate moved in my arms, a small moan escaping from her lips.

Slowly her eyelids opened.

I gasped.

Once golden, flecked with hues of green she had gleaned from our bonding, now Morgan's eyes had evolved into something truly ethereal.

Like the surface of an opal, a thousand rainbows seemed to glisten in her irises. Specks of azure, dots of topaz, and pinpricks of sapphire were all in her gaze.

I had never seen a fae with such eyes.

I opened my mouth to tell her, but she was pushing herself to her feet with surprising strength.

I tried to wrap an arm around her waist to support her but gently she pushed it away and turned to face me.

The look in her eyes was like a knife in my heart.

"What did he do to you?" I could hear my voice, rough and strained with desperation.

"Not now." Her eyes were pleading. "Not here. Not yet."

I nodded.

Later I would learn all that had transpired in this cursed place.

And later, I would help her heal.

But first, my silver one would do as she liked.

Bending down to pick up Excalibur, she walked slowly across the room to where the man hung on the wall.

"You've strung him up."

She did not comment on the bindings I had used. The dark shadows which furled and coiled like living, breathing things.

"I thought you would like to decide what to do with him." I wouldn't call it a gift. More like an offering. The least she was owed.

"I would. Thank you."

She stepped towards the man and he curled his bloody lips into a leer that made me want to smash his teeth in again and again.

"You cannot harm me," Morgan said softly, her eyes on his blue ones. "You cannot touch me. Not with my mate here. Not with them–" She gestured to all of the dead fae lying around us. "–here." She touched a hand to her heart and the man's eyes widened slightly.

"But first..." She turned back to where the breastplate lay behind her. "This horror you created should never have existed."

A burning ball of flame shot from her hand and ignited the piece of armor.

In an instant, it was a steaming pile of ash.

"That's what you'll be soon, Fenyx," she said simply as she stared at the ashes.

Let the bastard's name be unwritten from the history of the world. It could not happen soon enough.

Fenyx was snarling and writhing against his bindings. I knew it would be of no use.

"He's only mortal," I said to my mate as she continued to stare. I reached out to touch her arm, then withdrew it. Trying to remember that she had asked me not to touch her. "Flesh and blood. He has no power over you."

She nodded. "Nothing but the power of evil inside of him." She turned and pointed across the room. "My uncle."

My eyes swept to where she had gestured. The elderly man with the white beard, his chest cavity cut open.

"You *ate* him," she said to the man on the wall. There was revulsion mixed with horrible pain in her voice. "You killed these people." She stepped closer still and I resisted the urge to follow her every step. This I knew she had to do alone. "Hear me now. Hear my words. You do not deserve to live. They did. *They did.*"

The man on the wall smirked contemptuously through blood-tinged lips and began to open his mouth.

I would not, I swore to myself, intervene. He was hers alone.

I need not have feared. By my side, my mate raised her hand.

"No more of that. No more words." There was a strange power to her utterance.

The blond man's eyes bulged as if in shock as his lips pressed closed.

"Your victims asked for vengeance. So vengeance is what I will give them." She looked at me with reluctance. "It will be over far too quickly."

"Drawing out pain is for the likes of worms like him," I said quietly. "It is not for you, Morgan."

She nodded, then squared her shoulders and lifted her hands.

A whimpering sound was already coming from the dead man's throat.

Fire, they said, was the great purifier. Leaving only the essence behind. Making space for new growth and renewal.

When my mate had finished, we ascended the ancient, stone steps leading from the chamber together as the flames danced wildly behind us, swirling over the walls and filling the once-oppressive darkness with a brilliant, cleansing light.

CHAPTER 39 - MORGAN

B eneath the shroud of a warm spring night, we hastened through the haunted lanes
of my once-proud city.

The acrid scent of burning timber and the sharp sting of smoke assailed our senses as
we passed quickly through the castle, leaving the outer bailey, moving over the bridged
moat and down into the streets of Camelot.

As we reached the streets below the castle, we could hear the clash of swords and shouts
of battle. Fiery tongues licked at shops and houses, painting a mosaic of light on the
cobblestone.

The lifeless forms of soldiers and civilians lay strewn across the road. Makeshift barri-
cades had been erected in many of the streets but were now left abandoned.

A ruthless violence was sweeping through the city.

Over the sounds of fighting and fire, there came the worst one of all.

A chorus of voices wailing in unspeakable grief was drifting through the dark. The
anguished cries of parents weeping for their infants.

We turned a corner and I raised a hand to shield my face as a stifling miasma of blistering
heat rose up. A massive bonfire raged in the road. There were bodies piled high at its
center.

The thud of armored boots on cobblestones came from ahead. Draven pulled me back
into the shadows of a building just in time as a troop of soldiers came marching down the
street. Many were bleeding. Their faces were drawn and soot-stained.

I watched the faces in silence. Many were no more than youths. Had they participated
in this madness? Had they done as their king had asked tonight and slaughtered the
offspring of their neighbors, their friends, even their own families?

I choked back a sob as I caught sight of a woman sitting on the steps of a house across the way. Her gaze was anguished as she cradled a small bundle, rocking it back and forth in her arms.

Beside me I felt Draven's body tense as he saw her. Waves of pain radiated off his hulking frame. I understood. Camelot's pain was his pain now, too, as it was mine.

A hand touched my shoulder and I gasped, whirling around.

Draven's blade was already out, but as his eyes took in the figure beckoning to us, he began to sheath it.

A woman stood in the doorway behind us, a finger to her lips. Her eyes were wide and panicked.

"Please. Help me. There is a child."

Hearing that last word, Draven was already moving past me into the house. He glanced over his shoulder to see if anyone had noticed us, but the street was empty.

Inside the house, it was dark and quiet.

If there was a child there, I wondered, should it not have been crying?

I glanced at the white apron the woman wore and noticed it was flecked with spots of red.

My heart sank. Perhaps there had been a child. But it must already have been dead.

"This way," the woman urged.

We followed her into the back room where a single candle burned in a lantern that had been placed on the floor to avoid casting any light out into the street.

The woman hurried across the room to a cradle and then turned back to us holding a wrapped bundle.

"I couldn't help the mother," she said. "But the child thrives. Here. You must take it. I cannot keep it safe."

But my eyes were already looking past her at the form of the woman who lay, very still, on the small bed in the corner.

The woman's face was ghostly, drained of all warmth. Even her once rosy lips were pale. Only her hair was still bright and vivid. The sweat-soaked amethyst strands lay spread out over the white pillowcase.

"Orcades!"

I flew across the room and knelt by the bed, taking one of her hands in mine. It was very cold.

"I think she's already gone," the woman said softly, moving to stand behind me. "She came to me in distress, far into her labor. I'm a midwife, you see. Something had gone wrong. She had tried to take care of it herself, but she was bleeding too heavily. I brought her inside and did what I could. But I could not stop the blood." She hesitated, then asked, "Did you know her?"

"*Did* I?" The words were a bare whisper. "Is she truly dead then?"

The midwife wavered. "I believe so. She is of fae blood, is she not?"

I nodded.

"I know they are different from us, but still, she has not drawn breath in a very long time."

I turned back to Draven. He was holding something in his arms. An infant in swaddling blankets.

"The baby is alive, Morgan," he said, his deep voice rasping. "A girl. A little baby girl."

Then his eyes widened as he looked over and past me. "Morgan, look."

I turned back to see my sister's chest rising and falling. More than that, she was trying to move her head.

"Orcades," I said, touching her hair gently. "What happened?"

Her violet eyes had opened. She looked back at me but made no sound.

"We can't leave her like this," I said. "Draven, I can't leave her. She's my sister."

Draven was already moving towards the bed. "Here. Take the baby. I'll carry her."

I leaned down to my sister's ear and whispered, "Orcades, Arthur has taken Kaye. He's planning to hurt him somehow." I could not even say the worst word. "Draven and I must find him."

"She's very weak," the midwife warned, clasping her hands nervously. "But yes, take her. Take the child. By the Three, I pray you may keep them safe."

"The city... The other babies... Do you know if...?"

The woman shook her head as if she did not wish to think about what she had seen and heard that night. "The king is cursed. For all time and always for what he has done here tonight in Camelot." She spat onto the worn wood floor. "Let his name be cursed in the land."

"This is his child," I said quietly, taking the baby from Draven. My mate began to lift Orcades, gently wrapping the sheet she lay on around her.

The midwife's eyes widened. "The king's child? But his queen..."

"This fae woman is his queen. And I am his sister."

The woman began to tremble.

"Fear not," I said gently. "When this is all over, I will return here to thank you properly for what you've done today."

The woman raised her hands. "There is no need. No need at all. Just keep the child safe."

I nodded. And then we were passing back through the little house, hovering in the doorway as we stood looking out into the street.

Fires still raged across the city. The smells of burning thatch and wood mixed with the aroma of fresh blood. An ashy residue carried on the wind filled my nostrils and made me cough into my sleeve.

I cradled Orcades' child against me, wrapping the cloak the woman had given me around us.

If anyone tried to touch my sister's child, they would die.

By my side, Draven appeared with Orcades in his arms. He nodded at me and we began to move down the street, this time staying very close to the shadows of the buildings.

We were nearing the temple now.

Over the next bridge that spanned the Greenbriar and there it was.

Not the Temple of the Three, but the Temple of Perun.

Standing on an island in the midst of the river, the building exuded an air of conquest and cruelty. Made of cold gray stone, the temple's facade was adorned with deep, symmetrical grooves that carved sharp patterns into the surface, evoking the sense of a fortress rather than a place of worship. Harsh, brutal lines and stark, towering columns rose up as if defying the very heavens. Above the entrance, a massive stone frieze depicted Perun battling his way through a tempest, a familiar blade in his hand.

It was a monument to a god without mercy and as we walked slowly over the bridge towards its entrance, I couldn't help but feel it reflected the darkness that had overtaken my kingdom.

Beneath the bridge, the Greenbriar flowed, dark and tranquil, a sharp contrast to the chaos and turmoil in the city beyond.

As we approached the massive columns framing the temple's entrance, a deep, rumbling suddenly filled the air.

I glanced at Draven, holding Orcades baby more tightly against my chest. A thunderstorm?

Draven shook his head, his face grim and turned his head towards the city gates in the distance.

Fire erupted over the sky.

A flaming projectile flew over the walls and into the city, exploding with a deafening roar. The blaring of war horns carried over the river's surface.

A siege.

Camelot was under attack.

The temple was eerily silent as we stepped inside. Only the faint echo of our footsteps could be heard as we moved through an immense entry hall, its walls covered with stone reliefs depicting scenes of brutal battle and conquest.

We moved into the central chamber where massive stone pillars reached upwards to support the stone ceiling. The hall was dimly lit with only a few narrow windows high above where moonlight streamed in forming small square patches on the black marble floors.

Our path led to the inner sanctum. But along the way, we encountered no one. No soldiers. No servants. No priests or supplicants.

I remembered what Fenyx had said. How Arthur had planned to use his own child for the ritual.

Where was my brother now? Would we find him inside?

Abruptly, Draven paused. A closed door lay ahead of us, a heavy wooden slab inlaid with gold plating.

A ringing sound was coming from within.

From under the door flooded bright light.

Draven kicked it in.

The door flew open, slamming into the opposite wall with a bang.

Inside the room, the walls were lined with weapons and shields, offerings and tributes to a war-like god.

On the far side of the sanctum stood a colossal statue of the deity. Perun's form was imposing, his features carved with a cruel expression. At his feet lay what I thought at first was a pool of blood. As we stepped closer, I realized it was a pile of roses.

An altar lay in the center of the room. Before the altar stood a man in the dark robes of a priest, his back to us, his arms raised in the air.

Set into the altar in each corner rested small stone bowls. A dark, crimson liquid filled each one.

Upon the altar lay Kaye. His eyes were closed, his chestnut hair tousled. His face was as pale as death, but as I watched, his chest rose and fell–first once, then again.

He was bound to the altar with rough-hewn ropes, each of his limbs fastened to the stone surface.

Above the altar hovered a wooden chalice, spinning endlessly in the air like a child's top that defied the laws of gravity.

I had seen the grail before. But the sight of it here, hovering above Kaye, as if it had been carved from the root of some malevolent tree, filled me with dread.

A brilliant, red light was radiating from the grail, casting a sickly glow across the chamber.

Before Draven and I could more than a few feet past the entryway, droplets began to rise from the four bowls.

Slowly, four crimson lines of blood ascended from the corners of the altar, rising and lengthening as they converged over the wooden chalice and began to drip into the cup.

They were feeding it, I realized with horror. Feeding it with my brother's blood.

Thin, precise cuts marred Kaye's delicate wrists. The gashes were not deep enough to cause fatal harm. Instead, they kept a steady stream of blood flowing into a narrow channel which lined the altar's rim.

As the drops of blood flowed from Kaye's wrists, they fell into the ridges, snaking their way to each corner of the altar and replenishing the stone bowls with crimson offerings.

My heart constricted in my chest.

My brother, bound and helpless, was being used as a sacrifice to feed some dark power. But I was there now. This all would stop. I would *make* it stop.

Behind me, Draven lay Orcades down very gently on the floor as I turned to pass the baby to him.

At the altar, the priest turned, noticing us for the first time.

At first, he was unrecognizable to me. He had the face of no one I knew. This must be the High Priest Cavan who Merlin had mentioned.

Then the man passed a hand over his face and suddenly he was no longer a stranger at all.

Tyre's portly face looked back at me with a genial smile.

Then the smile shifted, becoming something that was no longer warm or genial by any stretch of imagination.

I stepped towards him. Strapped to the belt at my hip, Excalibur began to emit a humming sound, as if calling out to the grail as it spun its dance of blood high in the air over the altar.

"You won't wish to come any closer," Tyre warned, holding up his hands calmly. "To do so would be truly fatal."

"Get the fuck out of my way, traitor." Pulling Excalibur from its sheath, I held the blade aloft as it gleamed golden.

But Tyre only studied the blade with appreciation. "You've brought the sword. Excellent."

My heart sank.

"Your brother will be pleased." The priest looked past me. "And the child, too. If you had arrived a little earlier, we might not have had to resort to your brother, no matter what the king said." Tyre raised his brows. "And Fenyx?"

"I believe the term is liquified," Draven offered from behind me.

"As you'll soon be," I snarled, not taking my eyes off the priest.

"If the god so wills it, certainly. But he has blessed me before now." Tyre's expression was disturbingly beatific.

"Who are you really?" I demanded. "Cavan or Tyre?"

The priest smiled and passed his hand over his face again, erasing Tyre's portly features and replacing them with a thin-faced man with hard dark eyes.

"There was a Tyre once. I'm told he was a charming fellow. I can only hope I did him credit."

"You killed him," I said flatly.

The priest who was not Tyre nodded. "It was easier that way. Your brother needed someone in the temple. Someone he could trust."

"And this?" I gestured at Kaye. As Cavan momentarily glanced back at the altar, I sidled closer.

"Ah, yes. We feed the grail to feed the sword. Once the grail has drunk its fill, we'll bathe Excalibur in its glory."

I ground my teeth. "In Kaye's blood, you mean."

"He is an offering. Nothing more. The babe would have been better." He looked longingly at the child cradled securely in my mate's arms then glanced at Draven's horns and shook his head as if realizing it was useless. "Blood of the king. Blood of his kin. There is a deep and ancient power in it. I suppose it is too late now."

"You aren't laying a hand on that baby. Kaye isn't dead and he's not your fucking offering. Neither is the child."

"You touch your brother at your peril," Cavan warned, his dark eyes narrowing as he saw how close to the altar I'd approached. "Anyone who interrupts the ritual now that it has begun will not live to see its final glory."

"I don't care about glory, I care about my brother." I took another step towards the altar.

And then everything seemed to happen all at once.

I lifted Excalibur. As I did so, I realized the blade and the grail were not the same. The red light from the chalice and the golden light from the sword danced towards one another and where they met, there was a blinding flash.

A man ran into the room.

Darting past Draven, he brushed up against me, nearly knocking me to the ground. As he ran past I caught a glimpse of a pointed black beard and a long cloak of onyx and gold.

No, not a cloak.

Wings.

The man leaped towards the altar, forcefully knocking Cavan out of the way.

The High Priest of Perun snarled with rage as he crashed to the floor but it was too late.

Javer was rising, leaping into the air, his wings spreading out and beating loudly as he lifted off the ground just high enough to snatch the chalice from over the altar.

For a moment, he seemed to hang in suspension, his hand upon the rim of the goblet. And then it spilled.

Blood poured downwards, drenching Javer, the altar, and Kaye.

With a cry of agony, Javer's wings collapsed and he fell back onto the floor in a heap, the cup falling beside him with a dull clatter, the red light pulsing once, twice, then growing dim. He was dead.

I rushed towards my brother as Cavan did the same.

"We must resume the ritual," the priest shrieked. "You know not what you do."

"Damn your ritual." I whirled with my blade. "The Sword of Perun serves me now."

Ferrum deae. It was the iron of the goddess. There was no place for the god here tonight. Not even in his own temple.

The blade cut through the air with a menacing whoosh.

There was a sickening sound as the sword sliced through bone and flesh.

Cavan's head tumbled to the ground, his eyes rolling upwards.

The bounds holding Kaye to the altar were next. I cut them carefully one by one, then lifted my brother off the wretched slab of stone. He was heavier than I remembered. I pulled him onto the floor, cradling him in my lap.

Across the room, Draven's eyes met mine. He held the child in his arms. I held my brother in mine.

I could almost read his thoughts. What now?

My entire body felt weary with pain and relief.

Yet still it was not over. Outside, a battle raged. We had to get out of the temple.

But what would we emerge to? Where could we go with Arthur's child and with Kaye?

On the ground, beside Draven, Orcades began to cough.

Setting the sleeping newborn carefully on the floor beside its mother, Draven carefully lifted my sister to a sitting position, cupping her head with infinite gentleness to try to help her breathe more easily.

Turning her head with great effort, Orcades looked over at me and tried to smile. "Sister. A dark birthright indeed." Her voice was tinged with irony as she quoted from the prophecy. "Arthur still lives?"

"As far as we know," I told her. "You will, too."

She grimaced, pain clouding her face. "No. I think not."

"Did you know?" I was angry suddenly. Angry with her for leaving me. "Did you know this would be the price?"

Slowly, she shook her head. "You think too highly of me if you believe that." The child beside her let out a faint whimpering sound in its sleep. Gently she reached out a hand to touch the baby's cheek. "When springtime blooms, the babe is blessed," she whispered, quoting again. "Will you be blessed, little one?"

She raised her eyes to mine. "Medra. Her name is Medra."

"Medra," I repeated.

"You need not ever fear for your child." Draven's voice was rough. "No harm will come to her."

Orcades looked up at the man who supported her, as if seeing him for the first time. Her eyes widened, then she glanced back at me. "A Siabra. Your mate?"

"My mate," I said with pride.

She sighed a little. "There is no helping it, I suppose. I thank you," she said to Draven. "She will have need of protectors."

Orcades eyes were moving around the room. As she caught sight of the grail on the floor behind me, lying in a pool of Kaye's blood, she gasped.

"You know what this means." Moving a hand to her mouth she coughed again. There was more blood this time.

I nodded. I hadn't wished to think about it. But there was no denying the implications. There was only one way my brother could have gotten his hands on the grail.

"The death of kings," Orcades breathed. "Will she deliver it?"

"She won't have to," I said darkly. "Medra won't have to kill our father, Orcades. Because I swear to you I will do it myself."

None of this was accidental. Gorlois and the Valtain had been involved in Pendrath's affairs all along.

"The evils of the world at the feet of one man." Orcades eyes were filled with an unnatural brightness that somehow I knew could not last long. "Even in this, he has thwarted me." There was sorrow in her words. She was fading now. "You must go home, Sister. You must destroy them all."

"The three objects of power."

"Yes. But you must be very careful." She paused, gasping for breath. "He wants you back. He always has."

"What will happen if I do destroy them?"

"I do not know. You may find yourself. Or lose everything."

Something evil had begun here today. A darkness was rising. Something deep inside me told me it had happened once before. And that the world could not endure it if this evil rose again.

"There was another inscription," Orcades said suddenly. "Written upon the pedestal. I scratched it off."

Anticipation coiled in my chest. "What did it say?"

Orcades smiled, her lovely lips rimmed heartbreakingly with blood. "Whosoever pulls the sword from this stone shall be the rightful ruler of all Aercanum."

I couldn't tell if she was joking or not. The inscription was too momentous to believe.

"Who wrote it?" I demanded. "Who put the sword there in the first place? And why? Tell me that much."

But Orcades was looking down at her sleeping daughter. The brightness in her eyes was dimming like a candle. Already she slumped against Draven. He held her propped up with the utmost tenderness.

My mate had, I realized, been very silent through all of this. Now I saw the grief that constricted his face. He was reliving the worst moment of his life.

But this time, the baby would live. We had that much comfort.

"Who meets their death devoid of love shall surely face their end," Orcades murmured as she brushed her hand over the sleeping baby's cheek. "But one who gives their soul away, eternity extends."

"Orcades..." My voice caught.

"Oh, Medra," I heard my sister murmur. "You are the most beautiful thing I have ever seen in this or any world."

The light in her eyes faded. She was gone.

In my arms, Kaye stirred but did not waken.

I looked at Draven. His green eyes were calm and steady. Slowly he set down Orcades body and picked up the slumbering child, holding it closely against him like a balm to his heart.

I felt something in me start to blaze and burn. Grief and fury filled my throat.

Merlin. Orcades. Kaye. Javer. Medra.

It was too much. Too much to bear.

And at the heart of it all...

"To this I will make a reply, though it may mean my death," I said very clearly.

My voice rang out through the inner sanctum just as the sound of marching boots filled the hall outside.

My other brother had arrived.

CHAPTER 40 - MORGAN

A rthur entered the room and froze as he took in the scene before him.

His wife, dead on the floor.

His high priest, decapitated.

A strange, winged man lying lifeless beside the grail.

Me, with a very-much-alive Kaye in my arms.

My mate had already risen to his feet. Medra cradled in one strong arm, his sword drawn in the other.

Arthur's eyes moved to the baby Draven held.

"That baby..."

"Your child," I said. "Your daughter."

Arthur's eyes widened. "A daughter? I had thought a son..."

"You thought wrongly," I exclaimed. "You have always, *always* thought wrongly, Arthur. And tonight, you will finally hear the truth. What have you done, Arthur? Out there, in the city, what the fuck have you done? Can you not even see what you've become? You're a monster, Arthur. You're hardly a man at all."

I could hear the whiff of hysteria in my voice as I held Kaye tighter. He was breathing. Kaye was still breathing, I reminded myself, trying to steady myself.

No one would take my youngest brother from me. I had already lost one brother long ago.

"You don't understand." They weren't the words I'd expected to hear.

Arthur's eyes were almost pleading as he looked down at me from across the sanctum. "Our enemies are encroaching. We are losing this war. We needed a sacrifice. A powerful one to charge the sword. This... This was the best way to do it. The child would have been better." Again his eyes darted to the infant, as if he could not believe she truly existed. Had survived. "But the prophecy…"

He paused as if he wasn't sure how much I knew.

"Oh, I know," I said bitterly. "I know all about the prophecy, Arthur. I don't care. Babies. They were babies." I was weeping now. "How could you? You are truly cursed by the Three. You will never be known for anything else for as long as you draw breath. You are no longer a Pendragon. You are only *the Childslayer*."

The word the midwife had used earlier that night spilled from my lips like a brand. I watched Arthur flinch as the title hit him full on.

Even the soldiers who stood behind him in the hall looked vastly uncomfortable. I wondered if they had participated in Arthur's crime. If so, they deserved to die just as much as their king did.

For a moment, Arthur's face was blank. Then he straightened his back and turned to his men. "We must resume the ritual. Cavan is gone, but we will fetch another priest. You." He pointed to one of the soldiers. "Go and find one. We'll use the boy. He looks half dead anyhow. It's not too late. We can still…"

"No," I shouted, my voice rattling the stones.

"No," Draven growled, stepping in front of me to shield Kaye and I.

He raised his blade. In his arms, Medra began to cry. A high-pitched, plaintive wail filled the room.

There was a clamor in the hall outside. I heard the sound of clashing swords.

My brother stood indecisively in the doorway, a single guard remaining to stand guard at his back.

Then with a strangled shout, the last, lone soldier was pulled out of the room.

Arthur stepped backwards into the sanctum, turning to face the door with his hand on the hilt of his own weapon.

"Enough." A woman's voice. Clear and commanding.

Guinevere entered the room. She was garbed in pale blue robes. Perched on her shoulder was a golden owl, its eyes deep wells of wisdom.

There was a serenity to Guinevere's presence that did not falter even in the face of my brother's senseless fury.

Arthur looked at her and, to my surprise, took a step back. Then another.

Guinevere moved past him without a glance and came to stand near me, looking down at Kaye.

"Evil things have been done in this place in the name of a god," she said quietly.

Crouching down beside me, she touched Kaye's brow. On her shoulder, Tuva let out a soft hoot.

"He will live," Guinevere murmured, straightening back up.

The strange thing was, I believed her. She was no healer. Not that I knew of. But I believed her without a shadow of doubt.

"But he will not awaken." Her soft, doe-like, brown eyes met mine.

My breath hitched. "What do you mean?"

"He is bound to the chalice. It holds him even now. He walks between life and death."

I had not thought she had noticed the grail lying untouched by Javer's body.

Now she followed my gaze towards the prone figure. "Your friend?"

"Yes." Javer had been my friend. I knew it now. Too little, too late. "He saved Kaye."

"I'm sorry."

There was another sound from the doorway, and a new group of people entered the room.

Rebels. All of them were armed. At the forefront were Galahad and Lancelet.

"The temple is secure," Lancelet announced. She was carrying a heavy spear which she rested on the floor as she spoke. Her left arm was splinted and in a sling, her face was still battered and bruised, but her eyes burned with an excited fervor. "Morgan, it's good to see you." Her gaze drifted to Draven, then to the baby he held.

"There will be time for talk later," Guinevere told her before the questions could begin. "But for now..."

She walked fearlessly towards Arthur, her blue robes sweeping the floor. Just as Merlin's used to do.

My brother tightened his grip on the hilt of his sword, but he did not draw it.

When they were facing one another, she stopped.

The room had become very quiet.

"I owe you nothing. I will not apologize," my brother said, raising his voice. But I could see he was shaking. "I am the king."

"You are the king," Guinevere said simply. "But what you owe me is your death. Until then, may you live with the true horror of what you have done."

Before he could react, she touched her fingertips to his eyes.

Arthur shouted, but it was too late. Guinevere was already moving away from him to stand by Lancelet and the others.

"You have been blinded, Arthur." She looked around the room, her eyes lingering on where my sister lay dead, her amethyst tresses spilling out around her, to Javer and the grail, then back to Kaye and I. "We all have."

My brother was blinking his eyes and shaking his head like a man who had been submerged in a lake. "What have you done to me?"

"The scales are falling from your eyes," Guinevere said. "It will be... painful."

Arthur was gazing around the chamber as if he had never seen it before. He looked at me and Kaye. Then to where Orcades sprawled, her eyes sightless now forever.

Finally, his glance fell upon Medra where she rested in Draven's arms.

My mate's grip on the baby tightened protectively, and he frowned.

"That child." Arthur's voice was hoarse.

"Your child," Guinevere said. "Do you understand now?"

"No." Arthur was shaking his head. "I couldn't have. It's not possible."

"You have done many things most would find impossible. Murdering children in their mother's arms is only one of them. Your wife fled from you. She is dead now." Guinevere's voice was very calm.

I looked between her and my brother. "I don't understand. What's going on?"

"A very long time ago, your brother sold himself at a very great price," Guinevere said. "Ask him."

Arthur stared at me. "No. I couldn't. I wouldn't..."

"Tell me," I said, my voice cold. "What did you do, Arthur?"

He looked around the room as if searching for a way out. "There was a man. A powerful man. He came to me after Father died. He offered me... so many things."

"In exchange for what?" I demanded.

"Nothing. Everything. My loyalty. And to promise to help him, when the need arose. He wished to... find certain things. Things he had lost."

"He never asked about your sister?" Guinevere's voice was quiet but persistent.

"No. Why should he? I met him when I was quite alone. A mirror. There was a mirror in Father's treasure room. I was in there, looking at all of the spectacular things. I touched it. And the man... appeared. At first, I thought I was imagining things. Having some sort of a vision. But after that, we spoke through the mirror many times. He became... a curse upon me." Arthur's breathing had become ragged.

My heart sank as I realized who the man must have been. The man who had led Arthur down this path, very slowly at first, then more swiftly, until he had reached this desperate end of ruin and desolation, with the powers of the sword and grail dangling just out of his reach.

"He helped you follow the deepest desires of your heart," Guinevere said.

"Yes. No! That can't be. This wasn't me. Isn't me. I would never."

"But you did." My voice was cold. "He didn't force you, Arthur. Did he?"

"No," my brother faltered. I could see the sweat on his brow. "Not force. But he made it so... so that I wouldn't see things the same way. I didn't want to. After Father, I didn't want to feel as much anymore. I didn't wish to care. Do you understand? He softened it. So that I wouldn't have to. It was... a kindness."

"A kindness? Is that what you call it?" I looked at him, horrified. "Whatever he did, whatever you let him do, allowed you to become... something terrible, Arthur."

"My child." His gaze was on Medra now. "I would have killed her."

"All because of a prophecy," I said bitterly. "Your stupid fears and suspicions. She's a baby. She can't hurt you, Arthur."

Arthur said nothing. Just kept looking at little Medra. The baby had quieted now. Her little fist was in her mouth as she looked up at Draven and cooed.

She must be hungry, I realized. She would need milk.

And a mother.

There was a disturbance outside in the hall, and a messenger ran in, her face red and breathless.

"The siege is broken," she panted, looking at Guinevere.

I didn't understand. "We've won? The attackers have left?"

"No." The messenger shook her head. "We've lost. They're inside the city. Armies from Tintagel and Lyonesse. They're encircling the island as we speak."

"I understand. Thank you," Guinevere said. Her serenity seemed unshaken. "It won't be long now."

The bird on her shoulder swiveled her head around to look at me from behind huge eyes, then rotated it again to look at Arthur.

My brother was weeping, I realized. Water glistened on his face.

I could not remember the last time I had seen him cry. If they were tears of remorse, however, they were far too late. My heart had hardened towards him.

"You understand now?" Guinevere spoke with shocking gentleness to the man who had wronged her so terribly. "You understand your crimes?"

Arthur gave a jerky bob of his head. "I nearly killed Kaye. I nearly killed my daughter. The grail, the sword. He gave them to me to use. He would have helped me overthrow my enemies."

"They are not your enemies, Arthur. They never were," I said.

If the man who had seduced my brother into wickedness had so generously lent his objects of power, then there must be a reason, a much darker one than we knew. I knew enough about Gorlois le Fay to understand that much.

"I know that now." He looked at Guinevere with a great weariness in his eyes. "I must go out to them. They will be expecting me."

She nodded. "You know what awaits."

"Yes." He looked at Medra. Her eyes were very blue. Most babies' eyes were blue, I remembered. "Kings will fall. There is no escaping it, is there?"

"No," Guinevere said, her voice still gentle.

He nodded. "It will be a relief, in some ways."

I watched as he walked out into the hall.

"I don't understand," I said hollowly. I looked at Guinevere. "Please. I still don't understand."

Guinevere's eyes were full of sorrow. "We will follow him now. Leave Kaye here, Morgan. He will be all right until we return. Someone will remain with him."

She turned to the door.

A man and woman immediately moved towards me, carefully taking Kaye from my arms.

Slowly, I walked towards the doorway.

Draven was waiting for me.

"Do you understand? Do you know what this is all about?"

He hesitated, then touched my cheek. "I believe so, love. I believe so."

We followed Guinevere down the hall. Ahead of her Arthur walked, his back straight and proud.

For once in his life, he looked truly kingly.

As we reached the entrance to the temple, he stepped out alone.

Guinevere stopped, hanging back in the shadows of the temple's overhang, the group of rebels spreading around her. Lancelet took up a position on her left. Draven and I came to stand by her right.

Across the bridge, on the other side of the river, an army waited.

Warriors wearing the blue and silver armor of Tintagel sat on battle horses side by side soldiers from Lyonesse dressed in gold and purple. The banners of both kingdoms were held aloft by riders on armored mounts, long strips of silk streaming in the cool night breeze.

At the base of the bridge, the armies' leaders sat astride their mounts. There were three of them.

I saw a tall man with gray and black hair dressed in the ornate armor of a king. His cape was a vivid blue edged with silver.

Beside him sat a young man and a much older woman. Both had the same honey-toned brown skin as Guinevere and the same dark, curling hair. They wore the colors of Lyonesse.

It was the elder of the trio who, with a gesture of her reins, stepped forward, capturing the attention of all who were gathered on both sides of the river.

Raising her voice, the older woman spoke clearly. "I am Lady Marjolijn of the Royal House of Lyonesse, sister to the late King Leodegrance. By my side sits Prince Taryn, my nephew, now heir to the throne of Lyonesse. In the company of King Mark of Tintagel, we come to Camelot not as enemies but as bearers of justice and reparation."

The words rang true. Still, I knew there must have been deaths on both sides tonight. The bitterness of kingdom battling kingdom had made enemies of those who had once been allies. The peace would not be restored in one night. Especially when these armies had now invaded our lands just as Arthur had done to theirs.

"Nearly one year ago, without rhyme or reason, King Arthur Pendragon of Pendrath descended upon our lands in a tempest of destruction and chaos," Lady Marjolijn continued. "He razed our villages, brought ruin to our people, and desecrated our sacred temples in a campaign of battle that knew no honor or chivalry."

The warriors on the river bank sat silently beneath the moonlight, still and statuesque.

"Tintagel and Lyonesse, lands sovereign in their own right, were defended. We fought for our people and our ways of life. Now we stand united, here in the heart of your capital, at the foot of your temple, to demand that the blood debt be paid and that justice be done."

Lady Marjolijn's steely gaze swept out over all those assembled, her voice unwavering. "We call for the death of King Arthur Pendragon. We demand he answer for his crimes. With his death, may the scales of reparation begin to be balanced and the cries of the innocent finally begin to be heard."

The air was heavy with anticipation.

Arthur stepped forward into the grassy courtyard of the temple and into full sight of the surrounding army.

"I am Arthur, King of Pendrath."

Lady Marjolijn looked at him, her expression unchanging. "So you are."

My brother cleared his throat. "I take full responsibility for my crimes. All that I ask—no—all that I beg is that you spare my child." He turned and gestured to Medra in Draven's arms.

Lady Marjolijn's face became disdainful. "We do not harm infants. Only you would do such a thing."

My heart twisted in my chest. My brother had ruled with iron-fisted brutality. His admission and his presence before the armies of his enemies was, in itself, the strangest and rarest spectacle, a twist of fate no one could ever have anticipated.

It was as if the Three themselves had reached through the veils of existence and touched his soul, allowing him to finally see the haunting visage of his own wickedness and the darkness that had consumed him.

Across the river, Lady Marjolijn was raising her hand.

Almost instantly, a deadly hail of arrows was released into the air.

The missiles cut through the night in a grim volley of retribution and converged upon my brother where he stood. Arthur Pendragon. King of Pendrath. The scourge of three kingdoms. The Childslayer.

Without exception, the deadly shafts found their mark.

Arthur staggered, then collapsed on the riverbank at the foot of the temple he had constructed to honor his cruel, warlike god.

But it wasn't over. Lady Marjolijn's voice was ringing out again, firm and resolute.

"By the laws of warfare and through the bloodshed brought upon these lands, we declare Pendrath to no longer be a sovereign kingdom," she declared, her words echoing over the water. "As a consequence of King Arthur's campaign of tyranny and aggression, this land is now under the dominion of Tintagel and Lyonesse. The Pendragon's throne, a symbol of former power and authority, shall be shattered, and henceforth, our two kingdoms shall jointly preside over Pendrath."

The words shocked me to my core. There was no room for negotiation or compromise in her declaration. Only the echoes of war-terms and the unyielding determination of the victors.

The fate of Pendrath seemed to hang in the balance as the weight of her pronouncement settled over us all.

I could feel myself shaking.

"No." I stepped forward. "No. The throne belongs to Kaye Pendragon."

Across the river bank, Lady Marjolijn was peering at me.

"Who is that? Who are you, girl?" She frowned. "Is that the sister? The fae-blood girl?"

"I am Morgan Pendragon," I said clearly, hearing my voice carry over the water. "Arthur Pendragon was my brother. And while he may have been a tyrant to your people and mine, my youngest brother has done nothing wrong and he *will* sit on the throne of Pendrath as is his due."

"You seem to believe you are entitled to a negotiation," the older woman replied drily. "Perhaps you think we should all sit at a table and discuss what is due. But there will be no negotiating."

"Then you are no better than my brother." I heard my words ring out and watched as she stiffened.

"Sir Ector, perhaps you should have a word with the girl." The words were spoken by King Mark. He was turning to someone behind him.

A man stepped out from in between the horses. A man in the armor of a Pendrath knight.

The look of defeat on Sir Ector's face told me everything I needed to know. He had helped this army reach Camelot. But he had not anticipated they would treat Pendrath with the same contempt Arthur had them.

"Hold." Guinevere stepped up next to me. "Greetings, Aunt. Brother."

A look of astonishment came over Guinevere's family members' faces.

Lady Marjolijn recovered first. "Niece, we had believed you to be dead."

"No thanks to my father and brother, but I am very much alive," Guinevere said.

Her aunt looked at her, taking in the robes, the owl.

"When the High Priestess Merlin died, she appointed me her successor," Guinevere explained, seeing her aunt's gaze.

My eyes widened, but I said nothing. It made a great deal of sense.

Guinevere looked at me. "They cannot touch us here," she murmured. "Not on this island of Avalon. The seat of the goddesses' power. Where this temple should never, ever have been built."

"Be that as it may." Lady Marjolijn's face was returning to its hardened set. "The Three have no place here, Guinevere. The terms have been set. Pendrath will capitulate and comply in every way."

Guinevere remained unruffled. She reached a hand up to gently stroke the head of the owl on her shoulder.

Two huge shadows swooped overhead.

A cry went up as the beating of wings filled the air.

I looked up. Two colossal battlecats, their enormous wings casting vast shadows, were descending upon the temple grounds.

Across the river, the gathered onlookers gazed in awe. Whispers of shock and fear rippled through the crowd of soldiers.

And then, from across the river, the armies of Tintagel and Lyonesse began to stir and shift.

A second horde of troops was marching in from behind.

Fae soldiers resplendent in armor of deepest black, regal gold, and emerald green marched in unison until they completely encircled the Lyonesse and Tintagel forces, then came to a halt.

The air seemed to crackle with tension as the two armies faced one another.

My mate stepped forward.

"Lady Marjolijn," he called, as he came to stand at my side. "I believe Morgan Pendragon was far too modest when she introduced herself to you a moment ago."

His deep, resonant voice carried easily and could be heard by all.

The three monarchs turned back towards the temple, their eyes on us once again.

"She was born a Pendragon, it is true," my mate continued. "But she has taken on other names since then. Among them, first and foremost, the title of Empress of Myntra. She is also my wife. I stand before you, Prince Kairos Draven of the Royal House Venator of the Siabra Court of Umbral Flames."

A murmur went up amongst the three monarchs as they took in his height, his breadth, his horns.

"And these soldiers," Lady Marjolijn said, gesturing to the army which stood behind her own. "They are hers, I presume?"

"They are," Draven said easily. "As are these impressive creatures you see by her side."

As if to reinforce things, Nightclaw let out a loud growl that echoed across the river.

"Exmoors, I believe they are called," Lady Marjolijn said a little begrudgingly. But there was keen interest in her eyes. Had she, too, perhaps once read a tome of magical creatures beneath her bed, before she became the formidable lady I now saw before me?

"The forces you see behind you are only a small taste of what the empire of Myntra has to offer," Draven said.

Lady Marjolijn sniffed. "In other words, you back your wife with your realm."

"My wife backs herself with her own realm. I am merely thankful to be by her side," Draven answered.

"Negotiations are back on the table, I suppose," Lady Marjolijn said, looking at me.

I nodded. "Indeed, I believe they are."

"Very well. We will quarter our troops just outside of the city. Treaty talks can begin in the morning."

"My brother Kaye is currently very ill," I said quickly.

"Then you shall take his place or appoint a regent in his stead until he is recovered," Lady Marjolijn suggested.

I nodded my agreement.

"In the morning then." She turned away, and in a moment, a horn blew, and the troops from Lyonesse and Tintagel began to move out.

I turned to face Draven. He was empty-handed. I glanced behind us to see Galahad holding Medra. A bottle of milk had been acquired from somewhere and he was feeding it to her.

Guinevere had moved away from us. I looked over to the edge of the bridge and saw her removing the silk cloak she wore and draping it over Arthur's body.

"She is truly full of grace," Draven said quietly, watching with me.

I nodded. My throat was suddenly too constricted to form words.

My feelings were a maelstrom of contradictions. My brother's hands had been stained with the blood of countless innocents, Guinevere herself among them.

And yet for most of my life, I had believed him to be my flesh and blood. One didn't escape that so easily.

It was the greatest of ironies that in his final moments, my brother had almost returned to me and been forced to face the dark abyss he had become.

I took a deep breath. "The prophecy came true."

Draven's eyes formed a question.

"He died because of Medra. He died believing he was saving her from something worse. From himself."

"This." Draven gestured to the retreating army across the river "It might have all been much worse. Your brother spared his city that much, at least. It was a better death than he deserved."

I knew he was right.

"But now there is something much worse than Arthur to face," he said quietly.

I nodded, slipped my hand into his warm and strong one, and together, we turned back to face our friends.

EPILOGUE

T he cradle swayed gently back and forth. Inside, Medra lay wrapped in a soft, wool blanket. Her cherubic face was serene, her tiny rosebud lips softly parted. With her eyes closed, only the hint of her pointed ears revealed her mixed fae and mortal lineage.

I watched as the baby breathed a contented little sigh, then curled her tiny hands against her chest. Leaning over, I smoothed a downy lock of her hair. For now, its color was brown. Like Arthur's.

Across the room, in the bed that used to be Orcades', Kaye slumbered.

The calico cat and her litter of kittens had been brought back up from the stables. It was stupid, really, but part of me had hoped that if Kaye could hear them, feel them... that he might wake up.

The kittens pounced and played and slept at the foot of Kaye's bed. But he did not wake.

Draven touched my shoulder. "We should go now. They'll be waiting."

I nodded, then lifted a hand in farewell to Kasie, the healer from the temple who was watching over Kaye and Medra for us. She sat in a chair by the bedside, reading a book about herbal lore while her patients slept. I glanced at the clock on the wall. Medra's wet nurse was due to arrive for another feeding soon. The baby had a voracious appetite.

"They'll be fine," she mouthed, so as not to wake Medra. She smiled and made an ushering gesture. "Go."

I followed Draven out into the hall, my hand clasped in his much larger one.

We were going back to where, in some ways, you might say it had all begun...

The chorus of merry voices and the rich aroma of spiced ale and hearty stew spilled out as we pushed open the door of The Bear and Mermaid. Inside, the tavern was alive with activity.

I glanced across the room and saw familiar faces seated at a long, wooden table.

There was Hawl, with their sleek, brown fur rippling in the firelight. Their intelligent, amber eyes glimmered with humor as they opened their muzzle in a loud, growling laugh.

Beside Hawl sat a robust, red-haired man with rugged features. Gawain grinned as he gripped a frothy tankard.

Leaning against his side was a slender, ebony-skinned man with a disarming smile and kind, intelligent eyes ... which lit up as he caught sight of me standing in the entranceway with Draven.

"Morgan!" Crescent shouted, standing up and waving. "Get over here."

The blonde young woman across from him turned her head and paused what she'd been saying to look over at me with a small smile. My dear Lancelet.

Beside her sat Guinevere and Galahad.

And further down the table was Lady Marjolijn, sipping from her own large tankard of ale.

Of course, there had already been a more formal gathering than this one. Also at a very large table.

That morning, at the Round Table in the Temple of the Three, we had all sat down together—the rebels from Pendrath, the Siabra, and the representatives from Tintagel and Lyonesse.

Guinevere and Draven had taken up places on either side of me as we sat down at the Table. It had seemed fitting—the representative of the true temple and the Prince of the Siabra.

For hours, we had remained there, discussing everything from reparations to the release of prisoners of war. At times, things had turned heated. Understandably, Tintagel and Lyonesse were not so easy to satisfy after all they had suffered. But the reparations Pendrath would make were generous and would be supplemented by Myntra. Furthermore, I had done my best to reassure all parties that this would be a lasting peace and that all hostilities would cease immediately.

During the night, Draven, Sir Ector, and I had sent out riders to all of the Pendrath war camps, letting them know that Pendrath was withdrawing and surrendering unconditionally. Within days, the troops that had once fought our neighbors would be marching back to Camelot and then, hopefully, returning to their homes and their ordinary lives.

But it would be a long time before life could truly get back to normal.

Pendrath had experienced incredible losses.

We had lost our High Priestess, our queen, and our king.

But more than anything, the people of Camelot had to confront the bitter truth of their king's ultimate betrayal—his merciless decree to butcher their defenseless children.

Guinevere was already preparing to lead a memorial for the children, Merlin, and the queen.

Arthur would not be included.

Instead, my brother's body would be put to rest in a quiet, private ceremony. There would be no funeral procession, no forced show of public mourning. The pain of Arthur's perfidy was still too raw for any of that.

Camelot needed time to heal from the collective guilt and pain of Arthur's reign.

Beyond the peace talks, there were other pressing questions to be answered. How had they done it? How had Gawain, Hawl, and Crescent gotten the entire Siabra army to Camelot in time? And how had Guinevere and Galahad narrowly avoided being caught in the web of Tyre's—Cavan's—treachery?

A day into their mountain journey, Gawain and the other Siabra had been beset by a powerful blizzard that threatened to trap them in a narrow pass. According to Ulpheas and Crescent, there hadn't been any other choice. They could have stayed and waited out the snow, possibly for days or weeks while rations ran low and the cold slowly destroyed morale.

Or they could take a bold risk...and stitch.

Ulpheas had been the first volunteer.

When he had returned, unharmed, they had begun transporting the others. Anyone who volunteered, horses and all. A few chose to remain. These were instructed to return to the ships and help to guard them. But most had decided to take their chances, and to Crescent and Ulpheas's relief, there had been few losses despite the vast distance. By the end, they were fatigued and near collapsing, but they had done it. They had transported an army to the outskirts of Camelot.

But such a heroic feat would hopefully not be required again. Upon hearing their story, Draven had commanded Crescent and Ulpheas to begin a new project—the creation of gates linking Myntra to Pendrath. The fae of old had created the first ones, he'd said. Why couldn't we learn how to do so again?

As for Guinevere and Galahad's success both at the tournament and last night, it seemed we had my uncle to thank. Despite Tyre's insistence that all messages be passed through him, my uncle had been skirting that for quite some time due to suspicions of his own. Before he had come to my room, he had sent a brief, cryptic message to the rebels alerting them to the danger Kaye might be in.

He had not known about the children then. If he had, perhaps Arthur might have been stopped in time.

As it was, the rebels had swarmed out of their hiding places when they'd realized what was happening. At Guinevere and Galahad's command, they had joined the uprising against Arthur's soldiers alongside civilians who were doing the same. There had been many casualties—but along the way, some of the infants had been saved.

Now, trying to smile, I made my way across the room to the wooden table, with Draven by my side.

There were a few curious glances—at me and at the diverse group I was joining. The people of Pendrath were not used to seeing fae so openly. They were certainly not used to seeing horned men or talking bears.

But in time, I hoped they would accept all of the strangeness and newness for what it was. A new chapter for our kingdom. One in which differences no longer set us apart but made us stronger together.

"How is your arm?" I asked quietly, sliding into a spot on the bench beside Lancelet. Draven dropped down beside me, his hand briefly caressing my waist.

I reached out my hand to squeeze his.

"The healers saw to it. I'm fine," Lancelet said so quickly, I knew she hadn't even thought about the words. She grimaced, then looked at me. "Truly, I'm fine. Now."

I nodded. I doubted either of us were truly fine after all we had gone through. But I was glad she felt well enough to claim to be.

"You did something with the sword when I was down in the arena to help me. Didn't you?" Lancelet asked softly.

But she had not lowered her voice quite enough.

Lady Marjolijn with her hawklike hearing perked up down the table. "The sword? Ah, yes, we have heard of this sword Arthur found. The rumors are hard to believe. Did it truly wipe out hundreds of the king's own people with a blinding light at this tournament?"

I shifted uncomfortably. "I'm not sure about hundreds, but yes, it did kill everyone in the first few rows of the arena when it was... in the wrong hands."

"I'd say any Pendragon's hands were the wrong hands," Lady Marjolijn muttered loudly enough for me to hear.

My eyes flashed. "You need not worry about the sword. It will not be used against you. We plan to dispose of it."

Draven's fingers tightened around mine. He knew what I meant.

Lady Marjolijn's face softened slightly. "Good." She paused. "I hope you understand our position this morning. Concerning the child, I mean."

She meant Medra.

Orcades and Arthur's child could not, Lady Marjolijn and King Mark insisted, be permitted to rule Pendrath. Many at the Round Table on our side had agreed with them.

The people would revolt, Dame Halyna had said quietly, to have Arthur's surviving baby become their queen when their own children had been killed. Medra would be a constant reminder.

Kaye or I. That was who should be on the throne, said Sir Ector stoutly.

And as I didn't want it, the crown would fall to Kaye.

When he woke up.

In the meantime, Medra's future was still in flux. Some wished to see her raised in the temple. Others suggested she be sent to the Court of Umbral Flames in Myntra, for after all, was she not half-fae?

"I understood your reasoning," I said, forcing a terse smile.

Lady Marjolijn had just opened her mouth to reply and I was bracing for her words when the door to the tavern flew open and a group of soldiers from Tintagel and Lyonesse entered.

For a moment, my heart was in my throat. Had the peace talks this morning been a sham?

King Mark stepped forward with Prince Taryn beside him.

"Lady Marjolijn," the king of Tintagel said. "We must leave Camelot at once."

The eminent lady was already on her feet. "Why? What has happened?"

"We're under attack," Prince Taryn said.

Lady Marjolijn let out a hissing sound as her eyes shot towards me.

"Not," King Mark said hastily, "from Pendrath, Marjolijn.

Lady Marjolijn's eyes narrowed. "Then from where? Who dares to attack us now?"

The king of Tintagel hesitated. "Two attacks were reported in the night. One to Tintagel's west and the other to Lyonesse's northwest. From what we can gather, the attacks came from Rheged. But..." He hesitated. "They were not ordinary troops."

"What do you mean?" I asked. "Not ordinary?"

"It may be hard to believe—" I thought he said this for Lady Marjolijn's sake. "But our soldiers report dark, shadowy beings. Not...human. Monstrous creatures."

I glanced at Draven. My mate's body was tense. He had told me about the ambush on the beach when they'd made landfall.

Lady Marjolijn's face was red with anger. "Impossible. What nonsense is this?"

King Mark shrugged helplessly. "Perhaps it is nonsense and nothing more. But I am returning to see, either way. Immediately."

I rose to my feet. "Pendrath stands ready to come to Tintagel's aid should you need it." I looked at Lady Marjolijn. "And to Lyonesse's. Whatever we have left to give, we shall give it."

The dark-haired king nodded his appreciation, while Lady Marjolijn simply looked flinty-eyed.

Draven applied gentle pressure to my hand, reminding me.

"Myntra's forces are at your disposal also," I added quickly.

King Mark frowned. "Siabra forces?"

"A new day is dawning," my mate said evenly by my side. "Not all change must be evil. Perhaps this will herald a new time for Eskira, when fae and mortals fight side by side against their foes."

"Perhaps," said Lady Marjolijn. She did not look entirely convinced. She marched towards the door, then paused. "We will send word. Of whatever we find."

I nodded. "Thank you. And good luck."

When they had departed, I glanced at my mate.

Around the table, our friends were quiet, watching us.

"You'll be leaving soon then, I suppose," Crescent said, breaking the silence.

I whipped my head around to look at him. "How did you—?"

"Oh, it's written all over your faces," Lancelet said, waving a hand and wrinkling her nose. "Of course you wouldn't invite any of us either. Typical."

"Invite you? But I—"

"On the greatest quest that may have ever been?" Hawl's voice boomed. "And you would not take a friend?"

"It will be very dangerous. We aren't even sure—" But I was interrupted once again.

"We won't be left behind," Lancelet snapped. "We aren't children."

I rolled my eyes. "I know that. But I need you here. Did you ever think of that?"

My friend—for she was and always would be—narrowed her beautiful blue eyes. "What do you mean?"

"I was going to ask you to act as regent on Kaye's behalf, of course. And to look after him and Medra for me."

Her cheeks pinkened slightly. "Oh."

"Yes, oh." I sighed and sat back down by the table. "You know what we must do then?"

"Destroy the grail and the sword," Guinevere said softly from her place.

I nodded. And the spear, too, if we could locate it. The weapons of gods. With luck, we would also find Rychel and bring her back with us. "But we've lost anyone who truly knew anything about the past. Who could tell us more about the objects of power."

"Not everyone," Guinevere said, raising a hand to touch the owl resting on her shoulder. "Not everyone."

In the waning hours of the night, the tavern had emptied. Only a few stragglers remained, nursing their mugs and talking quietly.

The dwindling candlelight cast long shadows over the worn floorboards as the notes of a soft melody drifted from the lone musician left playing a harp in the corner.

I thought of Orcades and her harp and how she would never play again.

Draven's hand rested gently at the small of my back as we danced, my anchor in the night.

My mate had been quiet for a while, lost in his own thoughts. But his gaze never strayed from me. His protectiveness was a force that wrapped around me, shielding me from the outside world.

My silken gown brushed against the rough fabric of his tunic as he drew me closer against him, his touch possessive. As the song drew to a close, my mate guided my steps with a practiced ease, then finally pulled me into an embrace with a sigh.

"Tired?" I asked with sympathy. "It's been a long day."

He kissed the top of my head. "Tired and not tired, silver one."

"Are you going to keep calling me that?" I asked curiously.

"That depends. Do you like it?"

I nodded and pressed up more closely against him. "I like everything about you and how you talk to me."

I felt him smile.

"Should we go back to the castle?" I suggested. We had hardly slept since the night before last. I had closed my eyes for a few restless hours of sleep on the chaise in Orcades's chamber. Draven had sat on the floor, leaning against the couch, watching Medra and Kaye. I didn't think he had slept at all.

He hesitated. "Do you feel as if you need to return to them?"

He meant to Kaye and Medra.

"I suppose they'll be all right for a little while longer," I said cautiously. "Why? What did you have in mind?"

"They have rooms above, I'm told." The invitation in his eyes was unmistakable.

"I'm sure they're all booked up by now," I said. Still, I could feel the surface of my body where it pressed against him begin to simmer with anticipation.

"Not quite. I took the liberty of reserving a room while you were speaking to Galahad earlier." The corners of his lips curled upward, coaxing my heart to skip a beat in response.

"Come," he said softly, drawing me by the hand towards a staircase in the corner of the tavern.

His green eyes held a hint of mischief and an unspoken promise.

I followed him, of course. He was impossible to resist. Every line and contour of his face was burned into my heart. Who knew what waited around the corner for us when morning dawned? The road ahead was long and dark.

But in the meantime, here was light. Here was hope.

Here in the arms of my mate, my beloved mate.

My Draven.

THE END

Knight of the Goddess, Book 4 in the Blood of a Fae series, is coming in 2024. Preorder it on Amazon.

Not ready to say goodbye to Morgan, Draven, and the world of Aercanum?

Wishing this book had even more steam?

Head over to my website to sign-up for my newsletter and receive a bonus steamy scene. This special scene offers a spicy "what if?" moment for Draven and Morgan.

Grab the FREE bonus scene and hear about the latest new releases, giveaways, and other bookish treats:

https://briarboleyn.com

AUTHOR'S NOTE

"Then king Arthur let send for all the children born on May-day [...] and all were put in a ship to the sea, and some were four weeks old, and some less. And so by fortune the ship drove unto a castle, and was all to-riven, and destroyed..."
– from *Le Morte Darthur* by Sir Thomas Malory

In today's popular culture, King Arthur enjoys a glowing reputation as a medieval hero. Few people are aware of the May Day Massacre mentioned in the foremost King Arthur legend by Sir Thomas Malory.

In the legend, the story goes as follows: King Arthur has unwittingly slept with his half-sister, Morgause (in some versions she is named Orcades) and she becomes pregnant. Merlin comes to Arthur and tells him that his sister is carrying a child that will destroy him and all of the knights of his realm.

Fearing the destruction of the Knights of the Round Table, Arthur sends for all of the children born on May Day and has them put into a boat and set out to sea. The boat capsizes and all of the infants are drowned.

However, Arthur's own child miraculously survives: A son named Mordred.

It is King Arthur's greatest crime and one which haunts him until his dying day. At least, in that story.

Interestingly, many scholars believe the May Day Massacre was inspired directly by the Massacre of the Infants from the Biblical Gospel of Matthew.

I always knew I would be including a variation of the May Day Massacre in this series, with my own spin. Because it's a heartbreaking thing to write and to read, I thought it was important to let readers know it was not included for gratuitous reasons but because it is a key part of the legend.

TRIGGER WARNINGS

Abduction

Abuse

Alcohol Consumption

Amputation

Animal Abuse

Animal Death

Bullying / Harassment

Cannibalism

Child Abuse

Child Death

Childhood Trauma

Decapitation

Deceased Family Member

Domestic Violence

Drug Use

Homophobia

Infant Death

Murder

Physical Abuse / Torture

Poisoning

Sexual Assault

Violence / Gore

ALSO BY BRIAR BOLEYN

Blood of a Fae Series

Queen of Roses

Court of Claws

Empress of Fae

Knight of the Goddess (Forthcoming 2024)

Written as Fenna Edgewood...

The Gardner Girls Series

Masks of Desire (The Gardner Girls' Parents' Story)

Mistakes Not to Make When Avoiding a Rake (Claire's Story)

To All the Earls I've Loved Before (Gwen's Story)

The Seafaring Lady's Guide to Love (Rosalind's Story)

Once Upon a Midwinter's Kiss (Gracie's Story)

The Gardner Girls' Extended Christmas Epilogue (Caroline & John's Story – Available to Newsletter Subscribers)

Must Love Scandal Series

How to Get Away with Marriage (Hugh's Story)

The Duke Report (Cherry's Story)

A Duke for All Seasons (Lance's Story)

The Bluestocking Beds Her Bride (Fleur & Julia's Story)

Blakeley Manor Series

The Countess's Christmas Groom
Lady Briar Weds the Scot
Kiss Me, My Duke
My So-Called Scoundrel

ABOUT THE AUTHOR

B riar Boleyn is the fantasy romance pen name of USA TODAY bestselling author Fenna Edgewood. Briar rules over a kingdom of feral wildling children with a dark fae prince as her consort. When she isn't busy bringing new worlds to life, she can be found playing RPG video games, watching the birds at her bird feeder and pretending she's Snow White, or being sucked into a captivating book. Her favorite stories are the ones full of danger, magic, and true love.

Find Briar around the web at:

https://www.instagram.com/briarboleynauthor/

https://www.bookbub.com/profile/briar-boleyn

https://www.tiktok.com/@authorbriarboleyn

Made in United States
Troutdale, OR
10/25/2024

24064741R00246